OXFORD WORLD'S

ADELINE MOWBRAY

AMELIA OPIE, née Alderson, was born 12 November 1769 in Norwich, the only child of Dr James Alderson and his wife Amelia (née Briggs). She came of age during the years of the French Revolution, and by her early twenties was part of a circle of radical writers that included William Godwin, Mary Wollstonecraft, Thomas Holcroft, and Elizabeth Inchbald. In 1798 she married John Opie, a fashionable London portrait painter, and with his encouragement pursued an incipient literary career. She published *The Father and Daughter* in 1801, a sentimental tale that established her celebrity, followed by *Poems* (1802) and *Adeline Mowbray, or The Mother and Daughter* (1805). During the first two decades of the nineteenth century Opie was a literary lion, holding court at the centre of the artistic and social world of London, and almost equally celebrated in Paris. Following her husband's death in 1807 she continued to write and publish regularly, dividing her time between London and her father's house in Norwich, where she maintained a close relationship with the strict Quaker Gurney family, which included Elizabeth Fry. In 1825, shortly before the death of her father, she was admitted to the Society of Friends. The Quaker censure of the worldliness of fiction led her to shift to more didactic works, including books for children and prose essays on moral subjects and her travels. In her seventies she revised and reissued her two novels of enduring interest, *The Father and Daughter* and *Adeline Mowbray*, as well as a twelve-volume collection of her shorter works under the title *Miscellaneous Tales*. Her later life was devoted to active participation in benevolent organizations, especially the Abolitionist movement, Bible societies, and local charities in Norwich. She died on 2 December 1853, and was buried in the same grave as her father at the Friends' Cemetery.

SHELLEY KING is Assistant Professor of English Language and Literature at Queen's University, Kingston, Canada, where she specializes in Nineteenth-Century Fiction and Victorian Literature.

JOHN B. PIERCE is Associate Professor of English Language and Literature at Queen's University, Kingston, Canada. He is the author of articles on Richardson, Shelley, and Blake, and of *Flexible Design: Revisionary Poetics in Blake's 'Vala' or 'The Four Zoas'*.

OXFORD WORLD'S CLASSICS

For almost 100 years Oxford World's Classics have brought readers closer to the world's great literature. Now with over 700 titles—from the 4,000-year-old myths of Mesopotamia to the twentieth century's greatest novels—the series makes available lesser-known as well as celebrated writing.

The pocket-sized hardbacks of the early years contained introductions by Virginia Woolf, T. S. Eliot, Graham Greene, and other literary figures which enriched the experience of reading. Today the series is recognized for its fine scholarship and reliability in texts that span world literature, drama and poetry, religion, philosophy and politics. Each edition includes perceptive commentary and essential background information to meet the changing needs of readers.

OXFORD WORLD'S CLASSICS

AMELIA OPIE

Adeline Mowbray

Edited with an Introduction and Notes by
SHELLEY KING *and* JOHN B. PIERCE

OXFORD
UNIVERSITY PRESS

OXFORD
UNIVERSITY PRESS

Great Clarendon Street, Oxford OX2 6DP

Oxford University Press is a department of the University of Oxford.
It furthers the University's objective of excellence in research, scholarship,
and education by publishing worldwide in

Oxford New York

Athens Auckland Bangkok Bogotá Buenos Aires Calcutta
Cape Town Chennai Dar es Salaam Delhi Florence Hong Kong Istanbul
Karachi Kuala Lumpur Madrid Melbourne Mexico City Mumbai
Nairobi Paris São Paulo Singapore Taipei Tokyo Toronto Warsaw

with associated companies in Berlin Ibadan

Oxford is a registered trade mark of Oxford University Press
in the UK and in certain other countries

Published in the United States
by Oxford University Press Inc., New York

British Library Cataloguing in Publication Data

Data available

Library of Congress Cataloging in Publication Data

Data available

ISBN 0–19–283330–8

1 3 5 7 9 10 8 6 4 2

Typeset by RefineCatch Limited, Bungay, Suffolk
Printed in Great Britain by
Cox & Wyman Ltd., Reading, Berkshire

CONTENTS

ACKNOWLEDGEMENTS

We would like to thank the Advisory Research Committee of Queen's University for a travel grant that enabled us to do research in Britain for this project. We also gratefully acknowledge permission from the following to print previously unpublished Opie materials: Lord Abinger, for Opie's correspondence with Godwin and Wollstonecraft on deposit at the Bodleian Library, Oxford; and the Norfolk Record Office, for letters concerning the revisions to the novel in 1844. We also thank the Thomas Fisher Rare Book Library at the University of Toronto for permission to reproduce the title-page of the first edition. We have benefited greatly from the assistance of the following individuals and research libraries: Dr Bruce Barker-Benfield and the staff at Duke Humphrey's Library and the Bodleian; the British Library; Dr Williams's Library; the Thomas Fisher Rare Book Library; and the Norfolk Record Office, Norwich, especially Mr Clive Wilkins-Jones, Assistant Senior Librarian at the Norwich Public Library, who shared its extensive collection of Opie editions. Judith Luna of Oxford University Press has also been extremely helpful at all stages of the project, and deserves special thanks. For generous assistance with various elements of the edition we would also like to thank Claire Grogan, Fred Lock, Ruth Perry, Phillip Rogers, and Yaël Schlick. And finally, thanks to Peter Sabor for his enthusiasm for editing and his practical advice in the early stages of this project.

INTRODUCTION

Readers who do not wish to learn details of the plot will prefer to treat the Introduction as an Epilogue.

From their first appearance, the works of Amelia Alderson Opie inspired a remarkable diversity of responses. After reading *The Father and Daughter*, Sir Walter Scott wept. Dorothy Wordsworth read *Adeline Mowbray*, and afterwards wrote to William, 'it made us quite sick before we got to the end of it'.[1] At the same time an anonymous reviewer of *Adeline Mowbray* thought its second volume 'perhaps the most pathetic, and the most natural in its pathos, of any fictitious narrative in the language'.[2] Thomas J. Hogg felt the novel's views on marriage so affecting that he gave a copy of it to Percy Shelley in a successful attempt to persuade him to marry Harriet Westbrook. More recently, Gary Kelly, in *English Fiction of the Romantic Period, 1789–1830*, has contextualized Opie's importance for current studies in the history of the novel, pointing out that during the first two decades of the nineteenth century 'Opie was generally considered second only to Edgeworth among new fiction writers who wrote something more than "the trash of the circulating libraries"'.[3] Her reputation waned with the rise of Jane Austen, but Kelly further notes that 'her tales contain brilliant touches of dialogue, characterization, and incident, equal at times to Austen and very similar in character'.[4]

Although almost unknown today, Amelia Opie was one of the most popular and celebrated writers of the opening decades of the nineteenth century. Her marriage to the fashionable portrait painter John Opie brought her into the artistic circles of London, where she associated with Joshua Reynolds, James Northcote, and Benjamin Haydon. Her own literary accomplishments made her part of a circle including novelist and dramatist Elizabeth Inchbald, actress

---

[1] Dorothy Wordsworth to William Wordsworth, 23 April 1812, in *The Letters of William and Dorothy Wordsworth, 1812–1820*, ed. Ernest De Selincourt, revised by Mary Moorman and Alan G. Hill, 2nd edn. (Oxford, 1970), 7.

[2] *Edinburgh Review*, 8 (1806), 465.

[3] (Longman, 1989), 83.

[4] Ibid. 84.

Elizabeth Siddons, and novelist Mary Russell Mitford. Nor was her celebrity limited to London—in Paris she attended soirées with Lafayette and Madame de Staël, and captivated David, the foremost artist of Revolutionary Paris, who later cast a medal of her likeness. In later life she became a Quaker, and a close family friend and correspondent of prison reformer Elizabeth Fry. Her own work for the abolition of slavery led to correspondence with both British politicians such as Lord Brougham, and American feminists such as Elizabeth Cady Staunton. Yet, when near the end of her life she reflected on her past, it was the revolutionary ferment of the 1790s that stood out: 'from my loophole of retreat I am looking, with pleasure, *not* on the world as it is, but on the world as it was. The occurrences of the year 1794 have lately been pressing with such power on my remembrance, demanding from me a decided confession that it was the most interesting period of my long life.'[5] And it was to this period of intellectual ferment that she turned in writing *Adeline Mowbray*, her most political novel.

Adeline Mowbray is of special interest to the modern reader in that its account of the scandalous relationship between Adeline and Frederic Glenmurray is loosely based on the complex and often stormy relationship of Mary Wollstonecraft and William Godwin. While in many respects the story of Adeline and Glenmurray departs significantly from that of Wollstonecraft and Godwin, the parallels are suggestive. Mary Wollstonecraft was the well-known author of a series of radical tracts, including *A Vindication of the Rights of Men*—a response to the reactionary politics of Edmund Burke's *Reflections on the Revolution in France*—and *A Vindication of the Rights of Woman*—an early feminist response to Bishop Talleyrand, a supporter of the French Revolution, but one who ignored the question of the rights of women in a revolutionary republic. Educated, independent, intelligent, and wedded to the ideal of rationality, Adeline is the model of the woman of strength Wollstonecraft idealized in *A Vindication of the Rights of Woman* and strove to be in her own life; her emancipation perhaps even goes beyond that suggested by Wollstonecraft, in that she is 'convinced that she . . . had a right to be an author, a politician, and a philosopher' (p. 16). Wollstonecraft's future husband, William Godwin,

---

[5] Cecilia Lucy Brightwell, *Memorials of the Life of Amelia Opie, Selected and Arranged from her Letters, Diaries, and Other Manuscripts* (Norwich and London, 1854), 52.

was well known as one of the chief voices of radical thought in Britain at the time. His radical position on the abolition of all forms of restriction on personal expression made him a hero to the supporters of the French Revolution and a danger to the upholders of the status quo. Glenmurray, Opie's fictional version of Godwin, is a writer and philosopher as well, though in a more isolated philosophical and political position at the beginning of the novel: after years of early fame, he finds that his own writings have 'prejudiced the world against him in so unconquerable a degree, that to him almost every door and every heart was shut' (p. 20). What the actual and the fictional couples hold in common, besides an interest in radical politics, is a suspicion regarding the institution of marriage. Wollstonecraft had argued that marriage was the ultimate expression of society's tendency to teach women only to please men, while Godwin saw it as an odious monopoly that artificially restricted human choice. Ironically enough, it was this common suspicion that both brought them together and caused their downfall. Although they first met in 1791, it was not until Wollstonecraft's return to England in 1796, following a disastrous relationship with Gilbert Imlay in France, that the two began a serious affair. By that time she had an illegitimate child and had been forced to adopt the fiction of a marriage to Imlay. Her sexual relationship with Godwin began in 1796 with no thought of marriage, but when Wollstonecraft became pregnant in late December of that year the situation became more complicated. In a direct compromise of their own philosophical tenets, the two married for very practical purposes on 29 March 1797. Wollstonecraft's situation was such that the appearance of a second illegitimate child would have placed her clearly outside the confines of social acceptability.[6]

Amelia Alderson, later Opie, viewed these events not as a dispassionate observer but as one who knew both parties well and sympathized deeply with the problem of philosophical compromise they faced. She had met Godwin in 1794, at the height of his fame and notoriety, and their friendship was marked by intense intellectual engagement and frank exchange. Godwin offered highly supportive critiques of her early attempts to write for the stage; Amelia, in her turn, flattered his intellect, writing, 'you have often been in my

---

[6] For more on the relationship between Godwin and Wollstonecraft, see William St. Clair, *The Godwins and the Shelleys* (London, 1989), 157–88.

thoughts, & I have been continually endeavouring to profit by the labours of your wonderful mind'. Yet her letters also contained startlingly sharp rebukes: 'I hate you for always throwing *Coquette* in my teeth [she writes,] it is a bad habit & you have lately acquired some— you called me a bitch the last time I saw you.'[7] Their names were sometimes even linked in the gossip of radical circles. Alderson writes to her friend Mrs Taylor: 'Mrs. Inchbald says, the report of the world is that Mr. Holcroft is in love with her, *she* with Mr. Godwin, Mr. Godwin with *me*, and I am in love with Mr. Holcroft. A pretty story indeed! This report Godwin brings to me.'[8] By 1796 Amelia had met Mary Wollstonecraft, and in a letter of that year she wrote frankly and passionately to her:

I remember the time when my desire of seeing you was repressed by fear—but as soon as I read your letters from Norway, the cold awe which the philosopher had excited, was lost in the tender sympathy call'd forth by the *woman*—I saw nothing but the interesting creature of feeling, & imagination & I resolved if possible, to become acquainted with one who had alternately awakened my sensibility, & gratified my judgement—I *saw* you, & you are one of the few objects of my curiosity, who in gratifying— have not disappointed it also. You, & the *Lakes of Cumberland* have exceeded my expectations.[9]

On the marriage of the two, she wrote to her close friend Mrs Taylor: 'Heighho! what charming things would sublime theories be, if one could make one's practice keep up with them; but I am convinced it is impossible, and am resolved to make the best of every-day nature.'[10] This recognition of the conflict between 'sublime theories' and 'one's practice' underlies Opie's fictional retelling of the Wollstonecraft–Godwin union.

When she came to write *Adeline Mowbray*, Opie, herself an early enthusiast for radical philosophy and a close friend of its central proponents, knew at first hand the virtues of the individuals and ideals of their vision of social change. Yet she was equally familiar with their inability to mesh theory and practice, and personally sceptical of the practical impact of the new philosophy on women.

---

[7] Letter to Godwin, 1 November 1796, Oxford, Bodleian Library [Abinger deposit] Dep. b. 210/6.

[8] Letter to Mrs Taylor, 1796, quoted in Brightwell, *Memorials*, 60.

[9] Letter to Mrs Imlay, 28 August 1796 [Abinger deposit] Dep. b. 210/6.

[10] Letter to Mrs Taylor, 1797, quoted in Brightwell, *Memorials*, 63.

'Sublime theories' are, as Opie says, 'charming things', but social forces—the world of 'one's practice', of 'every-day nature'—wreak havoc on the individual life. This distinction between theory and practice finds its expression in the novel and in the period generally as a conflict between 'the world as it is' and 'a world as it *ought* to be' (p. 14). The distance between 'the world as it is'—a world constrained by the overwhelming force of public opinion and the maintenance of the status quo—and 'a world as it ought to be'—a utopian vision of rational, utilitarian citizens who balance individual happiness and liberty within a system of mutual benefit—provides the basis for her satire in general, and in particular for her satire on the status and education of women. The novel is, after all, entitled *Adeline Mowbray*, and finds its specialized focus in examining the experience of the radical and intellectual woman. 'The world as it is' offers protection to those who conform to its regulations concerning courtship, marriage, and motherhood, but severely limits the range of sexual, economic, and intellectual expression women have. Glenmurray's 'world as it ought to be' offers an elusive promise for Adeline of intellectual autonomy and the freedom to pursue rational desire, but this promise becomes a curse when put into effect in a world not ready for radical change and deviations from a socially defined norm. The group of female figures appearing at the novel's close, however, implies that some mediation between practice and theory might be possible through the development of what Opie calls a community of 'amiable women' (p. 68). The novel's subtitle, '*the Mother and Daughter*', indicates that the roots of such a community grow from a specific set of female relationships and that significant aspects of female identity can be examined in the light of this filial connection, for the attention of the novel centres on a series of very different mothers and daughters in one family. Mrs Woodville, Editha, Adeline, and Adeline's daughter, Editha, offer a series of permutations on the experience of what it is to be a mother or daughter or both in late-eighteenth-century England.

Mothers and Daughters: Mrs Woodville and Editha Mowbray

In Mrs Woodville and Editha Mowbray, the first mother-and-daughter pair presented in the novel, Opie establishes two contrasting modes of female conduct: good sense and genius. Framing these predispositions in terms of their relation to 'the world as it is' and 'the world as it ought to be', Hannah More, in *Essays on Various Subjects Principally Designed for Young Ladies* (1777), contrasts these same qualities: 'As it is the character of *Genius* to penetrate with a lynx's beam into unfathomable abysses and uncreated worlds, and to see what is *not*, so it is the property of *Good Sense* to distinguish perfectly, and judge accurately, what really *is*.'[11] More extols the virtues of '*Good Sense*' over the extravagances of '*Genius*'. The almost sublime penetration of genius is limited to the ephemeral or non-existent, while good sense grounds itself in judgement, the standard of pragmatic stability. Opie's approach to these contrasting aspects of female character, however, is somewhat more complex. In *Adeline Mowbray* the single-minded devotion to one or the other receives a severe critique, and Opie suggests that a balance of both is necessary to proper psychological and social development.

Mrs Woodville's practical and domestic skills make her an obvious figure of good sense. Described as the 'sole surviving daughter of an opulent merchant in London' (p. 3) married to a respectable country gentleman, Mrs Woodville represents the most practical match of new urban money and old rural property. Her marriage is primarily a financial exchange establishing economic security for the interests of both families, including Mrs Woodville herself and, ideally, her own offspring. It links capitalist wealth to aristocratic heritage, securing the link to the landed gentry desired by the *nouveau riche* on her side, and on the other the fluid capital needed by the aristocratic Woodvilles in order to maintain their estates in a growing market economy. The financial success of the marriage is consolidated when their daughter Editha is successfully married, 'merely to oblige her parents' (p. 5), to Mr Mowbray, the heir of Rosevalley.

The relative happiness of Mr and Mrs Woodville's marriage of convenience should not be taken as a model for marital satisfaction and evidence of conservative bias on Opie's part. As Wollstonecraft comments in *A Vindication of the Rights of Woman*, such practical unions, though pleasant enough, fall short of what she argues ought to be the ideal of marriage: 'whoever has cast a benevolent eye on society, must often have been gratified by the sight of a humble mutual love, not dignified by sentiment, or strengthened by a union

[11] New rev. edn. (Edinburgh, 1820), 121.

in intellectual pursuits ... yet, has not the sight of this moderate felicity excited more tenderness than respect?'[12] Wollstonecraft is even more critical of marriages based solely on sentiment: 'To speak disrespectfully of love is, I know, high treason against sentiment and fine feelings; but I wish to speak the simple language of truth, and rather to address the head than the heart.'[13] She advocates instead a relationship based on respect, intellectual stimulation, and mutual affection. Opie herself describes such a relationship as a 'rational though enthusiastic preference, which is deserving of the name of true love' (pp. 215–16).

Mrs Woodville herself is clearly celebrated for her active benevolence and practical management, and above all for her education of Adeline in household duties, the keeping of accounts, and the importance of charity. However, she is by no means a feminine ideal. Grammatical infelicities mark her speech, but betray her bourgeois origins as the least serious of her flaws. Her inability to read more than three pages of Locke's *Essay on Human Understanding* is more than a satiric jibe at philosophical writing. The couple's choice of 'cribbage and draughts' over philosophy and astronomy relegates the Woodvilles to an anti-intellectual sphere incompatible with the ultimate interests of Editha and Adeline (and Opie). Because Mrs Woodville so firmly rejects intellectual exercise, she becomes in part responsible for Editha's excesses: 'Happy would it have been for miss [Editha] Woodville, if the merits of the works which she so much admired could have been canvassed in her presence by rational and unprejudiced persons: but, her parents and friends being too ignorant to discuss philosophical opinions or political controversies, the young speculator was left to the decisions of her own inexperienced enthusiasm' (p. 4). For mothers to remain uninvolved in matters of intellect and political debate is to eschew maternal responsibility and to fail in an important element of the education of a daughter. And because Editha's intellect is unregulated, in part by her mother's naive and uninformed belief in her daughter's genius, she becomes so imbued with abstract theories that she fails in matters of practical benevolence: 'and while imagining systems for the good of society, and the furtherance of general philanthropy, she allowed

[12] Janet Todd and Marilyn Butler (eds.), *The Works of Mary Wollstonecraft*, 7 vols. (London, 1989), v. 94.
[13] Ibid. 96.

individual suffering in her neighborhood to pass unobserved and unrelieved' (p. 4).

In her portrait of Mrs Woodville's daughter, Editha, Opie draws a stereotype of all the vices conservative writers attributed to women who pursued a life of intellect—she neglects her 'proper' feminine domestic duties, she is intellectually assertive, and she is egotistical rather than modest. She is described as 'a showing-off woman', aiming 'to convert every drawing-room into an arena for the mind, and all her guests into intellectual gladiators' (p. 15). Yet this critical portrait of Editha ought not to suggest that Opie condemns intellectual women in general. Both biographical and literary evidence suggest a strong endorsement of female involvement in political discussion. Beyond her association with Godwin and Wollstonecraft, she counted herself among the blue-stockings—a term developed in the eighteenth century to describe women who participated in salons or mixed social gatherings for the purpose of intellectual discussion. She writes with great enthusiasm of attending 'blue' parties, and in *Detraction Displayed* offers a pointed defence of the blue-stocking. While still critical of what she terms 'a *woman of display*'[14] or one who pursues knowledge for the sake of dominating conversation, she insists that women should claim the term 'blue-stocking' as a mark of excellence rather than conceding it as an insult. Opie makes clear elsewhere that women should participate in intellectual pursuits. If they do not, she argues, 'it . . . seems to throw a stigma on cultivation of the mind in their own sex . . . [and] has moreover a tendency to deprive many individuals of the other, of the necessary stimulus to cultivate theirs'.[15] Editha, however, dominates rather than engages with others through her intellectual exertions, and while her example inspires Adeline to the proper exercise of mind, she also seems to sacrifice her daughter to the development of abstract educational theories.

Editha's genius and Mrs Woodville's good sense render them an incompatible mother-and-daughter combination. In her desire to improve her mother's intellect, and to make her a more fitting mother for genius, Editha strains the relationship. Mrs Woodville laments that the consequence of Editha's genius is her own exclusion from a comfortable social life with the other members, especially the

---

[14] *Detraction Displayed* (London, 1828), 263.
[15] Ibid. 262.

female members, of her society: 'And though, to be sure, the squires' ladies about are none of the brightest, and not to compare with my Edith, yet still they would have done very well for me and my dear good man to gossip a bit with' (p. 12). And in Mrs Woodville's dying hours, mother and daughter, though reciprocally loving, have so little in common that exchange is silenced. The irony, of course, is that Mrs Woodville's sensible ability to see 'what is' fails only in relation to her daughter, where she perceives her genius, but not its flaws. Yet in the absence provided by Editha's abstraction, Mrs Woodville is given a second chance to educate not a daughter but a granddaughter, and transmits to Adeline those skills and values her awe of genius made it impossible for her to teach Editha. In the portrait of this mother and daughter, the opening of the novel thus strikes the middle ground Opie will occupy throughout the narrative, apparently endorsing the conservative critique of women who pursue theoretical politics, but equally warning against the dangers of a female failure to engage with those same ideas.

In her role as mother Editha Mowbray's character develops further complexity. Aware of the random nature of her own education, she turns her thoughts to the education of her own daughter, striving to produce the perfect system, with predictably problematic results. Her attempt is, of course, doomed to failure as her undisciplined genius can settle on no coherent plan, and the narrator describes Adeline as 'tormented by the experimental philosophy of her mother' (p. 5) as she matures. Always immersed in theoretical approaches and the thought of her own future fame as the author of such a system, Editha is an inconsistent parent, often neglecting the immediate needs and the practical education of her daughter. Yet during her daughter's illness she watches over Adeline with a tenderness and 'unremitting attention' that eradicates all Editha's pretensions and apparent coldness: 'like the most common-place woman of her acquaintance, she lived to the present moment:—and she was rewarded for her cares by the recovery of her daughter, and by that daughter's most devoted attachment' (p. 8). Throughout her life Adeline retains this image of maternal devotion which supersedes any doubts she may entertain of her mother's parenting.

Adeline thus inherits two antithetical models of female conduct and unites them in herself. From her mother she derives a passionate interest in affairs of the intellect and a desire to be valued for her intellectual abilities; from her grandmother she learns 'all the ideas of œconomy and housewifery' (p. 9) which Mrs Woodville had been taught. Adeline also inherits her grandmother's desire for the company of other women; in her case, however, it is not the egotism of genius that renders her unacceptable to the community, but her attitude towards marriage, acquired through philosophical study with her mother. Thus, as a character Adeline poses a challenge for the conservative reader; constructed so as to fulfil every virtue required by conservative models of femininity, she fails only in one crucial point—she believes she can love chastely and honourably outside marriage.

Mothers and Daughters: Editha and Adeline

The next mother-and-daughter pairing—that of Editha and Adeline—moves beyond the antithesis of genius and common sense into an examination of how the commodification of women through sexual competition and marriage becomes a site for the near destruction of the mother–daughter relationship. Wollstonecraft had warned in *A Vindication of the Rights of Woman* of the danger posed to mothers and daughters by society's education of women to be sexual playthings first and foremost. She imagines the case of a woman who has never been educated to rational independence, but rather only to depend upon and to please men, who subsequently becomes a widowed mother:

What is then to become of her? She . . . falls an easy prey to some mean fortune-hunter, who defrauds her children of their parental inheritance, and renders her miserable. . . . The mother will be lost in the coquette, and, instead of making friends of her daughters, [she will] view them with eyes askance, for they are rivals—rivals more cruel than any other, because they invite a comparison, and drive her from the throne of beauty, who has never thought of a seat on the bench of reason.[16]

This is precisely the situation Opie constructs in the novel. Although in her early life Editha appears to have escaped the traditional emphasis in female education on dress, accomplishments, and coquetry, in middle age she succumbs to a desire to experience sentimental passion, and to the fortune-hunting Sir Patrick

---

[16] *Vindication of the Rights of Woman, Works of Mary Wollstonecraft*, v. 117–18.

O'Carrol. The consequences of this seduction are as much economic as personal. When Mrs Woodville dies she laments the fact that she has no material wealth to leave to Adeline, as a tangible expression of her recognition of her granddaughter's worth. She comforts herself, however, with the thought that Adeline's economic well-being is assured as her mother's only child. Thus, when Sir Patrick O'Carrol appears in Bath, he disrupts more than the emotional equilibrium of the mother and daughter. His marriage to Editha effectively removes financial control of the substantial Mowbray estates from feminine hands, and begins Adeline's economic woes. Though at first this figures simply as the erosion of her ability to perform her charitable and benevolent social function (a matter serious enough), it ends with Adeline experiencing directly the economic constraints of women who choose to live outside accepted social sexual norms. Fleeing Sir Patrick's sexual advances, she turns to Glenmurray, who provides her with an intellectually, emotionally, and sexually fulfilling (but unmarried) relationship. The independence she finds with him offers some compensation to Adeline, yet because she has been his mistress, she is later barred from access even to the small sum Glenmurray is able to leave her in his unwitnessed will, and from the one form of labour to which she is most suited, teaching young children.

When Sir Patrick's libertine interest in his wife's daughter leads to a physical assault on Adeline, mother and daughter can no longer escape the role he casts them in as sexual competitors. Because she is infatuated with Sir Patrick, Editha persuades herself that Adeline's perceptions are mistaken, and remains loyal to her lover. When Sir Patrick himself articulates his sexual preference for the younger woman, he initiates the emotional breach between mother and daughter that dominates the novel. He exploits the sexual economy in which the two women are trapped by trading upon Editha's desire for a courtly romantic love leading to marriage and Adeline's ingenuous belief in a Godwinian union of rationally minded individuals outside the confines of wedlock. He exchanges his appearance as an elegant lover for Editha's 'large independent fortune', but his attempt to gain 'possession of the daughter's person' (p. 27) involves a far more complex and costly negotiation, one that brings into contention 'the world as it is' and 'the world as it ought to be'. An intractable conflict emerges as Sir Patrick and Adeline negotiate the meaning behind the gendered codes of honour in place at the end of the eighteenth century. Male honour is defined by personal courage, socially produced through the institution of the duel; female honour is defined as sexual purity, socially produced through the institution of marriage. This division was a commonplace of the period: Jane West, for example, speaks of 'chastity' and 'its male concomitant courage'.[17] By setting these ideas against each other, Opie illustrates the difficult shift taking place in the masculine code, as society moves towards establishing 'the world as it ought to be', while questioning the impossibility of a shift in feminine codes, particularly as they are attached to the institution of marriage, which demonstrate the intractability and force of 'the world as it is'. Although unable to bring himself to refuse the duel with Sir Patrick, Glenmurray later in the novel does follow his principles in refusing Major Douglas's challenge to a duel over introducing Adeline to his sisters. This refusal takes the form of a negotiation that results in acceptance and understanding of Glenmurray's position. Despite acting outside the code of honour, he retains both his reputation and social standing. Adeline's attempts to apply his principles concerning marriage are not so easily accommodated.

Once Adeline clearly enters society as a sexual being, involved in a liaison with Glenmurray, the rules of social interaction change radically. Her choice to embrace Glenmurray's theories has two distinct negative consequences: first, its effect on her relationship with other men; second, its effect on her relationships with women. The men whom she meets invariably assume that because she entertains a sexual relationship with one man outside wedlock, she is necessarily eager to engage with other men as well. Adeline's adoption of Glenmurray's Godwinian ideas of chaste love without marriage leads to an emphasis on the ways in which her individual conduct is interpreted by the rest of society. Her mere articulation of her belief in this theory results in Sir Patrick's assumption that her discourse is a thin disguise for the lubricious desire he has suspected in women all along. Indeed, it is Sir Patrick's attempt to engage Adeline in a sexual liaison that leads her to make her practice fit her theory and begin her life as Glenmurray's lover. From this point on other men read her position as granting them licence to petition for her

---

[17] *Letters Addressed to a Young Lady*, 3 vols., 2nd edn. (London, 1806), iii. 146.

sexual favours. When she goes to consult the lawyer, Langley, his knowledge of her position leads him to make unwelcome advances, including a forcible kiss on her ungloved hand. When she leaves his office in distress, 'so disappointed, so ashamed, and so degraded', she is accosted by two young men who recognize her as 'that sweet creature who lived at Richmond with that crazy fellow, Glenmurray'. Thus confident of her identity, the young men make physical contact, patting her on the back and putting an arm around her waist. The dialogue makes clear their misogyny, as the young lawyers laugh at her distress and inquire whether her 'favours are all bespoken' (pp. 178–9). Only when Adeline tells them she is on the eve of marriage do they lose their sexual aggression and treat her with respect. In a parallel scene late in the novel Adeline is again threatened, this time by 'some young men of *ton*' (p. 206); her chance rescue in this instance by Colonel Mordaunt points to the precariousness of her status in relation to a violent masculine subculture.

Such conduct is not limited to strangers in the street and professional acquaintances. Even those of her own class with personal knowledge of both Adeline and Glenmurray find it difficult to discriminate between a chaste monogamous attachment without marriage and indiscriminate sexual availability. When Adeline meets Glenmurray's old friend Mr Maynard, he believes she is Glenmurray's wife and initially responds to her with praise and admiration. When he learns she is his mistress, however, he immediately contemplates rivalling Glenmurray for her affections. But by far the most important male figure who struggles to interpret the meaning of Adeline's conduct is Colonel Mordaunt. Initially introduced in the novel as a potential suitor, he is shown as a libertine who shares many characteristics with Sir Patrick, but who is capable of moderating his conduct. Aware of his attraction to Adeline and his own vision of himself as 'not a *marrying man*' (p. 21), he leaves Bath before the affair goes beyond initial mutual attraction. When he sees Adeline again in Richmond, he believes that he now has the opportunity to possess her on his own terms. More delicate than Sir Patrick, Mordaunt disdains both physical force and pressing his suit while Glenmurray still lives. Similarly, when he appears later in the novel to rescue Adeline from a rough encounter with men in the street, he professes his passion once more, only to be shocked by her revelation of her marriage to Berrendale, for 'libertine as he confessed himself to be, he had never yet allowed himself to address the wife of another' (p. 210). Yet his passionate declarations, perhaps more than anything else in the novel, bring home to Adeline the world's interpretation of her conduct. She asks, 'is it then given to a wife only to be secure from being insulted by offers horrible to the delicacy, and wounding to the sensibility, like those which I have heard from you?' (p. 115). In 'the world as it is' Adeline's deduction is correct.

Perhaps more distressing than the insults she meets with from the male community is the isolation from female community which results directly from her political social choices. Foremost, of course, is her isolation from her mother. Though precipitated primarily by the sexual competition fostered by Sir Patrick, the rift between mother and daughter also arises from their unexpected conflict concerning Glenmurray's theories. In another ironic inversion, Editha reveals that, despite her abstract genius, in this instance she sees 'what is' with a sensible clarity worthy of her mother, and warns Adeline that social theories such as those propounded by Glenmurray are for intellectual exercise and amusement only, not for practical application:

Little did I think that you were so romantic as to see no difference between amusing one's imagination with new theories and new systems, and acting upon them in defiance of common custom, and the received usages of society. . . . The poetical philosophy which I have so much delighted to study, has served me to ornament my conversation, and make persons less enlightened than myself wonder at the superior boldness of my fancy, and the acuteness of my reasoning powers. . . . No; though I think all they say true, I believe the purity they inculcate too much for this world. (pp. 40–1)

In one of her most rhetorically playful gestures, Opie places in the mouth of the much-satirized Editha the pragmatic understanding that Adeline herself will rationally come to through her unfortunate experiences in the subsequent chapters. Ultimately Editha herself proves unable to transcend the central taboo of contemporary feminine conduct. Although almost ready to become reconciled with her daughter, when she at last perceives Adeline's pregnant form she reacts with horror and repudiation, despite Dr Norberry's sensible admonition: 'Is it a greater crime to be in a family way, than to live with a man as his mistress? — You knew your daughter had done the last: therefore 'tis nonsense to be so affected at the former' (p. 105).

Adeline's body becomes the visible emblem of the pragmatic consequences of her theoretical beliefs, confirming the breach begun in sexual jealousy and competition.

Although most haunted by the loss of her mother, Adeline also loses the society of other women. Throughout the novel she laments that her appearance of vice prohibits interchange with a female community, and longs for the society of 'amiable women'. Adeline's servant Mary Warner, like Sir Patrick, is unable to distinguish the rational and virtuous relationship of Adeline with Glenmurray from any other unsanctioned union, and bluntly expresses the grounds of Adeline's isolation. When Mary refers to her as a 'kept miss', Adeline asks her to define the term. 'Why, a lady who lives with a man without being married to him, I take it; and that I take to be your case . . .', she replies. When Adeline tries to discriminate, noting 'But mistresses, or kept ladies in general, are women of bad character, and would live with any man; but I never loved, nor ever shall love, any man but Mr Glenmurray', Mary insists that 'if master is inclined to make an honest woman of you, you had better take him at his word' (p. 117). Indeed, in the world as it is, with its tendency to rigid social definitions, Opie spares no pains to reveal the lack of 'amiability' in many of the women who enforce the status quo. From Mrs Norberry's initial sense of Adeline as competition for her own daughters to her eventual reading of Adeline as sexual competition for Dr Norberry's attentions, Adeline becomes an often unknowing and always unwilling participant in the contemporary sexual economy. Although Mrs Norberry is ultimately revealed, for all her self-conscious pride, as a woman capable of intercepting correspondence and lying to her husband, her judgements are not atypical. Mr Maynard's sisters, Mrs Wallington and Miss Emily Maynard, evince a mixture of contempt and jealousy in their responses to their brother's praise of Adeline. Glenmurray's cousins are equally problematic. Although they do not meet directly with Adeline or even speak in the novel, they pass judgement with only 'the bold unfeeling stare of imagined superiority' (p. 127). Adeline is judged in terms of social and sexual violations; her impropriety attacks the securities provided by marriage, and her intellectual individuality, her free choice to live outside social boundaries, gives her an autonomy and consequently an attractiveness that engages the interest of men and arouses jealousy among many of the women in the novel.

Mothers and Daughters: Adeline and Editha

Adeline's personal experience of motherhood draws her out of the
arena of sexual competition with her own mother and into the
self-reflective struggle over the social, economic, and intellectual
costs of being a mother but not a wife. Wollstonecraft had expressed
her vision of the duty of women in her *Vindication*: 'speaking of
women at large, their first duty is to themselves as rational creatures,
and the next, in point of importance, as citizens, is that, which
includes so many, of a mother.'[18] In pursuing her relationship with
Glenmurrary, Adeline is true to herself as a rational creature, following that course which her intellect and her philosophical enquiry
have convinced her is most virtuous. It is only when her duty as a
mother comes into conflict with her duty to herself as an individual
that Adeline begins to reconsider her ideas. The first glimmerings
of doubt appear when she is pregnant with Glenmurray's child, and
experiences two events in Richmond that shake her confidence. In
the first, she learns of the economic hardship of a young woman
with a child born out of wedlock, who is left destitute by the death
of her lover. Though momentarily distraught by the thought that
such a fate would be hers, she regains her resolution: 'But is the
possession of property, then . . . so supreme a good, that the want
of it, through the means of his mother, should dispose a child to
curse that mother?—No: my child shall be taught to consider nothing valuable but virtue, nothing disgraceful but *vice*.—Fool that I
am! a bugbear frightened me; and to my foolish fears I was about to
sacrifice my own principles, and the respectability of Glenmurray'
(p. 129). The second encounter brings even greater confusion, for
she meets a bastard boy teased and ostracized by his fellows, and
observes at first hand the social burden that such a child bears.
Resolving to spare her own child such pain, she returns eager to
marry Glenmurray, but when the child miscarries, 'with her hopes of
being a mother vanished her wishes to become a wife, and all her
former reasons against marriage recurred in their full force' (p. 132).

   With Glenmurray's demise and her exclusion from economic
productivity because of her sexual past, Adeline begins to reconsider
her ideas, and agrees to marry Charles Berrendale. As she becomes a
mother herself, her professed attitudes to marriage undergo serious

[18] *Vindication of the Rights of Woman*, v. 216.

transformations as thoughts of the place of her daughter, named Editha after her estranged mother, become a central concern for her. Despite the idyllic nature of her 'rational though enthusiastic' relationship with Glenmurray and the suffering she undergoes during her marriage to Berrendale, Adeline ultimately endorses marriage as both a necessary and desirable institution. She does so in a series of exchanges with Colonel Mordaunt, in which she articulates her surrender of her former opinions. Jealous of her intellectual integrity, Adeline strives to make clear that neither financial necessity nor her personal need is responsible for her change of opinion; her marriage to Berrendale, she explains, arose 'from change of principle, on assurance of error, and not from interest, or necessity' (p. 216). She candidly acknowledges that her experience might well lead to the conclusion that indissoluble marriages should be abolished, but offers instead a rational plea for their continuation.

Her final letter to Mordaunt seems to be a rejection, not so much of Godwinian philosophy, as of Godwinian optimism concerning human nature. Adeline not only endorses marriage as an institution central to society, but insists on marriage without divorce. In his *Enquiry Concerning Political Justice* Godwin had argued that, even in the absence of formal marriage, monogamous attachment would be the social norm: 'It is a question of some moment whether the intercourse of the sexes, in a reasonable state of society, would be promiscuous, or whether each man would select for himself a partner to whom he will adhere as long as that adherence shall continue to be the choice of both parties. Probability seems to be greatly in favour of the latter.'[19] Opie bluntly refutes this assumption in Adeline's argument:

It has been said, that, were we free to dissolve at will a connection formed by love, we should not wish to do it, as constancy is natural to us, and there is in all of us a tendency to form an exclusive attachment. But though I believe, from my own experience, that the few are capable of unforced constancy, and could love for life one dear and honoured object, still I believe that the many are given to the love of change;—that, in men especially, a new object can excite new passion . . . (pp. 237–8)

Certainly the majority of the men Adeline encounters confirm this

[19] Penguin edn., ed. Isaac Kramnick (Harmondsworth, 1985), bk. VIII, ch. viii, app., p. 763.

observation: Sir Patrick is capable of wedding the mother and attempting to rape the daughter; Berrendale intrigues with a servant while the mother of his child is absent for the sake of its health, then subsequently commits bigamy; even Colonel Mordaunt can readily assuage the loss of Adeline for a while in the arms of 'a faded but attractive woman of quality' (p. 227).

Adeline's argument for marriage ultimately rests on the welfare of the children produced by a union. The optimistic Godwin had projected a communal interest in their well-being:

It may be imagined that the abolition of the present system of marriage would make education, in a certain sense, the affair of the public. . . . First, the personal cares which the helpless state of an infant requires. These will probably devolve upon the mother . . . and then it will be amicably and willingly participated by others. Secondly, food and other necessary supplies. These will easily find their true level, and spontaneously flow, from the quarter in which they abound, to the quarter that is deficient.[20]

Adeline's vision is far more bleak:

What then, in such a state of society, would be the fate of the children born in it?—What would their education be?—Parents continually engrossed in the enervating but delightful egotism of a new and happy love, lost in selfish indulgence, the passions awake, but the affections slumbering, and the sacred ties of parental feeling not having time nor opportunity to fasten on the heart,—their offspring would either die the victims of neglect, and the very existence of the human race be threatened; or, without morals or instruction, they would grow up to scourge the world by their vices, till the whole fabric of civilized society was gradually destroyed. (p. 238)

While Adeline does not deny the possibility of ideal and rational conduct, she does not see it as the norm of human behaviour. Indeed, the description of a parent 'continually engrossed in the enervating but delightful egotism of a new and happy love' might seem an accurate representation of Editha in the throes of her infatuation with Sir Patrick, and her commitment to a relationship that threatens the interest of her only child.

Ultimately, however, Adeline changes her view of marriage as a consequence of social forces in the world which, as she writes to

[20] *Enquiry Concerning Political Justice*, bk. VIII, ch. viii, app., 765.

Mordaunt, make her 'an example of vice, when I believed myself the champion of virtue' (p. 238). This recantation, if it can be called such, is exceedingly complex. The conflict between self-recrimination and self-justification finds its clearest expression in a powerful and troubling apologia:

True it is, that I did not act in defiance of the world's opinion, from any depraved feelings, or vicious inclinations: but the world could not be expected to believe this, since motives are known only to our own hearts, and the great Searcher of hearts: therefore, as far as example goes, I was as great a stumbling block to others as if the life I led had been owing to the influence of lawless desires; and society was right in making, and in seeing, no distinction between me and any other woman living in an unsanctioned connection. (p. 239)

Here Adeline insists on the purity of her original motives while acknowledging the inexorable force of social mores. Her state verges on the tragic: the individual heart, however pure, remains hidden and impotent in articulating and defending its actions upon the larger stage of the world, while the vast impersonal forces of 'society' are 'right' in eradicating forms of individual expression which threaten the continuities of 'the world as it is'. Thus, the virtuous motives of Adeline and the interested and vicious inclinations of Mary Warner are assigned the same moral value by such a world. Adeline's apologia therefore frames her change of opinion as a struggle between capitulation to and condemnation of society.

Neither response, however, is acceptable to her. The most 'horrible and overwhelming thought' for Adeline is the awareness 'of having by my example led another into the path of sin' (p. 240). The other here is Mary Warner, who tells Adeline that her relationship with Glenmurray taught her 'that marriage was all nonsense' (p. 204), and by extension that sexual relationships outside marriage were entirely acceptable. Adeline, like Wollstonecraft, is keenly aware of the importance of setting a moral example for her servants: Wollstonecraft writes 'Above all, we owe them a good example. . . . We cannot make our servants wise or good, but we may teach them to be decent and orderly; and order leads to some degree of morality.'[21] While Warner's accusations are misleading and prey upon Adeline's ingenuous virtue, they do awaken a sincere concern

---

[21] *Thoughts on the Education of Daughters, Works of Mary Wollstonecraft*, iv. 38–9.

for her own daughter's future. Adeline's example, now fixed in the
eyes of the world (and her own conscience) as an instance of error
and vice, may determine the contexts within which young Editha
will be received. At best, her fate may be to live in shame over her
mother's past; at worst, she may repeat her mother's example.
Instead of undercutting completely the validity of her earlier views,
Adeline grounds her change of view on a future vision of the 'two
ways in which a mother can be of use to her daughter'. As she goes
on to argue, 'the one is by instilling into her mind virtuous principles, and by setting her a virtuous example: the other is, by being to
her in her own person an awful warning,—a melancholy proof of the
dangers which attend a deviation from the path of virtue'. Adeline
finds herself unwilling to choose either path, however. Through
Adeline, Editha 'will learn that the woman who feels justly, yet has
been led even into the practice of vice, however she may be forgiven
by others, can never forgive herself' (pp. 238-9). The harshness
of Adeline's own judgement upon herself seems to exceed and over-
shadow her own censure of society. A more moderate view is presented in the community of amiable women who respond to Adeline
throughout the novel, and who surround her at its conclusion.

While 'the world as it is' contains libertines and coquettes,
hypocrites and bigamists, it also contains individuals whose integrity
and compassion render them exemplars of 'the world as it ought to
be'. There is a society of amiable women present in the novel,
women of thought and feeling who understand and sympathize with
Adeline's plight. They understand the moral paradox that Adeline
presents and hold out to her the hope of re-entry into an accepting
community. Beyond the mothers and daughters in the novel is the
community of amiable women who provide Adeline with guidance
and affection, and offer through their community with her the best
hope for women in the novel; Savanna, Mrs Pemberton, and Emma
Douglas are important representations of this community.

The Community of Women

If respectable women of her own class like Mrs Norberry, Mrs Beauclerc, Mrs Wallington, and Miss Emily Maynard eschew Adeline's
company, others are not so constrained. One of the key members of
the community of women surrounding Adeline is the mulatto,

Savanna. Adeline first encounters her in the streets of Richmond, where her husband is being dragged to jail by the bailiff for debt. Ravaged by illness, incarceration appears to mean certain death for William, and Adeline is faced with a trying dilemma: to save Savanna and her family by paying a portion of the debt they owe, or to satisfy the cravings of her own dying lover for the taste of pineapple. Difficult though it is for her affection to deny Glenmurray anything, Adeline chooses to practise social benevolence, and thus gains the loyal support of Savanna. Some readers, echoing Savanna herself, may wonder at Adeline's choice to disappoint her lover in this instance. Her actions, however, confirm the benevolent philosophy advocated by Wollstonecraft: 'Women too often confine their love and charity to their own families. They fix not in their minds the precedency of moral obligations, or make their feelings give way to duty. Goodwill to all the human race should dwell in our bosoms, nor should love to individuals induce us to violate this first of duties, or make us sacrifice the interest of any fellow-creature, to promote that of another, whom we happen to be more partial to.'[22] The rationally benevolent Adeline makes the only possible moral choice when faced with Savanna's dilemma, and is rewarded with one of the truest friends she finds in the narrative.

The name selected for this character suggests a resonance of family history. Opie's mother, Amelia Briggs, was born in India, but returned to England at an early age when orphaned by the death of both parents within eight months of each other. Accompanying her on the voyage home was her nurse, who subsequently returned to India, and was a subject of concern expressed in a letter from the orphan's uncle and guardian to the sea-captain who accompanied her on the voyage:

The black girl, her nurse, is not reconciled to England; and, thinking she never shall be so, she is determined to return to Bengal by the Christmas ships. As my mother will give her entire liberty to be at her own disposal, I believe her design is to enter into service, as other free women do. If it be in your power, you are very much desired by all my niece's friends to prevent Savannah's being bought or sold as a negro.[23]

Opie's own involvement with issues of black oppression dates from

---

[22] *Thoughts on the Education of Daughters*, 44.
[23] Brightwell, *Memorials*, 8.

an early age. As a child, she recollects, she was naturally fearful and
was frightened of, among other things, a black man, the footman of
one of her neighbours. She details her own tantrum in response to
his friendly overtures, and the measures her parents took to correct
her behaviour:

But as soon as my parents heard of this ill behaviour they resolved to put a
stop to it, and missey was forced to shake hands with the black the next
time he approached her, and thenceforward we were very good friends.
Nor did they fail to make me acquainted with negro history; as soon as
I was able to understand, I was shewn on the map where their native
country was situated; I was told the sad tale of negro wrongs and negro
slavery; and I believe that my early and ever-increasing zeal in the cause of
emancipation was founded and fostered by the kindly emotions which I
was encouraged to feel for my friend Aboar and all his race.[24]

   Opie took an active interest throughout her life in the issue of
emancipation, both through her literary works and through political
discussion. Her 'Negro Boy's Tale' and *The Black Man's Lament;
or, How to Make Sugar* attempt to raise awareness of the suffering of
slaves and to evoke sympathy and pity, and ultimately political action
from her English readers. Opie herself attended the Anti-Slavery
Convention of 1840 in London as an observer from Norwich.[25] Like
many of her contemporaries, she used strategies in her construction
of blacks that make today's readers uncomfortable. She relied heavily
on dialect speech to stress both the otherness of slaves and their
separation from the discourse of power. And for the most part, she
portrays them in her poetry as victims of oppression and passive
objects of pity.
   In *Adeline Mowbray*, however, the character of Savanna offers a
more complex representation which both participates in and at times
transcends the stereotype. Certainly Savanna's mode of speech
reflects the pidgin dialect associated with blacks in the period. Her
first words to Glenmurray—'Oh! when she gave tree guinea for me,
metought she mus be rich lady, but now dey say she be poor, and me

[24] Brightwell, *Memorials*, 13.
[25] Opie's intense engagement with the movement for the abolition of slavery is
reflected in her detailed account of the events of the first day of the Convention,
including the heated debate concerning the right of women to serve as delegates. This
extensive manuscript (roughly 30 pages in length) is extant in the Chapin Library,
Williams College, Williamstown, Massachusetts.

mus work for her' (p. 144)—are typical of the representation of black speech in the late eighteenth and early nineteenth century. Juba, the black servant in Maria Edgeworth's *Belinda* (1801), expresses himself almost identically. But ultimately the ideas Savanna expresses become more powerful than the disempowered forms of her discourse. Though Adeline remains silenced by the duty she believes a virtuous wife owes even to the worst of husbands, Savanna has no such inhibitions in her indictment of Berrendale's conduct: 'she poured forth all her long concealed wrath in a torrent of broken English, but plain enough to be well understood.—"You man!" she cried at last, "you will kill her; she pine at your no kindness;—and if she die, mind me, man! never you marry aden.—You marry, forsoot! you marry a lady! true bred lady like mine! No, man!—You best get a cheap miss from de street and be content—"' (p. 187). Though both race and class combine to disempower Savanna in the household (she is forced to apologize for her outburst and guards against future transgressions), she is nevertheless permitted to articulate the moral outrage felt by the reader at Berrendale's systematic persecution and deception of his wife. It is on her bosom that Adeline breathes her last, and it is she who provides the unconditional love and constant support that might otherwise have been expected of Editha.

If Savanna is at Adeline's side as a figure of constant affection and support, Rachel Pemberton is there as a figure of rational sympathy and instruction. Although Opie had not yet joined the Society of Friends when she wrote the novel, she was familiar with their beliefs through her friendship with the Gurney family of Norwich. A Christian sect that arose in the seventeenth century, the Quakers were defined by their desire to look inward to the promptings of conscience and their rejection of the world and the worldly, and came to be respected for their plain-speaking and truth-telling.[26] Thus Rachel Pemberton shares many of Adeline's ideals, and an understanding, despite her disagreement, of her need to follow the dictates of conscience rather than the regulations of society. Pemberton also reflects the sympathy that marked Quaker conduct: 'Throughout the developing Quaker conscience ran a persistent strain of humane compassion. In the words of John Bellers in 1695, "It is not he that

---

[26] On their background, see James Walvin, *The Quakers: Money and Morals* (London, 1997), 124.

dwells nearest that is only our neighbour, but he that wants our help
also claims that name and our love." [27] Thus, rather than rejecting
Adeline for her sexual transgression, Rachel Pemberton attempts to
argue rationally with her concerning her choice and her conscience,
and offers her support should Adeline be in need.

Mrs Pemberton's truth-telling and plain-speaking also perform
the important function of instructing Editha Mowbray concerning
her responsibility for Adeline's education and subsequent conduct.
Editha's long-awaited recognition that the autonomy and egotism of
genius must not compromise a woman's commitment to understanding and support of others in her community may be the most
important moral development in the novel. When Editha chooses to
remain with Miss Woodville, despite her transgressions, she demon-
strates both conscious responsibility for her role in shaping the
other's actions, and compassionate responsibility to place the needs
of another ahead of her own. Like Rachel Pemberton, she can hate
the sin but not the sinner, and can continue to offer compassion to a
fellow creature in need. Editha's growth in understanding in turn
renders her a viable choice to continue the education of the younger
Editha, and like her mother before her, she is given a second chance
to raise a granddaughter. Her exchanges with Rachel Pemberton also
set the stage for the long-awaited reconciliation of mother and
daughter.

There is, however, one important female figure who does not form
part of the loving circle at the conclusion of the novel, though one
might argue her right to be there in spirit. If any character serves as
the exemplary figure Adeline desires to be, it is Emma Douglas. A
woman of more character than beauty, she escapes society's school-
ing in coquetry and thus is able to focus her mind on issues other
than her own marketability within the sexual economy. This in turn
allows her to engage with Adeline's ideology more thoroughly than
do other characters. Perhaps most important, her flexible intellect
allows her to redefine 'the world' in order to meet and exchange ideas
with Adeline. Emma Douglas and her sister-in-law, for example, are
prepared to meet with Adeline in Portugal, where they argue that
because of the limited nature of their social world, certain decorums
may be overruled. Moreover, her refusal to participate in the petty

---

[27] Walvin, *The Quaker*, 125.

detraction so ardently practised by the Maynard sisters permits her instead to continue to recognize publicly Adeline's virtue while pragmatically arguing against her practice. Emma's refusal to participate in the worst of female communities is rewarded inevitably by her marriage to the reformed libertine Mordaunt, who sees in her an unfallen Adeline. As always in this novel, this is a resolution not untinged with irony: Mordaunt is both a desirable match and an exemplar of the limitations of society. The first object of sexual desire for Adeline, he leaves the field open to Glenmurray when he consciously espouses libertine values and rejects an identity as 'a *marrying man*'. Though ultimately brought to recognize the limitation of those values through his exchanges with Adeline, he nevertheless remains throughout the novel incapable of understanding completely Adeline's sexual virtue despite her relationship with Glenmurray. Thus Emma is sufficiently like Adeline to attract his interest, yet pure enough by conventional standards to satisfy his sense of female propriety. Emma, with her recognition of Adeline's virtue and pragmatic sense of what is possible for women in 'the world as it is', complements Mordaunt, and perhaps together they represent a potential for social renovation.

The novel thus asserts that the world has the power to determine women's lives, yet it also insists that it ought not therefore to go unquestioned. Those who are prepared to redefine 'the world' and who recognize the need to distinguish motive and to discriminate among apparently similar acts on a moral basis offer hope for a critique of social mores. Mrs Pemberton agrees to disagree with Adeline's view of marriage but does not shun her; Savanna also exhibits a ferocious loyalty that disregards all forms of social sanction in favour of individual moral worth. Although Anne Mellor describes the novel's conclusion as a 'feminotopia', this reading elides the importance of a significant male presence.[28] Throughout the novel, the sentimental Dr Norberry stands as an exemplar of humane compassion and forgiveness, a masculine figure who admires and respects intellect in women and who possesses valued qualities of loyalty and friendship. Although the novel emphasizes female communities, it is important to note the inclusiveness of this final

---

[28] ' "Am I Not a Woman, and a Sister?": Slavery, Romanticism, and Gender', in Alan Richardson and Sonia Hofkosh (eds.), *Romanticism, Race, and Imperial Culture, 1780–1839* (Bloomington, Ind., 1996), 323.

scene. The figures who surround Adeline are those who can combine
compassion with an ability to explore ideology. *Adeline Mowbray* asks
of its readers a similar flexibility of mind and ability to discriminate
complex moral issues.

NOTE ON THE TEXT

The present text is based on the first edition, published in 1805 in London in three volumes by Longman, Hurst, Rees, and Orme, and in Edinburgh by A. Constable and Co. While establishing the date of first publication for *Adeline Mowbray* has been somewhat problematic (with critical sources suggesting dates ranging from 1802 to 1804 to 1805), records from the Longman's Archives record the costs for paper, printing, and advertising for December of 1804 and the first advertisements marketing the novel appear in early January. It is likely, therefore, that the novel was completed in late 1804 and published in 1805.

The second edition is also problematic, but for different reasons. Advertisements for a second edition of the novel appear in July 1805, but the Longman Archives do not indicate costs for production of a second edition. It is quite possible that, with a print-run of 2,000 copies, of which 920 were left by 5 June 1805, Longman readvertised a phantom second edition to draw further attention to the book and encourage sales.[1]

The publication history of the third edition in three volumes, again by Longman, Hurst, Rees, Orme, and Brown, is less problematic. The Longman Archive record of 30 August 1810 shows a print-run of 500 copies for the third edition. Most variants in this edition are confined to the correction of errors in spelling and punctuation (one unfortunate error introduced is a date of 1801 on the title-page of the second volume). In addition to these minor changes, Opie consistently removed Dr Norberry's use of 'd——d'. This particular change may have been introduced in response to reviews of the first edition which complained about Opie's 'use of coarse and disgusting language'.[2] To all appearances, this edition sold slowly. For instance, by 1 February 1813 only 286 copies had been sold.

The final edition printed in Opie's lifetime appeared in 1844 in one volume as part of a scheme by the Grove & Sons printing-house

---

[1] See Jan Fergus and Janice Farrar Thaddeus, 'Women, Publishers, and Money, 1790–1820', *Studies in Eighteenth-Century Culture*, 17 (1987), 191–207.

[2] e.g. the *British Critic* (1805), 625.

to republish several of her works, which by this time were now all long out of print. The edition appeared with the Longman imprint on the title-page, but W. Grove & Sons acted as the printers. Opie herself made revisions to the text for this edition. On 27 August 1843 she wrote to her friend and Norwich printer, Simon Wilkin, of their importance: ' I sent up to W. Grove my Father and Daughter & Adeline Mowbray corrected by myself & in the last, two pages, as I think crossed out. . . .—the latter alterations [for *Adeline Mowbray*] I should be very unhappy not to have made—& would willingly pay for a cancel to have these made.'[3] As the letter indicates, most changes in this edition were in the nature of deletions or slight 'alterations' to the third edition. The omissions include such matters as the physical touching of Adeline by the ruffians in the street, Dr Norberry's recurrent 'Zounds', and, most importantly, a substantial passage in which she advocates Adeline's reading of Rousseau's *Julie*. This 'New and Illustrated Edition' included 'The Welcome Home' and 'The Quaker and the Young Man of the World', two works previously included in the 1818 *New Tales*. Some variants for the 1844 edition appear in the Textual Notes. Opie's revisions show a sensitivity to the changed sensibility of a Victorian reading audience and to her immediate circle of fellow Quakers.

This edition of the 1805 text is based on a copy in the Bodleian Library, Oxford (reproduced in the Woodstock Books edition), and a copy in the Thomas Fisher Rare Book Library, University of Toronto. In reproducing the text, we have normalized the positioning and use of quotation marks. Spellings consistent with eighteenth-century use (such as *antient, connexion, œconomy, phrensy, sooth* (for 'soothe'), and *villany*) have been retained.

---

[3] Norfolk Public Records Office, MS 4281, fo. 143.

SELECT BIBLIOGRAPHY

Modern Editions and Reproductions of Adeline Mowbray

Adeline Mowbray; or, The Mother and Daughter, introductions by Gina Luria. 3 vols. (New York: Garland Publishers, 1974) [Vol. 1 = 1805 edn; vols. 2 and 3 = 1810 edn. (vol. 2 title-page reads '1801', a printer's error for 1810): British Library copy].

Adeline Mowbray or The Mother and Daughter, introduction by Jeanette Winterson (London: Pandora Press, 1986) [1844 edn.].

Adeline Mowbray (New York: Woodstock Books, 1995) [1805 edn.: Bodleian Library copy].

Biographies

Cecilia Lucy Brightwell, *Memorials of the Life of Amelia Opie, Selected and Arranged from her Letters, Diaries, and Other Manuscripts* (Norwich: Fletcher and Alexander; London: Longman, Brown, & Co., 1854).

Margaret E. Macgregor, 'Amelia Alderson Opie: Worldling and Friend', *Smith College Studies in Modern Languages*, 14/1 and 2 (1932–3), pp. i–xi, 1–145 [contains a useful bibliography].

Jacobine Menzies-Wilson and Helen Lloyd, *Amelia: The Tale of a Plain Friend* (London: Oxford University Press, 1937).

Anne Thackeray Ritchie, *A Book of Sibyls* (London: Smith, Elder, & Co., 1883) [biography of Opie, 149–96].

William St Clair, *The Godwins and the Shelleys: The Biography of a Family* (London, Faber & Faber, 1989) [while devoted mainly to the Godwins and Shelleys, this biography offers authoritative commentary on Opie's relationship with Godwin and Wollstonecraft].

Recent Criticism

Roxanne Eberle, 'Amelia Opie's *Adeline Mowbray*: Diverting the Libertine Gaze; or, The Vindication of a Fallen Woman', *Studies in the Novel*, 26/2 (Summer 1994), 121–52.

Jan Fergus and Janice Farrar Thaddeus, 'Women, Publishers, and Money, 1790–1820', *Studies in Eighteenth-Century Culture*, 17 (1987), 191–207.

Carol Howard, '"The Story of the Pineapple": Sentimental Abolitionism and Moral Motherhood in Amelia Opie's *Adeline Mowbray*', *Studies in the Novel*, 30 (1998), 355–76.

Gary Kelly, 'Amelia Opie, Lady Caroline Lamb, and Maria Edgeworth: Official and Unofficial Ideology', *Ariel: A Review of International English Literature*, 12/4 (Oct. 1981), 3–24.

——'Discharging Debts: The Moral Economy of Amelia Opie's Fiction', *The Wordsworth Circle*, 11 (1980), 198–203.

—— *English Fiction of the Romantic Period* (London: Longman, 1989).

Further Reading in Oxford World's Classics

Godwin, William, *Caleb Williams*, ed. David McCracken.

—— *St Leon*, ed. Pamela Clemit.

Wollstonecraft, Mary, *Mary and The Wrongs of Woman*, ed. Gary Kelly.

—— *Political Writings*, ed. Janet Todd.

A CHRONOLOGY OF
AMELIA ALDERSON OPIE

1769   (12 November) born in Norwich, England; only child of James and Amelia (Briggs) Alderson.

1784   (31 December) mother dies; Amelia enters society and assumes control of her father's household; among their friends are the Gurney family, including children John Joseph, who was to become a leading figure in Quaker circles, and Elizabeth, who after her marriage to Joseph Fry became a leading advocate for prison reform.

1786   Writes *Adelaide*, a five-act play; social circle includes Mrs John Taylor, as well as Dr Aiken and his sister, Anna Letitia Barbauld; meets Sarah Siddons, the actress, in Norwich (September).

1789   (14 July) beginning of the French Revolution, greeted with enthusiasm by circle in Norwich.

1790   *The Dangers of Coquetry*, her first novel, published anonymously by Minerva Press.

1791   (4, 6 January) *Adelaide* produced at private theatre in Norwich, with Amelia Alderson playing a principal role.

1792   (May) Royal proclamation against circulation of seditious writings, beginning of anti-radical persecution in England.

1794   Meets William Godwin at a dinner given in his honour by her father in Norwich.

        Visits Godwin in London; attends treason trial of radicals Horne Tooke, Thomas Holcroft, Thomas Hardy, and John Thelwall; she and her father consider emigrating to America should the trial end in conviction.

1795   Fifteen poems printed in volumes 1–3 of the Norwich *Cabinet*, a radical periodical.

1796   Meets Mary Wollstonecraft; a close friendship ensues.

1798   Marries painter John Opie (May); social circle includes women of fashion such as Lady Cork and Lady Caroline Lamb, artists such as James Northcote and Joshua Reynolds, and writers such as Elizabeth Inchbald.

1799   Four poems published in first *Annual Anthology*, favourably reviewed.

1801   *The Father and Daughter* published (Longman, Hurst, Rees, Orme & Brown: two editions within the year).

1802   (August–October) visits Paris, meets Maria Edgeworth, Benjamin West, and J. M. W. Turner as well as Helen Maria Williams; songs solicited by George Thomson for his collection of Welsh airs; *Poems* published in the autumn; also *An Elegy to the Memory of the Late Duke of Bedford*.

1805   (January) *Adeline Mowbray, or The Mother and Daughter* published.

1806   *Simple Tales*, a collection of stories, published.

1807   (9 April) John Opie dies, buried in St Paul's Cathedral, 20 April; Amelia returns to Norwich where she edits her husband's *Lectures and Memoirs*; *The Warrior's Return and Other Poems* published.

1809   Ferdinando Paër, Italian composer of more than forty operas, creates opera *L'Agnese*, based on *The Father and Daughter*.

1810   Returns to London, meets Madame de Staël.

1812   *Temper; or, Domestic Scenes: A Tale*, published; quotes four lines from William Hayley's 1781 poem *The Triumph of Temper*, leading to sustained correspondence.

1813   *Tales of Real Life* published.

1814   Leaves Unitarian church and begins attending Quaker services.

1816   *Valentine's Eve* published; *Smiles and Tears*, a play by Mrs Kemble based on *The Father and Daughter*, produced in London; meets Sir Walter Scott, who tells her he wept on reading *The Father and Daughter*.

1818   *New Tales* published.

1820   *Tales of the Heart* published.

1821   (September) *Gerald Durald, the Bandit of Belemia*, a play based on 'The Ruffian Boy' from *New Tales*, produced at Drury Lane; it had earlier been dramatized and produced at Norwich by Edward Fitzball.

1822   *Madeline: A Tale* published (her last novel).

1825   (11 August) application accepted for admission to the Society of Friends, cementing a long friendship with the Gurney family; because of Quaker prohibitions concerning the worldliness of fiction, Opie shifts to more didactic works; publishes *Lying in All its Branches* as well as *Tales of the Pemberton*

Family (for children); (20 October) death of her father, James Alderson.

1826   *The Black Man's Lament* published (anti-slavery poem for children).

1828   *Detraction Displayed* published.

1829   Visits Paris: profile medal sculpted by Jacques-Louis David, entertained in social circle of Lafayette; she records that she was 'courted for . . . [her] *past*, not . . . [her] *recent* writings'.

1830   (August) news of civil unrest leads to her return to Paris.

1832   Visits Cornwall.

1834   *Lays for the Dead* published; (August) visits Scotland.

1835   Visits the Continent.

1839   'The Novice: A True Story' solicited for *Finden's Tableaux*, ed. M. R. Mitford.

1840   Anti-Slavery Convention in London, sits for Benjamin Haydon for his group portrait of the convention; 'Recollections of Days in Belgium' published in *Tait's Edinburgh Magazine*.

1844   Revises and reissues *Adeline Mowbray* (Grove edition).

1851   (May) attends Great Exhibition in London, where she suggests a wheelchair race to a fellow invalid.

1853   (2 December) dies in Norwich; buried in her father's grave in the Friends' Cemetery.

ADELINE MOWBRAY,

OR THE

MOTHER AND DAUGHTER:

A Tale,

IN THREE VOLUMES.

———

BY MRS. OPIE.

———

VOL. I.

═══

LONDON:

PRINTED FOR LONGMAN, HURST, REES, & ORME,

PATERNOSTER ROW;

AND A. CONSTABLE AND CO. EDINBURGH.

———

1805.

VOLUME I

CHAPTER I

In an old family mansion, situated on an estate in Gloucestershire known by the name of Rosevalley, resided Mrs Mowbray, and Adeline her only child.

Mrs Mowbray's father, Mr Woodville, a respectable country gentleman, married, in obedience to the will of his mother, the sole surviving daughter of an opulent merchant in London, whose large dower paid off some considerable mortgages on the Woodville estates, and whose mild and unoffending character soon gained that affection from her husband after marriage, which he denied her before it.

Nor was it long before their happiness was increased, and their union cemented, by the birth of a daughter; who continuing to be an only child, and the probable heiress of great possessions, became the idol of her parents, and the object of unremitted attention to those who surrounded her. Consequently, one of the first lessons which Editha Woodville learnt was that of egotism, and to consider it as the chief duty of all who approached her, to study the gratification of her whims and caprices.

But, though rendered indolent in some measure by the blind folly of her parents, and the homage of her dependents, she had a taste above the enjoyments which they offered her.

She had a decided passion for literature, which she had acquired from a sister of Mr Woodville, who had been brought up amongst literary characters of various pursuits and opinions; and this lady had imbibed from them a love of free inquiry, which she had little difficulty in imparting to her young and enthusiastic relation.

But, alas! that inclination for study, which, had it been directed to proper objects, would have been the charm of miss Woodville's life, and the safeguard of her happiness, by giving her a constant source of amusement within herself, proved to her, from the unfortunate direction which it took, the abundant cause of misery and disappointment.

For her, history, biography, poetry, and discoveries in natural philosophy,* had few attractions, while she pored with still unsatisfied delight over abstruse systems of morals and metaphysics, or new theories in politics;* and scarcely a week elapsed in which she did not receive, from her aunt's bookseller in London, various tracts on these her favourite subjects.

Happy would it have been for miss Woodville, if the merits of the works which she so much admired could have been canvassed in her presence by rational and unprejudiced persons: but, her parents and friends being too ignorant to discuss philosophical opinions or political controversies, the young speculator was left to the decisions of her own inexperienced enthusiasm. To her, therefore, whatever was bold and uncommon seemed new and wise; and every succeeding theory held her imagination captive till its power was weakened by one of equal claims to singularity.

She soon, however, ceased to be contented with reading, and was eager to become a writer also. But, as she was strongly imbued with the prejudices of an antient family, she could not think of disgracing that family by turning professed author: she therefore confined her little effusions to a society of admiring friends, secretly lamenting the loss which the literary world sustained in her being born a gentlewoman.

Nor is it to be wondered at, that, as she was ambitious to be, and to be thought, a deep thinker, she should have acquired habits of abstraction, and absence, which imparted a look of wildness to a pair of dark eyes, that beamed with intelligence, and gave life to features of the most perfect regularity.

To reverie, indeed, she was from childhood inclined; and her life was long a life of reverie. To her the present moment had scarcely ever existence; and this propensity to lose herself in a sort of ideal world, was considerably increased by the nature of her studies.

Fatal and unproductive studies! While, wrapt in philosophical abstraction, she was trying to understand a metaphysical question on the mechanism of the human mind, or what constituted the true nature of virtue, she suffered day after day to pass in the culpable neglect of positive duties; and while imagining systems for the good of society, and the furtherance of general philanthropy, she allowed individual suffering in her neighbourhood to pass unobserved and unrelieved. While professing her unbounded love for the great family of the world, she suffered her own family to pine under the consciousness of her neglect; and viciously devoted those hours to the vanity of abstruse and solitary study, which might have been better spent in amusing the declining age of her venerable parents, whom affection had led to take up their abode with her.

Let me observe, before I proceed further, that Mrs Mowbray scrupulously confined herself to theory, even in her wisest speculations; and being too timid, and too indolent, to illustrate by her conduct the various and opposing doctrines which it was her pride to maintain by turns, her practice was ever in opposition to her opinions.

Hence, after haranguing with all the violence of a true whig on the natural rights of man, or the blessings of freedom, she would 'turn to a tory in her elbow chair,'* and govern her household with despotic authority; and after embracing at some moments the doubts of the sceptic, she would often lie motionless in her bed, from apprehension of ghosts, a helpless prey to the most abject superstition.

Such was the mother of ADELINE MOWBRAY! such was the woman who, having married the heir of Rosevalley, merely to oblige her parents, saw herself in the prime of life a rich widow, with an only child, who was left by Mr Mowbray, a fond husband, but an ill-judging parent, entirely dependent on her!

At the time of Mr Mowbray's death, Adeline Mowbray was ten years old, and Mrs Mowbray thirty; and like an animal in an exhausted receiver,* she had during her short existence been tormented by the experimental philosophy of her mother.*

Now it was judged right that she should learn nothing, and now that she should learn every thing. Now, her graceful form and well-turned limbs were to be free from any bandage, and any clothing save what decency required,—and now they were to be tortured by stiff stays, and fettered by the stocks and the back-board.

All Mrs Mowbray's ambition had settled in one point, one passion, and that was EDUCATION. For this purpose she turned over innumerable volumes in search of rules on the subject, on which she might improve, anticipating with great satisfaction the moment when she should be held up as a pattern of imitation to mothers, and be prevailed upon, though with graceful reluctance, to publish her system, without a name, for the benefit of society.

But, however good her intentions were, the execution of them was continually delayed by her habits of abstraction and reverie. After having over night arranged the tasks of Adeline for the next day,— lost in some new speculations for the good of her child, she would lie in bed all the morning, exposing that child to the dangers of idleness.

At one time Mrs Mowbray had studied herself into great nicety with regard to the diet of her daughter; but, as she herself was too much used to the indulgencies of the palate to be able to set her in reality an example of temperance, she dined in appearance with Adeline at one o'clock on pudding without butter,* and potatoes without salt; but while the child was taking her afternoon's walk, her own table was covered with viands fitted for the appetite of opulence.

Unfortunately, however, the servants conceived that the daughter as well as the mother had a right to regale clandestinely; and the little Adeline used to eat for her supper, with a charge not to tell her mamma, some of the good things set by from Mrs Mowbray's dinner.

It happened that, as Mrs Mowbray was one evening smoothing Adeline's flowing curls, and stroking her ruddy cheek, she exclaimed triumphantly, raising Adeline to the glass, 'See the effect of temperance and low living! If you were accustomed to eat meat, and butter, and drink any thing but water, you would not look so healthy, my love, as you do now. O the excellent effects of a vegetable diet!'

The artless girl, whose conscience smote her during the whole of this speech, hung her blushing head on her bosom:—it was the confusion of guilt; and Mrs Mowbray perceiving it earnestly demanded what it meant, when Adeline, half crying, gave a full explanation.

Nothing could exceed the astonishment and mortification of Mrs Mowbray; but, though usually tenacious of her opinions, she in this case profited by the lesson of experience. She no longer expected any advantage from clandestine measures:—but Adeline, her appetites regulated by a proper exertion of parental authority, was allowed to sit at the well-furnished table of her mother, and was precluded, by a judicious and open indulgence, from wishing for a secret and improper one; while the judicious praises which Mrs Mowbray bestowed on Adeline's ingenuous confession endeared to her the practice of truth, and laid the foundation of a habit of ingenuousness which formed through life one of the ornaments of her character... Would that Mrs Mowbray had always been equally judicious!

Another great object of anxiety to her was the method of clothing children; whether they should wear flannel, or no flannel;* light shoes, to give agility to the motions of the limbs; or heavy shoes, in order to strengthen the muscles by exertion;—when one day, as she was turning over a voluminous author on this subject, the nursery-maid hastily entered the room, and claimed her attention, but in vain; Mrs Mowbray went on reading aloud:—

'Some persons are of opinion that thin shoes are most beneficial to health; others, equally worthy of respect, think thick ones of most use: and the reasons for these different opinions we shall class under two heads...'

'Dear me, ma'am!' cried Bridget, 'and in the mean time miss Adeline will go without any shoes at all.'

'Do not interrupt me, Bridget,' cried Mrs Mowbray, and proceeded to read on. 'In the first place, it is not clear, says a learned writer, whether children require any clothing at all for their feet.'*

At this moment Adeline burst open the parlour door, and, crying bitterly, held up her bleeding toes to her mother.

'Mamma, mamma!' cried she, 'you forget to send for a pair of new shoes for me; and see, how the stones in the gravel have cut me!'

This sight, this appeal, decided the question in dispute. The feet of Adeline bleeding on a new Turkey carpet proved that some clothing for the feet was necessary; and even Mrs Mowbray for a moment began to suspect that a little experience is better than a great deal of theory.

CHAPTER II

Meanwhile, in spite of all Mrs Mowbray's eccentricities and caprices, Adeline, as she grew up, continued to entertain for her the most perfect respect and affection.

Her respect was excited by the high idea which she had formed of her abilities,—an idea founded on the veneration which all the family seemed to feel for her on that account,—and her affection was excited even to an enthusiastic degree by the tenderness with which Mrs Mowbray had watched over her during an alarming illness.

For twenty-one days Adeline had been in the utmost danger; nor is it probable that she would have been able to struggle against the force of the disease, but for the unremitting attention of her mother. It was then, perhaps, for the first time that Mrs Mowbray felt herself a mother:—all her vanities, all her systems, were forgotten in the danger of Adeline,—she did not even hazard an opinion on the medical treatment to be observed. For once she was contented to obey instructions in silence; for once she was never caught in a reverie; but, like the most common-place woman of her acquaintance, she lived to the present moment:—and she was rewarded for her cares by the recovery of her daughter, and by that daughter's most devoted attachment.

Not even the parents of Mrs Mowbray, who, because she talked on subjects which they could not understand, looked up to her as a superior being, could exceed Adeline in deference to her mother's abilities; and when, as she advanced in life, she was sometimes tempted to think her deficient in maternal fondness, the idea of Mrs Mowbray bending with pale and speechless anxiety over her sleepless pillow used to recur to her remembrance, and in a moment the recent indifference was forgotten.

Nor could she entirely acquit herself of ingratitude in observing this seeming indifference: for, whence did the abstraction and apparent coldness of Mrs Mowbray proceed? From her mind's being wholly engrossed in studies for the future benefit of Adeline. Why did she leave the concerns of her family to others? why did she allow her infirm but active mother to superintend all the household duties? and why did she seclude herself from all society, save that of her own family, and Dr Norberry, her physician and friend, but that she might devote every hour to endeavours to perfect a system of education for her beloved and only daughter, to whom the work was to be dedicated?

'And yet,' said Adeline mentally, 'I am so ungrateful sometimes as to think she does not love me sufficiently.'

But while Mrs Mowbray was busying herself in plans for Adeline's education, she reached the age of fifteen, and was in a manner educated; not, however, by her,—though Mrs Mowbray would, no doubt, have been surprised to have heard this assertion.

Mrs Mowbray, as I have before said, was the spoiled child of rich parents; who, as geniuses were rarer in those days than they are now, spite of their own ignorance, rejoiced to find themselves the parents of a genius; and as their daughter always disliked the usual occupations of her sex, the admiring father and mother contented themselves with allowing her to please herself; saying to each other, 'She must not be managed in a common way; for you know, my dear, she is one of your geniuses,—and they are never like other folks.'

Mrs Woodville, the mother, had been brought up with all the ideas of œconomy and housewifery which at that time of day prevailed in the city, and influenced the education of the daughters of citizens.

'My dear,' said she one day to Adeline, 'as you are no genius, you know, like your mother, (and God forbid you should! for one is quite enough in a family,) I shall make bold to teach you every thing that young women in my young days used to learn, and my daughter may thank me for it some time or other: for you know, my dear, when I and my good man die, what in the world would come of my poor Edith, if so be she had no one to manage for her! for, Lord love you! she knows no more of managing a family, and such-like, than a new-born babe.'

'And can you, dear grandmother, teach me to be of use to my mother?' said Adeline.

'To be sure, child; for, as you are no genius, no doubt you can learn all them there sort of things that women commonly know:—so we will begin directly.'

In a short time Adeline, stimulated by the ambition of being useful, (for she had often heard her mother assert that utility was the foundation of all virtue,) became as expert in household affairs as Mrs Woodville herself: even the department of making pastry was now given up to Adeline, and the servants always came to her for orders, saying, that 'as their mistress was a learned lady, and that, and so could not be spoken with except here and there on occasion, they wished their young mistress, who was more easy spoken, would please to order:' and as Mr and Mrs Woodville's infirmities increased every day, Adeline soon thought it right to assume the entire management of the family.

She also took upon herself the office of almoner to Mrs Woodville, and performed it with an activity unknown to her; for she herself carried the broth and wine that were to comfort the infirm cottager; she herself saw the medicine properly administered that was to preserve his suffering existence: the comforts the poor required she purchased herself; and in sickness she visited, in sorrow she wept with them. And though Adeline was almost unknown personally to the neighbouring gentry, she was followed with blessings by the surrounding cottagers; while many a humble peasant watched at the gate of the park to catch a glimpse of his young benefactress, and pray God to repay to the heiress of Rosevalley the kindness which she had shewn to him and his offspring.

Thus happy, because usefully employed, and thus beloved and respected, because actively benevolent, passed the early years of Adeline Mowbray; and thus was she educated, before her mother had completed her system of education.

It was not long before Adeline took on herself a still more important office. Mrs Mowbray's steward was detected in very dishonest practices; but, as she was too much devoted to her studies to like to look into her affairs with a view to dismiss him, she could not be prevailed upon to discharge him from her service. Fortunately, however, her father on his death-bed made it his request that she would do so; and Mrs Mowbray pledged herself to obey him.

'But what shall I do for a steward in Davison's place?' said she soon after her father died.

'Is one absolutely necessary?' returned Adeline modestly. 'Surely farmer Jenkins would undertake to do all that is necessary for half the money; and, if he were properly overlooked—'

'And pray who can overlook him properly?' asked Mrs Mowbray.

'My grandmother and I,' replied Adeline timidly: 'we both like business, and—'

'Like business... but what do you know of it?'

'Know!' cried Mrs Woodville, 'why, daughter, Lina is very clever at it, I assure you!'

'Astonishing! She knows nothing yet of accounts.'

'Dear me! how mistaken you are, child! She knows accounts perfectly.'

'Impossible!' replied Mrs Mowbray: 'who should have taught her? I have been inventing an easy method of learning arithmetic,* by which I was going to teach her in a few months.'

'Yes, child: but I, thinking it a pity that the poor girl should learn nothing, like, till she was to learn every thing, taught her according to the old way; and I cannot but say she took to it very kindly. Did not you, Lina?'

'Yes, grandmother,' said Adeline; 'and as I love arithmetic very much, I am quite anxious to keep all my mother's accounts, and overlook the accounts of the person whom she shall employ to manage her estates in future.'

To this Mrs Mowbray, half pleased and half mortified, at length consented; and Adeline and farmer Jenkins entered upon their occupations. Shortly after Mrs Woodville was seized with her last illness; and Adeline neglected every other duty, and Mrs Mowbray her studies, 'to watch, and weep, beside a parent's bed.'*

But watch and weep was all Mrs Mowbray did: with every possible wish to be useful, she had so long given way to habits of abstraction, and neglect of everyday occupations, that she was rather a hindrance than a help in the sick-room.

During Adeline's illness, excessive fear of losing her only child had indeed awakened her to unusual exertion; and as all that she had to do was to get down, at stated times, a certain quantity of wine and nourishment, her task though wearisome was not difficult: but to sooth the declining hours of an aged parent, to please the capricious appetite of decay, to assist with ready and skilful alacrity the shaking hand of the invalid, jealous of waiting on herself and wanting to be cheated into being waited upon;—these trifling yet important details did not suit the habits of Mrs Mowbray. But Adeline was versed in them all; and her mother, conscious of her superiority in these things, was at last contented to sit by inactive, though not unmoved.

One day, when Mrs Mowbray had been prevailed upon to lie down for an hour or two in another apartment, and Adeline was administering to Mrs Woodville some broth which she had made herself, the old lady pressed her hand affectionately, and cried, 'Ah! child, in a lucky hour I made bold to interfere, and teach you what your mother was always too clever to learn. Wise was I to think one genius enough in a family,—else, what should I have done now? Lord bless me! my daughter, though the best child in the world, could never have made such nice broth as this to comfort me, so hot, and boiled to a minute like! Lord bless her! she'd have tried, that she would, but ten to one but she'd have smoked it, overturned it, and scalt her fingers into the bargain.—Ah, Lina, Lina! mayhap the time will come, when you, should you have a sick husband or child to nurse, may bless your poor grandmother for having taught you to be useful.'

'Dear grandmother,' said Adeline tenderly, 'the time is come: I am, you see, useful to you; and therefore I bless you already for having taught me to be so.'

'Good girl, good girl! just what I would have you! And God forgive me, and you too, Lina, when I own that I have often thanked God for not making you a genius! Not but what no child can behave better than mine; for, with all her wit and learning, she was always so respectful, and so kind to me and my dear good man, that I am sure I could not but rejoice in such a daughter; though, to be sure, I used to wish she was more conversible like; for, as to the matter of a bit of chat, Lord help us and save us! we never gossiped together in our lives. And though, to be sure, the squires' ladies about are none of the brightest, and not to compare with my Edith, yet still they would have done very well for me and my dear good man to gossip a bit with. So I was vexed when my daughter declared she wanted all her time for her studies, and would not visit any body, no, not even Mrs Norberry, who is to be sure a very good sort of woman, though a little given to speak ill of her neighbours. But then so we are all, you know: and, as I say, why, if one spoke well of all alike, what would be the use of one person's being better than his neighbours, except for conscience' sake? But, as I was going to say, my daughter was pleased to compliment me, and declare she was sure I could amuse myself without visiting women so much inferior to me; and she advised my beginning a course of study, as she called it.'

'And did you?' asked Adeline with surprise.

'Yes. To oblige her, my good man and I began to read one Mr Locke on the conduct of the human understanding;* which my daughter said would teach us to think.'

'To think?' said Adeline.

'Yes.—Now, you must know, my poor husband did not look upon it as very respectful like in Edith to say that, because it seemed to say that we had lived all these years without having thought at all; which was not true, to be sure, because we were never thoughtless like, and my husband was so staid when a boy that he was called a little old man.'

'But I am sure', said Adeline, half smiling, 'that my mother did not mean to insinuate that you wanted proper thought.'

'No, I dare say not,' resumed the old lady, 'and so I told my husband, and so we set to study this book: but, dear me! it was Hebrew Greek to us—and so dull!'

'Then you did not get through it, I suppose?'

'Through it, bless your heart! No—not three pages! So my good man says to Edith, says he, "You gave us this book, I think, child, to teach us to think?" "Yes, sir," says she. "And it has taught us to think," says he:—"it has taught us to think that it is very dull and disagreeable." So my daughter laughed, and said her father was witty; but, poor soul! he did not mean it.

'Well, then: as, to amuse us, we liked to look at the stars sometimes, she told us we had better learn their names, and study astronomy; and so we began that: but that was just as bad as Mr Locke; and we knew no more of the stars and planets, than the man in the moon. Yet that's not right to say, neither; for, as he is so much nearer the stars, he must know more about them than any one whomsoever. So at last my daughter found out that learning was not our taste: so she left us to please ourselves, and play cribbage and draughts* in an evening as usual.'

Here the old lady paused, and Adeline said affectionately, 'Dear grandmother, I doubt* you exert yourself too much: so much talking can't be good for you.'

'O! yes, child!' replied Mrs Woodville: 'it is no trouble at all to me, I assure you, but quite natural and pleasant like: besides, you know I shall not be able to talk much longer, so let me make the most of my time now.'

This speech brought tears into the eyes of Adeline; and seeing her mother re-enter the room, she withdrew to conceal the emotion which she felt, lest the cheerful loquacity of the invalid, which she was fond of indulging, should be checked by seeing her tears. But it had already received a check from the presence of Mrs Mowbray, of whose superior abilities Mrs Woodville was so much in awe, that, concluding her daughter could not bear to hear her nonsense, the old lady smiled kindly on her when with a look of tender anxiety she hastened to her bedside, and then, holding her hand, composed herself to sleep.

In a few days more, she breathed her last on the supporting arm of Adeline; and lamented in her dying moments, that she had nothing valuable in money to leave, in order to show Adeline how sensible she was of her affectionate attentions: 'but you are an only child,' she added, 'and all your mother has will be yours.'

'No doubt,' observed Mrs Mowbray eagerly; and her mother died contented.

CHAPTER III

At this period Adeline's ambition had led her to form new plans, which Mrs Woodville's death left her at liberty to put in execution. Whenever the old lady reminded her that she was no genius, Adeline had felt as much degraded as if she had said that she was no con-juror;* and though she was too humble to suppose that she could ever equal her mother, she was resolved to try to make herself more worthy of her, by imitating her in those pursuits and studies on which were founded Mrs Mowbray's pretensions to superior talents.

She therefore made it her business to inquire what those studies and pursuits were; and finding that Mrs Mowbray's noted superi-ority was built on her passion for abstruse speculations, Adeline eagerly devoted her leisure hours to similar studies: but, unfor-tunately, these new theories, and these romantic reveries, which only served to amuse Mrs Mowbray's fancy, her more enthusiastic daughter resolved to make conscientiously the rules of her practice. And while Mrs Mowbray expended her eccentric philosophy in words, as Mr Shandy did his grief,* Adeline carefully treasured up hers in her heart, to be manifested only by its fruits.

One author in particular, by a train of reasoning captivating though sophistical, and plausible though absurd, made her a delighted convert to his opinions, and prepared her young and impassioned heart for the practice of vice, by filling her mind, ardent in the love of virtue, with new and singular opinions on the subject of moral duty. On the works of this writer Adeline had often heard her mother descant in terms of the highest praise; but she did not feel herself so completely his convert on her own conviction, till she had experienced the fatal fascination of his style, and been conveyed by his bewitching pen from the world as it is, into a world as it *ought* to be.

This writer, whose name was Glenmurray, amongst other insti-tutions, attacked the institution of marriage;* and after having elaborately pointed out its folly and its wickedness, he drew so delightful a picture of the superior purity, as well as happiness, of an union cemented by no ties but those of love and honour, that Adeline, wrought to the highest pitch of enthusiasm for a new order of things, entered into a solemn compact with herself to act, when she was introduced into society, according to the rules laid down by this writer.

Unfortunately for her, she had no opportunity of hearing these opinions combated by the good sense and sober experience of Dr Norberry, then their sole visitant; for at this time the American war* was the object of attention to all Europe: and as Mrs Mowbray, as well as Dr Norberry, were deeply interested in this subject, they scarcely ever talked on any other; and even Glenmurray and his theories were driven from Mrs Mowbray's remembrance by political tracts and the eager anxieties of a politician. Nor had she even leisure to observe, that while she was feeling all the generous anxiety of a citizen of the world for the sons and daughters of American independence, her own child was imbibing, through her means, opinions dangerous to her well-being as a member of any civilized society, and laying, perhaps, the foundation to herself and her mother of future misery and disgrace. Alas! the astrologer in the fable* was but too like Mrs Mowbray!

But even had Adeline had an opportunity of discussing her new opinions with Dr Norberry, it is not at all certain that she would have had the power.

Mrs Mowbray was, if I may be allowed the expression, a showing-off woman,* and loved the information which she acquired, less for its own sake than for the supposed importance which it gave her amongst her acquaintance, and the means of displaying her superiority over other women. Before she secluded herself from society in order to study education, she had been the terror of the ladies in the neighbourhood; since, despising small talk, she would always insist on making the gentlemen of her acquaintance (as much terrified sometimes as their wives) engage with her in some literary or political conversation. She wanted to convert every drawing-room into an arena for the mind, and all her guests into intellectual gladiators. She was often heard to interrupt two grave matrons in an interesting discussion of an accouchement, by asking them if they had read a new theological tract, or a pamphlet against the minister? If they softly expatiated on the lady-like fatigue of body which they had endured, she discoursed in choice terms on the energies of the mind; and she never received or paid visits without convincing the company that she was the most wise, most learned, and most disagreeable of companions.

But Adeline, on the contrary, studied merely from the love of study, and not with a view to shine in conversation; nor dared she venture to expatiate on subjects which she had often heard Mrs Woodville say were very rarely canvassed, or even alluded to, by women. She remained silent, therefore, on the subject nearest her heart, from choice as well as necessity, in the presence of Dr Norberry, till at length she imbibed the political mania herself, and soon found it impossible to conceal the interest which she took in the success of the infant republic. She therefore one day put into the doctor's hands some bouts rimés* which she had written on some recent victory of the American arms; exclaiming with a smile, 'I, too, am a politician!'* and was rewarded by an exclamation of 'Zounds! girl—I protest you are as clever as your mother!'

This unexpected declaration fixed her in the path of literary ambition: and though wisely resolved to fulfil, as usual, every feminine duty, Adeline was convinced that she, like her mother, had a right to be an author, a politician, and a philosopher; while Dr Norberry's praises of her daughter convinced Mrs Mowbray, that almost unconsciously she had educated her into a prodigy, and confirmed her in her intention of exhibiting herself and Adeline to the admiring world during the next season at Bath;* for at Bath she expected to receive that admiration which she had vainly sought in London.

Soon after their marriage, Mr Mowbray had carried his lovely bride to the metropolis, where she expected to receive the same homage which had been paid to her charms at the assize-balls* in her neighbourhood. What then must have been her disappointment, when, instead of hearing as she passed, 'That is miss Woodville, the rich heiress—or the great genius—or the great beauty'—or, 'That is the beautiful Mrs Mowbray,' she walked unknown and unobserved in public and in private, and found herself of as little importance in the wide world of the metropolis, as the most humble of her acquaintance in a country ball-room. True, she had beauty, but then it was unset-off by fashion; nay, more, it was eclipsed by unfashionable and tasteless attire; and her manner, though stately

and imposing in an assembly where she was known, was wholly
unlike the manners of the world, and in a London party appeared
arrogant and offensive. Her remarks, too, wise as they appeared to
her and Mr Mowbray, excited little attention,—as the few persons to
whom they were known in the metropolis were wholly ignorant of
her high pretensions, and knew not that they were discoursing with a
professed genius, and the oracle of a provincial circle. Some persons,
indeed, surprised at hearing from the lips of eighteen, observations
on morals, theology, and politics, listened to her with wonder, and
even attention, but turned away, observing—

> Such things, 'tis true, are neither new nor rare,
> The only wonder is, how they got there:*

till at length, disappointed, mortified, and disgusted, Mrs Mowbray
impatiently returned to Rosevalley, where in beauty, in learning, and
in grandeur she was unrivalled, and where she might deal out her
dogmas, sure of exciting respectful attention, however she might fail
of calling forth a more flattering tribute from her auditors. But in the
narrower field of Bath she expected to shine forth with greater éclat
than in London, and to obtain admiration more worthy of her
acceptance than any which a country circle could offer.

To Bath, therefore, she prepared to go; and the young heart of
Adeline beat high with pleasure at the idea of mixing with that busy
world which her fancy had often clothed in the most winning
attractions.

But her joy, and Mrs Mowbray's, was a little overclouded at the
moment of their departure, by the sight of Dr Norberry's melancholy countenance. What was to be, as they fondly imagined, their
gain, was his loss, and with a full heart he came to bid them adieu.

For Adeline he had conceived not only affection, but esteem
amounting almost to veneration; for she appeared to him to unite
various and opposing excellencies. Though possessed of taste and
talents for literature, she was skilled in the minutest details of
housewifery and feminine occupations; and at the same time she
bore her faculties so meekly, that she never wounded the self-love of
any one, by arrogating to herself any superiority.

Such Adeline appeared to her excellent old friend; and his
affection for her was, perhaps, increased by the necessity which he
was under of concealing it at home. The praises of Mrs Mowbray

and Adeline were odious to the ears of Mrs Norberry and his daughters,—but especially the praises of the latter,—as the merit of Adeline was so uniform, that even the eye of envy could not at that period discover any thing in her vulnerable to censure: and as the sound of her name excited in his family a number of bad passions and corresponding expressions of countenance, the doctor wisely resolved to keep his feelings, with regard to her, locked up in his own bosom.

But he persisted in visiting at the Park daily; and it is no wonder, therefore, that the loss, even for a few months, of the society of its inhabitants should by him be anticipated as a serious calamity.

'Zounds!' cried he, as Adeline, with an exulting bound, sprung after her mother into the carriage, 'how gay and delighted you are! though my heart feels devilish queer and heavy.'

'My dear friend,' cried Mrs Mowbray, 'I must miss your society wherever I go.'—'I wish you were going too,' said Adeline: 'I shall often think of you.' 'Pshaw, girl! don't lie,' replied Dr Norberry, swallowing a sigh as he spoke: 'you will soon forget an old fellow like me.'—'Then I conclude that you will soon forget us.'—'He! how! what! think so at your peril.'—'I must think so, as we usually judge of others by ourselves.'—'Go to—go, miss mal-a-pert.—Well, but, drive on, coachman—this taking leave is plaguy disagreeable, so shake hands and be off.'

They gave him their hands, which he pressed very affectionately, and the carriage drove on.

'I am an old fool,' cried the doctor, wiping his eyes as the carriage disappeared. 'Well: God grant, sweet innocent, that you may return to me as happy and spotless as you now are!'

Mrs Mowbray had been married at a very early age, and had accepted in Mr Mowbray the first man who addressed her: consequently, that passion for personal admiration, so natural to women, had in her never been gratified, nor even called forth. But seeing herself, at the age of thirty-eight, possessed of almost undiminished beauty, she recollected that her charms had never received that general homage for which Nature intended them; and she who at twenty had disregarded, even to a fault, the ornaments of dress, was now, at the age of thirty-eight, eager to indulge in the extremes of decoration, and to share in the delights of conquest and admiration with her youthful and attractive daughter.

Attractive, rather than handsome, was the epithet best suited to describe Adeline Mowbray. Her beauty was the beauty of expression of countenance, not regularity of feature, though the uncommon fairness and delicacy of her complexion, the lustre of her hazel eyes, her long dark eyelashes, and the profusion of soft light hair which curled over the ever-mantling colour of her cheek, gave her some pretensions to what is denominated beauty. But her own sex declared she was plain—and perhaps they were right—though the other protested against the decision—and probably they were right also: but women criticize in detail, men admire in the aggregate. Women reason, and men feel, when passing judgment on female beauty: and when a woman declares another to be plain, the chances are that she is right in her opinion, as she cannot, from her being a woman, feel the charm of that power to please, that 'something than beauty dearer,'* which often throws a veil over the irregularity of features, and obtains, for even a plain woman, from men at least, the appellation of pretty.

Whether Adeline's face were plain or not, her form could defy even the severity of female criticism. She was indeed tall, almost to a masculine degree; but such were the roundness and proportion of her limbs, such the symmetry of her whole person, such the lightness and gracefulness of her movements, and so truly feminine were her look and manner, that her superior height was forgotten in the superior loveliness of her figure.

It is not to be wondered at, then, that miss Mowbray was an object of attention and admiration at Bath, as soon as she appeared, nor that her mother had her share of flattery and followers. Indeed, when it was known that Mrs Mowbray was a rich widow, and Adeline dependent upon her, the mother became, in the eyes of some people, much more attractive than her daughter.

It was impossible, however, that, in such a place as Bath, Mrs Mowbray and Adeline could make, or rather retain, a general acquaintance. Their opinions on most subjects were so very different from those of the world, and they were so little conscious, from the retirement in which they had lived, that this difference existed, or was likely to make them enemies, that not a day elapsed in which they did not shock the prejudices of some, and excite the contemptuous pity of others; and they soon saw their acquaintance coolly dropped by those who, as persons of family and fortune, had on their first arrival sought it with eagerness.

But this was not entirely owing to the freedom of their sentiments on politics, or on other subjects; but, because they associated with a well-known but obnoxious author;—a man whose speculations had delighted the inquiring but ignorant lover of novelty, terrified the timid idolater of antient usages, and excited the regret of the cool and rational observer:—regret, that eloquence so overwhelming, powers of reasoning so acute, activity of research so praise-worthy, and a love of investigation so ardent, should be thrown away on the discussion of moral and political subjects, incapable of teaching the world to build up again with more beauty and propriety, a fabric, which they were, perhaps, calculated to pull down: in short, Mrs Mowbray and Adeline associated with Glenmurray, that author over whose works they had long delighted to meditate, and who had completely led their imagination captive, before the fascination of his countenance and manners had come in aid of his eloquence.

CHAPTER IV

Frederic Glenmurray was a man of family, and of a small independent estate, which, in case he died without children, was to go to the next male heir; and to that heir it was certain it would go, as Glenmurray on principle was an enemy to marriage, and consequently not likely to have a child born in wedlock.

It was an unfortunate circumstance for Glenmurray, that, with the ardour of a young and inexperienced mind, he had given his eccentric opinions to the world as soon as they were conceived and arranged,—as he, by so doing, prejudiced the world against him in so unconquerable a degree, that to him almost every door and every heart was shut; and he by that means excluded from every chance of having the errors of his imagination corrected by the arguments of the experienced and enlightened—and corrected, no doubt, they would have been, for he had a mild and candid spirit, and a mind open to conviction.

'I consider myself', he used to say, 'as a sceptic, not as a man really certain of the truth of any thing which he advances. I doubt of all things, because I look upon doubt as the road to truth; and do but convince me what is the truth, and at whatever risk, whatever sacrifice, I am ready to embrace it.'

But, alas! neither the blamelessness of his life, nor even his active virtue, assisted by the most courteous manners, were deemed sufficient to counteract the mischievous tendency of his works; or rather, it was supposed impossible that his life could be blameless and his seeming virtues sincere:—and unheard, unknown, this unfortunate young man was excluded from those circles which his talents would have adorned, and forced to lead a life of solitude, or associate with persons unlike to him in most things, except in a passion for the bold in theory, and the almost impossible in practice.

Of this description of persons he soon became the oracle—the head of a sect, as it were; and those tenets which at first he embraced, and put forth more for amusement than from conviction, as soon as he began to suffer on their account, became as dear to him as the cross to the christian martyr: and deeming persecution a test of truth, he considered the opposition made to him and his doctrines, not as the result of dispassionate reason striving to correct absurdity, but as selfishness and fear endeavouring to put out the light which showed the weakness of the foundation on which were built their claims to exclusive respect.

When Mrs Mowbray and Adeline first arrived at Bath, the latter had attracted the attention and admiration of colonel Mordaunt, an Irishman of fortune, and an officer in the guards; and Adeline had not been insensible to the charms of a very fine person and engaging manners, united to powers of conversation which displayed an excellent understanding improved by education and reading. But colonel Mordaunt was not a *marrying man*, as it is called: therefore, as soon as he began to feel the influence of Adeline growing too powerful for his freedom, and to observe that his attentions were far from unpleasing to her,—too honourable to excite an attachment in her which he was resolved to combat in himself, he resolved to fly from the danger, which he knew he could not face and overcome; and after a formal but embarrassed adieu to Mrs Mowbray and Adeline, he suddenly left Bath.

This unexpected departure both surprised and grieved Adeline; but, as her feelings of delicacy were too strong to allow her to sigh for a man who, evidently, had no thoughts of sighing for her, she dismissed colonel Mordaunt from her remembrance, and tried to find as much interest still in the ball-rooms, and the promenades, as his presence had given them: nor was it long before she found in them an attraction and an interest stronger than any which she had yet felt.

It is naturally to be supposed that Adeline had often wished to know personally an author whose writings delighted her as much as Glenmurray's had done, and that her fancy had often portrayed him: but though it had clothed him in a form at once pleasing and respectable,—still, from an idea of his superior wisdom, she had imagined him past the meridian of life, and not likely to excite warmer feelings than those of esteem and veneration: and such continued to be Adeline's idea of Glenmurray, when he arrived at Bath, having been sent thither by his physicians for the benefit of his health.

Glenmurray, though a sense of his unpopularity had long banished him from scenes of public resort in general, was so pleased with the novelties of Bath, that, though he walked wholly unnoticed except by the lovers of genius in whatsoever shape it shows itself, he frequented daily the pump-room, and the promenades; and Adeline had long admired the countenance and dignified person of this young and interesting invalid, without the slightest suspicion of his being the man of all others whom she the most wished to see.

Nor had Glenmurray been slow to admire Adeline: and so strong, so irresistible was the feeling of admiration which she had excited in him, that, as soon as she appeared, all other objects vanished from his sight; and as women are generally quick-sighted to the effect of their charms, Adeline never beheld the stranger without a suffusion of pleasurable confusion on her cheek.

One morning at the pump-room, when Glenmurray, unconscious that Adeline was near, was reading the newspaper with great attention, and Adeline for the first time was looking at him unobserved, she heard the name of Glenmurray pronounced, and turned her head towards the person who spoke, in hopes of seeing Glenmurray himself; when Mrs Mowbray, turning round and looking at the invalid, said to a gentleman next her, 'Did you say, sir, that that tall, pale, dark, interesting-looking young man is Mr Glenmurray, the celebrated author?'

'Yes, ma'am,' replied the gentleman with a sneer: 'that is Mr Glenmurray, the celebrated author.'

'Oh! how I should like to speak to him!' cried Mrs Mowbray.

'It will be no difficult matter,' replied her informant: 'the gentle-man is always quite as much at leisure as you see him now; for *all* persons have not the same taste as Mrs Mowbray.'

So saying, he bowed and departed, leaving Mrs Mowbray, to whom the sight of a great author was new, so lost in contemplating Glenmurray, that the sarcasm with which he spoke entirely escaped her observation.

Nor was Adeline less abstracted: she too was contemplating Glenmurray, and with mixed but delightful feelings.

'So then he is young and handsome too!' said she mentally: 'it is a pity he looks so *ill*,' added she *sighing*: but the sigh was caused rather by his looking so *well*—though Adeline was not conscious of it.

By this time Glenmurray had observed who were his neighbours, and the newspaper was immediately laid down.

'Is there any news to-day?' said Mrs Mowbray to Glenmurray, resolved to make a bold effort to become acquainted with him. Glenmurray, with a bow and a blush of mingled surprise and pleas-ure, replied that there was a great deal,—and immediately presented to her the paper which he had relinquished, setting chairs at the same time for her and Adeline.

Mrs Mowbray, however, only slightly glanced her eye over the paper:—her desire was to talk to Glenmurray; and in order to accomplish this point, and prejudice him in her favour, she told him how much she rejoiced in seeing an author whose works were the delight and instruction of her life. 'Speak, Adeline,' cried she, turning to her blushing daughter; 'do we not almost daily read and daily admire Mr Glenmurray's writings?'—'Yes, certainly,' replied Adeline, unable to articulate more, awed no doubt by the presence of so superior a being; while Glenmurray, more proud of being an author than ever, said internally, 'Is it possible that that sweet creature should have read and admired my works?'

But in vain, encouraged by the smiles and even by the blushes of Adeline, did he endeavour to engage her in conversation. Adeline was unusually silent, unusually bashful. But Mrs Mowbray made ample amends for her deficiency; and Mr Glenmurray, flattered and amused, would have continued to converse with her and look at Adeline, had he not observed the impertinent sneers and rude laughter to which conversing so familiarly with him exposed Mrs

Mowbray. As soon as he observed this, he arose to depart; for Glenmurray was, according to Rochefoucault's maxim,* so exquisitely selfish, that he always considered the welfare of others before his own; and heroically sacrificing his own gratification to save Mrs Mowbray and Adeline from further censure, he bowed with the greatest respect to Mrs Mowbray, sighed as he paid the same compliment to Adeline, and, lamenting his being forced to quit them so soon, with evident reluctance left the room.

'What an elegant bow he makes!' exclaimed Mrs Mowbray. Adeline had observed nothing but the sigh; and on that she did not choose to make any comment.

The next day Mrs Mowbray, having learned Glenmurray's address, sent him a card for a party at her lodgings. Nothing but Glenmurray's delight could exceed his astonishment at this invitation. He had observed Mrs Mowbray and Adeline, even before Adeline had observed him; and, as he gazed upon the fascinating Adeline, he had sighed to think that she too would be taught to avoid the dangerous and disreputable acquaintance of Glenmurray. To him, therefore, this mark of attention was a source both of consolation and joy. But, being well convinced that it was owing to her ignorance of the usual customs and opinions of those with whom she associated, he was too generous to accept the invitation, as he knew that his presence at a rout* at Bath would cause general dismay, and expose the mistress to disagreeable remarks at least: but he endeavoured to make himself amends for his self-denial, by asking leave to wait on them when they were alone.

CHAPTER V

A day or two after, as Adeline was leaning on the arm of a young lady, Glenmurray passed them, and to his respectful bow she returned a most cordial salutation. 'Gracious me! my dear,' said her companion, 'do you know who that man is?'

'Certainly:—it is Mr Glenmurray.'

'My good gracious! and do you speak to him?'

'Yes:—why should I not?'

'Dear me! Why, I am sure! Why... don't you know what he is?'

'Yes; a celebrated writer, and a man of genius.'

'Oh, that may be, miss Mowbray: but they say one should not notice him, because he is—'

'He is what?' said Adeline eagerly.

'I do not exactly know what; but I believe it is a French spy, or a Jesuit.'

'Indeed?' replied Adeline laughing. 'But I am used to have better evidence against a person than a *they say* before I neglect an acknowledged acquaintance: therefore, with your leave, I shall turn back and talk a little to poor Mr Glenmurray.'

It so happened that *poor Mr Glenmurray* heard every word of this conversation; for he had turned round and followed Adeline and her fair companion, to present to the former the glove which she had dropped; and as they were prevented from proceeding by the crowd on the parade, which was assembled to see some unusual sight, he, being immediately behind them, could distinguish all that passed; so that Adeline turned round to go in search of him, before the blush of grateful admiration for her kindness had left his cheek.

'Then she seeks me because I am shunned by others!' said Glenmurray to himself. In a moment the world to him seemed to contain only two beings, Adeline Mowbray and Frederic Glenmurray; and that Adeline, starting and blushing with joyful surprise at seeing him so near her, was then coming in search of him!—of him, the neglected Glenmurray! Scarcely could he refrain catching the lovely and ungloved hand next him to his heart; but he contented himself with keeping the glove that he was before so eager to restore, and in a moment it was lodged in his bosom.

Nor could 'I can't think what I have done with my glove,' which every now and then escaped Adeline, prevail on him to own that he had found it. At last, indeed, it became unnecessary; for Adeline, as she glanced her eye towards Glenmurray, discovered it in the hiding-place: but, as delicacy forbade her to declare the discovery which she had made, he was suffered to retain his prize;* though a deep and sudden blush which overspread his cheek, and a sudden pause which she made in her conversation, convinced Glenmurray that she had detected his secret. Perhaps he was not sorry—nor Adeline; but certain it is that Adeline was for the remainder of the morning more lost in reverie than ever her mother had been; and that from that day every one, but Adeline and Glenmurray, saw that they were mutually enamoured.

Glenmurray was the first of the two lovers to perceive that they were so; and he made the discovery with a mixture of pain and pleasure. For what could be the result of such an attachment? He was firmly resolved never to marry; and it was very unlikely that Adeline, though she had often expressed to him her approbation of his writings and opinions, should be willing to sacrifice every thing to love, and become his mistress. But a circumstance took place which completely removed his doubts on this subject.

Several weeks had elapsed since the first arrival of the Mowbrays at Bath, and in that time almost all their acquaintances had left them one by one; but neither Mrs Mowbray nor Adeline had paid much attention to this circumstance. Mrs Mowbray's habits of abstraction, as usual, made her regardless of common occurrences; and to these were added the more delightful reveries occasioned by the attentions of a very handsome and insinuating man, and the influence of a growing passion. Mrs Mowbray, as we have before observed, married from duty, not inclination; and to the passion of love she had remained a total stranger, till she became acquainted at Bath with sir Patrick O'Carrol. Yes; Mrs Mowbray was in love for the first time when she was approaching her fortieth year! and a woman is never so likely to be the fool of love, as when it assails her late in life, especially if a lover be as great a novelty to her as the passion itself. Though not, alas! restored to a second youth, the tender victim certainly enjoys a second childhood, and exhibits but too openly all the little tricks and *minauderies** of a lovesick girl, without the youthful appearance that in a degree excuses them. This was the case with Mrs Mowbray; and while, regardless of her daughter's interest and happiness, she was lost in the pleasing hopes of marrying the agreeable baronet, no wonder the cold neglect of her Bath associates was not seen by her.

Adeline, engrossed also by the pleasing reveries of a first love, was as unconscious of it as herself. Indeed she thought of nothing but love and Glenmurray; else, she could not have failed to see, that, while sir Patrick's attentions and flatteries were addressed to her mother, his ardent looks and passionate sighs were all directed to herself.

Sir Patrick O'Carrol was a young Irishman, of an old family but an encumbered estate; and it was his wish to set his estate free by marrying a rich wife, and one as little disagreeable as possible. With this view he came to Bath; and in Mrs Mowbray he not only beheld a woman of large independent fortune, but possessed of great personal beauty, and young enough to be attractive. Still, though much pleased with the wealth and appearance of the mother, he soon became enamoured of the daughter's person; and had he not gone so far in his addresses to Mrs Mowbray as to make it impossible she should willingly transfer him to Adeline, and give her a fortune at all adequate to his wants, he would have endeavoured honourably to gain her affections, and entered the lists against the favoured Glenmurray.

But, as he wanted the mother's wealth, he resolved to pursue his advantage with her, and trust to some future chance for giving him possession of the daughter's person. In his dealings with men, sir Patrick was a man of honour; in his dealings with women, completely the reverse: he considered them as a race of subordinate beings, formed for the service and amusement of men; and that if, like horses, they were well lodged, fed, and kept clean, they had no right to complain.

Constantly therefore did he besiege Mrs Mowbray with his conversation, and Adeline with his eyes; and the very libertine gaze with which he often beheld her, gave a pang to Glenmurray which was but too soon painfully increased.

Sir Patrick was the only man of fashion who did not object to visit at Mrs Mowbray's on account of her intimacy with Glenmurray; but he had his own private reasons for going thither, and continued to visit at Mrs Mowbray's though Glenmurray was generally there, and sometimes he and the latter gentleman were the whole of their company.

One evening they and two ladies were drinking tea at Mrs Mowbray's lodgings, when Mrs Mowbray was unusually silent and Adeline unusually talkative. Adeline scarcely ever spoke in her mother's presence, from deference to her abilities; and whatever might be Mrs Mowbray's defects in other respects, her conversational talents and her uncommon command of words were indisputable. But this evening, as I before observed, Adeline, owing to her mother's tender abstractions, was obliged to exert herself for the entertainment of the guests.

It so happened, also, that something was said by one of the party which led to the subject of marriage, and Adeline was resolved not to let so good an opportunity pass of proving to Glenmurray how sincerely she approved his doctrine on that subject. Immediately, with an unreserve which nothing but her ignorance of the world, and the strange education which she had received, could at all excuse, she began to declaim against marriage, as an institution at once absurd, unjust, and immoral, and to declare that she would never submit to so contemptible a form, or profane the sacred ties of love by so odious and unnecessary a ceremony.

This extraordinary speech, though worded elegantly and delivered gracefully, was not received by any of her hearers, except sir Patrick, with any thing like admiration. The baronet, indeed, clapped his hands, and cried 'Bravo! a fine spirited girl, upon my soul!' in a manner so loud, and so offensive to the feelings of Adeline, that, like the orator of old, she was tempted to exclaim, 'What foolish thing can I have said, that has drawn forth this applause?'*

But Mrs Mowbray, though she could not help admiring the eloquence of her daughter,—eloquence which she attributed to her example,—was shocked at hearing Adeline declare that her practice should be consonant to her theory; while Glenmurray, though Adeline had only expressed his sentiments, and his reason approved what she had uttered, felt his delicacy and his feelings wounded by so open and decided an avowal of her opinions, and intended conduct in consequence of them: and he was still more hurt when he saw how much it delighted sir Patrick, and offended the rest of the company; who, after a silence the result of surprise and disgust, suddenly rose, and, coldly wishing Mrs Mowbray good night, left the house.

By Mrs Mowbray the cause of this abrupt departure was unsuspected: but Adeline, who had more observation, was convinced that she was the cause of it; and sighing deeply at the prejudices of the world, she sought to console herself by looking at Glenmurray, expecting to find in his eyes an expression of delight and approbation. To her great disappointment, however, his countenance was sad; while sir Patrick, on the contrary, had an expression of impudent triumph in his look, which made her turn blushing from his ardent gaze, and indignantly follow her mother, who was then leaving the room.

As she passed him, sir Patrick caught her hand rapturously to his lips (an action which made Glenmurray start from his chair), and exclaimed, 'Upon my soul, you are the only honest little woman I ever knew! I always was sure that what you just now said was the opinion of all your sex, though they were so confoundedly coy they would not own it.'

'Own what, sir?' asked the astonished Adeline.

'That they thought marriage a cursed bore, and preferred leading the life of honour, to be sure.'

'The life of honour! What is that?' demanded Adeline, while Glenmurray paced the room in agitation.

'The life, my dear girl, which you mean to lead;—love and liberty with the man of your heart.'

'Sir Patrick,' cried Glenmurray impatiently, 'this conversation is—'

'Prodigiously amusing to me,' returned the baronet, 'especially as I never could hold it to a modest woman before.'

'Nor shall you now, sir,' fiercely interrupted Glenmurray.

'Shall not, sir?' vociferated sir Patrick.

'Pray, gentlemen, be less violent,' exclaimed the terrified and astonished Adeline. 'I can't think what could offend you, Mr Glenmurray, in sir Patrick's original observation: the life of honour appears to me a very excellent name for the pure and honourable union which it is my wish to form; and—'

'There; I told you so;' triumphantly interrupted sir Patrick: 'and I never was better pleased in my life:—sweet creature! at once so lovely, so wise, and so liberal!'

'Sir,' cried Glenmurray, 'this is a mistake: your life of honour and miss Mowbray's are as different as possible; you are talking of what you are grossly ignorant of.'

'Ignorant! I ignorant! Look you, Mr Glenmurray, do you pretend to tell me I know not what the life of honour is, when I have led it so many times with so many different women?'

'How, sir!' replied Adeline: 'many times? and with many different women? My life of honour can be led with one only.'

'Well, my dear soul, I only led it with one at a time.'

'O sir! you are indeed ignorant of my meaning,' she rejoined: 'it is the individuality of an attachment that constitutes its chastity; and—'

'Ba-ba-bu, my lovely girl! what has chastity to do in the business?'

'Indeed, sir Patrick,' meekly returned Adeline, 'I—'

'Miss Mowbray,' angrily interrupted Glenmurray, 'I beg, I conjure you to drop this conversation: your innocence is no match for—'

'For what, sir?' furiously demanded sir Patrick.

'Your licentiousness,' replied Glenmurray.

'Sir, I wear a sword,' cried the baronet.—'And I a cane,' said Glenmurray calmly, 'either to defend myself or chastise insolence.'

'Mr Glenmurray! Sir Patrick!' exclaimed the agitated Adeline: 'for my sake, for pity's sake, desist!'

'For the present I will, madam,' faltered out sir Patrick;—'but I know Mr Glenmurray's address, and he shall hear from me.'

'Hear from you! Why, you do not mean to challenge him? you can't suppose Mr Glenmurray would do so absurd a thing as fight a duel? Sir, he has written a volume to prove the absurdity of the custom.*—No, no, thank God! you threaten his life in vain,' she added, giving her hand to Glenmurray; who, in the tenderness of the action and the tone of her voice, forgot the displeasure which her inadvertency had caused, and, pressing her hand to his lips, secretly renewed his vows of unalterable attachment.

'Very well, madam,' exclaimed sir Patrick in a tone of pique: 'then, so as Mr Glenmurray's life is safe, you care not what becomes of mine!'

'Sir,' replied Adeline, 'the safety of a fellow creature is always of importance in my eyes.'

'Then you care for me as a fellow creature only,' retorted sir Patrick, 'not as sir Patrick O'Carrol?—Mighty fine, truly, you dear ungrateful—' seizing her hand; which he relinquished, as well as the rest of his speech, on the entrance of Mrs Mowbray.

Soon after Adeline left the room, and Glenmurray bowed and retired; while sir Patrick, having first repeated his vows of admiration to the mother, returned home to muse on the charms of the daughter, and the necessity of challenging the moral Glenmurray.

Sir Patrick was a man of courage, and had fought several duels: but as life at this time had a great many charms for him, he resolved to defer at least putting himself in the way of getting rid of it; and after having slept late in the morning, to make up for the loss of sleep in the night, occasioned by his various cogitations, he rose, resolved go to Mrs Mowbray's, and, if he had an opportunity, indulge himself in some practical comments on the singular declaration made the evening before by her lovely daughter.

Glenmurray meanwhile had passed the night in equal watchfulness and greater agitation. To fight a duel would be, as Adeline
observed, contrary to his principles; and to decline one, irritated as
he was against sir Patrick, was repugnant to his feelings.

To no purpose did he peruse and reperuse nearly the whole of his
own book against duelling; he had few religious restraints to make
him resolve on declining a challenge, and he felt moral ones of little
avail: but in vain did he sit at home till the morning was far
advanced, expecting a messenger from sir Patrick;—no messenger
came:—he therefore left word with his servant, that, if wanted, he
might be found at Mrs Mowbray's, and went thither, in hopes of
enjoying an hour's conversation with Adeline; resolving to hint to
her, as delicately as he could, that the opinions which she had
expressed were better confined, in the present dark state of the
public mind, to a select and discriminating circle.

CHAPTER VI

Sir Patrick had reached Mrs Mowbray's some time before him, and
had, to his great satisfaction, found Adeline alone; nor did it escape
his penetration that her cheeks glowed, and her eyes sparkled with
pleasure, at his approach.

But he would not have rejoiced in this circumstance, had he
known that Adeline was pleased to see him merely because she considered his appearance as a proof of Glenmurray's safety; for, in spite
of his having written against duelling, and of her confidence in his
firmness and consistency, she was not quite convinced that the
reasoning philosopher would triumph over the feeling man.

'You are welcome, sir Patrick!' cried Adeline, as he entered, with a
most winning smile: 'I am very glad to see you: pray sit down.'

The baronet, who, audacious as his hopes and intentions were,
had not expected so kind a reception, was quite thrown off his guard
by it, and, catching her suddenly in his arms, endeavoured to obtain
a still kinder welcome. Adeline as suddenly disengaged herself from
him, and, with the dignity of offended modesty, desired him to quit
the room, as, after such an insolent attempt, she could not think
herself justified in suffering him to remain with her.

But her anger was soon changed into pity, when she saw sir

Patrick lay down his hat, seat himself, and burst into a long deliberate laugh.

'He is certainly mad!' she exclaimed; and, leaning against the chimney-piece, she began to contemplate him with a degree of fearful interest.

'Upon my soul! now,' cried the baronet, when his laugh was over, 'you do not suppose, my dear creature, that you and I do not understand one another! Telling a young fellow to leave the house on such occasions, means, in the pretty no meaning of your sex, "Stay, and offend again," to be sure.'

'He is certainly mad!' said Adeline, more confirmed than before in her idea of his insanity, and immediately endeavoured to reach the door: but in so doing she approached sir Patrick, who, rather roughly seizing her trembling hand, desired her to sit down, and hear what he had to say to her. Adeline, thinking it not right to irritate him, instantly obeyed.

'Now, then, to open my mind to you,' said the baronet, drawing his chair close to hers: 'From the very first moment I saw you, I felt that we were made for one another; though, being bothered by my debts, I made up to the old duchess, and she nibbled the bait directly,—deeming my clean inches (six feet one, without shoes) well worth her dirty acres.'

'How dreadfully incoherent he is!' thought Adeline, not suspecting for a moment that, by the old duchess, he meant her still blooming mother.

'But, my lovely love!' continued sir Patrick, most ardently pressing her hand, 'so much have your sweet person, and your frank and liberal way of thinking, charmed me, that I here freely offer myself to you, and we will begin the life of honour together as soon as you please.'

Still Adeline, who was unconscious how much her avowed opinions had exposed her to insult, continued to believe sir Patrick insane; a belief which the wildness of his eyes confirmed. 'I really know not,—you surprise me, sir Patrick,—I—'

'Surprise you, my dear soul! How could you expect anything else from a man of my spirit, after your honest declaration last night?... All I feared was, that Glenmurray should get the start of me.'

Adeline, though alarmed, bewildered, and confounded, had still recollection enough to know that, whether sane or insane, the words and looks of sir Patrick were full of increasing insult. 'I believe, I think I had better retire,' faltered out Adeline.

'Retire!... Aye, by all means,' exclaimed the baronet, rudely seizing her.

This outrage restored Adeline to her usual spirit and self-possession; and bestowing on him the epithet of 'mean-soul'd ruffian!' she had almost freed herself from his grasp, when a quick step was heard on the stairs, and the door was thrown open by Glenmurray. In a moment Adeline, bursting into tears, threw herself into his arms, as if in search of protection.

Glenmurray required no explanation of the scene before him: the appearance of the actors in it was explanation sufficient; and while with one arm he fondly held Adeline to his bosom, he raised the other in a threatening attitude against sir Patrick, exclaiming as he did it, 'Base, unmanly villain!'

'Villain!' echoed sir Patrick... 'but it is very well—very well for the present—Good morning to you, sir!' So saying, he hastily withdrew.

As soon as he was gone, Glenmurray for the first time declared to Adeline the ardent passion with which she had inspired him; and she, with equal frankness, confessed that her heart was irrevocably his.

From this interesting tête-à-tête Adeline was summoned to attend a person on business to her mother; and during her absence Glenmurray received a challenge from the angry baronet, appointing him to meet him that afternoon at five o'clock, about two miles from Bath. To this note, for fear of alarming the suspicions of Adeline, Glenmurray returned only a verbal message, saying he would answer it in two hours: but as soon as she returned he pleaded indispensable business; and before she could mention any fears respecting the consequences of what had passed between him and sir Patrick, he had left the room, having, to prevent any alarm, requested leave to wait on her early the next day.

As soon as Glenmurray reached his lodgings, he again revolved in his mind the propriety of accepting the challenge. 'How can I expect to influence others by my theories to act right, if my practice sets them a bad example?' But then again he exclaimed, 'How can I expect to have any thing I say attended to, when, by refusing to fight, I put it in the power of my enemies to assert I am a poltroon,* and worthy only of neglect and contempt? No, no; I must fight:—even

Adeline herself, especially as it is on her account, will despise me if I do not:'—and then, without giving himself any more time to deliberate, he sent an answer to sir Patrick, promising to meet him at the time appointed.

But after he had sent it he found himself a prey to so much self-reproach, and after he had forfeited his claims to consistency of conduct, he felt himself so strongly aware of the value of it, that, had not the time of the meeting been near at hand, he would certainly have deliberated upon some means of retracting his consent to it.

Being resolved to do as little mischief as he could, he determined on having no second* in the business; and accordingly repaired to the field accompanied only by a trusty servant, who had orders to wait his master's pleasure at a distance.

Contrary to Glenmurray's expectations, sir Patrick also came unattended by a second; while his servant, who was with him, was, like the other, desired to remain in the back ground.

'I wish, Mr Glenmurray, to do every thing honourable,' said the baronet, after they had exchanged salutations: 'therefore, sir, as I concluded you would find it difficult to get a second, I am come without one, and I *conclude* that I *concluded* right.—Aye, men of your principles can have but few friends.'

'And men of your practice ought to have none, sir Patrick,' retorted Glenmurray: 'but, as I don't think it worth while to explain to you my reasons for not having a second, as I fear that you are incapable of understanding them, I must desire you to take your ground.'

'With all my heart,' replied his antagonist; and then taking aim, they agreed to fire at the same moment.

They did so; and the servants, hearing the report of the pistols, ran to the scene of action, and saw sir Patrick bleeding in the sword-arm, and Glenmurray, also wounded, leaning against a tree.

'This is cursed unlucky,' said sir Patrick coolly: 'as you have disabled my right arm I can't go on with this business at present; but when I am well again, command me. Your wound, I believe, is as slight as mine; but as I can walk, and you cannot, and as I have a chaise, and you not, you shall use it to convey you and your servant home, and I and mine will go on foot.'

To this obliging offer Glenmurray was incapable of giving a denial; for he became insensible from loss of blood, and with the assistance of his antagonist was carried to the chaise, and, supported by his terrified servant, conveyed back to Bath.

It is not to be supposed that an event of this nature should be long unknown. It was soon told all over the city that sir Patrick O'Carrol and Mr Glenmurray had fought a duel, and that the latter was dangerously wounded; the quarrel having originated in Mr Glenmurray's scoffing at religion, king, and constitution, before the pious and loyal baronet.

This story soon reached the ears of Mrs Mowbray, who, in an agony of tender sorrow, and in defiance of all decorum, went in person to call on her admired sir Patrick; and Adeline, who heard of the affair soon after, as regardless of appearances as her mother, and more alarmed, went in person to inquire concerning her wounded Glenmurray.

By the time that she had arrived at his lodgings, not only his own surgeon but sir Patrick's had seen him, as his antagonist thought it necessary to ascertain the true state of his wound, that he might know whether he ought to stay, or fly his country.*

The account of both the surgeons was, however, so favourable, and Glenmurray in all respects so well, that sir Patrick's alarms were soon quite at an end; and the wounded man was lying on a sopha, lost in no very pleasant reflections, when Adeline knocked at his door. Glenmurray at that very moment was saying to himself, 'Well;—so much for principle and consistency! Now, my next step must be to marry, and then I shall have made myself a complete fool, and the worst of all fools,—a man presuming to instruct others by his precepts, when he finds them incapable even of influencing his own actions.'

At this moment his servant came up with 'miss Mowbray's compliments, and, if he was well enough to see her, she would come up and speak to him.'

In an instant all his self-reproaches were forgotten; and when Adeline hung weeping and silent on his shoulder, he could not but rejoice in an affair which had procured him a moment of such heart-felt delight. At first Adeline expressed nothing but terror at the consequences of his wound, and pity for his sufferings; but when she found that he was in no danger, and in very little pain, the tender mistress yielded to the severe monitress, and she began to upbraid Glenmurray for having acted not only in defiance of her wishes and principles, but of his own; of principles laid down by him to the world in the strongest point of view, and in a manner convincing to every mind.

'Dearest Adeline, consider the provocation,' cried Glenmurray;— 'a gross insult offered to the woman I love!'

'But who ever fought a duel without provocation, Glenmurray? If provocation be a justification, your book was unnecessary; and did not you offer an insult to the understanding of the woman you love, in supposing that she could be obliged to you for playing the fool on her account?'

'But I should have been called a coward had I declined the challenge; and though I can bear the world's hatred, I could not its contempt:—I could not endure the loss of what the world calls honour.'

'Is it possible,' rejoined Adeline, 'that I hear the philosophical Glenmurray talking thus, in the silly jargon of a man of the world?'

'Alas! I am a man, not a philosopher, Adeline!'

'At least be a sensible one;—consistent I dare not now call you. But have you forgotten the distinction which, in your volume on the subject of duels, you so strongly lay down between real and apparent honour? In which of the two classes do you put the honour of which, in this instance, you were so tenacious? What is there in common between the glory of risking the life of a fellow-creature, and testimony of an approving conscience?'

'An excellent observation that of yours, indeed, my sweet monitress,' said Glenmurray.

'An observation of mine! It is your own,' replied Adeline: 'but see, I have the book in my muff; and I will punish you for the badness of your practice, by giving you a dose of your theory.'

'Cruel girl!' cried Glenmurray, 'I am not ordered a sleeping draught!'

Adeline was however resolved; and, opening the book, she read argument after argument with unyielding perseverance, till Glenmurray, who, like the eagle in the song, saw on the dart that wounded him his own feathers, cried 'Quarter!'*

'But tell me, dear Adeline,' said Glenmurray, a little piqued at her too just reproofs, 'you, who are so severe on my want of consistency, are you yourself capable of acting up in every respect to your precepts?'

'After your weakness,' replied Adeline, smiling, 'it becomes me to doubt my own strength; but I assure you that I make it a scruple of conscience, to show by my conduct my confidence in the truth of my opinions.'

'Then, in defiance of the world's opinion, that opinion which I, you see, had not resolution to brave, you will be mine—not according to the ties of marriage, but with no other ties or sanction than those of love and reason?'

'I will,' said Adeline: 'and may that God whom I worship' (raising her fine eyes and white arms to heaven) 'desert me when I desert you!'

Who that had seen her countenance and gesture at that moment, could have imagined she was calling on heaven to witness an engagement to lead a life of infamy? Rather would they have thought her a sublime enthusiast breathing forth the worship of a grateful soul.

It may be supposed that Glenmurray's heart beat with exultation at this confession from Adeline, and that he forgot, in the promised indulgence of his passion, to confine himself within those bounds which strict decorum required. But Glenmurray did her justice; he beheld her as she was—all purity of feeling and all delicacy; and, if possible, the slight favours by which true passion is long contented to be fed, though granted by Adeline with more conscious emotion, were received by him with more devoted respect: besides, he again felt that mixture of pain with pleasure, on this assurance of her love, which he had experienced before. For he knew, though Adeline did not, the extent of the degradation into which the step which her conscience approved would necessarily precipitate her; and experience alone could convince him that her sensibility to shame, when she was for the first time exposed to it, would not overcome her supposed fortitude and boasted contempt of the world's opinion, and change all the roses of love into the thorns of regret and remorse.

And could he who doted on her;—he, too, who admired her as much for her consummate purity as for any other of her qualities;— could he bear to behold this fair creature, whose open eye beamed with the consciousness of virtue, casting her timid glances to the earth, and shrinking with horror from the conviction of having in the world's eye forfeited all pretensions to that virtue which alone was the end of her actions! Would the approbation of her own mind be sufficient to support her under such a trial, though she had with such sweet earnestness talked to him of its efficacy! These reflections had for some time past been continually occurring to him, and now they came across his mind blighting the triumphs of successful passion:—nay, but from the dread of incurring yet more ridicule, on account of the opposition of his practice to his theory, and perhaps the indignant contempt of Adeline, he could have thrown himself at her feet, conjuring her to submit to the degradation of being a wife.*

But, unknown to Glenmurray, perhaps, another reason prompted him to desire this concession from Adeline. We are never more likely to be in reality the slaves of selfishness, than when we fancy ourselves acting with most heroic disinterestedness.—Egotism loves a becoming dress, and is always on the watch to hide her ugliness by the robe of benevolence. Glenmurray thought that he was willing to marry Adeline merely for *her* sake; but I suspect it was chiefly for *his*. The true and delicate lover is always a monopolizer, always desirous of calling the woman of his affections his own: it is not only because he considers marriage as a holy institution that the lover leads his mistress to the altar; but because it gives him a right to appropriate the fair treasure to himself,—because it sanctions and perpetuates the dearest of all monopolies,* and erects a sacred barrier to guard his rights,—around which, all that is respectable in society, all that is most powerful and effectual in its organization, is proud and eager to rally.

But while Glenmurray, in spite of his happiness, was sensible to an alloy of it, and Adeline was tenderly imputing to the pain of his wound the occasionally mournful expression of his countenance, Adeline took occasion to declare that she would live with Glenmurray only on condition that such a step met with her mother's approbation.

'Then are my hopes for ever at an end,' said Glenmurray:—'or,— or' (and spite of himself his eyes sparkled as he spoke) '—or we must submit to the absurd ceremony of marriage.'

'Marriage!' replied the astonished Adeline: 'can you think so meanly of my mother, as to suppose her practice so totally opposite to her principles, that she would require her daughter to submit to a ceremony which she herself regards with contempt?—Impossible. I am sure, when I solicit her consent to my being yours, she will be pleased to find that her sentiments and observations have not been thrown away on me.'

Glenmurray thought otherwise: however, he bowed and was silent; and Adeline declared that, to put an end to all doubt on the subject, she would instantly go in search of Mrs Mowbray and propose the question to her: and Glenmurray, feeling himself more weak and indisposed than he chose to own to her, allowed her, though reluctantly, to depart.

CHAPTER VII

Mrs Mowbray was but just returned from her charitable visit when Adeline entered the room. 'And pray, miss Mowbray, where have you been?' she exclaimed, seeing Adeline with her hat and cloak on.

'I have been visiting poor Mr Glenmurray,' she replied.

'Indeed!' cried Mrs Mowbray: 'and without my leave! and pray who went with you?'

'Nobody, ma'am.'

'Nobody!—What! visit a man alone at his lodgings, after the education which you have received!'

'Indeed, madam,' replied Adeline meekly, 'my education never taught me that such conduct was improper; nor, as you did the same this afternoon, could I have dared to think it so.'

'You are mistaken, miss Mowbray,' replied her mother: 'I did not do the same; for the terms which I am upon with sir Patrick made my visiting him no impropriety at all.'

'If you think I have acted wrong,' replied Adeline timidly, 'no doubt I have done so; though you were quite right in visiting sir Patrick, as the respectability of your age and character, and sir Patrick's youth, warranted the propriety of the visit:—but, surely the terms which I am upon with Mr Glenmurray—'

'The terms which you are upon with Mr Glenmurray! and my age and character! what can you mean?' angrily exclaimed Mrs Mowbray.

'I hoped, my dear mother,' said Adeline tenderly, 'that you had long ere this guessed the attachment which subsists between Mr Glenmurray and me;—an attachment cherished by your high opinion of him and his writings; but which respect has till now made me hesitate to mention to you.'

'Would to heaven!' replied Mrs Mowbray, 'that respect had made you for ever silent on the subject! Do you suppose that I would marry my daughter to a man of small fortune,—but more especially to one who, as sir Patrick informs me, is shunned for his principles and profligacy by all the world?'

'To what sir Patrick says of Mr Glenmurray I pay no attention,' answered Adeline; 'nor are you, my dear mother, capable, I am sure, of being influenced by the prejudices of the world.—But you are quite mistaken in supposing me so lost to consistency, and so regardless of your liberal opinions and the books which we have studied, as to think of *marrying* Mr Glenmurray.'

'Grant me patience!' cried Mrs Mowbray: 'why, to be sure you do not think of living with him *without* being married?'

'Certainly, madam; that you may have the pleasure of beholding one union founded on rational grounds and cemented by rational ties.'

'How!' cried Mrs Mowbray, turning pale. 'I!—I have pleasure in seeing my daughter a kept mistress!—You are mad, quite mad.—*I* approve such unhallowed connections!'

'My dearest mother,' replied Adeline, 'your agitation terrifies me,—but indeed what I say is strictly true; and see here, in Mr Glenmurray's book, the very passage which I so often have heard you admire.' As she said this, Adeline pointed to the passage; but in an instant Mrs Mowbray seized the book and threw it on the fire.

Before Adeline had recovered her consternation Mrs Mowbray fell into a violent hysteric; and long was it before she was restored to composure. When she recovered she was so exhausted that Adeline dared not renew the conversation; but leaving her to rest, she made up a bed on her floor in her mother's room, and passed a night of wretchedness and watchfulness,—the first of the kind which she had ever known.—Would it had been the last!

In the morning Mrs Mowbray awoke, refreshed and calm; and, affected at seeing the pale cheek and sunk eye of Adeline, indicative of a sleepless and unhappy night, she held her hand out to her with a look of kindness; Adeline pressed it to her lips, as she knelt by the bed-side, and moistened it with tears of regret for the past and alarm for the future.

'Adeline, my dear child,' said Mrs Mowbray in a faint voice, 'I hope you will no longer think of putting a design in execution so fraught with mischief to you, and horror to me. Little did I think that you were so romantic as to see no difference between amusing one's imagination with new theories and new systems, and acting upon them in defiance of common custom, and the received usages of society. I admire the convenient trowsers and graceful dress of the Turkish women; but I would not wear them myself, lest it should expose me to derision.'

'Is there no difference', thought Adeline, 'between the importance of a dress and an opinion!—Is the one to be taken up, and laid down again, with the same indifference as the other!' But she continued silent, and Mrs Mowbray went on.

'The poetical philosophy which I have so much delighted to study, has served me to ornament my conversation, and make persons less enlightened than myself wonder at the superior boldness of my fancy, and the acuteness of my reasoning powers;—but I should as soon have thought of making this little gold chain round my neck fasten the hall-door, as act upon the precepts laid down in those delightful books. No; though I think all they say true, I believe the purity they inculcate too much for this world.'

Adeline listened in silent astonishment and consternation. Conscience, and the conviction of what is right, she then for the first time learned, were not to be the rule of action; and though filial tenderness made her resolve never to be the mistress of Glenmurray, she also resolved never to be his wife, or that of any other man; while, in spite of herself, the great respect with which she had hitherto regarded her mother's conduct and opinions began to diminish.

'Would to heaven, my dear mother,' said Adeline, when Mrs Mowbray had done speaking, 'that you had said all this to me ere my mind had been indelibly impressed with the truth of these forbidden doctrines; for now my conscience tells me that I ought to act up to them!'

'How!' exclaimed Mrs Mowbray, starting up in her bed, and in a voice shrill with emotion, 'are you then resolved to disobey me, and dishonour yourself?'

'Oh! never, never!' replied Adeline, alarmed at her mother's violence, and fearful of a relapse. 'Be but the kind affectionate parent that you have ever been to me; and though I will never marry, out of regard to my own principles, I will also never contract any other union, out of respect to your wishes,—but will lead with you a quiet, if not a *happy*, life; for never, never can I forget Glenmurray.'

'There speaks the excellent child I always thought you to be!'

replied Mrs Mowbray; 'and I shall leave it to time and good counsels to convince you, that the opinions of a girl of eighteen, as they are not founded on long experience, may possibly be erroneous.'

Mrs Mowbray never made a truer observation; but Adeline was not in a frame of mind to assent to it.

'Besides,' continued Mrs Mowbray, 'had I ever been disposed to accept of Mr Glenmurray as a son-in-law, it is very unlikely that I should be so now; as the duel took place not only, I find, from the treasonable opinions which he put forth, but from some disrespectful language which he held concerning me.'

'Who could dare to invent so infamous a calumny!' exclaimed Adeline.

'My authority is unquestionable, miss Mowbray: I speak from sir Patrick himself.'

'Then he adds falsehood to his other villanies!' returned Adeline, almost inarticulate with rage:—'but what could be expected from a man who could dare to insult a young woman under the roof of her mother with his licentious addresses?'

'What mean you?' cried Mrs Mowbray, turning pale.

'I mean that sir Patrick yesterday morning insulted me by the grossest familiarities, and—'

'My dear child,' replied Mrs Mowbray laughing, 'that is only the usual freedom of his manner; a manner which your ignorance of the world led you to mistake. He did not mean to insult you, believe me. I am sure that, spite of his ardent passion for me, he never, even when alone with me, hazarded any improper liberty.'

'The ardent passion which he feels for you, madam!' exclaimed Adeline, turning pale in her turn.

'Yes, miss Mowbray! What, I suppose you think me too old to inspire one!—But, I assure you, there are people who think the mother handsomer than the daughter!'

'No doubt, dear mother, every one ought to think so,—and would to heaven sir Patrick were one of those! But he, unfortunately—'

'Is of that opinion,' interrupted Mrs Mowbray angrily: 'and to convince you—so tenderly does he love me, and so fondly do I return his passion, that in a few days I shall become his wife.'

Adeline, on hearing this terrible information, fell insensible on the ground. When she recovered she saw Mrs Mowbray anxiously watching by her, but not with that look of alarm and tenderness with which she had attended her during her long illness; that look which was always present to her grateful and affectionate remembrance. No; Mrs Mowbray's eye was cast down with a half-mournful, half-reproachful, and half-fearful expression, when it met that of Adeline.

The emotion of anguish which her fainting had evinced was a reproach to the proud heart of Mrs Mowbray, and Adeline felt that it was so; but when she recollected that her mother was going to marry a man who had so lately declared a criminal passion for herself, she was very near relapsing into insensibility. She however struggled with her feelings, in order to gain resolution to disclose to Mrs Mowbray all that had passed between her and sir Patrick. But as soon as she offered to renew the conversation, Mrs Mowbray sternly commanded her to be silent; and insisting on her going to bed, she left her to her own reflections, till wearied and exhausted she fell into a sound sleep: nor, as it was late in the evening when she awoke, did she rise again till the next morning.

Mrs Mowbray entered her room as she was dressing, and inquired how she did, with some kindness.

'I shall be better, dear mother, if you will but hear what I have to say concerning sir Patrick,' replied Adeline, bursting into tears.

'You can say nothing that will shake my opinion of him, miss Mowbray,' replied her mother coldly: 'so I advise you to reconcile yourself to a circumstance which it is not in your power to prevent.' So saying, she left the room; and Adeline, convinced that all she could say would be vain, endeavoured to console herself, by thinking that, as soon as sir Patrick became the husband of her mother, his wicked designs on her would undoubtedly cease; and that, therefore, in one respect, this ill-assorted union would be beneficial to her.

Sir Patrick, meanwhile, was no less sanguine in his expectations from his marriage. Unlike the innocent Adeline, he did not consider his union with the mother as a necessary check to his attempts on the daughter; but, emboldened by what to him appeared the libertine sentiments of Adeline, and relying on the opportunities of being with her, which he must infallibly enjoy under the same roof in the country, he looked on her as his certain prey. Though he believed Glenmurray to be at that moment preferred to himself, he thought it impossible that the superior beauty of his person should not, in the end, have its due weight; as a passion founded in esteem, and the admiration of intellectual beauty, could not, in his opinion, subsist: besides, Adeline appeared in his eyes not a deceived enthusiast, but a susceptible and forward girl, endeavouring to hide her frailty under fine sentiments and high-sounding theories. Nor was sir Patrick's inference an unnatural one. Every man of the world would have thought the same; and on very plausible grounds.

CHAPTER VIII

As sir Patrick was not 'punctual as lovers to the moment sworn,'* Mrs Mowbray resolved to sit down and write immediately to Glenmurray; flattering herself at the same time, that the letter which was designed to confound Glenmurray would delight the tender baronet;—for Mrs Mowbray piqued herself on her talents for letter-writing, and was not a little pleased with an opportunity of displaying them to a celebrated author. But never before did she find writing a letter so difficult a task. Her eager wish of excelling deprived her of the means; and she who, in a letter to a friend or relation, would have written in a style at once clear and elegant, after two hours' effort produced the following specimen of the obscure, the pedantic, and affected.

'SIR,

'The light which cheers and attracts, if we follow its guidance, often leads us into bogs and quagmires:—Verbum sapienti.* Your writings are the lights, and the practice to which you advise my deluded daughter is the bog and the quagmire. I agree with you in all you have said against marriage;—I agree with the savage nations in the total uselessness of clothing; still I condescend to wear clothes, though neither becoming nor useful, because I respect public opinion; and I submit to the institution of marriage for reasons equally cogent. Such being my sentiments, sir, I must desire you never to see my daughter more. Nor could you expect to be received with open arms by me, whom the shafts of your ridicule have pierced, though warded off by the shield of love and gallantry;—but for this I thank you! Now shall I possess, owing to your baseness, at once a declared lover and a tried avenger; and the chains of Hymen* will be rendered more charming by gratitude's having blown the flame, while love forged the fetters.

'But with your writings I continue to amuse my imagination.— Lovely is the flower of the nightshade, though its berry be poison. Still shall I admire and wonder at you as an author, though I avoid and detest you as a man.

'EDITHA MOWBRAY.'

This letter was just finished when sir Patrick arrived, and to him it was immediately shown.

'Heh! what have we here?' cried he laughing violently as he perused it. 'Here you talk of being pierced by shafts which were warded off. Now, had *I* said that, it would have been called a bull.* As to the concluding paragraph—'

'O! that, I flatter myself,' said Mrs Mowbray, 'will tear him with remorse.'

'He must first understand it,' cried sir Patrick: 'I can but just comprehend it, and am sure it will be all botheration to him.'

'I am sorry to find such is your opinion,' replied Mrs Mowbray; 'for I think that sentence the best written of any.'

'I did not say it was not fine writing,' replied the baronet, 'I only said it was not to be understood.—But, with your leave, you shall send the letter, and we'll drop the subject.'

So said, so done, to the great satisfaction of sir Patrick, who felt that it was for his interest to suffer the part of Mrs Mowbray's letter which alluded to Glenmurray's supposed calumnies against her to remain obscurely worded, as he well knew that what he had asserted on this subject was wholly void of foundation.

Glenmurray did not receive it with equal satisfaction. He was indignant at the charge of having advised Adeline to become his mistress rather than his wife; and as so much of the concluding passage as he could understand seemed to imply that he had calumniated her mother, to remain silent a moment would have been to confess himself guilty: he therefore answered Mrs Mowbray's letter immediately. The answer was as follows:

'MADAM,

'To clear myself from the charge of having advised miss Mowbray to a step contrary to the common customs, however erroneous, of

society at this period, I appeal to the testimony of miss Mowbray
herself; and I here repeat to you the assurance which I made to her,
that I am willing to marry her when and where she chooses. I love
my system and my opinions, but the respectability of the woman
of my affections *more*. Allow me, therefore, to make you a little
acquainted with my situation in life:

'To you it is well known, madam, that wealth, honours, and titles
have no value in my eyes; and that I reverence talents and virtues,
though they wear the garb of poverty, and are born in the most
obscure stations. But you, or rather those who are so fortunate as to
influence your determinations, may consider my sentiments on this
subject as romantic and absurd. It is necessary, therefore, that I
should tell you, as an excuse in their eyes for presuming to address
your daughter, that, by the accident of birth, I am descended from an
antient family, and nearly allied to a noble one; and that my paternal
inheritance, though not large enough for splendour and luxury, is
sufficient for all the purposes of comfort and genteel affluence. I
would say more on this subject, but I am impatient to remove from
your mind the prejudice which you seem to have imbibed against
me. I do not perfectly understand the last paragraph in your letter. If
you will be so kind as to explain it to me, you may depend on my
being perfectly ingenuous: indeed, I have no difficulty in declaring,
that I have neither encouraged a feeling, nor uttered a word, capable
of giving the lie to the declaration which I am now going to make—
That I am,

    'With respect and esteem,

      'Your obedient servant,

        'F. GLENMURRAY.'

This letter had an effect on Mrs Mowbray's feelings so much in
favour of Glenmurray, that she was almost determined to let him
marry Adeline. She felt that she owed her some amends for contract-
ing a marriage so suddenly, and without either her knowledge or
approbation; and she thought that, by marrying her to the man of
her heart, she should make her peace both with Adeline and herself.
But, unfortunately, this design, as soon as it began to be formed, was
communicated to sir Patrick.

'So, then!' exclaimed he, 'you have forgotten and forgiven the
impertinent things which the puppy said!—things which obliged me

to wear this little useless appendage in a sling thus' (pointing to his wounded arm).

'O! no, my dear sir Patrick! But though what Mr Glenmurray said might alarm the scrupulous tenderness of a lover, perhaps it was a remark which might only suit the sincerity of a friend. Perhaps, if Mr Glenmurray had made it to me, I should have heard it with thanks, and with candour have approved it.'

'My sweet soul!' replied sir Patrick, 'you may be as candid and amiable as ever you please, but, "by St. Patrick!" never shall sir Patrick O'Carrol be father-in-law to the notorious and infamous Glenmurray—that subverter of all religion and order, and that scourge of civilized society!'

So saying, he stalked about the room; and Mrs Mowbray, as she gazed on his handsome person, thought it would be absurd for her to sacrifice her own happiness to her daughter's, and give up sir Patrick as her husband in order to make Glenmurray her son. She therefore wrote another letter to Glenmurray, forbidding him any further intercourse with Adeline, on any pretence whatever; and delayed not a moment to send him her final decision.

'That is acting like the sensible woman I took you for,' said sir Patrick: 'the fellow has now gotten his quietus,* I trust, and the dear little Adeline is reserved for a happier fate. Sweet soul! you do not know how fond she will be of me! I protest that I shall be so kind to her, it will be difficult for people to decide which I love best, the daughter or the mother.'

'But I hope *I* shall always know, sir Patrick,' said Mrs Mowbray gravely.

'You!—O yes, to be sure. But I mean that my fatherly attentions shall be of the warmest kind. But now do me the favour of telling me at what hour to-morrow I may appoint the clergyman to bring the license?'

The conversation that followed, it were needless and tedious to describe. Suffice, that eight o'clock the next morning was fixed for the marriage; and Mrs Mowbray, either from shame or compassion, resolved that Adeline should not accompany her to church, nor even know of the ceremony till it was over.

Nor was this a difficult matter. Adeline remained in her own apartment all the preceding day, endeavouring, but in vain, to reconcile herself to what she justly termed the degradation of her mother. She felt, alas! the most painful of all feelings, next to that of self-abasement,—the consciousness of the abasement of one to whom she had all her life looked up with love and veneration. To write to Glenmurray while oppressed by such contending emotions she knew to be impossible; she therefore contented herself with sending a verbal message, importing that he should hear from her the next day: and poor Glenmurray passed the rest of that day and the night in a state little better than her own.

The next morning Adeline, who had not closed her eyes till day-light, woke late, and from a sound but unrefreshing sleep. The first object she saw was her maid, smartly dressed, sitting by her bed-side; and she also saw that she had been crying.

'Is my mother ill, Evans?' she exclaimed.

'O! no, miss Adeline, quite well,' replied the girl, sighing.

'Thank God!' replied Adeline. The girl sighed still more deeply. 'But why are you so much dressed?' demanded Adeline.

'I have been out,' answered the maid.

'Not on unpleasant business?'

'That's as it may be,' she cried, turning away; and Adeline, from delicacy, forebore to press her further.

''Tis very late—is it not?' asked Adeline, 'and time for me to rise?'

'Yes, miss—I believe you had better get up.'

Adeline immediately rose.—'Give me the dark gown I wore yesterday,' said she.

'I think, miss, you had better put on your new white one,' returned the maid.

'My new white one!' exclaimed Adeline, astonished at an interference so new.

'Yes, miss—I think it will be taken kinder, and look better.'

At these words Adeline's suspicions were awakened. 'I see, Evans,' she cried, 'you have something extraordinary to tell me:—I partly guess; I,—my mother—' Here, unable to proceed, she lay down on the bed which she had just quitted.

'Yes, miss Adeline—'tis very true; but pray compose yourself. I am sure I have cried enough on your account, that I have.'

'What is true, my good Evans?' said Adeline faintly.

'Why, miss, my lady was married this morning to sir Patrick O'Carrol!—Mercy on me, how pale you look! I am sure I wish the villain was at the bottom of the sea, so I do.'

'Leave me,' said Adeline faintly, struggling for utterance.

'No—that I will not,' bluntly replied Evans; 'you are not fit to be left; and they are rejoicing below with sir Pat's great staring servant. But, for my part, I had rather stay here and cry with you than laugh with them.'

Adeline hid her face in the pillow, incapable of further resistance, and groaned aloud.

'Who should ever have thought my lady would have done so!' continued the maid.—'Only think, miss! they say, and I doubt it is too true, that there have been no writings, or settlements, I think they call them, drawn up; and so sir Pat have got all,* and he is over head and ears in debt, and my lady is to pay him out on't!'

At this account, which Adeline feared was a just one, as she had seen no preparations for a wedding going on, and had observed no signs of deeds, or any thing of the kind, she started up in an agony of grief—'Then has my mother given me up, indeed!' she exclaimed, clasping her hands together, 'and the once darling child may soon be a friendless outcast!'

'You want a friend, miss Adeline!' said the kind girl, bursting into tears.—'Never, while I live, or any of my fellow-servants.' And Adeline, whose heart was bursting with a sense of forlornness and abandonment, felt consoled by the artless sympathy of her attendant; and, giving way to a violent flood of tears, she threw her arms round her neck, and sobbed upon her bosom.

Having thus eased her feelings, she recollected that it was incumbent on her to exert her fortitude; and that it was a duty which she owed her mother not to condemn her conduct openly herself, nor suffer any one else to do it in her presence: still, at that moment, she could not find in her heart to reprove the observations by which, in spite of her sense of propriety, she had been soothed and gratified; but she hastened to dress herself as became a bridal dinner, and dismissed, as soon as she could, the affectionate Evans from her presence. She then walked up and down her chamber, in order to summon courage to enter the drawing-room.—'But how strange, how cruel it was,' said she, 'that my mother did not come to inform me of this important event herself!'

In this respect, however, Mrs Mowbray had acted kindly. Reluctant, even more than she was willing to confess to her own heart, to meet Adeline alone, she had chosen to conclude that she was still asleep, and had desired she might not be disturbed; but soon after her return from church, being assured that she was in a sound slumber, she had stolen to her bed-side and put a note under her pillow, acquainting her with what had passed: but this note Adeline in her restlessness had, with her pillow, pushed on the floor, and there unseen it had remained. But, as Adeline was pacing to and fro, she luckily observed it; and, by proving that her mother had not been so very neglectful of her, it tended to fortify her mind against the succeeding interview. The note began:—'My *dearest* child! to spare you, in your present weak state, the emotion which you would necessarily feel in attending me to the altar, I have resolved to let the ceremony be performed unknown to you. But, my beloved Adeline, I trust that your affection for me will make you rejoice in a step which you may, perhaps, at present disapprove, when convinced that it was absolutely necessary to my happiness, and can, in no way, be the means of diminishing yours.

'I remain

'Your ever affectionate mother.'

'She loves me still then!' cried Adeline, shedding tears of tenderness, 'and I accused her unjustly.—O my dear mother, if this event should indeed increase your happiness, never shall I repine at not having been able to prevent it.' And then, after taking two or three hasty turns round the room, and bathing her eyes to remove in a degree the traces of her tears, she ventured into the drawing-room.

But the sight of her mother seated by sir Patrick, his arm encircling her waist, in that very room which had so lately witnessed his profligate attempts on herself, deprived her of the little resolution which she had been able to assume, and pale and trembling she sunk speechless with emotion on the first chair near her.

Mrs Mowbray, or, as we must at present call her, lady O'Carrol, was affected by Adeline's distress, and, hastening to her, received the almost fainting girl in her arms; while even sir Patrick, feeling compassion for the unhappiness which he could more readily understand than his bride, was eager to hide his confusion by calling for water, drops, and servants.

'I want neither medicine nor assistance now,' said Adeline, gently raising her head from her mother's shoulder: 'the first shock is over, and I shall, I trust, behave in future with proper self-command.'

'Better late than never,' muttered lady O'Carrol, on whom the word *shock* had not made a pleasant impression; while sir Patrick, approaching Adeline, exclaimed, 'If you have not self-command, miss Mowbray, it is the only command which you cannot boast; for your power of commanding others no one can dispute, who has ever had the happiness of beholding you.'

So saying, he took her hand; and, as her mother's husband, claimed the privilege of saluting her,—a privilege which Adeline, though she almost shrunk with horror from his touch, had *self-command* enough not to deny him: immediately after he claimed the same favour from his bride; and they resumed their position on the sopha.

But so embarrassing was the situation of all parties that no conversation took place; and Adeline, unable any longer to endure the restraint to which she was obliged, rose, to return to her own room, in order to hide the sorrow which she was on the point of betraying, when her mother in a tone of reproach exclaimed, 'It grieves me to the soul, miss Mowbray, to perceive that you appear to consider as a day of mourning the day which I consider as the happiest of my life.'

'Oh! my dearest mother!' replied Adeline, returning and approaching her, 'it is the dread of your deceiving yourself, only, that makes me sad at a time like this: if this day in its consequences prove a happy one—'

'And wherefore should you doubt that it will, miss Mowbray?'

'Miss Mowbray, do you doubt my honour?' cried sir Patrick hastily.

Adeline instantly fixed her fine eyes on his face with a look which he knew how to *interpret*, but not how to support; and he cast his to the ground with painful consciousness.

She saw her triumph, and it gave her courage to proceed:—'O sir!' she cried, 'it is in your power to convert all my painful doubts into joyful certainties; make but my mother happy, and I will love and bless you ever.—Promise me, sir,' she continued, her enthusiasm and affection kindling as she spoke, 'promise me to be kind and indulgent to her;—she has never known contradiction; she has been through life the darling object of all who surrounded her; the pride of her parents, her husband, and her child: neglect, injury, and unkindness she would inevitably sink under: and I conjure you' (here she dropped on her knees and extended her arms in an attitude of entreaty), 'by all your hopes of happiness hereafter, to give her reason to continue to name this the happiest day of her life.'

Here she ceased, overcome by the violence of her emotions; but continued her look and attitude of entreaty, full of such sweet earnestness, that the baronet could hardly conceal the variety of feelings which assailed him; amongst which, passion for the lovely object before him predominated. To make a jest of Adeline's seriousness he conceived to be the best way to conceal what he felt; and while Mrs Mowbray, overcome with Adeline's expressions of tenderness, was giving way to them by a flood of tears, and grasping in both hers the clasped hands of Adeline, he cried, in an ironical tone,—'You are the most extraordinary motherly young creature that I ever saw in my life, my dear girl! Instead of your mother giving the nuptial benediction to you, the order of nature is reversed, and you are giving it to her. Upon my soul I begin to think, seeing you in that posture, that you are my bride begging a blessing of mamma on our union, and that I ought to be on my knees too.'

So saying, he knelt beside Adeline at lady O'Carrol's feet, and in a tone of mock solemnity besought her to bless both her affectionate children: and as he did this, he threw his arm round the weeping girl, and pressed her to his bosom. This speech, and this action, at once banished all self-command from the indignant Adeline, and in an instant she sprung from his embrace; and forgetting how much her violence must surprise, if not alarm and offend, her mother, she rushed out of the room, and did not stop till she reached her own chamber.

When there, she was alarmed lest her conduct should have occasioned both pain and resentment to lady O'Carrol; and it was with trembling reluctance that she obeyed the summons to dinner; but her fears were groundless. The bride had fallen into one of her reveries during sir Patrick's strange speech, from which she awakened only at the last words of it, viz. 'affectionate children:' and seeing sir Patrick at her feet, with a very tender expression on his face, and hearing the words 'affectionate children,' she conceived that he was expressing his hopes of their being blest with progeny, and that a selfish feeling of fear at such a prospect had hurried Adeline out of the room. She was therefore disposed to regard her daughter with pity, but not with resentment, when she entered the dinner-room, and Adeline's tranquillity in a degree returned: but when she retired for the night she could not help owning to herself, that that day, her mother's wedding-day, had been the most painful day of her existence—and she literally sobbed herself to sleep.

The next morning a new trial awaited her; she had to write a final farewell to Glenmurray. Many letters did she begin, many did she finish, and many did she tear; but recollecting that the longer she delayed sending him one, the longer she kept him in a state of agitating suspense, she resolved to send the last written, even though it appeared to her not quite so strong a transcript of her feelings as the former ones. Whether it were so or not, Glenmurray received it with alternate agony and transport;—with agony, because it destroyed every hope of Adeline's being his,—and with transport, because every line breathed the purest and yet most ardent attachment, and convinced him that, however long their separation, the love of Adeline would experience no change.

Many days elapsed before Glenmurray could bear any companion but the letter of Adeline; and during that time she was on the road with the bride and bridegroom to a beautiful seat in Berkshire, called the Pavilion, hired by sir Patrick, the week before his marriage, of one of his profligate friends. As the road lay through a very fine country, Adeline would have thought the journey a pleasant one, had not the idea of Glenmurray ill and dejected continually haunted her. Sir Patrick appeared to be engrossed by his bride, and she was really wholly wrapt up in him; and at times the beauties of the scenery around had power to engage Adeline's attention: but she immediately recollected how much Glenmurray would have participated in her delight, and the contemplation of the prospect ended in renewed recollections of him.

CHAPTER IX

At length they arrived at the place of their destination; and sir Patrick, warmly embracing his bride, bade her welcome to her new abode; and immediately approaching Adeline, he bestowed on her an embrace no less cordial:—or, to say the truth, so ardent seemed the welcome, even to the innocent Adeline, that she vainly endeavoured to persuade herself that, as her father-in-law, sir Patrick's tenderness was excusable.

Spite of her efforts to be cheerful she was angry and suspicious,

and had an indistinct feeling of remote danger; which though she
could not define even to herself, it was new and painful to her to
experience. But as the elastic mind of eighteen soon rebounds from
the pressure of sorrow, and forgets in present enjoyment the prospect of evil, Adeline gazed on the elegant apartment she was in with
joyful surprise; while, through folding doors on either side of it,
she beheld a suite of rooms, all furnished with a degree of tasteful
simplicity such as she had never before beheld: and through the
windows, which opened on a lawn that sloped to the banks of a rapid
river, she saw an amphitheatre of wooded hills, which proved that,
how great soever had been the efforts of art to decorate their new
habitation, the hand of Nature had done still more to embellish it;
and all fear of sir Patrick was lost in gratitude for his having chosen
such a retirement.

With eager curiosity Adeline hurried from room to room; admired
in the western apartments the fine effect of the declining sun shining
through rose-coloured window-curtains; gazed with delight on the
statues and pictures that every where met the eye, and reposed with
unsuspecting gaiety on the couches of eider down which were in
profusion around. Every thing in the house spoke it to be the temple
of Pleasure: but the innocent Adeline and her unobservant mother
saw nothing but elegant convenience in an abode in which the disciples of Epicurus* might have delighted; and while Æolian harps*
in the windows, and perfumes of all kinds, added to the enchantment
of the scene, the bride only beheld in the choice of the villa a proof of
her husband's desire of making her happy; and Adeline sighed for
virtuous love and Glenmurray, as all that was wanting to complete
her fascination.

Sir Patrick, meanwhile, was not blind to the impressions made on
Adeline by the beauty of the spot which he had chosen, though he
was far from suspecting the companion she had pictured to herself as
most fitted to enjoy and embellish it; and pleased because she was
pleased, and delighted to be regarded by her with such unusual
looks of complacency, he gave himself up to his natural vivacity; and
Adeline passed a merry, if not a happy, evening with the bride and
bridegroom.

But the next morning she arose with the painful conviction as
fresh as ever on her mind, that day would succeed to day, and yet she
should not behold Glenmurray; and that day would succeed to day,

and still should she see O'Carrol, still be exposed to his noisy mirth, to his odious familiarities, which, though she taught herself to believe they proceeded merely from the customs of his country, and the nearness of their relationship, it was to her most painful to endure.

Her only resource, therefore, from unpleasant thoughts was reading; and she eagerly opened the cases of books in the library, which were unlocked. But, on taking down some of the books, she was disappointed to find none of the kind to which she had been accustomed. Mrs Mowbray's peculiar taste had led her, as we have before observed, to the perusal of nothing but political tracts, systems of philosophy, and Scuderi's and other romances.* Scarcely had the works of our best poets found their way to her library; and novels, plays, and works of a lighter kind she was never in the habit of reading herself, and consequently had not put in the hands of her daughter. Adeline had, therefore, read Rousseau's Contrat Social, but not his Julie; Montesquieu's Esprit des Loix, but not his Lettres Persannes; and had glowed with republican ardour over the scenes of Voltaire's Brutus, but had never had her pure mind polluted by the pages of his Candide.*

Different had been the circumstances, and consequently the practice, of the owner of sir Patrick's new abode. Of all Rousseau's works, he had in his library only the New Heloise and his Confessions; of Montesquieu, none but the glowing letters above mentioned; and while Voltaire's chaste and moral tragedies were excluded, his profligate tales attracted the eye by the peculiar elegance of their binding; while dangerous French novels of all descriptions met the view under the downy pillows of the inviting sofas around, calculated to inflame the fancy and corrupt the morals.

But Adeline, unprepared by any reading of the kind to receive and relish the poison contained in them, turned with disgust from pages so uncongenial to her feelings; nor did her eye dwell delighted on any of the stores which the shelves contained, till she opened the Nouvelle Heloise; and as soon as she had read a few letters in that enchanting work, she seated herself in the apartment but the moment before become disgusting to her; and in a short time she forgot even Glenmurray himself,—or rather, she gave his form to the eloquent lover of Julie. But, unfortunately, the bride came in while her daughter was thus pleasantly engaged; and on being informed what her studies were, she peremptorily forbad her to read a book so pregnant with mischief; and though she had not read it, and consequently could not justly appreciate its character, she was sure, on the words of others, that such reading was improper for her daughter.

In vain did Adeline venture to say that Julie, like the works of Glenmurray, might be, perhaps, condemned by those who had never read a line of it. The book was prohibited; and Adeline, with a reluctant hand, restored it to its place.

Had she read it, the sacrifice which the guilty but penitent Julia makes to filial affection, and the respectable light in which the institution of marriage is held up to view, would have strengthened, no doubt, Adeline's resolution to obey her mother, and give up Glenmurray; and have led her to reconsider those opinions which taught her to think contemptible what ages and nations had been content to venerate. But it was decreed that every thing the mother of Adeline did should accelerate the fate of her devoted daughter.*

Disappointed in her hopes of finding amusement in reading, Adeline had recourse to walking; and none of the beautiful scenes around remained long unexplored by her. In her rambles she but too frequently saw scenes of poverty and distress, which ill contrasted with the beauty of the house which she inhabited; scenes, which even a small portion of the money expended there in useless decoration would have entirely alleviated: and they were scenes, too, which Adeline had been accustomed to relieve. The extreme of poverty in the cottage did not disgrace, on the Mowbray estate, the well-furnished mansion-house; but Adeline, as we have observed before, was allowed to draw on her mother for money sufficient to prevent industrious labour from knowing the distresses of want.

'And why should I not draw on her here for money for the same purposes?' cried Adeline to herself, as she beheld one spectacle of peculiar hardships.—'Surely my mother is not dependent on her husband? and even if she were, sir Patrick has not a hard heart, and will not refuse my prayer:' and therefore, promising the sufferers instant relief, she left them, saying she should soon reach the Pavilion and be back again; while the objects of her bounty were silent with surprise at hearing that their relief was to come from the Pavilion, a place hitherto closed to the solicitations of poverty, though ever open to the revels and the votaries of pleasure.

Adeline found her mother alone; and with a beating heart and a flushed cheek, she described the scene which she had witnessed, and begged to be restored to her old office of almoner on such occasions.

'A sad scene, indeed, my dear Adeline!' replied the bride in evident embarrassment, 'and I will speak to sir Patrick about it.'

'Speak to sir Patrick, madam! cannot you follow the impulse of humanity without consulting him?'

'I can't give the relief you ask without his assistance,' replied her mother; 'for, except a guinea or so, I have no loose cash about me for my own uses.—Sir Patrick's benevolence has long ago emptied his purse, and I gladly surrendered mine to him.'

'And shall you in future have no money for the purposes of charity but that you must claim from sir Patrick?' asked Adeline mournfully.

'O dear! yes,—I have a very handsome allowance settled on me; but then at present he wants it himself' (Adeline involuntarily clasped her hands together in an agony, and sighed deeply). 'But, however, child,' added the bride, 'as you seem to make such a point of it, take this guinea to the cottage you mention, *en attendant!*'*

Adeline took the guinea: but it was very insufficient to pay for medical attendance, to discharge the rent due to a clamorous land-lord, and to purchase several things necessary for the relief of the poor sufferers: therefore she added another guinea to it, and, not liking to relate her disappointment, sent the money to them, desiring the servant to say that she would see them the next morning, when she resolved to apply to sir Patrick for the relief which her mother could not give; feeling at the same time the mournful conviction, that she herself, as well as her mother, would be in future dependent on his bounty.

Though disposed to give way to mournful reflections on her own account, Adeline roused herself from the melancholy abstraction into which she was falling, by reflecting that she had still to plead the cause of the poor cottagers with sir Patrick; and hearing he was in the house, she hastened to prefer her petition.

Sir Patrick listened to her tone of voice, and gazed on her expressive countenance with delight: but when she had concluded her narration a solitary half-guinea was all he bestowed on her, saying, 'I am never roused to charity by the descriptions of others; I must always see the distress which I am solicited to relieve.'

'Then go with me to the cottage,' exclaimed Adeline; but to her great mortification he only smiled, bowed, and disappeared: and when he returned to supper, Adeline could scarcely prevail on herself to look at him without displeasure, and could not endure the unfeeling vivacity of his manner.

Mortified and unhappy she next morning went to the cottage, reluctant to impart to its expecting inhabitants the ill success which she had experienced. But what was her surprise when they came out joyfully to meet her, and told her that a gentleman had been there that morning very early, had discharged their debts, and given them a sum of money for their future wants!

'His name, his name?' eagerly inquired Adeline: but that they said he refused to give; and as he was in a horseman's large coat, and held a handkerchief to his face, they were sure they should not know him again.

A pleasing suspicion immediately came across Adeline's mind that this benevolent unknown might be Glenmurray; and the idea that he was perhaps unseen hovering round her, gave her one of the most exquisite feelings which she had ever known. But this agreeable delusion was soon dissipated by one of the children's giving her a card which the kind stranger had dropped from his pocket; and this card had on it 'Sir Patrick O'Carrol.'

At first it was natural for her to be hurt and disappointed at finding that her hopes concerning Glenmurray had no foundation in truth; but her benevolence, and indeed regard for her mother's happiness as well as her own, led her to rejoice in this unexpected proof of excellence in sir Patrick.—He had evidently proved that he loved to do good by stealth, and had withdrawn himself even from her thanks.

In a moment, therefore, she banished from her mind every trace of his unworthiness. She had done him injustice, and she sought refuge from the remorse which this consciousness inflicted on her, by going into the opposite extreme. From that hour, indeed, her complaisance to his opinions, and her attentions to him, were so unremitting and evident, that sir Patrick's passion became stronger than ever, and his hopes of a return to it seemed to be built on a very strong foundation.

Adeline had given all her former suspicions to the wind: daily instances of his benevolence came to her knowledge, and threw such a charm over all he said and did, that even the familiarity in his conduct, look, and manner towards her, appeared to her now nothing more than the result of the free manners of his countrymen;—and she sometimes could not help wishing sir Patrick to be known to, and intimate with, Glenmurray. But the moment was now at hand that was to unveil the real character of sir Patrick, and determine the destiny of Adeline.

One day sir Patrick proposed taking his bride to see a beautiful *ferme ornée** at about twelve miles' distance; and if it answered the expectations which he had formed of it, they were determined to spend two or three days in the neighbourhood to enjoy the beauty of the grounds;—in that case he was to return in the evening to the Pavilion, and drive Adeline over the next morning to partake in their pleasure.

To this scheme both the ladies gladly consented, as it was impossible for them to suspect the villanous design which it was intended to aid.

The truth was, that sir Patrick, having, as he fondly imagined, gained Adeline's affections, resolved to defer no longer the profligate attempt which he had long meditated; and had contrived this excursion in order to insure his wife's absence from home, and a tête-à-tête with her daughter,—not doubting but that opportunity was alone wanting to enable him to succeed in his abandoned wishes.

At an early hour the curricle was at the door, and sir Patrick, having handed his lady in, took leave of Adeline. He told her that he should probably return early in the evening, pressed her hand more tenderly than usual, and, springing into the carriage, drove off with a countenance animated with expected triumph.

Adeline immediately set out on a long walk to the adjoining villages, visited the cottages near the Pavilion, and, having dined at an early hour, determined to pass the rest of the day in reading, provided it was possible for her to find any book in the house proper for her perusal.

With this intention she repaired to an apartment called the library, but what in these times would be denominated a *boudoir*; and this, even in Paris, would have been admired for its voluptuous elegance.—On the table lay several costly volumes, which seemed to have been very lately perused by sir Patrick, as some of them were open, some turned down at particular passages: but as soon as she glanced her eye over their contents, Adeline indignantly threw them down again; and, while her cheek glowed with the blush of offended modesty she threw herself on a sofa, and fell into a long and mournful reverie on the misery which awaited her mother, in consequence of her having madly dared to unite herself for life to a young libertine, who could delight in no other reading but what was offensive to good morals and to delicacy. Nor could she dwell upon this subject without recurring to her former fears for herself; and so lost was she in agonizing reflections, that it was some time before she recollected herself sufficiently to remember that she was guilty of an indecorum, in staying so long in an apartment which contained books that she ought not even to be suspected of having had an opportunity to peruse.

Having once entertained this consciousness, Adeline hastily arose, and had just reached the door when sir Patrick himself appeared at it. She started back in terror when she beheld him, on observing in his countenance and manner evident marks not only of determined profligacy, but of intoxication. Her suspicions were indeed just. Bold as he was in iniquity, he dared not in a cool and sober moment put his guilty purpose in execution; and he shrunk with temporary horror from an attempt on the honour of the daughter of his wife, though he believed that she would be a willing victim. He had therefore stopped on the road to fortify his courage with wine; and, luckily for Adeline, he had taken more than he was aware of; for when, after a vehement declaration of the ardour of his passion, and protestations that she should that moment be his, he dared irreverently to approach her, Adeline, strong in innocence, aware of his intention, and presuming on his situation, disengaged herself from his grasp with ease; and pushing him with violence from her, he fell with such force against the brass edge of one of the sofas, that, stunned and wounded by the fall, he lay bleeding on the ground. Adeline involuntarily was hastening to his assistance: but recollecting how mischievous to her such an exertion of humanity might be, she contented herself with ringing the bell violently to call the servants to his aid. Then, in almost frantic haste, she rushed out of the house, ran across the park, and when she recovered her emotion she found herself, she scarcely knew how, sitting on a turf seat by the road side.

'Great God! what will become of me!' she wildly exclaimed: 'my mother's roof is no longer a protection to me;—I cannot absent myself from it without alleging a reason for my conduct, which will ruin her peace of mind for ever. Wretch that I am! whither can I go, and where can I seek for refuge?'

At this moment, as she looked around in wild dismay, and raised her streaming eyes to heaven, she saw a man's face peeping from between the branches of a tree opposite to her, and observed that he was gazing on her intently. Alarmed and fluttered, she instantly started from her seat, and was hastening away, when the man suddenly dropped from his hiding-place, and, running after her, called her by her name, and conjured her to stop; while, with an emotion of surprise and delight, she recognized in him Arthur, the servant of Glenmurray!

Instantly, scarcely knowing what she did, she pressed the astonished Arthur's rough hand in hers; and by this action confused and confounded the poor fellow so much, that the speech which he was going to make faltered on his tongue.

'Oh! where is your master?' eagerly inquired Adeline.

'My master have sent you this, miss,' replied Arthur, holding out a letter, which Adeline joyfully received; and, spite of her intended obedience to her mother's will, Glenmurray himself could not have met with a less favourable reception, for the moment was a most propitious one to his love: nor, as it happened, was Glenmurray too far off to profit by it. On his way from Bath he went a few miles out of his road, in order, as he said, and perhaps as he thought, to pay a visit to an old servant of his mother's, who was married to a respectable farmer; but, fortunately, the farm commanded a view of the Pavilion, and Glenmurray could from his window gaze on the house that contained the woman of his affections.

But to return to Adeline, who, while hastily tearing open the letter, asked Arthur where his master was, and heard with indescribable emotion that he was in the neighbourhood.

'Here! so providentially!' she exclaimed, and proceeded to read the letter; but her emotion forbade her to read it entirely. She only saw that it contained bank-notes; that Glenmurray was going abroad for his health; and, in case he should die there, had sent her the money which he had meant to leave her in his will,—lest she should be, in the meanwhile, any way dependent on sir Patrick.

Numberless conflicting emotions took possession of Adeline's heart while this new proof of her lover's attentive tenderness met her view; and, as she contrasted his generous and delicate attachment with the licentious passion of her mother's libertine husband, a burst of uncontrollable affection for Glenmurray agitated her bosom; and, rendered superstitious by her fears, she looked on him as sent by Providence to save her from the dangers of her home.

'This is the second time,' cried she, 'that Glenmurray, as my guardian angel, has appeared at the moment when I was exposed to danger from the same guilty quarter! Ah! surely there is more than accident in this! and he is ordained to be my guide and my protector!'

When once a woman has associated with an amiable man the idea of protection, he can never again be indifferent to her; and when the protector happens to be the chosen object of her love, his power becomes fixed on a basis never to be shaken.

'It is enough,' said Adeline in a faltering voice, pressing the letter to her lips, and bursting into tears of grateful tenderness as she spoke: 'Lead me to your master directly.'

'Bless my heart! will you see him then, miss?' cried Arthur.

'See him?' replied Adeline—'see the only friend I now can boast?—But let us be gone this moment, lest I should be seen and pursued.'

Instantly, guided by Arthur, Adeline set off full speed for the farm-house, nor stopped till she found herself in the presence of Glenmurray!

'O! I am safe now!' exclaimed Adeline, throwing herself into his arms; while he was so overcome with surprise and joy that he could not speak the welcome which his heart gave her: and Adeline, happy to behold him again, was as silent as her lover. At length Glenmurray exclaimed:

'Do we then meet again, Adeline!'

'Yes,' replied she; 'and we meet to part no more.'

'Do not mock me,' cried Glenmurray starting from his seat, and seizing her extended hand; 'my feelings must not be trifled with.'

'Nor am I a woman to trifle with them. Glenmurray, I come to you for safety and protection;—I come to seek shelter in your arms from misery and dishonour. You are ill, you are going into a foreign country: and from this moment look on me as your nurse, your companion;—your home shall be my home, your country my country!'

Glenmurray, too much agitated, too happy to speak, could only press the agitated girl to his bosom, and fold his arms round her, as if to assure her of the protection which she claimed.

'But there is not a moment to be lost,' cried Adeline: 'I may be missed and pursued: let us be gone directly.'

The first word was enough for Glenmurray: eager to secure the recovered treasure which he had thought for ever lost, his orders were given, and executed by the faithful Arthur with the utmost dispatch; and even before Adeline had explained to him the cause of her resolution to elope with him they were on their road to Cornwall, meaning to embark at Falmouth for Lisbon.

But Arthur, who was going to marry, and leave Glenmurray's service, received orders to stay at the farm till he had learned how sir Patrick was; and having obtained the necessary information, he was to send it to Glenmurray at Falmouth. The next morning he saw sir Patrick himself driving full speed past the farm; and having written immediately to his master, Adeline had the satisfaction of knowing that she had not purchased her own safety by the sufferings or danger of her persecutor, and the consequent misery of her mother.

CHAPTER X

But Glenmurray's heart needed no explanation of the cause of Adeline's elopement. She was with him—with him, as she said, for ever. True, she had talked of flying from misery and dishonour; but he knew they could not reach her in his arms,—not even dishonour according to the ideas of society,—for he meant to make Adeline legally his as soon as they were safe from pursuit, and his illness was forgotten in the fond transport of the present moment.

Adeline's joy was of a much shorter duration. Recollections of a most painful nature were continually recurring. True it was that it was no longer possible for her to reside under the roof of her mother:—but was it necessary for her to elope with Glenmurray? the man whom she had solemnly promised her mother to renounce! Then, on the other side, she argued that the appearance of love for Glenmurray was an excuse sufficient to conceal from her deluded parent the real cause of her elopement.

'It was my sole alternative,' said she mentally:—'my mother must either suppose me an unworthy child, or know sir Patrick to be an

unworthy husband; and it will be easier for her to support the knowledge of the one than of the other: then, when she forgives me, as no
doubt she will in time, I shall be happy: but that I could never be,
while convinced that I had made her miserable by revealing to her
the wickedness of sir Patrick.'

While this was passing in her mind, her countenance was full of
such anxious and mournful expression, that Glenmurray, unable to
keep silence any longer, conjured her to tell him what so evidently
weighed upon her spirits.

'The difficulty that oppressed me is past,' she replied, wiping
from her eyes the tears which the thought of having left her mother
so unexpectedly, and for the first time, produced. 'I have convinced
myself, that to leave home and commit myself to your protection was
the most proper and virtuous step that I could take: I have not
obeyed the dictates of love, but of reason.'

'I am very sorry to hear it,' said Glenmurray mournfully.

'It seems to me so very rational to love you,' returned Adeline
tenderly, shocked at the sad expression of his countenance, 'that
what seem to be the dictates of reason may be those of love only.'

To a reply like this, Glenmurray could only answer by those
incoherent yet intelligible expressions of fondness to the object of
them, which are so delightful to lovers themselves, and so uninterest-
ing to other people: nay, so entirely was Glenmurray again engrossed
by the sense of present happiness, that his curiosity was still suspended, and Adeline's story remained untold. But Adeline's pleasure
was damped by painful recollections, and still more by her not being
able to hide from herself the mournful consciousness that the ravages
of sickness were but too visible in Glenmurray's face and figure, and
that the flush of unexpected delight could but ill conceal the hollow
paleness of his cheek, and the sunk appearance of his eyes.

Meanwhile the chaise rolled on,—post succeeded to post; and
though night was far advanced, Adeline, fearful of being pursued,
would not consent to stop, and they travelled till morning. But
Glenmurray, feeling himself exhausted, prevailed on her, for his
sake, to alight at a small inn on the road side near Marlborough.

There Adeline narrated the occurrences of the past day; but with
difficulty could she prevail on herself to own to Glenmurray that she
had been the object of such an outrage as she had experienced from
sir Patrick.

A truly delicate woman feels degraded, not flattered, by being the object of libertine attempts; and, situated as Adeline and Glenmurray now were, to disclose the insult which had been offered to her was a still more difficult task: but to conceal it was impossible. She felt that, even to *him*, some justification of her precipitate and unsolicited flight was necessary; and nothing but sir Patrick's attempt could justify it. She therefore, blushing and hesitating, revealed the disgraceful secret: but such was its effect on the weak spirits and delicate health of Glenmurray, that the violent emotions which he underwent brought on a return of his most alarming symptoms;* and in a few hours Adeline, bending over the sick bed of her lover, experienced for the first time that most dreadful of feelings, fear for the life of the object of her affection.

Two days, however, restored him to comparative safety, and they reached a small and obscure village within a short distance from Falmouth, most conveniently situated. There they took up their abode, and resolved to remain till the wind should change, and enable them to sail for Lisbon.

In this retreat, situated in air as salubrious as that of the south of France, Glenmurray was soon restored to health, especially as happy love was now his, and brought back the health of which hopeless love had contributed to deprive him. The woman whom he loved was his companion and his nurse; and so dear had the quiet scene of their happiness become to them, that, forgetful there was still a danger of their being discovered, it was with considerable regret that they received a summons to embark, and saw themselves on their voyage to Portugal.

But before she left England Adeline wrote to her mother.

After a pleasant and short voyage the lovers found themselves at Lisbon; and Glenmurray, pursuant to his resolution, immediately proposed to Adeline to unite himself to her by the indissoluble ties of marriage.

Nothing could exceed Adeline's surprise at this proposal: at first she could not believe Glenmurray was in earnest; but seeing that he looked not only grave but anxious, and as if earnestly expecting an answer, she asked him whether he had convinced himself that what he had written against marriage was a tissue of mischievous absurdity.

Glenmurray, blushing, with the conceit of an author replied 'that he still thought his arguments unanswerable.'

'Then, if you still are convinced your theory is good, why let your practice be bad? It is incumbent on you to act up to the principles that you profess, in order to give them their proper weight in society—else you give the lie to your own declarations.'

'But it is better for me to do that, than for you to be the sacrifice to my reputation.'

'I', replied Adeline, 'am entirely out of the question: you are to be governed by no other law but your desire to promote general utility,* and are not to think at all of the interest of an individual.'

'How can I do so, when that individual is dearer to me than all the world beside?' cried Glenmurray passionately.

'And if you but once recollect that you are dearer to me than all the world beside, you will cease to suppose that my happiness can be affected by the opinion entertained of my conduct by others.' As Adeline said this, she twisted both her hands in his arms so affectionately, and looked up in his face with so satisfied and tender an expression, that Glenmurray could not bear to go on with a subject which evidently drew a cloud across her brow; and hours, days, weeks, and months passed rapidly over their heads before he had resolution to renew it.

Hours, days, weeks, and months spent in a manner most dear to the heart and most salutary to the mind of Adeline!—Her taste for books, which had hitherto been cultivated in a partial manner, and had led her to one range of study only, was now directed by Glenmurray to the perusal of general literature; and the historian, the biographer, the poet, and the novelist, obtained alternately her attention and her praises.

In her knowledge of the French and Italian languages, too, she was now considerably improved by the instructions of her lover; and while his occasional illnesses were alleviated by her ever watchful attentions, their attachment was cemented by one of the strongest of all ties—the consciousness of mutual benefit and assistance.

CHAPTER XI

One evening, as they were sitting on a bench in one of the public walks, a gentleman approached them, whose appearance bespoke him to be an Englishman, though his sun-burnt complexion showed that he had been for years exposed to a more ardent climate than that of Britain.

As he came nearer, Glenmurray thought his features were familiar to him; and the stranger, starting with joyful surprise, seized his hand, and welcomed him as an old friend. Glenmurray returned his salutation with great cordiality, and recognized in the stranger a Mr Maynard, an amiable man, who had gone to seek his fortune in India, and was returned a nabob,* but with an irreproachable character.

'So, then,' cried Mr Maynard gaily, 'this is the elegant young English couple that my servant, and even the inn-keeper himself, was so loud in praise of! Little did I think the happy man was my old friend,—though no man is more deserving of being happy: but I beg you will introduce me to your lady.'

Glenmurray, though conscious of the mistake he was under, had not resolution enough to avow that he was not married; and Adeline, unaware of the difficulty of Glenmurray's situation, received Mr Maynard's salutation with the utmost ease, though the tremor of her lover's voice, and the blush on his cheek as he said—'Adeline, give me leave to introduce to you Mr Maynard, an old friend of mine,'— were sufficient indications that the rencontre disturbed him.

In a few minutes Adeline and Mr Maynard were no longer strangers. Mr Maynard, who had not lived much in the society of well-informed women, and not at all in that of women accustomed to original thinking, was at once astonished and delighted at the variety of Adeline's remarks, at the playfulness of her imagination, and the eloquence of her expressions. But it was very evident, at length, to Mr Maynard, that in proportion as Adeline and he became more acquainted and more satisfied with each other, Glenmurray grew more silent and more uneasy. The consequence was unavoidable: as most men would have done on a like occasion, Mr Maynard thought Glenmurray was jealous of him.

But no thought so vexatious to himself, and so degrading to Adeline, had entered the confiding and discriminating mind of Glenmurray. The truth was, he knew that Mr Maynard, whom he had seen in the walks, though he had not known him again, had ladies of his party; and he expected that the more Mr Maynard admired his supposed wife, the more would he be eager to introduce her to his companions.

Nor was Glenmurray wrong in his conjectures.

'I have two sisters with me, madam,' said Mr Maynard, 'whom I shall be happy and proud to introduce to you. One of them is a widow, and has lived several years in India, but returned with me in delicate health, and was ordered hither: she is not a woman of great reading, but has an excellent understanding, and will admire you. The other is several years younger; and I am sure she would be happy in an opportunity of profiting by the conversation of a lady, who, though not older than herself, seems to have had so many more opportunities of improvement.'

Adeline bowed, and expressed her impatience to form this new acquaintance; and looked triumphantly at Glenmurray, meaning to express—'See, spite of the supposed prejudices of the world, here is a man who wants to introduce me to his sisters.' Little did she know that Maynard concluded she was a wife: his absence from England had made him ignorant of the nature of Glenmurray's works, or even that he was an author; so that he was not at all likely to suppose that the moral, pious youth, whom he had always respected, was become a visionary philosopher, and, in defiance of the laws of society, was living openly with a mistress.

'But my sister will wonder what is become of me,' suddenly cried Maynard; 'and as Emily is so unwell as to keep her room to-day, I must not make her anxious. But for her illness, I should have requested your company to supper.'

'And I should have liked to accept the invitation,' replied Adeline; 'but I will hope to see the ladies soon.'

'Oh! without fail, to-morrow,' cried Maynard: 'if Emily be not well enough to call on you, perhaps you will come to her apartments.'

'Undoubtedly: expect me at twelve o'clock.'

Maynard then shook his grave and silent friend by the hand and, departed,—his vanity not a little flattered by the supposed jealousy of Glenmurray.

'There now,' said Adeline, when he was out of hearing, 'I hope some of your tender fears are done away. You see there are liberal and unprejudiced persons in the world; and Mr Maynard, instead of shunning me, courts my acquaintance for his sisters.'

Glenmurray shook his head, and remained silent; and Adeline was distressed to feel by his burning hand that he was seriously uneasy.

'I shall certainly call on these ladies to-morrow,' continued Adeline:—'I really pine for the society of amiable women.'

Glenmurray sighed deeply: he dreaded to tell her that he could not allow her to call on them, and yet he knew that this painful task awaited him. Besides, she wished, she said, to know some amiable women; and, eager as he was to indulge all her wishes, he felt but too certainly that in this wish she could never be indulged. Even had he been capable of doing so dishonourable an action as introducing his mistress as his wife, he was sure that Adeline would have spurned at the deception; and silent and sad he grasped Adeline's hand as her arm rested within his, and, complaining of indisposition, slowly returned to the inn.

The next morning at breakfast, Adeline again expressed her eagerness to form an acquaintance with the sisters of Mr Maynard; when Glenmurray, starting from his seat, paced the room in considerable agitation.

'What is the matter?' cried Adeline, hastily rising and laying her hand on his arm.

Glenmurray grasped her hand, and replied with assumed firmness: 'Adeline, it is impossible for you to form an acquaintance with Mr Maynard's sisters: propriety and honour both forbid me to allow it.'

'Indeed!' exclaimed Adeline, 'are they not as amiable, then, as he described them? are they improper acquaintances for me? Well then—I am disappointed: but you are the best judge of what is right, and I am contented to obey you.'

The simple, ingenuous and acquiescent sweetness with which she said this, was a new pang to her lover:—had she repined, had she looked ill-humoured, his task would not have been so difficult.

'But what reason can you give for declining this acquaintance?' resumed Adeline.

'Aye! there's the difficulty,' replied Glenmurray: 'pure-minded and amiable as I know you to be, how can I bear to tell these children of prejudice that you are not my wife, but my mistress?'

Adeline started; and, turning pale, exclaimed, 'Are you sure, then, that they do not know it already?'

'Quite sure—else Maynard would not have thought you a fit companion for his sisters.'

'But surely he must know your principles; he must have read your works?'

'I am certain he is ignorant of both, and does not even know that I am an author.'

'Is it possible?' cried Adeline: 'is there any one so unfortunate as to be unacquainted with your writings?'

Glenmurray at another time would have been elated at a compliment like this from the woman whom he idolized; but at this moment he heard it with a feeling of pain which he would not have liked to define to himself, and casting his eyes to the ground he said nothing.

'So then,' said Adeline mournfully, 'I am an improper companion for *them*, not they for *me!*' and spite of herself her eyes filled with tears.—At this moment a waiter brought in a note for Glenmurray;—it was from Maynard, and as follows:

'MY DEAR FRIEND,

'Emily is better to-day; and both my sisters are so impatient to see, and know, your charming wife, that they beg me to present their compliments to Mrs Glenmurray and you; and request the honour of your company to a late breakfast:—at eleven o'clock we hope to see you,

'Ever yours,

'G.M.'

'We will send an answer,' said Glenmurray: but the waiter had been gone some minutes before either Adeline or Glenmurray spoke. At length Adeline, struggling with her feelings, observed, 'Mr Maynard seems so amiable a man, that I should think it would not be difficult to convince him of his errors: surely, therefore, it is your duty to call on him, state our real situation, and our reasons for it, and endeavour to convince him that our attachment is sanctioned both by reason and virtue.'

'But not by the church,' replied Glenmurray, 'and Maynard is of the old school: besides, a man of forty-eight is not likely to be convinced by the arguments of a young man of twenty-eight, and the example of a girl of nineteen.'*

'If age be necessary to give weight to arguments,' returned Adeline, 'I wonder that you thought proper to publish four years ago.'

'Would to God I never had published!' exclaimed Glenmurray, almost pettishly.

'If you had not, I probably should never have been yours,' replied Adeline, fondly leaning her head on his shoulder, and then looking up in his face. Glenmurray clasped her to his bosom; but again the pleasure was mixed with pain. 'All this time', rejoined Adeline, 'your friends are expecting an answer: you had better carry it in person.'

'I cannot,' replied Glenmurray, 'and there is only one way of getting out of this business to my satisfaction.'

'Name it; and rest assured that I shall approve it.'

'Then I wish to order horses immediately, and set off on our road to France.'

'So soon,—though the air agrees with you so well?'

'O yes;—for when the mind is uneasy no air can be of use to the body.'

'But why is your mind uneasy?'

'Here I should be exposed to see Maynard, and—and—he would see you too.'

'And what then?'

'What then?—Why, I could not bear to see him look on you with an eye of disrespect.'

'And wherefore should he?'

'O Adeline, the name of wife imposes restraint even on a libertine; but that of mistress—'

'Is Mr Maynard then a libertine?' said Adeline gravely: and Glenmurray, afraid of wounding her feelings by entering into a further explanation, changed the subject, and again requested her consent to leave Lisbon.

'I have often told you,' said Adeline sighing, 'that my will is yours; and if you will give strict orders to have letters sent after us to the towns that we shall stop at, I am ready to set off immediately.'

Glenmurray then gave his orders; wrote a letter explaining his situation to Maynard, and in an hour they were on their journey to France.

CHAPTER XII

In the mean while Mr Maynard, miss Maynard, and Mrs Wallington his widowed sister, were impatiently expecting Glenmurray's answer, and earnestly hoping to see him and his lovely companion,— but from different motives. Maynard was impatient to see Adeline because he really admired her; his sisters, because they hoped to find her unworthy of such violent admiration.

Their vanity had been piqued, and their envy excited, by the extravagant praises of their brother; and they had interrupted him by the first questions which all women ask on such occasions,—'Is she pretty?'

And he had answered, 'Very pretty.'

'Is she tall?'

'Very tall, taller than I am.'

'I hate tall women,' replied miss Maynard (a little round girl of nineteen).

'Is she fair?'

'Exquisitely fair.'

'I like brown women,' cried the widow: 'fair people always look silly.'

'But Mrs Glenmurray's eyes are hazel, and her eye-lashes long and dark.'

'Hazel eyes are always bold-looking,' cried miss Maynard.

'Not Mrs Glenmurray's; for her expression is the most pure and ingenuous that ever I saw. Some girls, indecent in their dress and very licentious in their manner, passed us as we sat on the walk; and the comments which I made on them provoked from Mrs Glenmurray some remarks on the behaviour and dress of women; and, as she commented on the disgusting expression of vice in women, and the charm of modest dignity both in dress and manners, her own dress, manners, and expression, were such an admirable comment on her words, and she shone so brightly, if I may use the expression, in the graceful awfulness of virtue, that I gazed with delight, and somewhat of apprehension lest this fair perfection should suddenly take flight to her native skies, toward which her fine eyes were occasionally turned.'

'Bless me! if our brother is not quite poetical! This prodigy has inspired him,' replied the widow with a sneer.

'For my part, I hate *prodigies*,' said miss Maynard: 'I feel myself unworthy to associate with them.'

When one woman calls another a prodigy, and expresses herself as unworthy to associate with her, it is very certain that she means to insult rather than compliment her; and in this sense Mr Maynard understood his sister's words: therefore, after having listened with tolerable patience to a few more sneers at the unconscious Adeline, he was provoked to say that, ill-disposed as he found they were towards his new acquaintance, he hoped that when they became acquainted with her they would still give him reason to say, as he always had done, that he was proud of his sisters; for, in his opinion, no woman ever looked so lovely as when she was doing justice to the merits and extenuating the faults of a rival.

'A rival!' exclaimed the sisters at once:—'And, pray, what rivalship could there be in this case?'

'My remark was a general one; but since you choose to make it a particular one, I will answer to it as such,' continued Mr Maynard. 'All women are rivals in one sense—rivals for general esteem and admiration; and she only shall have my suffrage in her favour, who can point out a beauty or a merit in another woman without insinuating at the same time a counterbalancing defect.'

'But Mrs Glenmurray, it seems, has *no* defects!'

'At least I have not known her long enough to find them out; but you, no doubt, will, when you know her, very readily spare me that trouble.'

How injudiciously had Maynard prepared the minds of his sisters to admire Adeline! It was a preparation to make them hate her; and they were very impatient to begin the task of depreciating both her *morale* and her *physique*, when Glenmurray's note arrived.

'It is not Glenmurray's hand,' said Maynard (indeed, from agitation of mind the writing was not recognizable). 'It must be hers then,' continued he, affecting to kiss the address with rapture.

'It is the hand of a sloven,' observed Mrs Wallington, studying the writing.

'But in dress she is as neat as a quaker,' retorted the brother, eagerly snatching the letter back, 'and her mind seems as pure as her dress.'

He then broke the seal, and read out what follows:

'"DEAR MAYNARD,

'"When you receive this, Adeline and I shall be on our road to France, and you,—start not!—are the occasion of our abrupt departure."'

'So, so, jealous indeed,' said Maynard to himself, and more

impressed than ever with the charms of Adeline; for he concluded that Glenmurray had discovered in her an answering prepossession.

'You the occasion, brother!' cried both sisters.

'Have patience.'

' "You saw Adeline; you admired her; and wished to introduce her to your sisters—this, honour forbad me to allow" '—(the sisters started from their seats) ' "for Adeline is not my wife, but my companion." '

Here Maynard made a full pause—at once surprised and confounded. His sisters, pleased as well as astonished, looked triumphantly at each other; and Mrs Wallington exclaimed, 'So, then, this angel of purity turns out to be a kept lady!' At this remark miss Maynard laughed heartily; but Maynard, to hide his confusion, commanded silence, and went on with the letter:

' "But, spite of her situation, strange as it may seem to you, believe me, no wife was ever more pure than Adeline." '

At this passage the sisters could no longer contain themselves, and they gave way to loud bursts of laughter, which Maynard could hardly help joining in; but being angry at the same time he uttered nothing but an oath, which I shall not repeat, and retreated to his chamber to finish the letter alone.

During his absence the laughter redoubled;—but in the midst of it Maynard re-entered, and desired they would allow him to read the letter to the end. The sisters immediately begged that he would proceed, as it was so amusing that they wished to hear more.— Glenmurray continued thus:

' "You have no doubt yet to learn that some few years ago I commenced author, and published opinions contrary to the established usage of society: amongst other things I proved the absurdity of the institution of marriage; and Adeline, who at an early age read my works, became one of my converts." '

'The man is certainly mad,' cried Maynard, 'and how dreadful it is that this angelic creature should have been his victim.'

'But perhaps this *fallen* angel, brother, for such you will allow she is, spite of her *purity*, was as wicked as he. I know people in general only blame the seducer, but I always blame the seduced equally.'

'I do not doubt it,' said her brother sneeringly, and going on with the letter.

'"No wonder then, that, being forced to fly from her maternal roof, she took refuge in my arms."

'Lucky dog!

'"But though Adeline was the victim neither of her own weakness nor of my seductions, but was merely urged by circumstances to act up to the principles which she openly professed, I felt so conscious that she would be degraded in your eyes after you were acquainted with her situation, though in mine she appears as spotless as ever, that I could not bear to expose her even to a glance from you less respectful than those with which you beheld her last night. I there-fore prevailed on her to leave Lisbon; nor had I any difficulty in so doing, when she found that your wish of introducing her to your sisters was founded on your supposition of her being my wife, and that all chance of your desiring her acquaintance for them would be over, when you knew the nature of her connection with me. I shall now bid you farewell. I write in haste and agitation, and have not time to say more than God bless you!

'"F.G."

'Yes, yes, I see how it is,' muttered Mr Maynard to himself when he had finished the letter, 'he was jealous of me. I wish' (raising his voice) 'that he had not been in such a confounded hurry to go away.'

'Why, brother,' replied Mrs Wallington, 'to be sure you would not have introduced us to this piece of angelic purity a little the worse for the wear!'

'No,' replied he; 'but I might have enjoyed her company myself.'

'And perhaps, brother, you might have rivalled the philosophic author in time,' observed miss Maynard.

'If I had not, it would have been from no want of good will on my part,' returned Maynard.

'Well, then I rejoice that the creature is gone,' replied Mrs Wallington, drawing up.

'And I too,' said miss Maynard disdainfully: 'but I think we had better drop this subject; I have had quite enough of it.'

'And so have I,' cried Mrs Wallington: 'but I must observe, before we drop it entirely, that when next my brother comes home and wearies his sisters by exaggerated praises of another woman, I hope he will take care that his goddess, or rather his angel of purity, does not turn out to be a kept mistress.'

So saying she left the room, and miss Maynard, tittering, followed her; while Maynard, too sore on this subject to bear to be laughed at, took his hat in a pet,* and, flinging the door after him with great violence, walked out to muse on the erring but interesting companion of Glenmurray.

CHAPTER XIII

While these conversations were passing at Lisbon, Glenmurray and Adeline were pursuing their journey to France; and insensibly did the charm of being together obliterate from the minds of each the rencontre which had so much disturbed them.

But Adeline began to be uneasy on a subject of much greater importance; she every day expected an answer from her mother, but no answer arrived; and they had been stationary at Perpignan some days, to which place they had desired their letters to be addressed, *poste restante*,* and still none were forwarded thither from Lisbon.

The idea that her mother had utterly renounced her now took possession of her imagination, and love had no charm to offer her capable of affording her consolation: the care which she had taken of her infancy, the affectionate attentions that had preserved her life, and the uninterrupted kindness which she had shown towards her till her attachment to sir Patrick took place,—all these pressed powerfully and painfully on her memory, till her elopement seemed wholly unjustifiable in her eyes, and she reprobated her conduct in terms of the most bitter self-reproach.

At these moments even Glenmurray seemed to become the object of her aversion. Her mother had forbidden her to think of him; yet, to make her flight more agonizing to her injured parent, she had eloped with *him*. But as soon as ever she beheld him he regained his wonted influence over her heart, and her self-reproaches became less poignant: she became sensible that sir Patrick's guilt and her mother's imprudent marriage were the causes of her own fault, and not Glenmurray; and could she but receive a letter of pardon from England, she felt that her conscience would again be at peace.

But soon an idea of a still more harassing nature succeeded and overwhelmed her. Perhaps her desertion had injured her mother's health; perhaps she was too ill to write; perhaps she was dead:—and when this horrible supposition took possession of her mind she used to avoid even the presence of her lover; and as her spirits commonly sunk towards evening, when the still renewed expectations of the day had been deceived, she used to hasten to a neighbouring church when the bell called to vespers, and, prostrate on the steps of the altar, lift up her soul to heaven in the silent breathings of penitence and prayer. Having thus relieved her heart she returned to Glenmurray, pensive but resigned.

One evening after she had unburthened her feelings in this manner, Glenmurray prevailed on her to walk with him to a public promenade; and being tired they sat down on a bench in a shady part of the mall. They had not sat long before a gentleman and two ladies seated themselves beside them.

Glenmurray instantly rose up to depart; but the gentleman also rose and exclaimed, ''Tis he indeed! Glenmurray, have you forgotten your old friend Willie Douglas?'

Glenmurray, pleased to see a friend whom he had once so highly valued, returned the salutation with marked cordiality; while the ladies with great kindness accosted Adeline, and begged she would allow them the honour of her acquaintance.

Taught by the rencontre at Lisbon, Adeline for a moment felt embarrassed; but there was something so truly benevolent in the countenance of both ladies, and she was so struck by the extreme beauty of the younger one, that she had not resolution to avoid, or even to receive their advances coldly; and while the gentlemen were commenting on each other's looks, and in an instant going over the occurrences of past years, the ladies, pleased with each other, had entered into conversation.

'But I expected to see you and your lady,' said major Douglas; 'for Maynard was writing to me from Lisbon when he laid by his pen and took the walk in which he met you; and on his return he filled up the rest of his letter with the praises of Mrs Glenmurray, and expressions of envy at your happiness.'

Glenmurray and Adeline both blushed deeply. 'So!' said Adeline to herself, 'here will be another letter to write when we get home;' for, though ingenuousness was one of her most striking qualities, she had not resolution enough to tell her new acquaintance that she was not married: besides, she flattered herself, that, could she once interest these charming women in her favour, they would not refuse her their society even when they knew her real situation; for she thought them too amiable to be prejudiced, as she called it, and was not yet aware how much the perfection of the female character depends on respect even to what may be called the prejudices of others.

The day began to close in; but major Douglas, though Glenmurray was too uneasy to answer him except by monosyllables, would not hear of going home, and continued to talk with cheerfulness and interest of the scenes of his and Glenmurray's early youth. He too was ignorant of his friend's notoriety as an author: he had lived chiefly at his estates in the Highlands; nor would he have left them, but because he was advised to travel for his health; and the lovely creature whom he had married, as well as his only sister, was anxious on his account to put the advice in execution. He therefore made no allusions to Glenmurray's opinions that could give him an opportunity of explaining his real situation; and he saw with confusion, that every moment increased the intimacy of Adeline and the wife and sister of his friend.

At length his feelings operated so powerfully on his weak frame, that a sudden faintness seized him, and supported by Adeline and the major, and followed by his two kind companions, he returned to the inn: there, to get rid of the Douglases and avoid the inquiries of Adeline, who suspected the cause of his illness, he immediately retired to bed.

His friends also returned home, lamenting the apparently declining health of Glenmurray, and expatiating with delight on the winning graces of his supposed wife; for these ladies were of a different class of women to the sisters of Maynard.—Mrs Douglas was so confessedly a beauty, so rich in acknowledged attractions, that she could afford to do justice to the attractions of another; and miss Douglas was so decidedly devoid of all pretensions to the lovely in person, that the idea of competition with the beautiful never entered her mind, and she was always eager to admire what she knew that she was incapable of rivalling. Unexposed, therefore, to feel those petty jealousies, those paltry competitions which injure the character of women in general, Emma Douglas's mind was the seat of benevolence and candour,—as was her beautiful sister's from a different cause; and they were both warmer even than the major in praise of Adeline.

But a second letter from Mr Maynard awaited major Douglas at the inn, which put a fatal stop to their self-congratulations at having met Glenmurray and his companion.

Mr Maynard, full of Glenmurray's letter, and still more deeply impressed than ever with the image of Adeline, could not forbear writing to the major on the subject; giving as a reason, that he wished to let him know the true state of affairs, in order that he might avoid Glenmurray... The letter came too late.

'And I have seen him, have welcomed him as a friend, and he has had the impudence to introduce his harlot to my wife and sister!'

So spoke the major in the language of passion,—and passion is never accurate.—Glenmurray had *not* introduced Adeline: and this was gently hinted by the kind and candid Emma Douglas; while the younger and more inexperienced wife sat silent with consternation, at having pressed with the utmost kindness the hand of a kept mistress.

Vain were the representations of his sister to sooth the wounded pride of major Douglas. Without considering the difficulty of such a proceeding, he insisted upon it that Glenmurray should have led Adeline away instantly, as unworthy to breathe the same air with his wife and sister.

'You find by that letter, brother,' said miss Douglas, 'that this unhappy Adeline is still an object of respect in his eyes, and he could not wound her feelings so publicly, especially as she seems to be more ill-judging than vicious.'

She spoke in vain.—The major was a soldier, and so delicate in his ideas of the honour of women, that he thought his wife and sister polluted from having, though unconsciously, associated with Adeline: being violently irritated therefore at the supposed insult offered him by Glenmurray, he left the room, and, having dispatched a challenge to him, told the ladies he had letters to write to England till bed-time arrived: then, after having settled his affairs in case he should fall in the conflict, he sat brooding alone over the insolence of his former friend.

There was a consciousness too which aggravated his resentment.

Calumny had been busy with his reputation; and, though he deserved it not, had once branded him with the name of coward. Besides, his elder sister had been seduced by a man of very high rank, and was then living with him as his mistress. Made still more susceptible therefore of affront by this distressing consciousness, he suspected that Glenmurray, from being acquainted with these circumstances, had presumed on them, and dared to take a liberty with him, situated as he then was, which in former times he would not have ventured to offer.

As Adeline and Glenmurray were both retired for the night when the major's note arrived, it was not delivered till morning,—nor then, luckily, till Adeline, supposing Glenmurray asleep, was gone to take her usual walk to the post-office: Glenmurray, little aware of its contents, opened it, and read as follows:

'SIR,

'For your conduct in introducing your mistress to my wife and sister, I demand immediate satisfaction. As you may possibly not have recovered your indisposition of last night, and I wish to take no unfair advantages, I do not desire you to meet me till evening; but at six o'clock, a mile out of the north side of the town, I shall expect you.—I can lend you pistols if you have none.'

'There is only one step to be taken,' said Glenmurray mentally, starting up and dressing himself: and in a few moments he was at major Douglas's lodgings.

The major had just finished dressing, when Glenmurray was announced. He started and turned pale at seeing him; then, dismissing his servant and taking up his hat and his pistols, he desired Glenmurray to walk out with him.

'With all my heart,' replied Glenmurray. But, recollecting himself, 'No no,' said he: 'I come hither now, merely to talk to you; and if, after what has passed, the ladies should see us go out together, they would be but too sure of what was going to happen, and might follow us.'

'Well, then sir,' cried the major, 'we had better separate till evening.'

'I shall not leave you, major Douglas,' replied Glenmurray solemnly, 'whatever harsh things you may say or do, till I have made you listen to me.'

'How can I listen to you, when nothing you can say can be a justification of your conduct?'

'I do not mean to offer any.—I am only come to tell you my story, with that of my companion, and my resolutions in consequence of my situation; and I conjure you, by the recollections of our early days, of our past pleasures and fatigues, those days when fatigue itself was a pleasure, and I was not the weak emaciated being that I am now, unable to bear exertion, and overcome even to female weakness by agitation of mind such as I experienced last night—'

'For God's sake sit down,' cried the major, glancing his eye over the faded form of Glenmurray.—Glenmurray sat down.

'I say, I conjure you by these recollections', he continued, 'to hear me with candour and patience. Weakness will render me brief.' Here he paused to wipe the damps from his forehead; and Douglas, in a voice of emotion, desired him to say whatever he chose, but to say it directly.

'I will,' replied Glenmurray; 'for indeed there is one at home who will be alarmed at my absence.'

The major frowned; and, biting his lip, said, 'Proceed, Mr Glenmurray,' in his usual tone.

Glenmurray obeyed. He related his commencing author,—the nature of his works,—his acquaintance with Adeline,—its consequences,—her mother's marriage,—sir Patrick's villany,—Adeline's elopement, her refusal to marry him, and the grounds on which it was founded. 'And now,' cried Glenmurray when his narration was ended, 'hear my firm resolve. Let the consequences to my reputation be what they may, let your insults be what they may, I will not accept your challenge; I will not expose Adeline to the risk of being left without a protector in a foreign land, and probably without one in her own. I fear that, in the natural course of things, I shall not continue with her long; but, while I can watch over her and contribute to her happiness, no dread of shame, no fear for what others may think of me, no selfish consideration whatever shall induce me to hazard a life which belongs to her, and on which at present her happiness depends. I think, Douglas, you are incapable of treating me with indignity; but even to that I will patiently submit, rather than expose my life; while, consoled by my motive, I will triumphantly exclaim—"See, Adeline, what I can endure for thy sake!"'

Here he paused; and the major, interested and affected, had

involuntarily put out his hand to him; but, drawing it back, he said, 'Then I may be sure that you meant no affront to me by suffering my wife and sister to converse with miss Mowbray?'

Glenmurray having put an end to these suspicions entirely, by a candid avowal of his feelings, and of his wish to have escaped directly if possible, the major shook him affectionately by the hand, and told him that though he firmly believed too much learning had made him mad, yet, that he was as much his friend as ever. 'But what vexes me is,' said he, 'that you should have turned the head of that sweet girl. The opinion of the world is every thing to a woman.'

'Aye, it is indeed,' replied Glenmurray; 'and, spite of ridicule, I would marry Adeline directly, as I said before, to guaranty her against reproach.—I wish you would try to persuade her to be mine legally.'

'That I will,' eagerly replied the major; 'I am sure I shall prevail with her. I am sure I shall soon convince her that the opinions she holds are nothing but nonsense.'

'You will find', replied Glenmurray, blushing, 'that her arguments are unanswerable notwithstanding.'

'What, though taken from the cursed books you mentioned?'

'You forget that I wrote these books.'

'So I did; and I wish she could forget it also: and then they would appear to her, as they must do no doubt to all people of common sense, and that is, abominable stuff.'

Glenmurray bit his lips,—but the author did not long absorb the lover, and he urged the major to return with him to his lodgings.

'Aye, that I will,' cried he: 'and what is more, my sister Emma, who writes admirably, shall write her a letter to convince her that she had better be married directly.'

'She had better converse with her,' said Glenmurray.

The major looked grave, and observed that they would do well to go and consult the women on the subject, and tell them the whole story. So saying, he opened the door of a closet leading to their apartment: but there, to their great surprise, they found Mrs Douglas and Emma, and as well informed of every thing as themselves;—for, expecting that a duel might be the consequence of the major's impetuosity, and hearing Mr Glenmurray announced, they resolved to listen to the conversation, and, if it took the turn which they expected, to rush in and endeavour to mollify the disputants.

'So, ladies! this is very pretty indeed! Eaves-droppers, I protest,' cried major Douglas: but he said no more; for his wife, affected by the recital which she had heard, and delighted to find that there would be no duel, threw her arms round his neck, and burst into tears. Emma, almost equally affected, gave her hand to Glenmurray, and told him nothing on her part should be omitted to prevail on Adeline to sacrifice her opinions to her welfare.

'I said so,' cried the major. 'You will write to her.'

'No; I will see her, and argue with her.'

'And so will I,' cried the wife.

'That you shall not,' bluntly replied the major.

'Why not? I think it my duty to do all I can to save a fellow creature from ruin; and words spoken from the heart are always more powerful than words written.'

'But what will the world say, if I permit you to converse with a kept mistress?'

'The world here to us, as we associate with none and are known to none, is Mr Glenmurray and miss Mowbray; and of their good word we are sure.'

'Aye,' cried Emma, 'and sure of succeeding with this interesting Adeline too; for if she likes us, as I think she does—'

'She adores you,' replied Glenmurray.

'So much the better:—then, when we shall tell her that we cannot associate with her, much as we admire her, unless she consents to become a wife, surely she will hear reason.'

'No doubt,' cried Mrs Douglas; 'and then we will go to church with her, and you, Emma, shall be bride's maid.'

'I see no necessity for that,' observed the major gravely.

'But I do,' replied Emma. 'She will repeat her vows with more heartfelt reverence, when two respectable women, deeply impressed themselves with their importance, shall be there to witness them.'

'But there is no protestant church here,' exclaimed Glenmurray: 'however, we can go back to Lisbon, and you are already resolved to return thither.'

This point being settled, it was agreed that Glenmurray should prepare Adeline for their visit; and with a lightened heart he went to execute his commission. But when he saw Adeline he forgot his commission and every thing but her distress; for he found her with an open letter in her hand, and an unopened one on the floor, in a state of mind almost bordering on phrensy.

VOLUME II

CHAPTER I

As soon as Adeline beheld Glenmurray, 'See!' she exclaimed in a hoarse and agitated tone, 'there is my letter to my mother, returned unopened, and here is a letter from Dr Norberry which has broken my heart:—however, we must go to England directly.'

The letter was as follows:

'You have made a pretty fool of me, deluded but still dear girl! for you have made me believe in forebodings, and be hanged to you. You may remember with what a full heart I bade you adieu, and I recollect what a devilish queer sensation I had when the park-gates closed on your fleet carriage. I swore a good oath at the postillions for driving so fast, as I wished to see you as long as I could; and now I protest that I believe I was actuated by a foreboding that at that house, and on that spot, I should never behold you again.' (Here a tear had fallen on the paper, and the word '*again*' was nearly blotted out.) 'Dear, lost Adeline, I prayed for you too! I prayed that you might return as innocent and happy as you left me. Lord have mercy on us! who should have thought it!—But this is nothing to the purpose, and I suppose you think you have done nought but what is right and clever.'

He then proceeded to inform Adeline, who had written to him to implore his mediation between her and her mother, 'that the latter had sent express for him on finding, by the hasty scrawl which came the day after Adeline's departure from the farm-house, that she had eloped, and who was the companion of her flight; that he found her in violent agitation, as sir Patrick, stung to madness at the success of his rival, had with an ingenuousness worthy a better cause avowed to her his ardent passion for her daughter, his resolution to follow the fugitives, and by every means possible separate Adeline from her lover; and that, after having thanked lady O'Carrol for her great generosity to him, he had taken his pistols, mounted his horse, attended by his groom also well armed, and vowed that he would never return unless accompanied by the woman whom he adored.'

'No wonder therefore,' continued the doctor, 'that I was an unsuccessful advocate for you,—especially as I was not inclined to manage the old bride's self-love; for I was so provoked at her cursed folly in marrying the handsome profligate, that, if she had not been in distress, I never meant to see her again. But, poor silly soul! she suffers enough for her folly, and so do you;—for her affections and her self-love, being equally wounded by sir Patrick's confession, you are at present the object of her aversion. To you she attributes all the misery of having lost the man on whom she still dotes; (an old blockhead!) and when she found from your last letter to me that you are not the wife but the mistress of Glenmurray, (by the bye, your letter to her from Lisbon she desires me to return unopened,) and that the child once her pride is become her disgrace, she declared her solemn resolution never to see you more, and to renounce you for ever—(Terrible words, Adeline, I tremble to write them). But a circumstance has since occurred which gives me hopes that she may yet forgive, and receive you on certain conditions. About a fortnight after sir Patrick's departure, a letter from Ireland, directed to him in a woman's hand, arrived at the Pavilion. Your mother opened it, and found it was from a wife of her amiable husband, whom he had left in the north of Ireland, and who, having heard of his second marriage, wrote to tell him that, unless he came quickly back to her, she would prosecute him for bigamy, as he knew very well that undoubted proofs of the marriage were in her possession. At first this new proof of her beautiful spouse's villany drove your mother almost to phrensy, and I was again sent for; but time, reflection, and perhaps my arguments, convinced her, that to be able to free herself from this rascal for ever, and consequently her fortune, losing only the ten thousand pounds which she had given him to pay his debts, was in reality a consoling circumstance. Accordingly, she wrote to the real lady O'Carrol, promising to accede quietly to her claim, and wishing that she would spare her and herself the disgrace of a public trial; especially as it must end in the conviction of sir Patrick. She then, on hearing from him that he had traced you to Falmouth, and was going to embark for Lisbon when the wind was favourable, enclosed him a copy of his wife's letter, and bade him an eternal farewell!—But be not alarmed lest this insane profligate should overtake and distress you. He is gone to his final account. In his hurry to get on board, overcome as he was with the great quantity of liquor which he had drunk to banish care, he sprung from the boat before it was near enough to reach the vessel; his foot slipped against the side, he fell into the water, and, going under the ship, never rose again. I leave you to imagine how the complicated distresses of the last three months, and this awful climax to them, have affected your mother's mind; even I cannot scold her, now, for the life of me: she is not yet, I believe, disposed in your favour; but were you here, and were you to meet, it is possible that, forlorn, lonely, and deserted as she now feels, the tie between you might be once more cemented; and much as I resent your conduct, you may depend on my exertions.—O Adeline, child of my affection, why must I blush to subscribe myself

'Your sincere friend,

'J.N.?'

Words cannot describe the feelings of anguish which this letter excited in Adeline: nor could she make known her sensations otherwise than by reiterated requests to be allowed to set off for England directly,—requests to which Glenmurray, alarmed for her intellects, immediately assented. Therefore, leaving a hasty note for the Douglases, they soon bade farewell to Perpignan; and after a long laborious journey, but a short passage, they landed at Brighton.

It was a fine evening; and numbers of the gay and fashionable of both sexes were assembled on the beach, to see the passengers land. Adeline and Glenmurray were amongst the first: and while heart-sick, fatigued, and melancholy, Adeline took the arm of her lover, and turned disgusted from the brilliant groups before her, she saw, walking along the shore, Dr Norberry, his wife, and his two daughters.

Instantly, unmindful of every thing but the delight of seeing old acquaintances, and of being able to gain some immediate tidings of her mother, she ran up to them; and just as they turned round, she met them, extending her hand in friendship as she was wont to do.— But in vain;—no hand was stretched out to meet hers, nor tongue nor look proclaimed a welcome to her; Dr Norberry himself coldly touched his hat, and passed on, while his wife and daughters looked scornfully at her, and, without deigning to notice her, pursued their walk.

Astonished and confounded, Adeline had not power to articulate a word; and, had not Glenmurray caught her in his arms, she would have fallen to the ground.

'Then now I am indeed an outcast! even my oldest and best friend renounces me,' she exclaimed.

'But I am left to you,' cried Glenmurray.

Adeline sighed. She could not say, as she had formerly done, 'and you are all to me.' The image of her mother, happy as the wife of a man she loved, could not long rival Glenmurray; but the image of her mother, disgraced and wretched, awoke all the habitual but dormant tenderness of years; every feeling of filial gratitude revived in all its force; and, even while leaning on the shoulder of her lover, she sighed to be once more clasped to the bosom of her mother.

Glenmurray felt the change, but, though grieved, was not offended:—'I shall die in peace,' he cried, 'if I can but see you restored to your mother's affection, even though the surrender of my happiness is to be the purchase.'

'You shall die in peace!' replied Adeline shuddering. The phrase was well-timed, though perhaps undesignedly so. Adeline clung close to his arm, her eyes filled with tears, and all the way to the inn she thought only of Glenmurray with an apprehension which she could not conquer.

'What do you mean to do now?' said Glenmurray.

'Write to Dr Norberry. I think he will at least have humanity enough to let me know where to find my mother.'

'No doubt; and you had better write directly.'

Adeline took up her pen. A letter was written,—and as quickly torn. Letter succeeded to letter; but not one of them answered her wishes. The dark hour arrived, and the letter remained unwritten.

'It is too soon to ring for candles,' said Glenmurray, putting his arm round her waist and leading her to the window. The sun was below the horizon, but the reflection of his beams still shone beautifully on the surrounding objects. Adeline, reclining her cheek on Glenmurray's arm, gazed in silence on the scene before her; when the door suddenly opened, and a gentleman was announced. It was now so dark that all objects were indistinctly seen, and the gentleman had advanced close to Adeline before she knew him to be Dr Norberry: and, before she could decide how she should receive him, she felt herself clasped to his bosom with the affection of a father.

Surprised and affected, she could not speak; and Glenmurray had ordered candles before Adeline had recovered herself sufficiently to say these words, 'After your conduct on the beach, I little expected this visit.'

'Pshaw!' replied the doctor: 'when a man out of regard to society has performed a painful task, surely he may be allowed, out of regard to himself, to follow the dictates of his heart.—I obeyed my head when I passed you so cavalierly, and I thought I should never have gone through my task as I did;—but then for the sake of my daughters, I gave a gulp, and called up a fierce look. But I told madam that I meant to call on you, and she insisted, very properly, that it should be in the dark hour.'

'But what of my mother?'

'She is a miserable woman, as she deserves to be—an old fool.'

'Pray do not call her so; to hear she is miserable is torment sufficient to me:—where is she?'

'Still at the Pavilion: but she is going to let Rosevalley, retire to her estate in Cumberland, and live unknown and unseen.'

'But will she not allow me to live with her?'

'What? as Mr Glenmurray's mistress? receive under her roof the seducer of her daughter?'

'Sir, I am no seducer.'

'No,' cried Adeline: 'I became the mistress of Mr Glenmurray from the dictates of my reason, not my weakness or his persuasions.'

'Humph!' replied the doctor, 'I should expect to find such reason in Moorfields:* besides, had not Mr Glenmurray's books turned your head, you would not have thought it pretty and right to become the mistress of any man: so he is your seducer, after all.'

'So far I plead guilty,' replied Glenmurray; 'but whatever my opinions are, I have ever been willing to sacrifice them to the welfare of miss Mowbray, and have, from the first moment that we were safe from pursuit, been urgent to marry her.'

'Then why the devil are you not married?'

'Because I would not consent,' said Adeline coldly.

'Mad, certainly mad,' exclaimed the doctor: 'but you, faith, you are an honest fellow after all,' turning to Glenmurray and shaking him by the hand; 'weak o' the head, not bad in the heart: burn your d——d books, and I am your friend for ever.'

'We will discuss that point another time,' replied Glenmurray: 'at present the most interesting subject to us is the question whether Mrs Mowbray will forgive her daughter or not?'

'Zounds, man, if I may judge of Mrs Mowbray by myself, one condition of her forgiveness will be your marrying her daughter.'

'O blest condition!' cried Glenmurray.

'I should think,' replied Adeline coldly, 'my mother must have had too much of marriage to wish me to marry; but if she should insist on my marrying, I will comply, and on no other account.'

'Strange infatuation! To me it appears only justice and duty. But your reasons, girl, your reasons?'

'They are few, but strong. Glenmurray, philanthropically bent on improving the state of society, puts forth opinions counteracting its received usages, backed by arguments which are in my opinion incontrovertible.'

'In your opinion!—Pray, child, how old are you?'

'Nineteen.'

'And at that age you set up for a reformer? Well,—go on.'

'But though it be important to the success of his opinions, and indeed to the respectability of his character, that he should act according to his precepts, he, for the sake of preserving to me the notice of persons whose narrowness of mind I despise, would conform to an institution which both he and I think unworthy of regard from a rational being.—And shall not I be as generous as he is? shall I scruple to give up for his honour and fame the petty advantages which marriage would give me? Never—his honour and fame are too dear to me; but the claims which my mother has on me are in my eyes so sacred that, for her sake, though not for my own, I would accept the sacrifice which Glenmurray offers. If, then, she says that she will never see or pardon me till I am become a wife, I will follow him to the altar directly; but till then I must insist on remaining as I am. It is necessary that I should respect the man I love; and I should not respect Glenmurray were he not capable of supporting with fortitude the consequences of his opinions; and could he, for motives less strong than those he avows, cease to act up to what he believes to be right. For, never can I respect or believe firmly in the truth of those doctrines, the followers of which shrink from a sort of martyrdom in support of them.'

'O Mr Glenmurray!' cried the doctor shaking his head, 'what have you to answer for! What a glorious champion would that creature have been in the support of truth, when even error in her looks so like to virtue!—And then the amiable disinterestedness of you both!—Zounds! what a powerful thing must true love be, when it can make a speculative philosopher indifferent to the interests of his system, and ready to act in direct opposition to it, rather than injure the respectability of the woman he loves! Well, well, the Lord forgive you, young man, for having taken it into your head to set up for a great author.'

Glenmurray answered by a deep-drawn sigh; and the doctor continued: 'Then there is that girl again, with a heart so fond and true that her love comes in aid of her integrity, and makes her think no sacrifice too great, in order to prove her confidence in the wisdom of her lover,—urging her to disregard all personal inconveniences rather than let him forfeit, for her sake, his pretensions to independence and consistency of character! 'Sdeath, girl! I can't help admiring you. But no more I could a Malabar widow, who with fond and pious enthusiasm, from an idea of duty, throws herself on the funeral pile of her husband.* But still I should think you a cursed fool, notwithstanding, for professing the opinions that led to such an exertion of duty. And now here are you, possessed of every quality both of head and heart to bless others and to bless yourself—owing to the foolish and pernicious opinions;—here you are, I say, blasted in reputation in the prime of your days, and doomed perhaps to pine through existence in—Pshaw! by the Lord I can't support the idea!' added he, gulping down a sob as he spoke, and traversing the room in great emotion.

Adeline and Glenmurray were both of them deeply and painfully affected; and the latter was going to express what he felt, when the doctor, seizing Adeline's hand, affectionately exclaimed, 'Well, my poor child! I will see your mother once more; I will go to London tomorrow—by this time she is there—and you had better follow me; you will hear of me at the Old Hummums;* and here is a card of address to an hotel near it, where I would advise you to take up your abode.'

So saying, he shook Glenmurray by the hand; when, starting back, he exclaimed 'Odzooks, man! here is a skin like fire, and a pulse like lightning. My dear fellow, you must take care of yourself.'

Adeline burst into tears.

'Indeed, doctor, I am only nervous.'

'Nervous!... What, I suppose you think you understand my profession better than I do. But don't cry, my child: when your mind is easier, perhaps, he will do very well; and, as one thing likely to give him immediate ease, I prescribe a visit to the altar of the next parish church.'

So saying he departed; and all other considerations were again swallowed up in Adeline's mind by the idea of Glenmurray's danger.

'Is it possible that my marrying you would have such a blessed effect on your health?' cried Adeline after a pause.

'It certainly would make my mind easier than it now is,' replied he.

'If I thought so,' said Adeline: 'but no—regard for my supposed interest merely makes you say so; and indeed I should not think so well of you as I now do, if I imagined that you could be made easy by an action by which you forfeited all pretensions to that consistency of character so requisite to the true dignity of a philosopher.'

A deep sigh from Glenmurray, in answer, proved that he was no philosopher.

In the morning the lovers set off for London, Dr Norberry having preceded them by a few hours. This blunt but benevolent man had returned the evening before slowly and pensively to his lodgings, his heart full of pity for the errors of the well-meaning enthusiasts whom he had left, and his head full of plans for their assistance, or rather for that of Adeline. But he entered his own doors again reluctantly—he knew but too well that no sympathy with his feelings awaited him there. His wife, a woman of narrow capacity and no talents or accomplishments, had, like all women of that sort, a great aversion to those of her sex who united to feminine graces and gentleness, the charms of a cultivated understanding and pretensions to accomplishments or literature.

Of Mrs Mowbray, as we have before observed, she had always been peculiarly jealous, because Dr Norberry spoke of her knowledge with wonder, and of her understanding with admiration; not that he entertained one moment a feeling of preference towards her, inconsistent with an almost idolatrous love of his wife, whose skill in all the domestic duties, and whose very pretty face and person, were the daily themes of his praise. But Mrs Norberry wished to engross all his panegyrics to herself, and she never failed to expatiate on Mrs Mowbray's foibles and flightiness as long as the doctor had expatiated on her charms.

Sometimes, indeed, this last subject was sooner exhausted than the one which she had chosen; but when Adeline grew up, and became as it were the rival of her daughters in the praises of her husband, she found it difficult, as we have said before, to bring faults in array against excellencies.

Mrs Norberry could with propriety observe, when the doctor was exclaiming, 'What a charming essay Mrs Mowbray has just written!'

'Aye,—but I dare say she can't write a market bill.'

When he said, 'How well she comprehends the component parts of the animal system!'

She could with great justice reply, 'But she knows nothing of the component parts of a plum pudding.'

But when Adeline became the object of the husband's admiration and the wife's enmity, Mrs Norberry could not make these pertinent remarks, as Adeline was as conversant with all branches of house-wifery as herself; and, though as learned in all systems as her mother, was equally learned in the component parts of puddings and pies. She was therefore at a loss what to say when Adeline was praised by the doctor; and all she could observe on the occasion was, that the girl might be clever, but was certainly very ugly, very affected, and very conceited.

It is not to be wondered at, therefore, that Mrs Mowbray's degrading and unhappy marriage, and Adeline's elopement, should have been sources of triumph to Mrs Norberry and her daughters; who, though they liked Mrs Mowbray very well, could not bear Adeline.

'So, Dr Norberry, these are your uncommon folks!'—exclaimed Mrs Norberry on hearing of the marriage and of the subsequent elopement;—'I suppose you are now well satisfied at not having a genius for your wife, or geniuses for your daughters?'

'I always was, my dear,' meekly replied the mortified and afflicted doctor, and dropped the subject as soon as possible; nor had it been resumed for some time when Adeline accosted them on the beach at Brighton. But her appearance called forth their dormant enmity; and the whole way to their lodgings the good doctor heard her guilt expatiated upon with as much violence as ever: but just as they got home he coldly and firmly observed, 'I shall certainly call on the poor deluded girl this evening.'

And Mrs Norberry, knowing by the tone and manner in which he spoke, that this was a point which he would not give up, contented herself with requiring only that he should go in the dark hour.

CHAPTER II

It was to a wife and daughters such as these that he was returning, with the benevolent wish of interesting them for the guilty Adeline.

'So, Dr Norberry, you are come back at last!' was his first salutation, 'and what does the creature say for herself?'

'The creature?—Your *fellow*-creature, my dear, says very little— grief is not wordy.'

'Grief!—So then she is unhappy, is she?' cries miss Norberry; 'I am monstrous glad of it.'

The doctor started; and an oath nearly escaped his lips. He did say, 'Why, zounds, Jane!—' but then he added, in a softer tone, 'Why do you rejoice in the poor girl's affliction?'

'Because I think it is for the good of her soul.'

'Good girl!' replied the father:—'But God grant, Jane,' (seizing her hand) 'that your soul may not need such a medicine!'

'It never will,' said her mother proudly: 'she has been differently brought up.'

'She has been well brought up, you might have added,' observed the doctor, 'had modesty permitted it. Mrs Mowbray, poor woman, had good intentions; but she was too flighty. Had Adeline, my children, had such a mother as yours, she would have been like you.'

'But not half so handsome,' interrupted the mother in a low voice.

'But as our faults and our virtues, my dear, depend so much on the care and instruction of others, we should look with pity as well as aversion on the faults of those less fortunate in instructors than we have been.'

'Certainly;—very true,' said Mrs Norberry, flattered and affected by this compliment from her husband: 'but you know, James Norberry,' laying her hand on his, 'I always told you you over-rated Mrs Mowbray; and that she was but a dawdle,* after all.'

'You always did, my good woman,' replied he, raising her hand to his lips.

'But you men think yourselves so much wiser than we are!'

'We do so,' replied the doctor.

The tone was equivocal—Mrs Norberry felt it to be so, and looked up in his face.—The doctor understood the look: it was one of doubt and inquiry; and, as it was his interest to sooth her in order to carry his point, he exclaimed, 'We men are, indeed, too apt to pride ourselves in our supposed superior wisdom: but I, you will own, my dear, have always done your sex justice; and you in particular.'

'You have been a good husband, indeed, James Norberry,' replied his wife in a faltering voice; 'and I believe you to be, to every one, a just and honourable man.'

'And I dare say, dame, I do no more than justice to you, when I think you will approve and further a plan for Adeline Mowbray's good, which I am going to propose to you.'

Mrs Norberry withdrew her hand; but returning it again:—'To be sure, my dear,' she cried. 'Any thing you wish; that is, if I see right to—'

'I will explain myself,' continued the doctor gently. 'I have promised this poor girl to endeavour to bring about a reconciliation between her and her mother: but though Adeline wishes to receive her pardon on any terms, and even, if it be required, to renounce her lover, I fear Mrs Mowbray is too much incensed against her, to see or forgive her.'

'Hard-hearted woman!' cried Mrs Norberry.

'Cruel, indeed!' cried her daughters.

'But a mother ought to be severe, very severe, on such occasions, young ladies,' hastily added Mrs Norberry: 'but go on, my dear.'

'Now it is but too probable,' continued the doctor, 'that Glenmurray will not live long, and then this young creature will be left to struggle unprotected with the difficulties of her situation; and who knows but that she may, from poverty and the want of a protector, be tempted to continue in the paths of vice?'

'Well, Dr Norberry, and what then?—Who or what is to prevent it?—You know we have three children to provide for; and I am a young woman as yet.'

'True, Hannah,' giving her a kiss, 'and a very pretty woman too.'

'Well, my dear love, any thing we can do with prudence I am ready to do; I can say no more.'

'You have said enough,' cried the doctor exultingly; 'then hear my plan: Adeline shall, in the event of Glenmurray's death, which though not certain seems likely... to be sure, I could not inquire into the nature of his nocturnal perspirations, his expectoration, and so forth...'

'Dear papa, you are so professional!' affectedly exclaimed his youngest daughter.

'Well, child, I have done; and to return to my subject:—if Glenmurray lives or dies, I think it advisable that Adeline should go into retirement to lie-in. And where can she be better than in my little cottage now empty, within a four miles ride of our house? If she wants protection, I can protect her; and if she wants money before her mother forgives her, you can give it to her.'

'Indeed, papa,' cried both the girls, 'we shall not grudge it.'

The doctor started from his chair, and embraced his daughters with joy mixed with wonder; for he knew they had always disliked Adeline.—True; but then she was prosperous, and their superior. Little minds love to bestow protection; and it was easy to be generous to the fallen Adeline Mowbray: had her happiness continued, so would their hatred.

'Then it is a settled point, is it not, dame?' asked the doctor, chucking his wife under the chin; when, to his great surprise and consternation, she threw his hand indignantly from her, and vociferated, 'She shall never live within a ride of our house, I can assure you, Dr Norberry.'

The doctor was petrified into silence, and the girls could only articulate 'La! mamma!' But what could produce this sudden and violent change? Nothing but a simple and natural operation of the human mind. Though a very kind husband, and an indulgent father, Dr Norberry was suspected of being a very gallant man:* and some of Mrs Norberry's good-natured friends had occasionally hinted to her their sorrow at hearing such and such reports; reports which were indeed destitute of foundation: but which served to excite suspicions in the mind of the tenacious Mrs Norberry. And what more likely to re-awaken them than the young and frail Adeline Mowbray living in a cottage of her husband's, protected, supported, and visited by him! The moment this idea occurred, its influence was unconquerable;

and with a voice and manner of determined hostility she made known her resolves in consequence of it.

After a pause of dismay and astonishment the doctor cried, 'Zounds, dame, what have you gotten in your head? What, all on a sudden, has had such a cursed ugly effect on you?'

'Second thoughts are best, doctor; and I now feel that it would be highly improper for you, with daughters grown up, to receive with such marked kindness a young woman at a cottage of yours, who is going to lie-in of a bastard child.'

'But, sdeath, my dear, it is a different case, when I do it to keep her out of the way of having any more.'

'That is more than I know, Dr Norberry,' replied the wife bridling, and fanning herself.

'Whew!' whistled the doctor; and then addressing his daughters, 'Girls, you had better go to bed; it grows late.'

The young ladies obeyed; but first hung round their mother's neck, as they bade her good night, and hoped she would not be so *cruel* to the poor deluded Adeline.

Mrs Norberry angrily shook them off, with a peevish—'Get along, girls.' The doctor cordially kissed, and bade God bless them; while the door closed and left the loving couple alone.

What passed it were tedious to repeat: suffice that after a long altercation, continued even after they were retired to rest, the doctor found his wife, on this subject, incapable of listening to reason, and that, as a finishing stroke, she exclaimed 'It does not signify talking, Dr Norberry,' (pushing her pillow vehemently towards the valence as she spoke,) 'while I have my senses, and can see into a mill-stone* a little, the hussey shall never come near us.'

The doctor sighed deeply; turned himself round, not to sleep but to think, and rose unrefreshed the next morning to go in search of Mrs Mowbray, dreading the interview which he was afterwards to have with Adeline; for he did not expect to succeed in his application to her mother, and he could not now soften his intelligence with a 'but,' as he intended. 'True,' he meant to have said to her, 'your mother will not receive you; but if you ever want a home or a place of retirement, I have a cottage, and so forth.'

'Pshaw!' cried the doctor to himself, as these thoughts came across him on the road, and made him hastily let down the front window of the post-chaise for air.

'Did your honour speak?' cries the post-boy.

'Not I. But can't you drive faster and be hanged to you?'

The boy whipped his horses.—The doctor then found that it was up hill—down went the glass again:—'Zounds, you brute, why, do you not see it is up hill?'—For find fault he must; and with his wife he could not, or dared not, even in fancy.

'Dear me! Why, your honour bade me put on.'

'Devilishly obedient,' muttered the doctor: 'I wish every one was like you in that respect.'—And in a state of mind not the pleasantest possible the doctor drove into town, and to the hotel where Mrs Mowbray was to be found.

Dr Norberry was certainly now not in a humour to sooth any woman whom he thought in the wrong, except his wife; and, whether from carelessness or design, he did not, unfortunately for Adeline, manage the self-love of her unhappy mother.

He found Mrs Mowbray with her heart shut up, not softened by sorrow. The hands once stretched forth with kindness to welcome him, were now stiffly laid one upon the other; and 'How are you, sir?' coldly articulated, was followed by as cold a 'Pray sit down.'

'Zounds!—Why, how ill you look!' exclaimed the doctor bluntly.

'I attend more to my feelings than my looks,' with a deep sigh answered Mrs Mowbray.

'Your feelings are as bad as your looks, I dare say.'

'They are worse, sir,' said Mrs Mowbray, piqued.

'There was no need of *that*,' replied the doctor: 'but I am come to point out to you one way of getting rid of some of your unpleasant feelings:—see, and forgive your daughter.'

Mrs Mowbray started, changed colour, and exclaimed with quickness, 'Is she in England?' but added instantly, 'I have no daughter:—she, who was my child, is my most inveterate foe; she has involved me in disgrace and misery.'

'With a little of your own help she has,' replied the doctor. 'Come, come, my old friend, you have both of you something to forget and forgive; and the sooner you set about it the better. Now do write, and tell Adeline, who is by this time in London, that you forgive her.'

'Never:—after having promised me not to hold converse with that villain without my consent? Had I no other cause of complaint against her;—had she not by her coquettish arts seduced the affections of the man I loved;—never, never would I forgive her having violated the sacred promise which she gave me.'

'A promise', interrupted the doctor, 'which she would never have violated, had not you first violated that sacred compact which you entered into at her birth.'

'What mean you, sir?'

'I mean, that though a parent does not, at a child's birth, solemnly make a vow to do all in his or her power to promote the happiness of that child,—still, as he has given it birth, he has tacitly bound himself to make it happy. This tacit agreement you broke, when at the age of forty, you, regardless of your daughter's welfare, played the fool and married a pennyless profligate, merely because he had a fine person and a handsome leg.'

Mrs Mowbray was too angry and too agitated to interrupt him, and he went on:

'Well; what was the consequence? The young fellow very naturally preferred the daughter to the mother; and, as he could not have her by fair, was resolved to have her by foul means; and so he—'

'I beg, Dr Norberry,' interrupted Mrs Mowbray in a faint voice, 'that you would spare the disgusting recital.'

'Well, well, I will. Now do consider the dilemma your child was in: she must either elope, or by her presence keep alive a criminal passion in her father-in-law, which you sooner or later must discover; and be besides exposed to fresh insults.—Well, Glenmurray by chance happened to be on the spot just as she escaped from that villanous fellow's clutches, and—'

'He is dead, Dr Norberry,' interrupted Mrs Mowbray; 'and you know the old adage, Do not speak ill of the dead.'

'And a devilish silly adage it is. I had rather speak ill of the dead than the living, for my part: but let me go on.—Well, love taking the name and habit of prudence and filial piety, (for she thought she consulted your happiness, and not her own,) bade her fly to and with her lover; and now there she is, owing to the pretty books which you let her read, living with him as his mistress, and glorying in it, as if it was a notable praise-worthy action.'

'And you would have me forgive her?'

'Certainly: a fault which both your precepts and conduct occasioned. Not but what the girl has been wrong—terribly wrong:—no

one ought to do evil that good may come.* You had forbidden her to
have any intercourse with Glenmurray; and she therefore knew that
disobeying you would make you unhappy—that was a certainty.
That fellow's persevering in his attempts, after the fine rebuff which
she had given him, was an uncertainty; and she ought to have run the
risk of it, and not committed a positive fault to avoid a possible evil.
But then hers was a fault which she could not have committed had
not you married that d——d dog. And as to her not being married to
Glenmurray, that is no fault of his: the good lad looks as ashamed of
what he has done as any modest miss in Christendom; and, with your
consent, will marry your daughter to-morrow morning. Lord! Lord!
that ever so good, cleanly-hearted a youth should have poked his
nose into the filthy mess of eccentric philosophy!'

'Have you done, doctor?' cried Mrs Mowbray haughtily: 'have you
said all that miss Mowbray and you have invented to insult me?'

'Your *child* send me to insult you!—She!—Adeline!—Why, the
poor soul came broken-hearted and post haste from France, when
she heard of your misfortunes, to offer her services to console you.'

'She console me?—she, the first occasion of them?—But for her,
I might still have indulged the charming delusion, even if it were
delusion, that love of me, not of my wealth, induced the man I doted
upon to commit a crime to gain possession of me.'

'Why, zounds!' hastily interrupted the doctor, 'every one saw that
he loved her long before he married you.'

The storm, long gathering, now burst forth; and rising, with the
tears, high colour, and vehement voice of unbridled passion, Mrs
Mowbray exclaimed, raising her arm and clenching her fist as she
spoke, 'And it is being the object of that cruel preference, which
I never, never will forgive her!'

The doctor, after ejaculating 'Whew!' as much as to say 'The
murder is out,'* instantly took his hat and departed, convinced his
labour was vain. 'Zounds!' muttered he as he went down stairs, 'two
instances in one day! Ah, ah!—that jealousy is the devil.' He then
slowly walked to the hotel, where he expected to find Adeline and
Glenmurray.

They had arrived about two hours before; and Adeline in a frame
of mind but ill fitted to bear the disappointment which awaited
her. For, with the sanguine expectations natural to her age, she had
been castle-building as usual; and their journey to London had been

rendered a very short one, by the delightful plans, for the future, which she had been forming and imparting to Glenmurray.

'When I consider,' said she, 'the love which my mother has always shown for me, I cannot think it possible that she can persist in renouncing me; and however her respect for the prejudices of the world, a world which she intended to live in at the time of her unfortunate connexion, might make her angry at my acting in defiance of its laws,—now that she herself, from a sense of injury and disgrace, is about to retire from it, she will no longer have a motive to act contrary to the dictates of reason herself, or to wish me to do so.'

'But your ideas of reason and hers may be so different—'

'No. Our practice may be different, but our theory is the same, and I have no doubt but that my mother will now forgive and receive us; and that, living in a romantic solitude, being the whole world to each other, our days will glide away in uninterrupted felicity.'

'And how shall we employ ourselves?' said Glenmurray smiling.

'You shall continue to write for the instruction of your fellow-creatures; while my mother and I shall be employed in endeavouring to improve the situation of the poor around us, and perhaps in educating our children.'

Adeline, when animated by any prospect of happiness, was irresistible: she was really Hope herself, as described by Collins—

> But thou, oh Hope! with eyes so fair,
> What was thy delighted measure!*

and Glenmurray, as he listened to her, forgot his illness; forgot every thing, but what Adeline chose to imagine. The place of their retreat was fixed upon. It was to be a little village near Falmouth, the scene of their first happiness. The garden was laid out; Mrs Mowbray's library planned; and so completely were they lost in their charming prospects for the future, that every turnpike-man had to wait a longer time than he was accustomed to for his money; and the postillion had driven into London in the way to the hotel, before Adeline recollected that she was, for the first time, in a city which she had long wished most ardently to see.

They had scarcely taken up their abode at the hotel recommended to them by Dr Norberry, when he knocked at the door. Adeline from the window had seen him coming; and sure as she thought herself to be of her mother's forgiveness, she turned sick and faint when the decisive moment was at hand; and, hurrying out of the room, she begged Glenmurray to receive the doctor, and apologize for her absence.

Glenmurray awaited him with a beating heart. He listened to his step on the stairs: it was slow and heavy; unlike that of a benevolent man coming to communicate good news. Glenmurray began immediately to tremble for the peace of Adeline; and, hastily pouring out a glass of wine, was on the point of drinking it when Dr Norberry entered.

'Gadzooks, give me a glass,' cried he: 'I want one, I am sure, to recruit my spirits.' Glenmurray in silence complied with his desire. 'Come, I'll give you a toast,' cried the doctor: 'Here is—'

At this moment Adeline entered. She had heard the doctor's last words, and she thought he was going to drink to the reconciliation of her mother and herself; and hastily opening the door she came to receive the good news which awaited her. But, at sight of her, the toast died unfinished on her old friend's lips; he swallowed down the wine in silence, and then taking her hand led her to the sofa.

Adeline's heart began to die within her; and before the doctor, after having taken a pinch of snuff, and blowed his nose full three times, was prepared to speak, she was convinced that she had nothing but unwelcome intelligence to receive; and she awaited in trembling expectation an answer to a 'Well, sir,' from Glenmurray spoken in a tone of fearful emotion.

'No, it is not well, sir,' replied the doctor; 'it is d——d ill, sir.'

'You have seen my mother,' said Adeline, catching hold of the arm of the sofa for support; and in an instant Glenmurray was by her side.

'I have seen Mrs Mowbray, but not your mother: for I have seen a woman dead to every graceful impulse of maternal affection, and alive only to a selfish sense of rivalship and hatred. My poor child! God forgive the deluded woman! But I declare she detests you!'

'Detests me?' exclaimed Adeline.

'Yes; she swears that she can never forgive the preference which that vile fellow gave you, and I am convinced that she will keep her word; and—Lord have mercy upon us!' cried the doctor, turning round and seeing the situation into which his words had thrown Adeline, who was then lying immoveable in Glenmurray's arms. But she did not long remain so, and with a frantic scream kept repeating the words 'She detests me!' till, unable to contend any longer with the acuteness of her feelings, she sunk, sobbing convulsively, exhausted on the bed to which they carried her.

'My good friend, my only friend,' cried Glenmurray, 'what is to be done? Will she scream again, think you, in that most dreadful and unheard-of manner? For, if she does, I must run out of the house.'

'What, then, she never treated you in this pretty way before, heh?'

'Never, never. Her self-command has always been exemplary.'

'Indeed?—Lucky fellow! My wife and daughters often scream just as loud, on very trifling occasions: but that scream went to my heart; for I well know how to distinguish between the shriek of agony and that of passion.'

When Adeline recovered, she ardently conjured Dr Norberry to procure her an interview with her mother; contending that it was absolutely impossible to suppose, that the sight of a child so long and tenderly loved should not renew a little of her now dormant affection.

'But you were her rival, as well as her child: remember that. However, you look so ill, that now, if ever, she will forgive you, I think: therefore I will go back to Mrs Mowbray; and while I am there do you come, ask for me, and follow the servant into the room.'

'I will,' replied Adeline: and leaning on the arm of her lover, she slowly followed the doctor to her mother's hotel.

CHAPTER III

'This is the most awful moment of my life,' said Adeline.

'And the most anxious one of mine,' replied Glenmurray. 'If Mrs Mowbray forgives you, it will be probably on condition that—'

'Whatever be the conditions, I must accept them,' said Adeline.

'True,' returned Glenmurray, wiping the cold dews of weakness from his forehead: 'but no matter—at any rate, I should not have been with you long.'

Adeline, with a look of agony, pressed the arm she held to her bosom.

Glenmurray's heart smote him immediately—he felt he had been ungenerous; and, while the hectic* of a moment passed across his cheek, he added, 'But I do not do myself justice in saying so. I believe my best chance of recovery is the certainty of your being easy. Let me but see you happy, and so disinterested is my affection, as I have often told you, that I shall cheerfully assent to any thing that may ensure your happiness.'

'And can you think,' answered Adeline, 'that my happiness can be independent of yours? Do you not see that I am only trying to prepare my mind for being called upon to surrender my inclinations to my duty?'

At this moment they found themselves at the door of the hotel. Neither of them spoke; the moment of trial was come; and both were unable to encounter it firmly. At last Adeline grasped her lover's hand, bade him wait for her at the end of the street, and with some degree of firmness she entered the vestibule, and asked for Dr Norberry.

Dr Norberry, meanwhile, with the best intentions in the world, had but ill prepared Mrs Mowbray's mind for the intended visit. He had again talked to her of her daughter, and urged the propriety of forgiving her; but he had at the same time renewed his animadversions on her own conduct.

'You know not, Dr Norberry,' observed Mrs Mowbray, 'the pains I took with the education of that girl; and I expected to be repaid for it by being styled the happiest as well as best of mothers.'

'And so you would, perhaps, had you not wished to be a wife as well as mother.'

'No more on that subject, sir,' haughtily returned Mrs Mowbray. —'Yes,—Adeline was indeed my joy, my pride.'

'Aye, and pride will have a fall; and a devilish tumble yours has had, to be sure, my old friend. Zounds, it has broke its knees—never to be sound again.'*

At this unpropitious moment 'a lady to Dr Norberry' was announced, and Adeline tottered into the room.

'What strange intrusion is this?' cried Mrs Mowbray: 'who is this woman?'

Adeline threw back her veil, and, falling on her knees, stretched out her arms in an attitude of entreaty: speak she could not, but her countenance was sufficiently expressive of her meaning; and her pale sunk cheek spoke forcibly to the heart of her mother.—At this moment, when a struggle which might have ended favourably for Adeline was taking place in the mind of Mrs Mowbray, Dr Norberry injudiciously exclaimed,

'There,—there she is! Look at her, poor soul! There is little fear, I think, of her ever rivalling you again.'

At these words Mrs Mowbray darted an angry look at the doctor, and desired him to take away that woman; who came, no doubt instigated by him, to insult her. 'Take her away,' she cried, 'and never let me see her again.'

'O my mother, hear me, in pity hear me!' exclaimed Adeline.

'As it is for the last time, I will hear you,' replied Mrs Mowbray; 'for never, no never will I behold you more! Hear me vow—'

'Mother, for God's sake, make not a vow so terrible!' cried Adeline, gathering courage from despair, and approaching her: 'I have grievously erred, and will cheerfully devote the rest of my life to endeavour, by the most submissive obedience and attention, to atone for my past guilt.'

'Atone for it! Impossible; for the misery which I owe to you, no submission, no future conduct can make me amends. Away! I say: your presence conjures up recollections which distract me, and I solemnly swear—'

'Hold, hold, if you have any mercy in your nature,' cried Adeline almost frantic: 'this is, I feel but too sensibly, the most awful and important moment of my life; on the result of this interview depends my future happiness or misery. Hear me, O my mother! You, who can so easily resolve to tear the heart of a child that adores you, hear me! reflect that, if you vow to abandon me for ever, you blast all the happiness and prospects of my life; and at nineteen 'tis hard to be deprived of happiness for ever. True, I may not long survive the anguish of being renounced by my mother, a mother whom I love with even enthusiastic fondness; but then could you ever know peace again with the conviction of having caused my death? Oh! no. Save then yourself and me from these miseries, by forgiving my past errors, and deigning sometimes to see and converse with me!'

The eager and animated volubility with which Adeline spoke made it impossible to interrupt her, even had Mrs Mowbray been inclined to do so: but she was not; nor, when Adeline had done speaking, could she find in her heart to break silence.

It was evident to Dr Norberry that Mrs Mowbray's countenance expressed a degree of softness which augured well for her daughter; and, as if conscious that it did so, she covered her face suddenly with her handkerchief.

'Now then is the time,' thought the doctor. 'Go nearer her, my child,' said he in a low voice to Adeline, 'embrace her knees.'

Adeline rose, and approached Mrs Mowbray: she seized her hand, she pressed it to her lips. Mrs Mowbray's bosom heaved violently: she almost returned the pressure of Adeline's hand.

'Victory, victory!' muttered the doctor to himself, cutting a caper behind Mrs Mowbray's chair.

Mrs Mowbray took the handkerchief from her face.

'My mother, my dear mother! look on me, look on me with kindness only one moment, and only say that you do not hate me!'

Mrs Mowbray turned round and fixed her eyes on Adeline with a look of kindness, and Adeline's began to sparkle with delight; when, as she threw back her cloak, which, hanging over her arm, embarrassed her as she knelt to embrace her mother's knees, Mrs Mowbray's eyes glanced from her face to her shape.

In an instant the fierceness of her look returned: 'Shame to thy race, disgrace to thy family!' she exclaimed, spurning her kneeling child from her: 'and canst thou, while conscious of carrying in thy bosom the proof of thy infamy, dare to solicit and expect my pardon?—Hence! ere I load thee with maledictions.'

Adeline wrapped her cloak round her, and sunk terrified and desponding on the ground.

'Why, what a ridiculous caprice is this!' cried the doctor. 'Is it a greater crime to be in a family way, than to live with a man as his mistress?—You knew your daughter had done the last: therefore 'tis nonsense to be so affected at the former.—Come, come, forget and forgive!'

'Never: and if you do not leave the house with her this moment, I will not stay in it. My injuries are so great that they cannot admit forgiveness.'

'What a horrible, unforgiving spirit yours must be!' cried Dr Norberry: 'and after all, I tell you again, that Adeline has something to forgive and forget too; and she sets you an example of christian charity in coming hither to console and comfort you, poor forsaken woman as you are!'

'Forsaken!' exclaimed Mrs Mowbray: 'aye; why, and for *whom*, was I forsaken? There's the pang! and yet you wonder that I cannot instantly forgive and receive the woman who injured me where I was most vulnerable.'

'O my mother!' cried Adeline, almost indignantly, 'and can that wretch, though dead, still have power to influence my fate in this dreadful manner? and can you still regret the loss of the affection of that man, whose addresses were a disgrace to you?'

At these unguarded words, and too just reproaches, Mrs Mowbray lost all self-command; and, in a voice almost inarticulate with rage, exclaimed:—'I loved that wretch, as you are pleased to call him. I gloried in the addresses which you are pleased to call my disgrace. But he loved you—he left me for you—and on your account he made me endure the pangs of being forsaken and despised by the man whom I adored. Then mark my words: I solemnly swear,' dropping on her knees as she spoke, 'and I call on God to witness my oath, by all my hopes of happiness hereafter, that until you shall have experienced the anguish of being forsaken and despised as I have been, till you shall be as wretched in love, and as disgraced in the eye of the world, I never will see you more, or pardon your many sins against me—No—not even were you on your death-bed. Yet, no; I am wrong there—Yes; on your death-bed,' she added, her voice faltering as she spoke, and passion giving way in a degree to the dictates of returning nature,—'yes, there; there I should—I should forgive you.'

'Then I feel that you will forgive me soon,' faintly articulated Adeline sinking on the ground; while Mrs Mowbray was leaving the room, and Dr Norberry was standing motionless with horror, from the rash oath which he had just heard. But Adeline's fall aroused him from his stupor.

'For God's sake, do not go and leave your daughter dying!' cried he: 'your vow does not forbid you to continue to see her now.' Mrs Mowbray turned back, and started with horror at beholding the countenance of Adeline.

'Is she really dying?' cried she eagerly, 'and have I killed her?' These words, spoken in a faltering tone, and with a look of anxiety, seemed to recall the fleeting spirit of Adeline. She looked up at her mother, a sort of smile quivered on her lip; and faintly articulating 'I am better,' she burst into a convulsive flood of tears, and laid her head on the bosom of her compassionate friend.

'She will do now,' cried he exultingly to Mrs Mowbray: 'you need alarm yourself no longer.'

But alarm was perhaps a feeling of enjoyment, to the sensations

which then took possession of Mrs Mowbray. The apparent danger
of Adeline had awakened her long dormant tenderness: but she
had just bound herself by an oath not to give way to it, except
under circumstances the most unwelcome and affecting, and had
therefore embittered her future days with remorse and unavailing
regret.—For some minutes she stood looking wildly and mournfully
on Adeline, longing to clasp her to her bosom, and pronounce her
pardon, but not daring to violate her oath. At length, 'I cannot bear
this torment,' she exclaimed, and rushed out of the room: and when
in another apartment, she recollected, and uttered a scream of agony
as she did so, that she had seen Adeline probably for the last time;
for, voluntarily, she was now to see her no more.

The same recollection occurred to Adeline; and as the door closed
on her mother, she raised herself up, and looked eagerly to catch the
last glimpse of her gown, as the door shut it from her sight. 'Let us
go away directly now,' said she, 'for the air of this room is not good
for me.'

The doctor, affected beyond measure at the expression of quiet
despair with which she spoke, went out to order a coach; and Adeline
instantly rose, and kissed with fond devotion the chair on which her
mother had sat. Suddenly she heard a deep sigh—it came from the
next room—perhaps it came from her mother; perhaps she could
still see her again: and with cautious step she knelt down and looked
through the key-hole of the door.

She did see her mother once more. Mrs Mowbray was lying on
the bed, beating the ground with her foot, and sighing as if her heart
would break.

'O! that I dare go in to her!' said Adeline to herself: 'but I can at
least bid her farewell here.' She then put her mouth to the aperture,
and exclaimed, 'Mother, dearest mother! since we meet now for
the last time—' (Mrs Mowbray started from the bed) 'let me thank
you for all the affection, all the kindness which you lavished on me
during eighteen happy years. I shall never cease to love and pray
for you.' (Mrs Mowbray sobbed aloud.) 'Perhaps, you will some
day or other think you have been harsh to me, and may wish that
you had not taken so cruel a vow.' (Mrs Mowbray beat her breast
in agony: the moment of repentance was already come.) 'It may
therefore be a comfort to you at such moments to know that I
sincerely, and from the bottom of my heart, forgive this rash

action:—and now, my dearest mother, hear my parting prayers for your happiness!'

At this moment a noise in the next room convinced Adeline that her mother had fallen down in a fainting fit, and the doctor entered the room.

'What have I done?' she exclaimed. 'Go to her this instant.'—He obeyed. Raising up Mrs Mowbray in his arms, he laid her on the bed, while Adeline bent over her in silent anguish, with all the sorrow of filial anxiety. But when the remedies which Dr Norberry administered began to take effect, she exclaimed, 'For the last time! Cruel, but most dear mother!' and pressed her head to her bosom, and kissed her pale lips with almost frantic emotion.

Mrs Mowbray opened her eyes: they met those of Adeline, and instantly closed again.

'She has looked at me for the last time,' said Adeline; 'and now this one kiss, my mother, and farewell for ever!' So saying she rushed out of the room, and did not stop till she reached the coach, and, springing into it, was received into the arms of Glenmurray.

'You are my all now,' said she. 'You have long been mine,' replied he: but respecting the anguish and disappointment depicted on her countenance, he forbore to ask for an explanation; and resting her pale cheek on his bosom, they reached the inn in silence.

Adeline had walked up and down the room a number of times, had as often looked out of the window, before Dr Norberry, whom she had been anxiously expecting and looking for, made his appearance. 'Thank God, you are come at last!' said she, seizing his hand as he entered.

'I left Mrs Mowbray,' replied he, 'much better both in mind and body.'

'A blessed hearing!' replied Adeline.

'And you, my child, how are you?' asked the doctor affectionately.

'I know not yet,' answered Adeline mournfully: 'as yet I am stunned by the blow which I have received: but pray tell me what has passed between you and my mother since we left the hotel.'

'What has passed?' cried Dr Norberry, starting from his chair, taking two hasty strides across the room, pulling up the cape of his coat, and muttering an oath between his shut teeth—'Why, this passed:—The deluded woman renounced her daughter; and her friend, her old and faithful friend, has renounced her.'

'Oh! my poor mother!' exclaimed Adeline.

'Girl! girl! don't be foolish,' replied the doctor; 'keep your pity for more deserving objects; and, as the wisest thing you can do, endeavour to forget your mother.'

'Forget her! Never.'

'Well, well, you will be wiser in time; and now you shall hear all that passed. When she recovered entirely, and found that you were gone, she gave way to an agony of sorrow, such as I never before witnessed; for I believe that I never beheld before the agony of remorse.'

'My poor mother!' cried Adeline, again bursting into tears.

'What! again!' exclaimed the doctor. (Adeline motioned to him to go on, and he continued.) 'At sight of this, I was weak enough to pity her; and, with the greatest simplicity, I told her, that I was glad to see that she felt penitent for her conduct, since penitence paved the way to amendment; when, to my great surprise, all the vanished fierceness and haughtiness of her look returned, and she told me, that so far from repenting she approved of her conduct; and that remorse had no share in her sorrow; that she wept from consciousness of misery, but of misery inflicted by the faults of others, not her own.'

'Oh! Dr Norberry,' cried Adeline reproachfully, 'I doubt, by awakening her pride, you destroyed the tenderness returning towards me.'

'May be so. However, so much the better; for anger is a less painful state of mind to endure than that of remorse; and while she thinks herself only injured and aggrieved, she will be less unhappy.'

'Then,' continued Adeline in a faltering voice, 'I care not how long she hates me.'

Dr Norberry looked at Adeline a moment with tears in his eyes, and evidently gulped down a rising sob. 'Good child! good child!' he at length articulated. 'Yet—no. Girl, girl, your virtue only heaps coals of fire on that devoted woman's head.'

'For pity's sake, Dr Norberry!' cried Adeline.

'Well, well, I have done. But she'll forget and forgive all in time, I do not doubt.'

'Impossible: remember her oath.'

'And do you really suppose that she will think herself bound to keep so silly and rash an oath; an oath made in the heat of passion?'

'Undoubtedly I do; and I know, that were she to break it, she would never be otherwise than wretched all her life after. Therefore, unless Glenmurray forsakes me' (she added, trying to smile archly as she spoke), 'and this I am not happy enough to expect, I look on our separation in this world to be eternal.'

'You do?—Then, poor devil, how miserable she will be, when her present resentment shall subside! Well; when that time comes I may perhaps see her again,' added the doctor, gulping again.

'Heaven bless you for that intention!' cried Adeline. 'But how could you ever have the heart to renounce her?'

'Zounds, girl! you are almost as provoking as your mother. Why, how could I have the heart to do otherwise, when she whitewashed herself and blackened you? To be sure, it did cause me a twinge or two to do it; and had she been an iota less haughty, I should have turned back and said, 'Kiss, and be friends again.' But she seemed so provokingly anxious to get rid of me, and waved me with her hand to the door in such a d——d tragedy queen sort of a manner, that, having told her very civilly to go to the devil her own way, I gulped down a sort of a tender choking in my throat, and made as rapid an exit as possible. And now another trial awaits me. I came to town, at some inconvenience to myself, to try to do you service. I have failed, and I have now no further business here: so we must part, and God knows when we shall meet again. For I rarely leave home, and may not see you again for years.'

'Indeed!' exclaimed Adeline. 'Surely,' looking at Glenmurray, 'we might settle in Dr Norberry's neighbourhood?'

Glenmurray said nothing, but looked at the doctor; who seemed confused, and was silent.

'Look ye, my dear girl,' said he at length: 'the idea of your settling near me had occurred to me, but—' here he took two hasty strides across the room—'in short, that's an impossible thing; so I beg you to think no more about it. If, indeed, you mean to marry Mr Glenmurray—'

'Which I shall not do,' replied Adeline coldly.

'There again, now!' cried the doctor pettishly: 'you, in your way, are quite as obstinate and ridiculous as your mother. However, I hope you will know better in time. But it grows late—'tis time I should be in my chaise, and I hear it driving up. Mr Glenmurray,' continued he in an altered tone of voice, 'to your care and your tenderness I leave this poor child: and, zounds, man! if you will but burn your books before her face, and swear they are d——d stuff, why, 'sdeath, I say,

I would come to town on purpose to do you homage.—Adeline, my child, God bless you! I have loved you from your infancy, and I wish, from my soul, that I left you in a better situation. But you will write to me, heh?'

'Undoubtedly.'

'Well, one kiss:—don't be jealous, Glenmurray. Your hand, man.—Woons, what a hand! My dear fellow, take care of yourself, for that poor child's sake: get the advice which I recommended, and good air.' A rising sob interrupted him—he hemmed it off, and ran into his chaise.

CHAPTER IV

'Now, then,' said Adeline, her tears dropping fast as she spoke, 'now, then, we are alone in the world; henceforward we must be all to each other.'

'Is the idea a painful one, Adeline?' replied Glenmurray reproachfully.

'Not so,' returned Adeline. 'Still I can't yet forget that I had a mother, and a kind one too.'

'And may have again.'

'Impossible:—there is a vow in heaven against it. No—My plans for future happiness must be laid unmindful and independent of her. They must have you and your happiness for their sole object; I must live for you alone: and you,' added she in a faltering voice, 'must live for me.'

'I will live as long as I can,' replied Glenmurray sighing, 'and as one step towards it I shall keep early hours: so to rest, dear Adeline, and let us forget our sorrows as soon as possible.'

The next morning Adeline's and Glenmurray's first care was to determine on their future residence. It was desirable that it should be at a sufficient distance from London, to deserve the name and have the conveniences of a country abode, yet sufficiently near it for Glenmurray to have the advice of a London physician if necessary.

'Suppose we fix at Richmond?' said Glenmurray: and Adeline, to whom the idea of dwelling on a spot at once so classical and beautiful was most welcome, joyfully consented; and in a few days they were settled there in a pleasant but expensive lodging.

But here, as when abroad, Glenmurray occasionally saw old acquaintances, many of whom were willing to renew their intercourse with him for the sake of being introduced to Adeline; and who, from a knowledge of her situation, presumed to pay her that sort of homage, which, though not understood by her, gave pangs unutterable to the delicate mind of Glenmurray. 'Were she my wife, they dared not pay her such marked attention,' said he to himself; and again, as delicately as he could, he urged Adeline to sacrifice her principles to the prejudices of society.

'I thought,' replied Adeline gravely, 'that, as we lived for each other, we might act independent of society, and serve it by our example even against its will.'

Glenmurray was silent.—He did not like to own how painful and mischievous he found in practice the principles which he admired in theory—and Adeline continued:

'Believe me, Glenmurray, ours is the very situation calculated to urge us on in the pursuit of truth. We are answerable to no one for our conduct; and we can make any experiments in morals that we choose. I am wholly at a loss to comprehend why you persist in urging me to marry you. Take care, my dear Glenmurray—the high respect I bear your character was shaken a little by your fighting a duel in defiance of your principles; and your eagerness to marry, in further defiance of them, may weaken my esteem, if not my love.'

Adeline smiled as she said this: but Glenmurray thought she spoke more in earnest than she was willing to allow; and, alarmed at the threat, he only answered, 'You know it is for your sake merely that I speak,' and dropped the subject; secretly resolving, however, that he would not walk with Adeline in the fashionable promenades, at the hours commonly spent there by the beau monde.

But, in spite of this precaution, they could not escape the assiduities of some gay men of fashion, who knew Glenmurray and admired his companion; and Adeline at length suspected that Glenmurray was jealous. But in this she wronged him; it was not the attention paid her, but the nature of it, that disturbed him. Nor is it to be wondered at that Adeline herself was eager to avoid the public walks, when it is known that one of her admirers at Richmond was the colonel Mordaunt whom she had become acquainted with at Bath.

Colonel Mordaunt, 'curst with every granted prayer,'* was just beginning to feel the tedium of life, when he saw Adeline unexpectedly at Richmond; and though he felt shocked at first, at beholding her in so different a situation from that in which he had first beheld her, still that very situation, by holding forth to him a prospect of being favoured by her in his turn, revived his admiration with more than its original violence, and he resolved to be, if possible, the lover of Adeline, after Glenmurray should have fallen a victim, as he had no doubt but he would, to his dangerous illness.

But the opportunities which he had of seeing her suddenly ceased. She no longer frequented the public walks; and him, though he suspected it not, she most studiously avoided; for she could not bear to behold the alteration in his manner when he addressed her, an alteration perhaps unknown to himself. True, it was not insulting; but Adeline, who had admired him too much at Bath not to have examined with minute attention the almost timid expression of his countenance, and the respectfulness of his manner when he addressed her, shrunk abashed from the ardent and impassioned expression with which he now met her,—an expression which Adeline used to call 'looking like sir Patrick;' and which indicated even to her inexperience, that the admiration which he then felt was of a nature less pure and flattering than the one which she excited before; and though in her own eyes she appeared as worthy of respect as ever, she was forced to own even to herself, that persons in general would be of a contrary opinion.

But in vain did she resolve to walk very early in a morning only, being fully persuaded that she should then meet with no one. Colonel Mordaunt was as wakeful as she was; and being convinced that she walked during some part of the day, and probably early in a morning, he resolved to watch near the door of her lodgings, in hopes to obtain an hour's conversation with her. The consequence was, that he saw Adeline one morning walk pensively and alone, down the shady road that leads from the terrace to Petersham.

This opportunity was not to be overlooked; and he overtook and accosted her with such an expression of pleasure on his countenance, as was sufficient to alarm the now suspicious delicacy of Adeline; and, conscious as she was that Glenmurray beheld colonel Mordaunt's attentions with pain, a deep blush overspread her cheek at his approach, while her eyes were timidly cast down.

Colonel Mordaunt saw her emotion, and attributed it to a cause flattering to his vanity; it even encouraged him to seize her hand;

and, while he openly congratulated himself on his good fortune in meeting her alone, he presumed to press her hand to his lips. Adeline indignantly withdrew it, and replied very coldly to his inquiries concerning her health.

'But where have you hidden yourself lately?' cried he,—'O miss Mowbray! loveliest and, I may add, most beloved of women, how have I longed to see you alone, and pour out my whole soul to you!'

Adeline answered this rhapsody by a look of astonishment only— being silent from disgust and consternation,—while involuntarily she quickened her pace, as if wishing to avoid him.

'O hear me, and hear me patiently!' he resumed. 'You must have noticed the effect which your charms produced on me at Bath; and may I dare to add that my attentions then did not seem displeasing to you?'

'Sir!' interrupted Adeline, sighing deeply, 'my situation is now changed; and—'

'It is so, I thank Fortune that it is so,' replied colonel Mordaunt; 'and I am happy to say, it is changed by no crime of mine.' (Here Adeline started and turned pale.) 'But I were unworthy all chance of happiness, were I to pass by the seeming opportunity of being blest, which the alteration to which you allude holds forth to me.'

Here he paused, as if in embarrassment, but Adeline was unable to interrupt him.

'Miss Mowbray,' he at length continued, 'I am told that you are not on good terms with your mother; nay, I have heard that she has renounced you: may I presume to ask if this be true?'

'It is,' answered Adeline trembling with emotion.

'Then, as before long it is probable that you will be without— without a protector—' (Adeline turned round and fixed her eyes wildly upon him.) 'To be sure,' continued he, avoiding her steadfast gaze, 'I could wish to call you mine this moment; but, unhappy as you appear to be in your present situation, I know, unlike many women circumstanced as you are, you are too generous and noble-minded to be capable of forsaking in his last illness the man whom in his happier moments you honoured with your love.' As he said this, Adeline, her lips parched with agitation, and breathing short, caught hold of his arm; and pressing her cold hand, he went on: 'Therefore, I will not venture even to wish to be honoured with a kind look from you till Mr Glenmurray is removed to a happier world. But *then*, dearest of women, you whom I loved without hope of possessing you, and whom now I dote upon to madness, I conjure you to admit my visits, and let my attentions prevail on you to accept my protection, and allow me to devote the remainder of my days to love and you!'

'Merciful heaven!' exclaimed Adeline clasping her hands together, 'to what insults am I reserved!'

'Insults!' echoed colonel Mordaunt.

'Yes sir,' replied Adeline: 'you have insulted me, grossly insulted me, and know not the woman whom you have tortured to the very soul.'

'Hear me, hear me, miss Mowbray!' exclaimed colonel Mordaunt, almost as much agitated as herself: 'by heaven I meant not to insult you! and perhaps I—perhaps I have been misinformed—No!—Yes, yes, it must be so;—your indignation proves that I have—You are, no doubt—and on my knees I implore your pardon—you are the wife of Mr Glenmurray.'

'And suppose I am *not* his wife,' cried Adeline, 'is it then given to a wife only to be secure from being insulted by offers horrible to the delicacy, and wounding to the sensibility, like those which I have heard from you?' But before colonel Mordaunt could reply, Adeline's thoughts had reverted to what he had said of Glenmurray's certain danger; and, unable to bear this confirmation of her fears, with the speed of phrensy she ran towards home, and did not stop till she was in sight of her lodging, and the still closed curtain of her apartment met her view.

'He is still sleeping, then,' she exclaimed, 'and I have time to recover myself, and endeavour to hide from him the emotion of which I could not tell the reason.' So saying, she softly entered the house, and by the time Glenmurray rose she had regained her composure. Still there was a look of anxiety on her fine countenance, which could not escape the penetrating eye of love.

'Why are you so grave this morning?' said Glenmurray, as Adeline seated herself at the breakfast table:—'I feel much better and more cheerful to-day.'

'But are you, indeed, better?' replied Adeline, fixing her tearful eyes on him.

'Or I much deceive myself,' said Glenmurray.

'Thank God!' devoutly replied Adeline. 'I thought—I thought—' Here tears choked her utterance, and Glenmurray drew from her a confession of her anxious fears for him, though she prudently resolved not to agitate him by telling him of the rencontre with colonel Mordaunt.

But when the continued assurances of Glenmurray that he was better, and the animation of his countenance, had in a degree removed her fears for his life, she had leisure to revert to another source of uneasiness, and to dwell on the insult which she had experienced from colonel Mordaunt's offer of protection.

'How strange and irrational', thought Adeline, 'are the prejudices of society! Because an idle ceremony has not been muttered over me at the altar, I am liable to be thought a woman of vicious inclinations, and to be exposed to the most daring insults.'

As these reflections occurred to her, she could scarcely help regretting that her principles would not allow her delicacy and virtue to be placed under the sacred shelter bestowed by that ceremony which she was pleased to call idle. And she was not long without experiencing still further hardships from the situation in which she had persisted so obstinately to remain. Their establishment con- sisted of a footman and a maid servant; but the latter had of late been so remiss in the performance of her duties, and so impertinent when reproved for her faults, that Adeline was obliged to give her warning.

'Warning, indeed!' replied the girl: 'a mighty hardship, truly! I can promise you I did not mean to stay long; it is no such favour to live with a kept miss;—and if you come to that, I think I am as good as you.'

Shocked, surprised, and unable to answer, Adeline took refuge in her room. Never before had she been accosted by her inferiors with- out respectful attention; and now, owing to her situation, even a servant-maid thought herself authorised to insult her, and to raise herself to her level!

'But surely,' said Adeline mentally, 'I ought to reason with her, and try to convince her that I am in reality as virtuous as if I were Glenmurray's wife, instead of his mistress.'

Accordingly she went back into the kitchen; but her resolution failed her when she found the footman there, listening with a broad grin on his countenance to the relation which Mary was giving him of the 'fine trimming' which she had given 'madam'.

Scarcely did the presence of Adeline interrupt or restrain her; but at last she turned round and said, 'And, pray, have you got any thing to say to me?'

'Nothing more now,' meekly replied Adeline, 'unless you will follow me to my chamber.'

'With all my heart,' cried the girl; and Adeline returned to her own room.

'I wish, Mary, to set you right', said Adeline, 'with respect to my situation. You called me, I think, a kept miss, and seemed to think ill of me.'

'Why, to be sure, ma'am,' replied Mary, a little alarmed—'every body say you are a kept lady, and so I made no bones of saying so; but I am sure if so be you are not so, why I ax pardon.'

'But what do you mean by the term kept lady?'

'Why, a lady who lives with a man without being married to him, I take it; and that I take to be your case, an't it, I pray?'

Adeline blushed and was silent:—it certainly was her case. However, she took courage and went on:

'But mistresses, or kept ladies in general, are women of bad character, and would live with any man; but I never loved, nor ever shall love, any man but Mr Glenmurray. I look on myself as his wife in the sight of God; nor will I quit him till death shall separate us.'

'Then if so be that you don't want to change, I think you might as well be married to him.'

Adeline was again silent for a moment, but continued—

'Mr Glenmurray would marry me to-morrow, if I chose.'

'Indeed! Well, if master is inclined to make an honest woman of you, you had better take him at his word, I think.'

'Gracious heaven!' cried Adeline, 'what an expression! Why will you persist to confound me with those deluded women who are victims of their own weakness?'

'As to that,' replied Mary, 'you talk too fine for me; but a fact is a fact—are you or are you not my master's wife?'

'I am not.'

'Why then you are his mistress, and a kept lady to all intents and purposes: so what signifies argufying the matter? I lived with a kept madam before; and she was as good as you, for aught I know.'

Adeline, shocked and disappointed, told her she might leave the room.

'I am going,' pertly answered Mary, 'and to seek for a place: but I must beg that you will not own you are no better than you should be, when a lady comes to ask my character; for then perhaps I should not get any one to take me: I shall call you Mrs Glenmurray.'

'But I shall not call *myself* so,' replied Adeline. 'I will not say what is not true, on any account.'

'There now, there's spite! and yet you pertend to call yourself a gentlewoman, and to be better than other kept ladies! Why, you are not worthy to tie the shoestrings of my last mistress—she did not mind telling a lie rather than lose a poor servant a place; and she called herself a married woman rather than hurt me.'

'Neither she nor you, then,' replied Adeline gravely, 'were sensible of what great importance a strict adherence to veracity is, to the interests of society.* I am;—and for the sake of mankind I will always tell the truth.'

'You had better tell one innocent lie for mine,' replied the girl pertly. 'I dare to say the world will neither know nor care any thing about it: and I can tell you I shall expect you will.'

So saying she shut the door with violence, leaving Adeline mournfully musing on the distresses attending on her situation, and even disposed to question the propriety of remaining in it.

The inquietude of her mind, as usual, showed itself in her countenance, and involved her in another difficulty: to make Glenmurray uneasy by an avowal of what had passed between her and Mary was impossible; yet how could she conceal it from him? And while she was deliberating on this point, Glenmurray entered the room, and tenderly inquired what had so evidently disturbed her.

'Nothing of any consequence,' she faltered out, and burst into tears.

'Could "nothing of consequence" produce such emotion?' answered Glenmurray.

'But I am ashamed to own the cause of my uneasiness.'

'Ashamed to own it to me, Adeline? To be sure, you have a great deal to fear from my severity!' said he, faintly smiling.

Adeline for a moment resolved to tell him the whole truth; but, fearful of throwing him into a degree of agitation hurtful to his weak frame, she, who had the moment before so nobly supported the necessity of a strict adherence to truth, condescended to equivocate and evade; and turning away her head, while a conscious blush overspread her cheek, she replied, 'You know that I look forward with anxiety and uneasiness to the time of my approaching confinement.'

Glenmurray believed her; and overcome by some painful feelings, which fears for himself and anxiety for her occasioned him, he silently pressed her to his bosom; and, choked with contending emotions, returned to his own apartment.

'And I have stooped to the meanness of disguising the truth!' cried Adeline, clasping her hands convulsively together: 'surely, surely, there must be something radically wrong in a situation which exposes one to such a variety of degradations!'

Mary, meanwhile, had gone in search of a place; and having found the lady to whom she had been advised to offer herself, at home, she returned to tell Adeline that Mrs Pemberton would call in half an hour to inquire her character. The half-hour, an anxious one to Adeline, having elapsed, a lady knocked at the door, and inquired, in Adeline's hearing, for Mrs Glenmurray.

'Tell the lady,' cried Adeline immediately from the top of the staircase, 'that miss Mowbray will wait on her directly.' The footman obeyed, and Mrs Pemberton was ushered into the parlour: and now, for the first time in her life, Adeline trembled to approach a stranger; for the first time she felt that she was going to appear before a fellow-creature, as an object of scorn, and, though an enthusiast for virtue, to be considered as a votary of vice. But it was a mortification which she must submit to undergo; and hastily throwing a large shawl over her shoulders, to hide her figure as much as possible, with a trembling hand she opened the door, and found herself in the dreaded presence of Mrs Pemberton.

Nor was she at all re-assured when she found that lady dressed in the neat, modest garb of a strict quaker—a garb which creates an immediate idea in the mind, of more than common rigidness of principles and sanctity of conduct in the wearer of it. Adeline curtsied in silence.

Mrs Pemberton* bowed her head courteously; then, with a countenance of great sweetness, and a voice calculated to inspire confidence, said, 'I believe thy name is Mowbray; but I came to see Mrs Glenmurray: and as on these occasions I always wish to confer with the principal, wouldst thou, if it be not inconvenient, ask the mistress of Mary to let me see her.'

'I am myself the mistress of Mary,' replied Adeline in a faint voice.

'I ask thine excuse,' answered Mrs Pemberton, re-seating herself: 'as thou art Mrs Glenmurray, thou art the person I wanted to see.'

Here Adeline changed colour, overcome with the consciousness that she ought to undeceive her, and the sense of the difficulty of doing so.

'But thou art very pale, and seemest uneasy,' continued the gentle quaker—'I hope thy husband is not worse.'

'Mr Glenmurray, but not my husband,' said Adeline, 'is better to-day.'

'Art thou not married?' asked Mrs Pemberton with quickness.

'I am not.'

'And yet thou livest with the gentleman I named, and art the person whom Mary called Mrs Glenmurray?'

'I am,' replied Adeline, her paleness yielding to a deep crimson, and her eyes filling with tears.

Mrs Pemberton sat for a minute in silence; then rising with an air of cold dignity, 'I fear thy servant is not likely to suit me,' she observed, 'and I will not detain thee any longer.'

'She can be an excellent servant,' faltered out Adeline.

'Very likely—but there are objections.' So saying she reached the door: but as she passed Adeline she stopped, interested and affected by the mournful expression of her countenance, and the visible effort she made to retain her tears.

Adeline saw, and felt humbled at the compassion which her countenance expressed: to be an object of pity was as mortifying as to be an object of scorn, and she turned her eyes on Mrs Pemberton with a look of proud indignation: but they met those of Mrs Pemberton fixed on her with a look of such benevolence, that her anger was instantly subdued; and it occurred to her that she might make the benevolent compassion visible in Mrs Pemberton's countenance serviceable to her discarded servant.

'Stay, madam,' she cried, as Mrs Pemberton was about to leave the room, 'allow me a moment's conversation with you.'

Mrs Pemberton, with an eagerness which she suddenly endeavoured to check, returned to her seat.

'I suspect', said Adeline, (gathering courage from the conscious kindness of her motive,) 'that your objection to take Mary Warner into your service proceeds wholly from the situation of her present mistress.'

'Thou judgest rightly,' was Mrs Pemberton's answer.

'Nor do I wonder', continued Adeline, 'that you make this objection, when I consider the present prejudices of society.'

'Prejudices!' softly exclaimed the benevolent quaker.

Adeline faintly smiled, and went on—'But surely you will allow, that in a family quiet and secluded as ours, and in daily contemplation of an union uninterrupted, faithful, and virtuous, and possessing all the sacredness of marriage, though without the name, it is not likely that the young woman in question should have imbibed any vicious habits or principles.'

'But in contemplating thy union itself, she has lived in the contemplation of vice; and thou wilt own, that, by having given it an air of respectability, thou hast only made it more dangerous.'

'On this point,' cried Adeline, 'I see we must disagree—I shall therefore, without further preamble, inform you, madam, that Mary, aware of the difficulty of procuring a service, if it were known that she had lived with a kept mistress, as the phrase is' (here an indignant blush overspread the face of Adeline), 'desired me to call myself the wife of Glenmurray: but this, from my abhorrence of all falsehood, I peremptorily refused.'

'And thou didst well,' exclaimed Mrs Pemberton, 'and I respect thy resolution.'

'But my sincerity will, I fear, prevent the poor girl's obtaining other reputable places; and I, alas! am not rich enough to make her amends for the injury which my conscience forces me to do her. But if you, madam, could be prevailed upon to take her into your family, even for a short time only, to wipe away the disgrace which her living with me has brought upon her—'

'Why can she not remain with thee?' asked Mrs Pemberton hastily.

'Because she neglected her duty, and, when reproved for it, replied in very injurious language.'

'Presuming probably on thy way of life?'

'I must confess that she has reproached me with it.'

'And this was all her fault?'

'It was:—she can be an excellent servant.'

'Thou hast said enough; thy conscience shall not have the

additional burthen to bear, of having deprived a poor girl of her maintenance—I will take her.'

'A thousand thanks to you,' replied Adeline: 'you have removed a weight off my mind; but my conscience, I bless God, has none to bear.'

'No?' returned Mrs Pemberton: 'dost thou deem thy conduct blameless in the eyes of that Being whom thou hast just blessed?'

'As far as my connection with Mr Glenmurray is concerned, I do.'

'Indeed!'

'Nay, doubt me not—believe me that I never wantonly violate the truth; and that even an evasion, which I, for the first time in my life, was guilty of to-day, has given me a pang to which I will not again expose myself.'

'And yet, inconsistent beings as we are,' cried Mrs Pemberton, 'straining at a gnat, and swallowing a camel,* what is the guilt of the evasion which weighs on thy mind, compared to that of living, as thou dost, in an illicit commerce? Surely, surely, thine heart accuses thee; for thy face bespeaks uneasiness, and thou wilt listen to the whispers of penitence, and leave, ere long, the man who has betrayed thee.'

'The man who has betrayed me! Mr Glenmurray is no betrayer— he is one of the best of human beings. No, madam: if I had acceded to his wishes, I should long ago have been his wife; but, from a conviction of the folly of marriage, I have preferred living with him without the performance of a ceremony which, in the eye of reason, can confer neither honour nor happiness.'

'Poor thing!' exclaimed Mrs Pemberton, rising as she spoke, 'I understand thee now—Thou art one of the enlightened, as they call themselves—Thou art one of those wise in their own conceit, who, disregarding the customs of ages, and the dictates of experience, set up their own opinions against the hallowed institutions of men and the will of the Most High.'

'Can you blame me', interrupted Adeline, 'for acting according to what I think right?'

'But hast thou well studied the subject on which thou hast decided? Yet, alas! to thee how vain must be the voice of admoni-tion!' (she continued, her countenance kindling into strong expres-sion as she spoke)—'From the poor victim of passion and persuasion, penitence and amendment might be rationally expected; and she, from the path of frailty, might turn again to that of virtue: but for one like thee, glorying in thine iniquity, and erring, not from the too tender heart, but the vain-glorious head,—for thee there is, I fear, no blessed return to the right way; and I, who would have tarried with thee even in the house of sin, to have reclaimed thee, penitent, now hasten from thee, and for ever—firm as thou art in guilt.'

As she said this she reached the door; while Adeline, affected by her emotion, and distressed by her language, stood silent and almost abashed before her.

But with her hand on the lock she turned round, and in a gentler voice said, 'Yet not even against a wilful offender like thee, should one gate that may lead to amendment be shut. Thy situation and thy fortunes may soon be greatly changed; affliction may subdue thy pride, and the counsel of a friend of thine own sex might then sound sweetly in thine ears. Should that time come, I will be that friend. I am now about to set off for Lisbon with a very dear friend, about whom I feel as solicitous as thou about thy Glenmurray; and there I shall remain some time. Here then is my address; and if thou shouldest want my advice or assistance write to me, and be assured that Rachel Pemberton will try to forget thy errors in thy distresses.'

So saying she left the room, but returned again, before Adeline had recovered herself from the various emotions which she had experienced during her address, to ask her christian name. But when Adeline replied, 'My name is Adeline Mowbray,' Mrs Pemberton started, and eagerly exclaimed, 'Art thou Adeline Mowbray of Gloucestershire—the young heiress, as she was called, of Rosevalley?'

'I was once', replied Adeline, sinking back into a chair, 'Adeline Mowbray of Rosevalley.'

Mrs Pemberton for a few minutes gazed on her in mournful silence: 'And art thou', she cried, 'Adeline Mowbray? Art thou that courteous, blooming, blessed being, (for every tongue that I heard name thee blessed thee) whom I saw only three years ago bounding over thy native hills, all grace, and joy, and innocence?'

Adeline tried to speak, but her voice failed her.

'Art thou she', continued Mrs Pemberton, 'whom I saw also leaning from the window of her mother's mansion, and inquiring with the countenance of a pitying angel concerning the health of a wan labourer who limped past the door?'

Adeline hid her face with her hands.

Mrs Pemberton went on in a lower tone of voice,—'I came with some companions to see thy mother's grounds, and to hear the night-ingales in her groves; but—' (here Mrs Pemberton's voice faltered) 'I have seen a sight far beyond that of the proudest mansion, said I to those who asked me of thy mother's seat; I have heard what was sweeter to my ear than the voice of the nightingale; I have seen a blooming girl nursed in idleness and prosperity, yet active in the discharge of every christian duty; and I have heard her speak in the soothing accents of kindness and of pity, while her name was followed by blessings, and parents prayed to have a child like her.— O lost, unhappy girl! such *was* Adeline Mowbray: and often, very often, has thy graceful image recurred to my remembrance: but, how art thou changed! Where is the open eye of happiness? where is the bloom that spoke a heart at peace with itself? I repeat it, and I repeat it with agony.—Father of mercies! is this thy Adeline Mowbray?'

Here, overcome with emotion, Mrs Pemberton paused; but Adeline could not break silence: she rose, she stretched out her hand as if going to speak, but her utterance failed her, and again she sunk on a chair.

'It was thine', resumed Mrs Pemberton in a faint and broken voice, 'to diffuse happiness around thee, and to enjoy wealth unhated, because thy hand dispensed nobly the riches which it had received bounteously: when the ear heard thee, then it blessed thee; when the eye saw thee, it gave witness to thee; and yet—'

Here again she paused, and raised her fine eyes to heaven for a few minutes, as if in prayer; then, pressing Adeline's hand with an almost convulsive grasp, she drew her bonnet over her face, as if eager to hide the emotion which she was unable to subdue, and suddenly left the house; while Adeline, stunned and overwhelmed by the striking contrast which Mrs Pemberton had drawn between her past and present situation, remained for some minutes motionless on her seat, a prey to a variety of feelings which she dared not venture to analyse.

But, amidst the variety of her feelings, Adeline soon found that sorrow, sorrow of the bitterest kind, was uppermost. Mrs Pemberton had said that she was about to be visited by affliction—alluding, there was no doubt, to the probable death of Glenmurray—And was his fate so certain that it was the theme of conversation at Richmond? Were only *her* eyes blind to the certainty of his danger?

On these ideas did Adeline chiefly dwell after the departure of her monitress; and in an agony unspeakable she entered the room where Glenmurray was sitting, in order to look at him, and form her own judgement on a subject of such importance. But, alas! she found him with the brilliant deceitful appearance that attends his complaint—a bloom resembling health on his cheek, and a brightness in his eye rivalling that of the undimmed lustre of youth. Surprised, delighted, and overcome by these appearances, which her inexperience rendered her incapable of appreciating justly, Adeline threw herself on the sofa by him; and, as she pressed her cold cheek to his glowing one, her tearful eye was raised to heaven with an expression of devout thankfulness.

'Mrs Pemberton paid you a long visit,' said Glenmurray, 'and I thought once, by the elevated tone of her voice, that she was preaching to you.'

'I believe she was,' cheerfully replied Adeline, 'and now I have a confession to make; the season of reserve shall be over, and I will tell you all the adventures of this day without *evasion*.'

'Aye, I thought you were not ingenuous with me this morning,' replied Glenmurray: 'but better late than never.'

Adeline then told him all that had passed between her and Mary and Mrs Pemberton, and concluded with saying, 'But the surety of your better health, which your looks give me, has dissipated every uneasiness; and if you are but spared to me, sorrow cannot reach me, and I despise the censure of the ignorant and the prejudiced.—The world approve! What is the world to me?—

'The conscious mind is its own awful world!'*

Glenmurray sighed deeply as she concluded her narration.

'I have only one request to make,' said he—'Never let that Mary come into my presence again; and be sure to take care of Mrs Pemberton's address.'

Adeline promised that both his requests should be attended to. Mary was paid her wages, and dismissed immediately; and a girl being hired to supply her place, the ménage went on quietly again.

But a new mortification awaited Glenmurray and Adeline. In spite of Glenmurray's eccentricities and opinions, he was still remembered with interest by some of the female part of his family; and two of his cousins, more remarkable for their beauty than their virtue, hearing that he was at Richmond, made known to him their intention of paying him a morning visit on their way to their country seat in the neighbourhood.

'Most unwelcome visiters, indeed!' cried Glenmurray, throwing the letter down; 'I will write to them and forbid them to come.'

'That's impossible,' replied Adeline, 'for by this time they must be on the road, if you look at the date of the letter: besides, I wish you to receive them; I should like to see any relations or friends of yours, especially those who have liberality of sentiment enough to esteem you as you deserve.'

'You!—you see them!' exclaimed Glenmurray, pacing the room impatiently: 'O Adeline, that is *impossible!*'

'I understand you,' replied Adeline, changing colour: 'they will not deem me worthy,' forcing a smile, 'to be introduced to them.'

'And therefore would I forbid their coming. I cannot bear to *exclude* you from my presence in order that I may receive them. No: when they arrive, I will send them word that I am unable to see them.'

'While they will attribute the refusal to the influence of the *creature* who lives with you! No, Glenmurray, for my sake I must insist on your not being denied to them; and, believe me, I should consider myself as unworthy to be the choice of your heart, if I were not able to bear with firmness a mortification like that which awaits me.'

'But you allow it to be a mortification?'

'Yes; it is mortifying to a woman who knows herself to be virtuous, and is an idolater of virtue, to pay the penalty of vice, and be thought unworthy to associate with the relations of the man whom she loves.'

'They shall not come, I protest,' exclaimed Glenmurray.

But Adeline was resolute; and she carried her point. Soon after this conversation the ladies arrived, and Adeline shut herself up in her own apartment, where she gave way to no very pleasant reflections. Nor was she entirely satisfied with Glenmurray's conduct:—true, he had earnestly and sincerely wished to refuse to see his unexpected and unwelcome guests; but he had never once expressed a desire of combating their prejudices for Adeline's sake, and an intention of requesting that she might be introduced to them; but, as any common man would have done under similar circumstances, he was contented to do homage to 'things as they are,'* without an effort to resist the prejudice to which he was superior.

'Alas!' cried Adeline, 'when can we hope to see society enlightened and improved, when even those who see and strive to amend its faults in theory, in practice tamely submit to the trammels which it imposes?'

An hour, a tedious hour to Adeline, having elapsed, Glenmurray's visiters departed; and by the disappointment that Adeline experienced at hearing the door close on them, she felt that she had had a secret hope of being summoned to be presented to them; and, with a bitter feeling of mortification, she reflected, that she was probably to the man whom she adored a shame and a reproach.

'Yet I should like to see them,' she said, running to the window as the carriage drove up, and the ladies entered it. At that moment they, whether from curiosity to see her, or accident, looked up at the window where she was. Adeline started back indignant and confused; for, thrusting their heads eagerly forward, they looked at her with the bold unfeeling stare of imagined superiority; and Adeline, spite of her reason, sunk abashed and conscious from their gaze.

'And this insult', exclaimed she, clasping her hands and bursting into tears, 'I experience from Glenmurray's *relations!* I think I could have borne it better from any one else.'

She had not recovered her disorder when Glenmurray entered the room, and, tenderly embracing her, exclaimed, 'Never, never again, my love, will I submit to such a sacrifice as I have now made;' when seeing her in tears, too well aware of the cause, he gave way to such a passionate burst of tenderness and regret, that Adeline, terrified at his agitation, though soothed by his fondness, affected the cheerfulness which she did not feel, and promised to drive the intruders from her remembrance.

Had Glenmurray and Adeline known the real character of the unwelcome visiters, neither of them would have regretted that Adeline was not presented to them. One of them was married, and to so accommodating a husband, that his wife's known gallant was his intimate friend; and under the sanction of his protection she was received every where, and visited by every one, as the world did not think proper to be more clear-sighted than the husband himself chose to be. The other lady was a young and attractive widow, who coquetted with many men, but intrigued with only one at a time; for which self-denial she was rewarded by being allowed to pass unquestioned through the portals of fashionable society. But these ladies would have scorned to associate with Adeline; and Adeline, had she known their private history, would certainly have returned the compliment.

The peace of Adeline was soon after disturbed in another way. Glenmurray finding himself disposed to sleep in the middle of the day, his cough having kept him waking all night, Adeline took her usual walk, and returned by the church-yard. The bell was tolling; and as she passed she saw a funeral enter the church-yard, and instantly averted her head.

In so doing her eyes fell on a decent-looking woman, who with a sort of angry earnestness was watching the progress of the procession.

'Aye, there goes your body, you rogue!' she exclaimed indignantly, 'but I wonder where your soul is now?—where I would not be for something.'

Adeline was shocked, and gently observed, 'What crime did the person of whom you are speaking, that you should suppose his soul so painfully disposed of?'

'What crime?' returned the woman: 'crime enough, I think:— why, he ruined a poor girl here in the neighbourhood; and then, because he never chose to make a will, there is she lying-in of a little by-blow,* with not a farthing of money to maintain her or the child, and the fellow's money is gone to the heir at law, scarce of kin to him, while his own flesh and blood is left to starve.'

Adeline shuddered:—if Glenmurray were to die, she and the child she bore would, she knew, be beggars.

'Well, miss, or madam, belike, by the look of you,' continued the woman glancing her eye over Adeline's person, 'what say you? Don't you think the fellow's soul is where we should not like to be? How-ever, he had his hell here too, to be sure! for, when speechless and unable to move his fingers, he seemed by signs to ask for pen and ink, and he looked in agonies; and there was the poor young woman cry-ing over him, and holding in her arms her poor destitute baby, who would as he grew up be taught, he must think, to curse the wicked father who begot him, and the naughty mother who bore him!'

Adeline turned very sick, and was forced to seat herself on a tomb-stone. 'Curse the mother who bore him!' she inwardly repeated,—'and will my child curse me? Rather let me undergo the rites I have despised!' and instantly starting from her seat she ran down the road to her lodgings, resolving to propose to Glenmurray their immediate marriage.

'But is the possession of property, then,' she said to herself as she stopped to take breath, 'so supreme a good, that the want of it, through the means of his mother, should dispose a child to curse that mother?—No: my child shall be taught to consider nothing valuable but virtue, nothing disgraceful but *vice*.—Fool that I am! a bugbear frightened me; and to my foolish fears I was about to sacrifice my own principles, and the respectability of Glenmurray. No—Let his property go to the heir at law—let me be forced to labour to support my babe, when its father—' Here a flood of tears put an end to her soliloquy, and slowly and pensively she returned home.

But the conversation of the woman in the church-yard haunted her while waking, and continued to distress her in her dreams that night; and she was resolved to do all she could to relieve the situation of the poor destitute girl and child, in whose fate she might possibly see an anticipation of her own: and as soon as breakfast was over, and Glenmurray was engaged in his studies, she walked out to make the projected inquiries.

The season of the year was uncommonly fine; and the varied scenery visible from the terrace was, at the moment of Adeline's approach to it, glowing with more than common beauty. Adeline stood for some minutes gazing on it in silent delight; when her reverie was interrupted by the sound of boyish merriment, and she saw, at one end of the terrace, some well-dressed boys at play.

> Alas! regardless of their doom,
> The little victims play!*

immediately recurred to her: for, contemplating the probable evils of existence, she was darkly brooding over the imagined fate of her own offspring, should it live to see the light; and the children at their sport, having no care of ills to come, naturally engaged her attention.

But these happy children ceased to interest her, when she saw standing at a distance from the group, and apparently looking at it with an eye of envy, a little boy, even better dressed than the rest; who was sobbing violently, yet ardently trying to conceal his grief. And while she was watching the young mourner attentively, he suddenly threw himself on a seat; and, taking out his handkerchief, indignantly and impatiently wiped away the tears that would no longer be restrained.

'Poor child!' thought Adeline, seating herself beside him; 'and has affliction reached thee so soon!'

The child was beautiful: and his clustering locks seemed to have been combed with so much care; the frill of his shirt was so fine, and had been so very neatly plaited; and his sun-burnt neck and hands were so very very clean, that Adeline was certain he was the darling object of some fond mother's attention. 'And yet he is unhappy!' she inwardly exclaimed. 'When my fate resembled his, how happy I was!' But from recollections like these she always hastened; and checking the rising sigh, she resolved to enter into conversation with the little boy.

'What is the matter?' she cried.—No answer.—'Why are you not playing with the young gentlemen yonder?'

She had touched the right string:—and bursting into tears, he sobbed out, 'Because they won't let me.'

'No? and why will they not let you?' To this he replied not; but sullenly hung his blushing face on his bosom.

'Perhaps you have made them angry?' gently asked Adeline. 'Oh! no, no,' cried the boy; 'but—' 'But what?' Here he turned from her, and with his nail began scratching the arm of the seat.

'Well; this is very strange, and seems very unkind,' cried Adeline: 'I will speak to them.' So saying, she drew near the other children, who had interrupted their play to watch Adeline and their rejected playmate. 'What can be the reason,' said she, 'that you will not let that little boy play with you?' The boys looked down, and said nothing.

'Is he ill-natured?'

'No.'

'Does he not play fair?'

'Yes.'

'Don't you like him?'

'Yes.'

'Then why do you make him unhappy, by not letting him join in your sport?'

'Tell the lady, Jack,' cries one; and Jack, the biggest boy of the party, said: 'Because he is not a gentleman's son like us, and is only a little bastard.'

'Yes,' cried one of the other children; 'and his mamma is so proud she dresses him finer than we are, for all he is base-born: and our papas and mammas don't think him fit company for us.'

They might have gone on for an hour—Adeline could not interrupt them. The cause of the child's affliction was a dagger in her heart; and, while she listened to the now redoubled sobs of the disgraced and proudly afflicted boy, she was driven almost to phrensy: for 'Such', she exclaimed, 'may one time or other be the pangs of my child, and so to him may the hours of childhood be embittered!'—Again she seated herself by the little mourner—and her tears accompanied his.

'My dear child, you had better go home,' said she, struggling with her feelings; 'your mother will certainly be glad of your company.'

'No, I won't go to her; I don't love her: they say she is a bad woman, and my papa a bad man, because they are not married.'

Again Adeline's horrors returned.—'But, my dear, they love you, no doubt; and you ought to love them,' she replied with effort.

'There, there comes your papa,' cried one of the boys; 'go and cry to him;—go.'

At these words Adeline looked up, and saw an elegant-looking man approaching with a look of anxiety.

'Charles, my dear boy, what has happened?' said he, taking his hand; which the boy sullenly withdrew. 'Come home directly,' continued his father, 'and tell me what is the matter, as we go along.' But again snatching his hand away, the proud and deeply wounded child resentfully pushed the shoulder next him forward, whenever his father tried to take his arm, and elbowed him angrily as he went.

Adeline felt the child's action to the bottom of her heart. It was a volume of reproach to the father; and she sighed to think what the parents, if they had hearts, must feel, when the afflicted boy told the cause of his grief. 'But, unhappy boy, perhaps my child may live to bless you!' she exclaimed, clasping her hands together: 'never, never will I expose my child to the pangs which you have experienced to-day.' So saying, she returned instantly to her lodgings; and having just strength left to enter Glenmurray's room, she faintly exclaimed: 'For pity's sake, make me your wife to-morrow!' and fell senseless on the floor.

On her recovery she saw Glenmurray pale with agitation, yet with an expression of satisfaction in his countenance, bending over her. 'Adeline! my dearest life!' he whispered as her head lay on his bosom, 'blessed be the words you have spoken, whatever be their cause! To-morrow you shall be my wife.'

'And then our child will be legitimate, will he not?' she eagerly replied.

'It will.'

'Thank God!' cried Adeline, and relapsed into a fainting fit. For it was not decreed that the object of her maternal solicitude should ever be born to reward it. Anxiety and agitation had had a fatal effect on the health of Adeline; and the day after her rencounter on the terrace she brought forth a dead child.

As soon as Adeline, languid and disappointed, was able to leave her room, Glenmurray, whom anxiety during her illness had rendered considerably weaker, urged her to let the marriage ceremony be performed immediately. But with her hopes of being a mother vanished her wishes to become a wife, and all her former reasons against marriage recurred in their full force.

In vain did Glenmurray entreat her to keep her lately formed resolution: she still attributed his persuasions to generosity, and the heroic resolve of sacrificing his principles, with the consistency of his character, to her supposed good, and it was a point of honour with her to be as generous in return: consequently the subject was again dropped; nor was it likely to be soon renewed; and anxiety of a more pressing nature disturbed their peace and engrossed their attention. They had been three months at Richmond, and had incurred there a considerable debt; and Glenmurray, not having sufficient money with him to discharge it, drew upon his banker for half the half-year's rents from his estate, which he had just deposited in his hands; when to his unspeakable astonishment he found that the house had stopped payment, and that the principal partner was gone off with the deposits!

Scarcely could the firm mind of Glenmurray support itself under this stroke. He looked forward to the certainty of passing the little remainder of his life not only in pain but in poverty, and of seeing increase as fast as his wants the difficulty of supplying them; while the woman of his heart bent in increased agony over his restless couch; for he well knew that to raise money on his estate, or to anticipate the next half-year's rents, was impossible, as he had only a life interest in it; and, as he held the fatal letter in his hand, his frame shook with agitation.

'I could not have believed,' cried Adeline, 'that the loss of any sum of money could have so violently affected you.'

'Not the loss of my all! my support during the tedious scenes of illness!'

'Your all!' faltered out Adeline; and when she heard the true state of the case she found her agitation equalled that of Glenmurray, and in hopeless anguish she leaned on the table beside him.

'What is to be done', said she, 'till the next half-year's rents become due? Where can we procure money?'

'Till the next half-year's rents become due!' replied he, looking at her mournfully: 'I shall not be distressed for money then.'

'No?' answered Adeline (not understanding him): 'our expenses have never yet been more than that sum can supply.'

Glenmurray looked at her, and, seeing how unconscious she was of the certainty of the evil that awaited her, had not the courage to distress her by explaining his meaning; and she went on to ask him what steps he meant to take to raise money.

'My only resource', said he, 'is dunning a near relation of mine who owes me three hundred pounds: he is now, I believe, able to pay it. He is in Holland, indeed, at present; but he is daily expected in England, and will come to see me here.—I have named him to you before, I believe. His name is Berrendale.'

It was then agreed that Glenmurray should write to Mr Berrendale immediately; and that, to prevent the necessity of incurring a further debt for present provisions and necessaries, some of their books and linen should be sold:—but week after week elapsed, and no letter was received from Mr Berrendale.

Glenmurray grew rapidly worse;—and their landlord was clamorous for his rent;—advice from London also became necessary to quiet Adeline's mind,—though Glenmurray knew that he was past cure: and after she had paid a small sum to quiet the demands of the landlord for a while, she had scarcely enough left to pay a physician: however, she sent for one, recommended by Dr Norberry, and by selling a writing-desk inlaid with silver, which she valued because it was the gift of her father, she raised money sufficient for the occasion.

Dr —— arrived, but not to speak peace to the mind of Adeline.

She saw, though he did not absolutely say so, that all chance of Glenmurray's recovery was over: and though with the sanguine feelings of nineteen she could 'hope though hope were lost',* when she watched Dr ——'s countenance as he turned from the bed-side of Glenmurray, she felt the coldness of despair thrill through her frame; and, scarcely able to stand, she followed him into the next room, and awaited his orders with a sort of desperate tranquillity.

After prescribing alleviations of the ill beyond his power to cure, Dr —— added that terrible confirmation of the fears of anxious affection.—'Let him have whatever he likes; nothing can hurt him now; and all your endeavours must be to make the remaining hours of his existence as comfortable as you can, by every indulgence possible: and indeed, my dear madam,' he continued, 'you must be prepared for the trial that awaits you.'

'Prepared! did you say?' cried Adeline in the broken voice of tearless and almost phrensied sorrow.—'O God! if he must die, in mercy let me die with him. If I have sinned,' (here she fell on her knees,) 'surely, surely the agony of this moment is atonement sufficient.'

Dr ——, greatly affected, raised her from the ground, and conjured her for the sake of Glenmurray, and that she might not make his last hours miserable, to bear her trial with more fortitude.

'And can you talk of his "last hours", and yet expect me to be composed?—O sir! say but that there is one little little gleam of hope for me, and I will be calm.'

'Well,' replied Dr ——, 'I *may* be mistaken; Mr Glenmurray is young, and—and—' here his voice faltered, and he was unable to proceed; for the expression of Adeline's countenance, changing as it instantly did from misery to joy,—joy of which he knew the fallacy,—while her eyes were intently fixed on him, was too much for a man of any feeling to support; and when she pressed his hand in the convulsive emotions of her gratitude, he was forced to turn away his head to conceal the starting tear.

'Well, I may be mistaken—Mr Glenmurray is young,' Adeline repeated again and again, as his carriage drove off; and she flew to Glenmurray's bed-side to impart to him the satisfaction which he rejoiced to see her feel, but in which he could not share.

Her recovered security did not, however, last long: the change in Glenmurray grew every day more visible; and to increase her distress, they were forced, to avoid disagreeable altercations, to give the landlord a draft on Mr Berrendale for the sum due to him, and remove to very humble lodgings in a closer part of the town.

Here their misery was a little alleviated by the unexpected receipt of twenty pounds, sent to Glenmurray by a tenant who was in arrears to him, which enabled Adeline to procure Glenmurray every thing that his capricious appetite required; and at his earnest entreaty, in order that she might sometimes venture to leave him, lest her health should suffer, she hired a nurse to assist her in her attendance upon him.

A hasty letter too was at length received from Mr Berrendale, saying, that he should very soon be in England, and should hasten to Richmond immediately on his landing. The terror of wanting money, therefore, began to subside: but day after day elapsed, and Mr Berrendale came not; and Adeline, being obliged to deny herself almost necessary sustenance that Glenmurray's appetite might be tempted, and his nurse, by the indulgence of hers, kept in good humour, resolved, presuming on the arrival of Mr Berrendale, to write to Dr Norberry and solicit the loan of twenty pounds.

Having done so, she ceased to be alarmed, though she found herself in possession of only three guineas to defray the probable expenses of the ensuing week; and, in somewhat less misery than usual, she, at the earnest entreaty of Glenmurray, set out to take a walk.

Scarcely conscious what she did, she strolled through the town, and seeing some fine grapes at the window of a fruiterer, she went in to ask the price of them, knowing how welcome fruit was to the feverish palate of Glenmurray. While the shopman was weighing the grapes, she saw a pine-apple on the counter, and felt a strong wish to carry it home as a more welcome present; but with unspeakable dissappointment she heard that the price of it was two guineas—a sum which she could not think herself justified in expending, in the present state of their finances, even to please Glenmurray, especially as he had not expressed a wish for such an indulgence: besides, he liked grapes; and, as medicine, neither of them could be effectual.

It was fortunate for Adeline's feelings that she had not overheard what the mistress of the shop said to her maid as she left it.

'I should have asked another person only a guinea; but as those sort of women never mind what they give, I asked two, and I dare say she will come back for it.'

'I have brought you some grapes,' cried Adeline as she entered Glenmurray's chamber, 'and I would have brought you a pine-apple, but that it was too dear.'

'A pine-apple!'* said Glenmurray languidly turning over the grapes, and with a sort of distaste putting one of them in his mouth, 'a pine-apple!—I wish you had bought it with all my heart! I protest that I feel as if I could eat a whole one.'

'Well,' replied Adeline, 'if you would enjoy it so much, you certainly ought to have it.'

'But the price, my dear girl!—what was it?'

'Only two guineas,' replied Adeline, forcing a smile.

'Two guineas!' exclaimed Glenmurray: 'No,—that is too much to give—I will not indulge my appetite at such a rate—but, take away the grapes—I can't eat them.'

Adeline, disappointed, removed them from his sight; and, to increase her vexation, Glenmurray was continually talking of pine-apples, and in a way that showed how strongly his diseased appetite wished to enjoy the gratification of eating one. At last, unable to bear to see him struggling with an ungratified wish, she told him that she believed they could afford to buy the pine-apple, as she had written to borrow some money of Dr Norberry, to be paid as soon as Mr Berrendale arrived. In a moment the dull eye of Glenmurray lighted up with expectation; and he, who in health was remarkable for self-denial and temperance, scrupled not, overcome by the influence of the fever which consumed him, to gratify his palate at a rate the most extravagant.

Adeline sighed as she contemplated this change effected by illness; and, promising to be back as soon as possible, she proceeded to a shop to dispose of her lace veil, the only ornament which she had retained; and that not from vanity, but because it concealed from the eye of curiosity the sorrow marked on her countenance. But she knew a piece of muslin would do as well; and for two guineas she sold a veil worth treble the sum; but it was to give a minute's pleasure to Glenmurray, and that was enough for Adeline.

In her way to the fruiterer's she saw a crowd at the door of a mean-looking house, and in the midst of it she beheld a mulatto woman, the picture of sickness and despair, supporting a young man who seemed ready to faint every moment, but whom a rough-featured man, regardless of his weakness, was trying to force from the grasp of the unhappy woman; while a mulatto boy, known in Richmond by the name of the Tawny Boy, to whom Adeline had often given halfpence in her walks, was crying bitterly, and hiding his face in the poor woman's apron.

Adeline immediately pressed forward to inquire into the cause of a distress only too congenial to her feelings; and as she did so, the tawny boy looked up, and, knowing her immediately, ran eagerly forward to meet her, seeming, though he did not speak, to associate with her presence an idea of certain relief.

'Oh! it is only a poor man', replied an old woman in answer to Adeline's inquiries, 'who can't pay his debts,—and so they are dragging him to prison—that's all.' 'They are dragging him to his death too,' cried a younger woman in a gentle accent; 'for he is only just recovering from a bad fever: and if he goes to jail the bad air will certainly kill him, poor soul!'

'Is that his wife?' said Adeline. 'Yes, and my mammy,' said the tawny boy, looking up in her face, 'and she so ill and sorry.'

'Yes, unhappy creatures,' replied her informant, 'and they have known great trouble; and now, just as they had got a little money together, William fell ill, and in doctor's stuff Savanna (that's the mulatto's name) has spent all the money she had earned, as well as her husband's; and now she is ill herself, and I am sure William's going to jail will kill her. And a hard-hearted, wicked wretch Mr Davis is, to arrest him—that he is—not but what it is his due, I cannot say but it is—but, poor souls! he'll die, and she'll die, and then what will become of their poor little boy?'

The tawny boy all this time was standing, crying, by Adeline's side, and had twisted his fingers in her gown, while her heart sympathized most painfully in the anguish of the mulatto woman. 'What is the amount of the sum for which he is taken up?' said Adeline.

'Oh! trifling: but Mr Davis owes him a grudge, and so will not wait any longer. It is in all only six pounds; and he says if they will pay half he will wait for the rest; but then he knows they could as well pay all as half.'

Adeline, shocked at the knowledge of a distress which she was not able to remove, was turning away as the woman said this, when she felt that the little boy pulled her gown gently, as if appealing to her generosity; while a surly-looking man, who was the creditor himself, forcing a passage through the crowd, said, 'Why, bring him along, and have done with it; here is a fuss to make indeed about that idle dog, and that ugly black b——h!'*

Adeline till then had not recollected that she was a mulatto; and this speech, reflecting so brutally on her colour,—a circumstance which made her an object of greater interest to Adeline,—urged her to step forward to their joint relief with an almost irresistible impulse; especially when another man reproached the fellow for his brutality, and added, that he knew them both to be hard-working, deserving persons. But to disappoint Glenmurray of his promised pleasure was impossible; and having put sixpence in the tawny boy's hand, she was hastening to the fruiterer's, when the crowd, who were following William and the mulatto to the jail, whither the bailiffs were dragging rather than leading him, fell back to give air to the poor man, who had fainted on Savanna's shoulder, and seemed on the point of expiring—while she, with an expression of fixed despair, was gazing on his wan cheek.

Adeline thought on Glenmurray's danger, and shuddered as she beheld the scene; she felt it but a too probable anticipation of the one in which she might soon be an actor.

At this moment a man observed, 'If he goes to prison he will not live two days, that every one may see;' and the mulatto uttered a shriek of agony.

Adeline felt it to her very soul; and, rushing forward, 'Sir, sir,' she exclaimed to the unfeeling creditor, 'if I were to give you a guinea now, and promise you two more a fortnight hence, would you release this poor man for the present?'

'No: I must have three guineas this moment,' replied he. Adeline sighed, and withdrew her hand from her pocket. 'But were Glenmurray here, he would give up his own indulgence, I am sure, to save the lives of, probably, two fellow-creatures,' thought Adeline; 'and he would not forgive me if I were to sacrifice such an opportunity to the sole gratification of his palate.'—But then again, Glenmurray eagerly expecting her with the promised treat, so gratifying to the feverish taste of sickness, seemed to appear before her, and she turned away: but the eyes of the mulatto, who had heard her words, and had hung on them breathless with expectation, followed her with a look of such sad reproach for the disappointment which she had occasioned her, and the little boy looked up so wistfully in her face, crying, 'Poor fader, and poor mammy!' that Adeline could not withstand the force of the appeal; but almost exclaiming 'Glenmurray would upbraid me if I did not act thus,' she gave the creditor the three guineas, paid the bailiffs their demand, and then made her way through the crowd, who respectfully drew back to give her room to pass, saying, 'God bless you, lady! God bless you!'

But William was too ill, and Savanna felt too much to speak; and the surly creditor said, sneeringly, 'If I had been you, I would, at least, have thanked the lady.' This reproach restored Savanna to the use of speech; and (but with a violent effort) she uttered in a hoarse and broken voice, '*I* tank her! God tank her! I never can:' and Adeline, kindly pressing her hand, hurried away from her in silence, though scarcely able to refrain exclaiming, 'You know not the sacrifice which you have cost me!' The tawny boy still followed her, as loth to leave her. 'God bless you, my dear!' said she kindly to him: 'there, go to your mother, and be good to her.' His dark face glowed as she spoke to him, and holding up his chin, 'Tiss me!' cried he, 'poor tawny boy love you!' She did so; and then, reluctantly, he left her, nodding his head, and saying 'Dood bye' till he was out of sight.

With him, and with the display of his grateful joy, vanished all that could give Adeline resolution to bear her own reflections at the idea of returning home, and of the trial that awaited her. In vain did she now try to believe that Glenmurray would applaud what she had done.—He was now the slave of disease, nor was it likely that even his self-denial and principled benevolence could endure with patience so cruel a disappointment—and from the woman whom he loved too!—and to whom the indulgence of his slightest wishes ought to have been the first object.

'What shall I do?' cried she: 'what will he say?—No doubt he is impatiently expecting me; and, in his weak state, disappointment may—' Here, unable to bear her apprehensions, she wrung her hands in agony; and when she arrived in sight of her lodgings she dared not look up, lest she should see Glenmurray at the window watching for her return. Slowly and fearfully did she open the door; and the first sound she heard was Glenmurray's voice from the door of his room, saying, 'So, you are come at last!—I have been so impatient!' And indeed he had risen and dressed himself, that he might enjoy his treat more than he could do in a sick-bed.

'How can I bear to look him in the face!' thought Adeline, lingering on the stairs.

'Adeline, my love! why do you make me wait so long?' cried Glenmurray. 'Here are knives and plates ready; where is the treat I have been so long expecting?'

Adeline entered the room and threw herself on the first chair, avoiding the sight of Glenmurray, whose countenance, as she hastily glanced her eyes over it, was animated with the expectation of a pleasure which he was not to enjoy. 'I have not brought the pine-apple,' she faintly articulated. 'No!' replied Glenmurray, 'how hard upon me!—the only thing for weeks that I have wished for, or could have eaten with pleasure! I suppose you were so long going that it was disposed of before you got there?'

'No,' replied Adeline, struggling with her tears at this first instance of pettishness in Glenmurray.

'Pardon me the supposition,' replied Glenmurray, recovering himself: 'more likely you met some dun* on the road, and so the two guineas were disposed of another way—If so, I can't blame you. What say you? Am I right?'

'No.' 'Then how was it?' gravely asked Glenmurray. 'You must have had a very powerful and sufficient reason, to induce you to disappoint a poor invalid of the indulgence which you had yourself excited him to wish for.'

'This is terrible, indeed!' thought Adeline, 'and never was I so tempted to tell a falsehood.'

'Still silent! You are very unkind, miss Mowbray,' said Glenmurray; 'I see that I have tired even *you* out.'

These words, by the agony which they excited, restored to Adeline all her resolution. She ran to Glenmurray; she clasped his burning hands in hers; and as succinctly as possible she related what had passed. When she had finished, Glenmurray was silent; the fretful-ness of disease prompted him to say, 'So then, to the relief of strangers you sacrificed the gratification of the man whom you love, and deprived him of the only pleasure he may live to enjoy!' But the habitual sweetness and generosity of his temper struggled, and struggled effectually, with his malady; and while Adeline, pale and trembling, awaited her sentence, he caught her suddenly to his bosom, and held her there a few moments in silence.

'Then you forgive me?' faltered out Adeline.

'Forgive you! I love and admire you more than ever! I know your heart, Adeline; and I am convinced that depriving yourself of the delight of giving me the promised treat, in order to do a benevolent action, was an effort of virtue of the highest order; and never, I trust, have you known, or will you know again, such bitter feelings as you this moment experienced.'

Adeline, gratified by his generous kindness, and charmed with his praise, could only weep her thanks. 'And now,' said Glenmurray, laughing, 'you may bring back the grapes—I am not like Sterne's dear Jenny;* if I cannot get pine-apple, I will not insist on eating crab.'

The grapes were brought; but in vain did he try to eat them. At this time, however, he did not send them away without highly commending their flavour, and wishing that he dared give way to his inclinations, and feast upon them.

'O God of mercy!' cried Adeline, bursting into an agony of grief as she reached her own apartment, and throwing herself on her knees by the bed-side, 'Must that benevolent being be taken from me for ever, and must I, must I survive him!'

She continued for some minutes in this attitude, and with her heart devoutly raised to heaven; till every feeling yielded to resignation, and she arose calm, if not contented; when, on turning round, she saw Glenmurray leaning against the door, and gazing on her.

'Sweet enthusiast!' cried he smiling: 'so, thus, when you are distressed, you seek consolation.'

'I do,' she replied: 'Sceptic, wouldst thou wish to deprive me of it?'

'No, by heaven!' warmly exclaimed Glenmurray; and the evening passed more cheerfully than usual.

The next post brought a letter not from Dr Norberry, but from his wife; it was as follows, and contained three pound-notes:

'Mrs Norberry's compliments to miss Mowbray, having opened her letter, poor Dr Norberry being dangerously ill of a fever, find her distress; of which shall not inform the Dr, as he feels so much for his friend's misfortunes, specially when brought on by misconduct. But, out of respect for your mother, who is a good sort of woman, though rather particular, as all learned ladies are, have sent three pound-notes; the miss Norberrys giving one a-piece, not to lend, but a gift, and they join Mrs Norberry in hoping miss Mowbray will soon see the error of her ways; and, if so be, no doubt Dr Norberry will use his interest to get her into the Magdalen.'*

This curious epistle would have excited in Glenmurray and Adeline no other feelings save those of contempt, but for the information it contained of the doctor's being dangerously ill; and, in fear for the worthy husband, they forgot the impertinence of the wife and daughters.

The next day, fortunately, Mr Berrendale arrived, and with him the 300*l*. Consequently, all Glenmurray's debts were discharged, better lodgings procured, and the three pound notes returned in a blank cover to Mrs Norberry. Charles Berrendale was first cousin to Glenmurray, and so like him in face, that they were, at first, mistaken for brothers: but to a physiognomist they must always have been unlike; as Glenmurray was remarkable for the character and expression of his countenance, and Berrendale for the extreme beauty of his features and complexion. Glenmurray was pale and thin, and his eyes and hair dark. Berrendale's eyes were of a light blue; and though his eye-lashes were black, his hair was of a rich auburn: Glenmurray was thin and muscular; Berrendale, round and corpulent: still they were alike; and it was not ill observed of them, that Berrendale was Glenmurray in good health.

But Berrendale could not be flattered by the resemblance, as his face and person were so truly what is called handsome, that, partial as our sex is said to be to beauty, any woman would have been excused for falling in love with him. Whether his mind was equal to his person we shall show hereafter.

The meeting between Berrendale and Glenmurray was affectionate on both sides; but Berrendale could scarcely hide the pain he felt on seeing the situation of Glenmurray, whose virtues he had always loved, whose talents he had always respected, and to whose active friendship towards himself he owed eternal gratitude.

But he soon learnt to think Glenmurray, in one respect, an object of envy, when he beheld the constant, skilful, and tender attentions of his nurse, and saw in that nurse every gift of heart, mind, and person, which could make a woman amiable.

Berrendale had heard that his eccentric cousin was living with a girl as odd as himself; who thought herself a genius, and pretended to universal knowledge: great then was his astonishment to find this imagined pedant, and pretender, not only an adept in every useful and feminine pursuit, but modest in her demeanour, and gentle in her manners: little did he expect to see her capable of serving the table of Glenmurray with dishes made by herself, not only tempting to the now craving appetite of the invalid but to the palate of an epicure,—while all his wants were anticipated by her anxious attention, and many of the sufferings of sickness alleviated by her inventive care.

Adeline, mean while, was agreeably surprised to see the good effect produced on Glenmurray's spirits, and even his health, by the arrival of his cousin; and her manner became even affectionate to Berrendale, from gratitude for the change which his presence seemed to have occasioned.

Adeline had now a companion in her occasional walks;— Glenmurray insisted on her walking, and insisted on Berrendale's accompanying her. In these tête-à-têtes Adeline unburthened her heart, by telling Berrendale of the agony she felt at the idea of losing Glenmurray; and while drowned in tears she leaned on his arm, she unconsciously suffered him to press the hand that leaned against him; nor would she have felt it a freedom to be reproved, had she been conscious that he did so. But these trifling indulgences were fewel to the flame that she had kindled in the heart of Berrendale; a flame which he saw no guilt in indulging, as he looked on Glenmurray's death as certain, and Adeline would then be free.

But though Adeline was perfectly unconscious of his attachment, Glenmurray had seen it even before Berrendale himself discovered it; and he only waited a favourable opportunity to make the discovery known to the parties. All he had as yet ventured to say was, 'Charles, my Adeline is an excellent nurse!—You would like such an one during your fits of the gout;' and Berrendale had blushed deeply while he assented to Glenmurray's remarks, because he was conscious that, while enumerating Adeline's perfections, he had figured her to himself warming his flannels, and leaning tenderly over his gouty couch.*

One day, while Adeline was reading to Glenmurray, and Berrendale was attending not to what she read, but to the beauty of her mouth while reading, the nurse came in, and said that 'a mulatto woman wished to speak to miss Mowbray.'

'Show her up,' immediately cried Glenmurray; 'and if her little boy is with her, let him come too.'

In vain did Adeline expostulate—Glenmurray wished to enjoy the mulatto's expressions of gratitude; and, in spite of all she could say, the mother and child were introduced.

'So!' cried the mulatto, (whose looks were so improved that Adeline scarcely knew her again,) 'So! me find you at last; and, please God! we not soon part more.' As she said this, she pressed the hem of Adeline's gown to her lips with fervent emotion.

'Not part from her again!' cried Glenmurray: 'What do you mean, my good woman?'

'Oh! when she gave tree guinea for me, metought she mus be rich lady, but now dey say she be poor, and me mus work for her.'

'And who told you I was poor?'

'Dat cross man where you live once—he say you could not pay him, and you go away—and he tell me dat your love be ill; and me so sorry, yet so glad! for my love be well aden, and he have got good employ; and now I can come and serve you, and nurse dis poor gentleman, and all for noting but my meat and drink; and I know dat great fat nurse have gold wages, and eat and drink fat beside,—I knowd her well.'

All this was uttered with great volubility, and in a tone between laughing and crying.

'Well, Adeline,' said Glenmurray when she had ended, 'you did not throw away your kindness on an unworthy and ungrateful object; so I am quite reconciled to the loss of the pine-apple; and I will tell your honest friend here the story,—to show her, as she has a tender heart herself, the greatness of the sacrifice you made for her sake.'

Adeline begged him to desist; but he went on; and the mulatto could not keep herself quiet on her chair while he related the circumstance.

'And did she do dat to save me?' she passionately exclaimed; 'Angel woman! I should have let poor man go to prison, before disappoint my William!'

'And did you forgive her immediately?' said Berrendale.

'Yes, certainly.'

'Well, that was heroic too,' returned he.

'And no one but Glenmurray would have been so heroic, I believe,' said Adeline.

'But, lady, you break my heart,' cried the mulatto, 'if you not take my service. My William and me, too poor to live togedder of some year perhaps. Here, child, tawny boy, down on knees, and vow wid me to be faithful and grateful to this our mistress, till our last day; and never to forsake her in sickness or in sorrow! I swear dis to my great God:—and now say dat after me.' She then clasped the little boy's hands, bade him raise his eyes to heaven, and made him repeat what she had said, ending it with 'I swear dis, to my great God.'

There was such an affecting solemnity in this action, and in the mulatto such a determined enthusiasm of manner incapable of being controlled, that Adeline, Glenmurray, and Berrendale observed what passed in respectful silence: and when it was over, Glenmurray said, in a voice of emotion, 'I think, Adeline, we must accept this good creature's offer; and as nurse grows lazy and saucy, we had better part with her: and as for your young knight there,' (the tawny boy had by this time nestled himself close to Adeline, who, with no small emotion, was playing with his woolly curls,) 'we must send him to school; for, my good woman, we are not so poor as you imagine.'

'God be thanked!' cried the mulatto.

'But what is your name?'

'I was christened Savanna,'* replied she.

'Then, good Savanna,' cried Adeline, 'I hope we shall both have reason to bless the day when first we met; and to-morrow you shall come home to us.' Savanna, on hearing this, almost screamed with joy, and as she took her leave Berrendale slipped a guinea into her hand: the tawny boy meanwhile slowly followed his mother, as if unwilling to leave Adeline, even though she gave him halfpence to spend in cakes: but on being told that she would let him come again the next day, he tripped gaily down after Savanna.

The quiet of the chamber being then restored, Glenmurray fell into a calm slumber; Adeline took up her work; and Berrendale, pretending to read, continued to feed his passion by gazing on the unconscious Adeline.

While they were thus engaged, Glenmurray, unobserved, awoke; and he soon guessed how Berrendale's eyes were employed, as the book which he held in his hand was upside down; and through the fingers of the hand which he held before his face, he saw his looks fixed on Adeline.

The moment was a favourable one for Glenmurray's purpose: and just as he raised himself from his pillow, Adeline had discovered the earnest gaze of Berrendale; and a suspicion of the truth that instant darting across her mind, disconcerted and blushing, she had cast her eyes on the ground.

'That is an interesting study which you are engaged in, Charles,' cried Glenmurray smiling.

Berrendale started; and, deeply blushing, faltered out, 'Yes.'

Adeline looked at Glenmurray, and, seeing a very arch and meaning expression on his countenance, suspected that he had made the same discovery as herself: yet, if so, she wondered at his looking so pleasantly on Berrendale as he spoke.

'It is a book, Charles,' continued Glenmurray, 'which the more you study the more you will admire; and I wish to give you a clue to understand some passages in it better than you can now do.'

This speech deceived Adeline, and made her suppose that Glenmurray really alluded to the book which lay before Berrendale: but it convinced *him* that Glenmurray spoke metaphorically; and as his manner was kind, it also made him think that he saw and did not disapprove his attachment.

For a few minutes, each of them being engrossed in different contemplations, there was a complete silence; but Glenmurray interrupted it by saying, 'My dear Adeline, it is your hour for walking; but, as I am not disposed to sleep again, will you forgive me if I keep your walking companion to myself to-day?—I wish to converse with him alone.'

'Oh! most cheerfully,' she replied with quickness: 'you know I love a solitary ramble of all things.'

'Not very flattering that to my cousin,' observed Glenmurray.

'I did not wish to flatter him,' said Adeline gravely; and Berrendale, fluttered at the idea of the coming conversation with Glenmurray, and mortified by Adeline's words and manner, turned to the window to conceal his emotion.

Adeline, then, with more than usual tenderness, conjured Glenmurray not to talk too much, nor do any thing to destroy the hopes on which her only chance of happiness depended, viz. the now possible chance of his recovery, and then set out for her walk; while, with a restraint and coldness which she could not conquer, she bade Berrendale farewell for the present.

The walk was long, and her thoughts perturbed:—'What could Glenmurray want to say to Mr Berrendale?'—'Why did Mr Berrendale sit with his eyes so intently and clandestinely, as it were, fixed on me?' were thoughts perpetually recurring to her: and half impatient, and half reluctant, she at length returned to her lodgings.

When she entered the apartment, she saw signs of great emotion in the countenance of both the gentlemen; and in Berrendale's eyes the traces of recent tears. The tone of Glenmurray's voice too, when he addressed her, was even more tender than usual, and Berrendale's attentions more marked, yet more respectful; and Adeline observed that Glenmurray was unusually thoughtful and absent, and that the cough and other symptoms of his complaint were more troublesome than ever.

'I see you have exerted yourself and talked too much during my absence,' cried Adeline, 'and I will never leave you again for so long a time.'

'You never shall,' said Glenmurray. 'I must leave *you* for so long a time at last, that I will be blessed with the sight of you as long as I can.'

Adeline, whose hopes had been considerably revived during the last few days, looked mournfully and reproachfully in his face as he uttered these words.

'It is even so, my dearest girl,' continued Glenmurray, 'and I say this to guard you against a melancholy surprise:—I wish to prepare you for an event which to me seems unavoidable.'

'Prepare me!' exclaimed Adeline wildly. 'Can there be any preparation to enable one to bear such a calamity? Absurd idea! However, I shall derive consolation from the severity of the stroke: I feel that I shall not be able to survive it.' So saying, her head fell on Glenmurray's pillow; and, for some time, her sorrow almost suspended the consciousness of suffering.

From this state she was aroused by Glenmurray's being attacked with a violent paroxysm of his complaint, and all selfish distress was lost in the consciousness of his sufferings: again he struggled through, and seemed so relieved by the effort, that again Adeline's hopes revived; and she could scarcely return, with temper, Berrendale's 'good night,' when Glenmurray expressed a wish to rest, because his spirits had not risen in any proportion to hers.

The nurse had been dismissed that afternoon; and Adeline, as Savanna was not to come home till the next morning, was to sit up alone with Glenmurray that night; and, contrary to his usual custom, he did not insist that she should have a companion.

For a few hours his exhausted frame was recruited by a sleep more than usually quiet, and but for a few hours only. He then became restless, and so wakeful and disturbed, that he professed to Adeline an utter inability to sleep, and therefore he wished to pass the rest of the night in serious conversation with her.

Adeline, alarmed at this intention, conjured him not to irritate his complaint by so dangerous an exertion.

'My mind will irritate it more,' replied he, 'if I refrain from it; for it is burthened, my Adeline, and it longs to throw off its burthen. Now then, ere my senses wander, hear what I wish to communicate to you, and interrupt me as little as possible.'

Adeline, oppressed and awed beyond measure at the unusual solemnity of his manner, made no answer; but, leaning her cheek on his hand, awaited his communication in silence.

'I think,' said Glenmurray, 'I shall begin with telling you Berrendale's history: it is proper that you should know all that concerns him.'

Adeline, raising her head, replied hastily,—'Not to satisfy any curiosity of mine; for I feel none, I assure you.'

'Well then,' returned Glenmurray, sighing, 'to please me, be it.— Berrendale is the son of my mother's sister, by a merchant in the neighbourhood of the 'Change,* who hurt the family pride so much by marrying a tradesman, that I am the only one of the clan who has noticed her since. He ran away, about four years ago, with the only child of a rich West Indian from a boarding-school. The consequence was, that her father renounced her; but, when, three years ago, she died in giving birth to a son, the unhappy parent repented of his displeasure, and offered to allow Berrendale, who from the bankruptcy and sudden death of both his parents had been left destitute, an annuity of 300*l.* for life,* provided he would send the child over to Jamaica, and allow him to have all the care of his education. To this Berrendale consented.'

'Reluctantly, I hope,' said Adeline, 'and merely out of pity for the feelings of the childless father.'

'I hope so too,' continued Glenmurray; 'for I do not think the chance of inheriting all his grandfather's property a sufficient reason to lead him to give up to another, and in a foreign land too, the society and education of his child: but, whatever were his reasons, Berrendale acceded to the request, and the infant was sent to

Jamaica; and ever since the 300*l.* has been regularly remitted to him: besides that, he has recovered two thousand and odd hundred pounds from the wreck of his father's property; and with œconomy, and had he a good wife to manage his affairs for him, Berrendale might live very comfortably.'

'My dear Glenmurray,' cried Adeline impatiently, 'what is this to me? and why do you weary yourself to tell me particulars so little interesting to me?'

Glenmurray bade her have patience, and continued thus: 'And now, Adeline,' (here his voice evidently faltered) 'I must open my whole heart to you, and confess that the idea of leaving you friendless, unprotected, and poor, your reputation injured, and your peace of mind destroyed, is more than I am able to bear, and will give me, in my last moments, the torments of the damned.' Here a violent burst of tears interrupted him; and Adeline, overcome with emotion and surprise at the sight of the agitation which his own sufferings could never occasion in him, hung over him in speechless woe.

'Besides,' continued Glenmurray, recovering himself a little, 'I— O Adeline!' seizing her cold hand, 'can you forgive me for having been the means of blasting all your fair fame and prospects in life?'

'For the sake of justice, if not of mercy,' exclaimed Adeline, 'forbear thus cruelly to accuse yourself. You know that from my own free, unbiassed choice I gave myself to you, and in compliance with my own principles.'

'But who taught you those principles?—who led you to a train of reasoning, so alluring in theory, so pernicious in practice? Had not I, with the heedless vanity of youth, given to the world the crude conceptions of four-and-twenty, you might at this moment have been the idol of a respectable society; and I, equally respected, have been the husband of your heart; while happiness would perhaps have kept that fatal disease at bay, of which anxiety has facilitated the approach.'

He was going on: but Adeline, who had till now struggled success-fully with her feelings, wound up almost to phrensy at the possibility that anxiety had shortened Glenmurray's life, gave way to a violent paroxysm of sorrow, which, for a while, deprived her of conscious-ness; and when she recovered she found Berrendale bending over her, while her head lay on Glenmurray's pillow.

The sight of Berrendale in a moment roused her to exertion;—his look was so full of anxious tenderness, and she was at that moment so ill disposed to regard it with complacency, that she eagerly declared she was quite recovered, and begged Mr Berrendale would return to bed; and Glenmurray seconding her request, with a deep sigh he departed.

'Poor fellow!' said Glenmurray, 'I wish you had seen his anxiety during your illness!'

'I am glad I did *not*,' replied Adeline: 'but, how can you persist in talking to me of any other person's anxiety, when I am tortured with yours? Your conversation of to-night has made me even more miserable than I was before. By what strange fatality do you blame yourself for the conduct worthy of admiration?—for giving to the world, as soon as produced, opinions which were calculated to enlighten it?'

'But,' replied Glenmurray, 'as those opinions militated against the experience and custom of ages, ought I not to have paused before I published, and kept them back till they had received the sanction of my maturer judgment?'

'And does your maturer judgment condemn them?'

'Four years cannot have added much to the maturity of my judgment,' replied Glenmurray: 'but I will own that some of my opinions are changed; and that, though I believe those which are unchanged are right in theory, I think, as the mass of society could never at *once* adopt them, they had better remain unacted upon, than that a few lonely individuals should expose themselves to certain distress, by making them the rules of their conduct.* You, for instance, you, my Adeline, what misery—!' Here his voice again faltered, and emotion impeded his utterance.

'Live—do but live,' exclaimed Adeline passionately, 'and I can know of misery but the name.'

'But I cannot live, I cannot live,' replied Glenmurray, 'and the sooner I die the better;—for thus to waste your youth and health in the dreadful solitude of a sick-room is insupportable to me.'

'O Glenmurray!' replied Adeline, fondly throwing herself on his neck, 'could you but live free from any violent pain, and were neither you nor I ever to leave this room again, believe me, I should not have a wish beyond it. To see you, to hear you, to prove to you how much I love you, would, indeed it would, be happiness sufficient for me!' After this burst of true and heartfelt tenderness, there was a pause of some moments: Glenmurray felt too much to speak, and Adeline was sobbing on his pillow. At length she pathetically again exclaimed, 'Live; only live! and I am blest!'

'But I *cannot* live, I *cannot* live,' again replied Glenmurray; 'and when I die, what will become of you?'

'I care not,' cried Adeline: 'if I lose you, may the same grave receive us!'

'But it *will* not, my dearest girl;—grief does not kill; and, entailed as my estate is, I have nothing to leave you: and though richly qualified to undertake the care of children, in order to maintain yourself, your unfortunate connection, and singular opinions, will be an eternal bar to your being so employed. O Adeline! these cutting fears, these dreadful reflections, are indeed the bitterness of death: but there is one way of alleviating my pangs.'

'Name it,' replied Adeline with quickness.

'But you must promise then to hear me with patience.—Had I been able to live through my illness, I should have conjured you to let me endeavour to restore you to your place in society, and consequently to your usefulness, by making you my wife: and young, and I may add innocent and virtuous, as you are, I doubt not but the world would at length have received you into its favour again.'

'But you must, you will, you shall live,' interrupted Adeline, 'and I shall be your happy wife.'

'Not *mine*,' replied Glenmurray, laying an emphasis on the last word.

Adeline started, and, fixing her eyes wildly on his, demanded what he meant.

'I mean,' replied he, 'to prevail on you to make my last moments happy, by promising, some time hence, to give yourself a tender, a respectable, and a legal protector.'

'O Glenmurray!' exclaimed Adeline, 'and can you insult my tenderness for you with such a proposal? If I can even survive you, do you think that I can bear to give you a successor in my affection? or, how can you bear to imagine that I shall?'

'Because my love for you is without selfishness, and I wish you to be happy even though another makes you so. The lover, or the husband, who wishes the woman of his affection to form no second attachment, is, in my opinion, a selfish, contemptible being. Perhaps I do not expect that you will ever feel, for another man, an attachment like that which has subsisted between us—the first affection of young and impassioned hearts; but I am sure that you may again feel love enough to make yourself and the man of your choice perfectly happy; and I hope and trust that you will be so.'

'And forget you, I suppose?' interrupted Adeline reproachfully.

'Not so: I would have you remember me always, but with a chastised and even a pleasing sorrow; nay, I would wish you to imagine me a sort of guardian spirit, watching your actions, and enjoying your happiness.'

'I have *listened* to you,' cried Adeline in a tone of suppressed anguish, 'and, I trust, with tolerable patience: there is one thing yet for me to learn—the *name* of the object whom you wish me to marry, for I suppose *he* is found.'

'He is,' returned Glenmurray. 'Berrendale loves you; and he it is whom I wish you to choose.'

'I thought so,' exclaimed Adeline, rising and traversing the room hastily, and wringing her hands.

'But wherefore does his name', said Glenmurray, 'excite such angry emotion? Perhaps self-love makes me recommend him,' continued he, forcing a smile, 'as he is reckoned like me, and I thought that likeness might make him more agreeable to you.'

'Only the more odious,' impatiently interrupted Adeline. 'To look like you, and not *be* you, Oh! insupportable idea!' she exclaimed, throwing herself on Glenmurray's pillow, and pressing his burning temples to her cold cheek.

'Adeline,' said Glenmurray solemnly, 'this is, perhaps, the last moment of confidential and uninterrupted intercourse that we shall ever have together; ' Adeline started, but spoke not; 'allow me, therefore, to tell you it is my *dying request*, that you would endeavour to dispose your mind in favour of Berrendale, and to become in time his wife. Circumstanced as you are, your only chance for happiness is becoming a wife: but it is too certain that few men worthy of you, in the most essential points, will be likely to marry you after your connection with me.'

'Strange prejudice!' cried Adeline, 'to consider as my disgrace, what I deem my glory!'

Glenmurray continued thus: 'Berrendale himself has a great deal of the old school about him, but I have convinced him that you are not to be classed with the frail of your sex; and that you are one of the purest as well as loveliest of human beings.'

'And did he want to be convinced of this?' cried Adeline indignantly; 'and *yet* you advise me to marry him?'

'My dearest love,' replied Glenmurray, 'in all cases the most we can expect is, to choose the best *possible* means of happiness. Berrendale is not perfect; but I am convinced that you would commit a fatal error in not making him your husband; and when I tell you it is my *dying request* that you should do so—'

'If you wish me to retain my senses,' exclaimed Adeline, 'repeat that dreadful phrase no more.'

'I will not say any more at all now,' faintly observed Glenmurray, 'for I am exhausted:—still, as morning begins to dawn, I should like to sit up in my bed, and gaze on it, perhaps for—' Here Adeline put her hand to his mouth: Glenmurray kissed it, sighed, and did not finish the sentence. She then opened the shutters to let in the rising splendor of day, and, turning round towards Glenmurray, almost shrieked with terror at seeing the visible alteration a night had made in his appearance; while the yellow rays of the dawn played on his sallow cheek, and his dark curls, once crisped and glossy, hung faint and moist on his beating temples.

'It is strange, Adeline,' said Glenmurray (but with great effort), 'that, even in my situation, the sight of morning, and the revival as it were of nature, seems to invigorate my whole frame. I long to breathe the freshness of its breeze also.'

Adeline, conscious for the first time that all hope was over, opened the window, and felt even her sick soul and languid frame revived by the chill but refreshing breeze. To Glenmurray it imparted a feeling of physical pleasure, to which he had long been a stranger: 'I breathe freely,' he exclaimed, 'I feel alive again!'—and, strange as it may seem, Adeline's hopes began to revive also.—'I feel as if I could sleep now,' said Glenmurray, 'the feverish restlessness seems abated; but, lest my dreams be disturbed, promise me, ere I lie down again, that you will behave kindly to Berrendale.'

'Impossible! The only tie that bound me to him is broken:—I thought he sincerely sympathized with me in my wishes for your recovery; but now that, as he loves me, his wishes must be in direct opposition to mine,—I cannot, indeed I cannot, endure the sight of him.'

Glenmurray could not reply to this natural observation: he knew that, in a similar situation, his feelings would have been like Adeline's; and, pressing her hand with all the little strength left him, he said 'Poor Berrendale!' and tried to compose himself to sleep; while Adeline, lost in sad contemplation, threw herself in a chair by his bed-side, and anxiously awaited the event of his reawaking.

But it was not long before Adeline herself, exhausted both in body and mind, fell into a deep sleep; and it was mid-day before she awoke: for no careless, heavy-treading, and hired nurse now watched the slumbers of the unhappy lovers; but the mulatto, stepping light as air, and afraid even of breathing lest she should disturb their repose, had assumed her station at the bed-side, and taken every precaution lest any noise should awake them. Hers was the service of the heart; and there is none like it.

At twelve o'clock Adeline awoke; and her first glance met the dark eyes of Savanna kindly fixed upon her. Adeline started, not immediately recollecting who it could be; but in a moment the idea of the mulatto, and of the service which she had rendered her, recurred to her mind, and diffused a sensation of pleasure through her frame. 'There is a being whom I have served,' said Adeline to herself, and, extending her hand to Savanna, she started from her seat, invigorated by the thought: but she felt depressed again by the consciousness that she, who had been able to impart so much joy and help to another, was herself a wretch for ever; and in a moment her eyes filled with tears, while the mulatto gazed on her with a look of inquiring solicitude.

'Poor Savanna!' cried Adeline in a low and plaintive tone.

There are moments when the sound of one's own voice has a mournful effect on one's feelings—this was one of those moments to Adeline; the pathos of her own tone overcame her, and she burst into tears: but Glenmurray slept on; and Adeline hoped nothing would suddenly disturb his rest, when Berrendale opened the door with what appeared unnecessary noise, and Glenmurray hastily awoke.

Adeline immediately started from her seat, and, looking at him with great indignation, demanded why he came in in such a manner, when he knew Mr Glenmurray was asleep.

Berrendale, shocked and alarmed at Adeline's words and expression, so unlike her usual manner, stammered out an excuse. 'Another time, sir,' replied Adeline coldly, 'I hope you will be more *careful*.'

'What is the matter?' said Glenmurray, raising himself in the bed. 'Are you scolding, Adeline? If so, let me hear you: I like novelty.'

Here Adeline and Berrendale both hastened to him, and Adeline almost looked with complacency on Berrendale; when Glenmurray, declaring himself wonderfully refreshed by his long sleep, expressed a great desire for his breakfast, and said he had a most voracious appetite.

But to all Berrendale's attentions she returned the most forbidding reserve; nor could she for a moment lose the painful idea, that the death of Glenmurray would be to him a source of joy, not of anguish. Berrendale was not slow to observe this change in her conduct; and he conceived that, as he knew Glenmurray had mentioned his pretensions to her, his absence would be of more service to his wishes than his presence; and he resolved to leave Richmond that afternoon,— especially as he had a dinner engagement at a tavern in London, which, in spite of love and friendship, he was desirous of keeping.

He was not mistaken in his ideas: the countenance of Adeline assumed less severity when he mentioned his intention of going away, nor could she express regret at his resolution, even though Glenmurray with anxious earnestness requested him to stay. But Glenmurray entreated in vain: used to consider his own interest and pleasure in preference to that of others, Berrendale resolved to go; and resisted the prayers of a man who had often obliged him with the greatest difficulty to himself.

'Well, then,' said Glenmurray mournfully, 'if you must go, God bless you! I wish you, Charles, all possible earthly happiness; nay, I have done all I can to ensure it to you: but you have disappointed me. I hoped to have joined your hand, in my last moments, to that of this dear girl, and to have bequeathed her in the most solemn manner to your care and tenderness; but, no matter, farewell! we shall probably meet no more.'

Here Berrendale's heart failed him, and he almost resolved to stay: but a look of angry repugnance which he saw on Adeline's countenance, even amidst her sorrow, got the better of his kind emotions, by wounding his self-love; and grasping Glenmurray's hand, and saying, 'I shall be back in a day or two,' he rushed out of the room.

'I am sorry Mr Berrendale is forced to go,' said Adeline involuntarily when the street-door closed after him.

'Had you condescended to tell him so, he would undoubtedly have staid,' replied Glenmurray rather peevishly. Adeline instantly felt, and regretted, the selfishness of her conduct. To avoid the sight of a disagreeable object, she had given pain to Glenmurray; or, rather, she had not done her utmost to prevent his being exposed to it.

'Forgive me,' said Adeline, bursting into tears: 'I own I thought only of myself, when I forbore to urge his stay. Alas! with you, and you alone, I believe, is the gratification of self always a secondary consideration.'

'You forget that I am a philanthropist,' replied Glenmurray, 'and cannot bear to be praised, even by you, at the expense of my fellow-creatures. But come, hasten dinner; my breakfast agreed with me so well, that I am impatient for another meal.'

'You certainly are better to-day,' exclaimed Adeline with unwonted cheerfulness.

'My feelings are more tolerable, at least,' replied Glenmurray: and Adeline and the mulatto began to prepare the dinner immediately. How often during her attendance on Glenmurray had she recollected the words of her grandmother, and blessed her for having taught her to be *useful!*

As soon as dinner was over, Glenmurray complained of being drowsy: still he declared he would not go to bed till he had seen the sun set, as he had that day, for the second time since his illness, seen it rise; and therefore, when it was setting, Adeline and Savanna led him into a room adjoining, which had a western aspect. Glenmurray fixed his eyes on the crimson horizon with a peculiar expression; and his lips seemed to murmur, 'For the last time! Let me breathe the evening air, too, once more,' said he.

'It is too chill, dear Glenmurray.'

'It will not hurt me,' replied Glenmurray; and Adeline complied with his request.

'The breeze of evening is not refreshing like that of morning,' he observed; 'but the beauty of the setting is, perhaps, superior to that of the rising sun:—they are both glorious sights, and I have enjoyed them both to-day, nor have I for years experienced so strong a feeling of devotion.'

'Thank God!' cried Adeline. 'O Glenmurray! there has been one thing only wanting to the completion of our union; and that was, that we should worship together.'

'Perhaps, had I remained longer here,' replied Glenmurray, 'we might have done so; for, believe me, Adeline, though my feelings have continually hurried me into adoration of the Supreme Being, I have often wished my homage to be as regular and as founded on immutable conviction as it once was: but it is too late now for amendment, though, alas! not for *regret*, *deep* regret: yet He who reads the heart knows that my intentions were pure, and that I was not fixed in the stubbornness of error.'

'Let us change this discourse,' cried Adeline, seeing on Glenmurray's countenance an expression of uncommon sadness, which he, from a regard to her feelings, struggled to cover. He did indeed feel sadness—a sadness of the most painful nature; and while Adeline hung over him with all the anxious and soothing attention of unbounded love, he seemed to shrink from her embrace with horror, and, turning away his head, feebly murmured, 'O Adeline! this faithful kindness wounds me to the very soul. Alas! alas! how little have I deserved it!'

If Glenmurray, who had been the means of injuring the woman he loved, merely by following the dictates of his conscience, and a love of what he imagined to be truth, without any view to his own benefit or the gratification of his personal wishes, felt thus acutely the anguish of self-upbraiding,—what ought to be, and what must be, sooner or later, the agony and remorse of that man, who, merely for the gratification of his own illicit desires, has seduced the woman whom he loved from the path of virtue, and ruined for ever her reputation and her peace of mind!

'It is too late now for you to sit at an open window, indeed it is,' cried Adeline, after having replied to Glenmurray's self-reproaches by the touching language of tears, and incoherent expressions of confiding and unchanged attachment; 'and as you are evidently better to-day, do not, by breathing too much cold air, run the risk of making yourself worse again.'

'Would I were really better! would I could live!' passionately exclaimed Glenmurray: 'but indeed I do feel stronger to-night than I have felt for many months.' In a moment the fine eyes of Adeline were raised to heaven with an expression of devout thankfulness; and, eager to make the most of a change so favourable, she hurried Glenmurray back to his chamber, and, with a feeling of renewed hope, sat by to watch his slumbers. She had not sat long before the door opened, and the little tawny boy entered. He had watched all day to see the good lady, as he called Adeline; but, as she had not left Glenmurray's chamber except to prepare dinner, he had been disappointed: so he was resolved to seek her in her own apartment. He had bought some cakes with the penny which Adeline had given him, and he was eager to give her a piece of them.

'Hush!' cried Adeline, as she held out her hand to him; and he in a whisper crying 'Bite,' held his purchase to her lips. Adeline tasted it, said it was very good, and, giving him a halfpenny, the tawny boy disappeared again: the noise he made as he bounded down the stairs woke Glenmurray. Adeline was sitting on the side of the bed; and as he turned round to sleep again he grasped her hand in his, and its feverish touch damped her hopes, and re-awakened her fears. For a short time she mournfully gazed on his flushed cheek, and then, gently sliding off the bed, and dropping on one knee, she addressed the Deity in the language of humble supplication.

Insensibly she ceased to pray in thought only, and the lowly-murmured prayer became audible. Again Glenmurray awoke, and Adeline reproached herself as the cause.

'My rest was uneasy,' cried he, 'and I rejoice that you woke me: besides, I like to hear you—Go on, my dearest girl; there is a some-thing in the breathings of your pious fondness that soothes me,' added he, pressing the hand he held to his parched lips.

Adeline obeyed: and as she continued, she felt ever and anon, by the pressure of Glenmurray's hand, how much he was affected by what she uttered.

'But must he be taken from me!' she exclaimed in one part of her prayer. 'Father, if it be possible, permit this cup to pass by me untasted.'* Here she felt the hand of Glenmurray grasp hers most vehemently; and, delighted to think that he had pleasure in hearing her, she went on to breathe forth all the wishes of a trembling yet confiding spirit, till overcome with her own emotions she ceased and arose, and leaning over Glenmurray's pillow was going to take his hand:—but the hand which she pressed returned not her pressure; the eyes were fixed whose approving glance she sought; and the horrid truth rushed at once on her mind, that the last convulsive grasp had been an eternal farewell, and that he had in that grasp expired.

Alas! what preparation however long, what anticipation however sure, can enable the mind to bear a shock like this! It came on Adeline like a thunder-stroke: she screamed not; she moved not; but, fixing a dim and glassy eye on the pale countenance of her lover, she seemed as insensible as poor Glenmurray himself; and hours might have elapsed—hours immediately fatal both to her senses and existence—ere any one had entered the room, since she had given orders to be disturbed by no one, had not the tawny boy, encouraged by his past success, stolen in again, unperceived, to give her a piece of the apple which he had bought with her last bounty.

The delighted boy tripped gaily to the bed-side, holding up his treasure; but he started back, and screamed in all the agony of terror, at the sight which he beheld—the face of Glenmurray ghastly, and the mouth distorted as if in the last agony, and Adeline in the stupor of despair.

The affectionate boy's repeated screams soon summoned the whole family into the room, while he, vainly hanging on Adeline's arm, begged her to speak to him: But nothing could at first rouse Adeline, not even Savanna's loud and extravagant grief. When, however, they tried to force her from the body, she recovered her recollection and her strength; and it was with great difficulty she could be carried out of the room, and kept out when they had accomplished their purpose.

But Savanna was sure that looking at such a sad sight would kill her mistress; for she should die herself if she saw William dead, she declared; and the people of the house agreed with her. They knew not that grief is the best medicine for itself; and that the overcharged heart is often relieved by the sight which standers-by conceive likely to snap the very threads of existence.

As Adeline and Glenmurray had both of them excited some interest in Richmond, the news of the death of the latter was immediately abroad; and it was told to Mrs Pemberton, with a pathetic account of Adeline's distress, just as the carriage was preparing to convey her and her sick friend on their way to Lisbon. It was a relation to call forth all the humanity of Mrs Pemberton's nature. She forgot Adeline's crime in her distress; and knowing she had no female friend with her, she hastened on the errand of pity to the abode of vice. Alas! Mrs Pemberton had learnt but too well to sympathize in grief like that of Adeline. She had seen a beloved husband expire in her arms, and had afterwards followed two children to the grave. But she had taken refuge from sorrow in the active duties of her religion, and in becoming a teacher of those truths to others, by which she had so much benefited herself.

Mrs Pemberton entered the room just as Adeline, on her knees, was conjuring the persons with her to allow her to see Glenmurray once more.

Adeline did not at all observe the entrance of Mrs Pemberton, who, in spite of the self-command which her principles and habits gave her, was visibly affected when she beheld the mourner's tearless affliction: and the hands which, on her entrance, were quietly crossed on each other, confining the modest folds of her simple cloke, were suddenly and involuntarily separated by the irresistible impulse of pity; while, catching hold of the wall for support, she leaned against it, covering her face with her hands. 'Let me see him! only let me see him once more!' cried Adeline, gazing on Mrs Pemberton, but unconscious who she was.

'Thou shalt see him,' replied Mrs Pemberton with considerable effort; 'give me thy hand, and I will go with thee to the chamber of death.' Adeline gave a scream of mournful joy at this permission, and suffered herself to be led into Glenmurray's apartment. As soon as she entered it she sprang to the bed, and, throwing herself beside the corpse, began to contemplate it with an earnestness and firmness which surprised every one. Mrs Pemberton also fixedly gazed on the wan face of Glenmurray: 'And art thou fallen!' she exclaimed, 'thou, wise in thine own conceit, who presumedst, perhaps, sometimes to question even the existence of the Most High, and to set up thy vain chimeras of yesterday against the wisdom and experience of centuries? Child of the dust! child of error! what art thou now, and whither is thy guilty spirit fled? But balmy is the hand of affliction; and she, thy mourning victim, may learn to bless the hand that chastizes her, nor add to the offences which will weigh down thy soul, a dread responsibility for hers!'

Here she was interrupted by the voice of Adeline; who, in a deep and hollow tone, was addressing the unconscious corpse. 'For God's sake, speak! for this silence is dreadful—it looks so like death.'

'Poor thing!' said Mrs Pemberton, kneeling beside her, 'and is it even thus with thee? Would thou couldst shed tears, afflicted one!'

'It is very strange,' continued Adeline: 'he loved me so tenderly, and he used to speak and look so tenderly, and now, see how he neglects me! Glenmurray, my love! for mercy's sake, speak to me!' As she said this, she laid her lips to his: but, feeling on them the icy coldness of death, she started back, screaming in all the violence of phrensy; and, recovered to the full consciousness of her misfortune, she was carried back to her room in violent convulsions.

'Would I could stay and watch over thee!' said Mrs Pemberton, as she gazed on Adeline's distorted countenance; 'for thou, young as thou art, wert well known in the chambers of sorrow and of sickness; and I should rejoice to pay back to thee part of the debt of those whom thy presence so often soothed: but I must leave thee to the care of others.'

'You leave her to my care,' cried Savanna reproachfully,—who felt even her violent sorrow suspended while Mrs Pemberton spoke in accents at once sad yet soothing,—'you leave her to my care, and who watch, who love her more than me?'

'Good Savanna!' replied Mrs Pemberton, pressing the mulatto's hand as she returned to her station beside Adeline, who was fallen into a calm slumber, 'to thy care, with confidence, I commit her. But perhaps there may be an immediate necessity for money, and I had better leave this with thee,' she added, taking out her purse: but Savanna assured her that Mr Berrendale was sent for, and to him all those concerns were to be left. Mrs Pemberton stood for a few moments looking at Adeline in silence, then slowly left the house.

When Adeline awoke, she seemed so calm and resigned, that her earnest request of being allowed to pass the night alone was granted, especially as Mrs Pemberton had desired that her wish, even to see Glenmurray again, should be complied with: but the faithful mulatto watched till morning at the door. No bed that night received the weary limbs of Adeline. She threw herself on the ground, and in alternate prayer and phrensy passed the first night of her woe: towards morning, however, she fell into a perturbed sleep. But when the light of day darting into the room awakened her to conscious-ness; and when she recollected that he to whom it usually summoned her existed no longer; that the eyes which but the preceding morning had opened with enthusiastic ardour to hail its beams, were now for ever closed; and that the voice which used to welcome her so tenderly, she should never, never hear again; the forlornness of her situation, the hopelessness of her sorrow burst upon her with a violence too powerful for her reason: and when Berrendale arrived, he found Glenmurray in his shrowd, and Adeline in a state of insanity.* For six months her phrensy resisted all the efforts of medicine, and the united care which Berrendale's love and Savanna's grateful attachment could bestow; while with Adeline's want of their care seemed to increase their desire of bestowing it, and their affection gathered new strength from the duration of her helpless malady. So true is it, that we become attached more from the aid which we give than that which we receive; and that the love of the obliger is more apt to increase than that of the obliged by the obligation conferred. At length, however, Adeline's reason slowly yet surely returned; and she, by degrees, learnt to contemplate with firmness, and even calmness, the loss which she had sustained. She even looked on Berrendale and his attentions not with anger, but gratitude and complacency; she had even pleasure in observing the likeness he bore Glenmurray; she felt that it endeared him to her. In the first paroxysms of her phrensy, the sight of him threw her into fits of raving; but as she grew better she had pleasure in seeing him: and when, on her recovery, she heard how much she was indebted to his persevering tenderness, she felt for him a decided regard, which Berrendale tried to flatter himself might be ripened into love.

But he was mistaken; the heart of Adeline was formed to feel violent and lasting attachments only. She had always loved her mother with a tenderness of a most uncommon nature; she had felt for Glenmurray the fondest enthusiasm of passion: she was now separated from them both. But her mother still lived; and though almost hopeless of ever being restored to her society, all her love for her returned; and she pined for that consoling fondness, those soothing attentions, which, in a time of such affliction, a mother on a widowed daughter can alone bestow.

'Yet, surely,' cried she in the solitude of her own room, 'her oath cannot now forbid her to forgive me; for, am I not as WRETCHED IN LOVE, nay more, far more so, than *she* has been? Yes—yes; I will write to her: besides HE wished me to do so' (meaning Glenmurray, whom she never named); and she did write to her, according to the address which Dr Norberry sent soon after he returned to his own house. Still week after week elapsed, and month after month, but no answer came.

Again she wrote, and again she was disappointed; though her loss, her illness in consequence of it, her pecuniary distress, and the large debt which she had incurred to Berrendale, were all detailed in a manner calculated to move the most obdurate heart. What then could Adeline suppose? Perhaps her mother was ill; perhaps she was dead: and her reason was again on the point of yielding to this horrible supposition, when she received her two letters in a cover, directed in her mother's hand-writing.

At first she was overwhelmed by this dreadful proof of the continuance of Mrs Mowbray's deep resentment; but, ever sanguine, the circumstance of Mrs Mowbray's having written the address herself appeared to Adeline a favourable symptom; and with renewed hope she wrote to Dr Norberry to become her mediator once more: but to this letter no answer was returned; and Adeline concluded her only friend had died of the fever which Mrs Norberry had mentioned in her letter.

'Then I have lost my only friend!' cried Adeline, wringing her hands in agony, as this idea recurred to her. 'Your only friend?' repeated Berrendale, who happened to be present, 'O Adeline!'

Her heart smote her as he said this. 'My oldest friend I should have said,' she replied, holding out her hand to him; and Berrendale thought himself supremely happy.

But Adeline was far from meaning to give the encouragement which this action seemed to bestow: wholly occupied by her affliction, her mind had lost its energy, and she would not have made an effort to dissipate her grief by employment and exertion, had not that virtuous pride and delicacy, which in happier hours had been the ornament of her character, rebelled against the consciousness of owing pecuniary obligations to the lover whose suit she was determined to reject, and urged her to make some vigorous attempt to maintain herself.

Many were the schemes which occurred to her; but none seemed so practicable as that of keeping a day-school in some village near the metropolis.—True, Glenmurray had said, that her having been his mistress would prevent her obtaining scholars; but his fears, perhaps, were stronger than his justice in this case. These fears, however, she found existed in Berrendale's mind also, though he ventured only to hint them with great caution.

'You think, then, no prudent parents, if my story should be known to them, would send their children to me?' said Adeline to Berrendale.

'I fear—I—that is to say, I am sure they would not.'

'Under such circumstances,' said Adeline, 'you yourself would not send a child to my school?'

'Why—really—I—as the world goes,'—replied Berrendale.

'I am answered,' said Adeline with a look and tone of displeasure; and retired to her chamber, intending not to return till Berrendale was gone to his own lodging. But her heart soon reproached her with unjust resentment; and, coming back, she apologized to Berrendale for being angry at his laudable resolution of acting according to those principles which he thought most virtuous, especially as she claimed for herself a similar right.

Berrendale, gratified by her apology, replied, 'that he saw no objection to her plan, if she chose to deny him the happiness of sharing his income with her, provided she would settle in a village where she was not likely to be known, and change her name.'

'Change my name! Never. Concealment of any kind almost always implies the consciousness of guilt; and while my heart does not condemn me, my conduct shall not seem to accuse me. I will go to whatever place you shall recommend; but I beg your other request may be mentioned no more.'

Berrendale, glad to be forgiven on any terms, promised to comply with her wishes; and he having recommended to her to settle at a village some few miles north of London, Adeline hired there a small but commodious lodging, and issued immediately cards of advertisement, stating what she meant to teach, and on what terms; while Berrendale took lodgings within a mile of her, and the faithful mulatto attended her as a servant of all-work.

Fortunately, at this time, a lady at Richmond, who had a son the age of the tawny boy, became so attached to him, that she was desirous of bringing him up to be the play-fellow and future attendant on her son; and the mulatto, pleased to have him so well disposed of, resisted the poor little boy's tears and reluctance at the idea of being separated from her and Adeline: and before she left Richmond she had the satisfaction of seeing him comfortably settled in the house of his patroness.

Adeline succeeded in her undertaking even beyond her utmost wishes. Though unknown and unrecommended, there was in her countenance and manner a something so engaging, so strongly inviting confidence, and so decisively bespeaking the gentlewoman, that she soon excited in the village general respect and attention: and no sooner were scholars intrusted to her care, than she became the idol of her pupils; and their improvement was rapid in proportion to the love which they bore her.

This fortunate circumstance proved a balm to the wounded mind of Adeline. She felt that she had recovered her usefulness;—that desideratum in morals and life, spite of her misfortunes, acquired a charm in her eyes. True it was, that she was restored to her capability of being useful, by being where she was unknown; and because the mulatto, unknown to her, had described her as reduced to earn her living, on account of the death of the man to whom she was about to be married: but she did not revert to the reasons of her being so generally esteemed; she contented herself with the consciousness of being so; and for some months she was tranquil, though not happy. But her tranquillity was destined to be of short duration.

VOLUME III

CHAPTER I

The village in which Adeline resided happened to be the native place of Mary Warner, the servant whom she had been forced to dismiss at Richmond; and who having gone from Mrs Pemberton to another situation, which she had also quitted, came to visit her friends.

The wish of saying lessening things of those of whom one hears extravagant commendations, is, I fear, common to almost every one, even where the object praised comes in no competition with oneself:—and when Mary Warner heard from every quarter of the grace and elegance, affability and active benevolence of the new comer, it was no doubt infinitely gratifying to her to be able to exclaim,—'Mowbray! did you say her name is? La! I dares to say it is my old mistress, who was kept by one Mr Glenmurray!' But so greatly were her auditors prepossessed in favour of Adeline, that very few of them could be prevailed upon to believe Mary's supposition was just; and so much was she piqued at the disbelief which she met with, that she declared she would go to church the next Sunday to shame the hussey, and go up and speak to her in the church-yard before all the people.

'Ah! do so, if you ever saw our miss Mowbray before,' was the answer: and Mary eagerly looked forward to the approaching Sunday. Mean while, as we are all of us but too apt to repeat stories to the prejudice of others, even though we do not believe them, this strange assertion of Mary was circulated through the village even by Adeline's admirers; and the next Sunday was expected by the unconscious Adeline alone with no unusual eagerness.

Sunday came; and Adeline, as she was wont to do, attended the service: but, from the situation of her pew, she could neither see Mary nor be seen by her till church was over. Adeline then, as usual, was walking down the broad walk of the church-yard, surrounded by the parents of the children who came to her school, and receiving from them the customary marks of respect, when Mary, bustling through the crowd, accosted her with—'So!—your sarvant, miss Mowbray, I am glad to see you here in such a respectable situation.'

Adeline, though in the gaily-dressed lady who accosted her she had some difficulty in recognizing her quondam* servant, recollected the pert shrill voice and insolent manner of Mary immediately; and involuntarily starting when she addressed her, from painful associations and fear of impending evil, she replied, 'How are you, Mary?' in a faltering tone.

'Then it is Mary's miss Mowbray,' whispered Mary's auditors of the day before to each other; while Mary, proud of her success, looked triumphantly at them, and was resolved to pursue the advantage which she had gained.

'So you have lost Mr Glenmurray, I find!' continued Mary.

Adeline spoke not, but walked hastily on:—but Mary kept pace with her, speaking as loud as she could.

'And did the little one live, pray?'

Still Adeline spoke not.

'What sort of a getting-up* had you, miss Mowbray?'

At this mischievously-intended question Adeline's other sensations were lost in strong indignation; and resuming all the modest but collected dignity of her manner, she turned round, and, fixing her eyes steadily on the insulting girl, exclaimed aloud, 'Woman, I never injured you either in thought, word or deed:—whence comes it, then, that you endeavour to make the finger of scorn point at me, and make me shrink with shame and confusion from the eye of observation?'

'Woman! indeed!' replied Mary—but she was not allowed to proceed; for a gentleman hastily stepped forward, crying, 'It is impossible for us to suffer such insults to be offered to miss Mowbray;—I desire, therefore, that you will take your daughter away' (turning to Mary's father); 'and, if possible, teach her better manners.' Having said this, he overtook the agitated Adeline; and, offering her his arm, saw her home to her lodgings: while those who had heard with surprise and suspicion the strange and impertinent questions and insolent tone of Mary, resumed in a degree their confidence in Adeline, and turned a disgusted and deaf ear to the hysterical vehemence with which the half-sobbing Mary defended herself, and vilified Adeline, as her father and brother-in-law, almost by force, led her out of the church-yard.

The gentleman who had so kindly stepped forward to the assistance of Adeline was Mr Beauclerc, the surgeon of the village, a man of considerable abilities and liberal principles; and when he bade Adeline farewell, he said, 'My wife will do herself the pleasure of calling on you this evening:' then, kindly pressing her hand, he with a respectful bow took his leave.

Luckily for Adeline, Berrendale was detained in town that day; and she was spared the mortification of showing herself to him, writhing as she then was under the agonies of public shame, for such it seemed to her. Convinced as she then was of the light in which she must have appeared to the persons around her from the malicious interrogatories of Mary;—convinced too, as she was more than beginning to be, of the fallacy of the reasoning which had led her to deserve, and even to glory in, the situation which she now blushed to hear disclosed;—and conscious as she was, that to remain in the village, and expect to retain her school, was now impossible—she gave herself up to a burst of sorrow and despondence; during which her only consolation was, that it was not witnessed by Berrendale.

It never for a moment entered into the ingenuous mind of Adeline, that her declaration would have more weight than that of Mary Warner; and that she might, with almost a certainty of being believed, deny her charge entirely: on the contrary, she had no doubt but that Mrs Beauclerc was coming to inquire into the grounds for Mary's gross address; and she was resolved to confess to her all the circumstances of her story.

After church in the afternoon Mrs Beauclerc arrived, and Adeline observed, with pleasure, that her manner was even kinder than usual; it was such as to ensure the innocent of the most strenuous support, and to invite the guilty to confidence and penitence.

'Never, my dear miss Mowbray,' said Mrs Beauclerc, 'did I call on you with more readiness than now; as I come assured that you will give me not only the most ample authority to contradict, but the fullest means to confute, the vile calumnies which that malicious girl, Mary Warner, has, ever since she entered the village, been propagating against you: but, indeed, she is so little respected in her rank of life, and you so highly in yours, that your mere denial of the truth of her statement will, to every candid mind, be sufficient to clear your character.'

Adeline never before was so strongly tempted to violate the truth;

and there was a friendly earnestness in Mrs Beauclerc's manner, which proved that it would be almost cruel to destroy the opinion which she entertained of her virtue. For a moment Adeline felt disposed to yield to the temptation, but it was only for a moment,— and in a hurried and broken voice she replied, 'Mary Warner has asserted of me nothing but—' Here her voice faltered.

'Nothing but falsehoods, no doubt,' interrupted Mrs Beauclerc triumphantly,—'I thought so.'

'Nothing but the TRUTH!' resumed Adeline.

'Impossible!' cried Mrs Beauclerc, dropping the cold hand which she held: and Adeline, covering her face, and throwing herself back in the chair, sobbed aloud.

Mrs Beauclerc was herself for some time unable to speak; but at length she faintly said—'So sensible, so pious, so well-informed, and so pure-minded as you seem!—to what strange arts, what wicked seductions, did you fall a victim?'

'To no arts—to no seductions'—replied Adeline, recovering all her energy at this insinuation against Glenmurray. 'My fall from virtue, as you would call it, was, I may say, from love of what I thought virtue; and if there be any blame, it attaches merely to my confidence in my lover's wisdom and my own too obstinate self-conceit. But you, dear madam, deserve to hear my whole story; and, if you can favour me with an hour's attention, I hope, at least, to convince you that I was worthy of a better fate than to be publicly disgraced by a malicious and ignorant girl.'

Mrs Beauclerc promised the most patient attention; and Adeline related the eventful history of her life, slightly dwelling on those parts of it which in any degree reflected on her mother, and extolling most highly her sense, her accomplishments, and her maternal tenderness. When she came to the period of Glenmurray's illness and death, she broke abruptly off, and rushed into her own chamber; and it was some minutes before she could return to Mrs Beauclerc, or before her visitor could wish her to return, as she was herself agitated and affected by the relation which she had heard:—and when Adeline came in she threw her arms round her neck, and pressed her to her heart with a feeling of affection that spoke consolation to the wounded spirit of the mourner.

She then resumed her narration;—and, having concluded it, Mrs Beauclerc, seizing her hand, exclaimed, 'For God's sake, marry Mr

Berrendale immediately; and abjure for ever, at the foot of the altar, those errors in opinion to which all your misery has been owing!'

'Would I could atone for them some other way!' she replied.

'Impossible! and if you have any regard for me you will become the wife of your generous lover; for then, and not till then, can I venture to associate with you.'

'I thought so,' cried Adeline; 'I thought all idea of remaining here, with any chance of keeping my scholars, was now impossible.'

'It would not be so,' replied Mrs Beauclerc, 'if every one thought like me: I should consider your example as a warning to all young people; and to preserve my children from evil I should only wish them to hear your story, as it inculcates most powerfully how vain are personal graces, talents, sweetness of temper, and even active benevolence, to ensure respectability and confer happiness, without a strict regard to the long-established rules for conduct, and a continuance in those paths of virtue and decorum which the wisdom of ages has pointed out to the steps of every one.—But others will, no doubt, consider, that continuing to patronise you, would be patronizing vice; and my rank in life is not high enough to enable me to countenance you with any chance of leading others to follow my example; while I should not be able to serve you, but should infallibly lose myself. But some time hence, as the wife of Mr Berrendale, I might receive you as your merits deserve: till then—' Here Mrs Beauclerc paused, and she hesitated to add, 'we meet no more.'

Indeed it was long before the parting took place Mrs Beauclerc had justly appreciated the merits of Adeline, and thought she had found in her a friend and companion for years to come: besides, her children were most fondly attached to her; and Mrs Beauclerc, while she contemplated their daily improvement under her care, felt grateful to Adeline for the unfolding excellencies of her daughters. Still, to part with her was unavoidable; but the pang of separation was in a degree soothed to Adeline by the certainty which Mrs Beauclerc's sorrow gave her, that, spite of her errors, she had inspired a real friendship in the bosom of a truly virtuous and respectable woman; and this idea gave a sensation of joy to her heart to which it had long been a stranger.

The next morning some of the parents, whom Mary's tale had not yet reached, sent their children as usual. But Adeline refused to enter upon any school duties, bidding them affectionately farewell, and telling them that she was going to write to their parents, as she was obliged to leave her present situation, and, declining keeping school, meant to reside, she believed, in London.

The children on hearing this looked at each other with almost tearful consternation; and Adeline observed, with pleasure, the interest which she had made to herself in their young hearts. After they were gone she sent a circular letter to her friends in the village, importing that she was under the necessity of leaving her present residence; but that, whatever her future situation might be, she should always remember, with gratitude, the favours which she had received at ——.

The necessity that drove her away was, by this time, very well understood by every one; but Mrs Beauclerc took care to tell those who mentioned the subject to her, the heads of Adeline's story;* and to add always, 'and I have reason to believe that, as soon as she is settled in town, she will be extremely well married.'

To the mulatto the change in Adeline's plans was particularly pleasing, as it would bring her nearer her son, and nearer William, from whom nothing but a sense of grateful duty to Adeline would so long have divided her. But Savanna imagined that Adeline's removal was owing to her having at last determined to marry Mr Berrendale; an event which she, for Adeline's sake, earnestly wished to take place, though for her own she was undecided whether to desire it or not, as Mr Berrendale might not, perhaps, be as contented with her services as Adeline was.

While these thoughts were passing in Savanna's mind, and her warm and varying feelings were expressed by alternate smiles and tears, Mr Berrendale arrived from town: and as Savanna opened the door to him, she, half whimpering half smiling, dropped him a very respectful curtsey, and looked at him with eyes full of unusual significance.

'Well, Savanna, what has happened?—Any thing new or extraordinary since my absence?' said Berrendale.

'Me tink not of wat have appen, but wat will appen,' replied Savanna.

'And what is going to happen?' returned Berrendale, seating himself in the parlour, 'and where is your mistress?'

'She dress herself, that dear missess,' replied Savanna, lingering with the door in her hand, 'and I,—I ope to ave a dear massa too.'

'What!' cried Berrendale, starting wildly from his seat, 'what did you say?'

'Why, me ope my missess be married soon.'

'Married! to whom?' cried Berrendale, seizing her hand, and almost breathless with alarm.

'Why, to you, sure,' exclaimed Savanna, 'and den me hope you will not turn away poor Savanna!'

'What reason you have, my dear Savanna, for talking thus, I cannot tell; nor dare I give way to the sweet hopes which you excite: but, if it be true that I may hope, depend on it you shall cook my wedding dinner, and then I am sure it will be a good one.'

'Can full joy eat?' asked the mulatto thoughtfully.

'A good dinner is a good thing, Savanna,' replied Berrendale, 'and ought never to be slighted.'

'Me good dinner day I marry, but I not eat it.—O sir, pity people look best in dere wedding clothes, but my William look well all day and every day, and perhaps you will too, sir; and den I ope to cook your wedding dinner, next day dinner, and all your dinners.'

'And so you shall, Savanna,' cried Berrendale, grasping her hand, 'and I—' Here the door opened, and Adeline appeared; who, surprised at Berrendale's familiarity with her servant, looked gravely, and stopped at the door with a look of cold surprise. Berrendale, awed into immediate respect—for what is so timid and respectful as a man truly in love?—bowed low, and lost in an instant all the hopes which had elevated his spirits to such an unusual degree.

Adeline with an air of pique observed, that she feared she interrupted them unpleasantly, as something unusually agreeable and enlivening seemed to occupy them as she came in, over which her entrance seemed to have cast a cloud.

The mulatto had by this time retreated to the door, and was on the point of closing it, when Berrendale stammered out, as well as he could, 'Savanna was, indeed, raising my hopes to such an unexpected height, that I felt almost bewildered with joy; but the coldness of your manner, miss Mowbray, has sobered me again.'

'And what did Savanna say to you?' cried Adeline.

'I—I say,' cried Savanna returning, 'dat is, he say, I should be let cook de wedding dinner.'

Adeline, turning even paler than she was before, desired her coldly to leave the room; and, seating herself at the greatest possible distance from Berrendale, leaned for some time in silence on her hand—he not daring to interrupt her meditations. But at last she said, 'What could give rise to this singular conversation between you and Savanna I am wholly at a loss to imagine: still I—I must own that it is not so ill-timed as it would have been some weeks ago. I will own, that since yesterday I have been considering your generous proposals with the serious attention which they deserve.'

On hearing this, which Adeline uttered with considerable effort, Berrendale in a moment was at her side, and almost at her feet.

'I—I wish you to return to your seat,' said Adeline coldly: but hope had emboldened him, and he chose to stay where he was.

'But, before I require you to renew your promises, or make any on my side, it is proper that I should tell you what passed yesterday; and if the additional load of obloquy which I have acquired does not frighten you from continuing your addresses—' Here Adeline paused:—and Berrendale, rather drawing back, then pushing his chair nearer her as he spoke, gravely answered, that his affection was proof against all trials.

Adeline then briefly related the scene in the church-yard, and her conversation with Mrs Beauclerc, and concluded thus:—'In consequence of this, and of the recollection of HIS advice, and HIS decided opinion, that by becoming the wife of a respectable man, I could alone expect to recover my rank in society, and, consequently, my usefulness, I offer you my hand; and promise, in the course of a few months, to become yours in the sight of God and man.'

'And from no other reason?—from no preference, no regard for me?' demanded Berrendale reproachfully.

'Oh! pardon me; from decided preference; there is not another being in the creation whom I could bear to call husband.'

Berrendale, gratified and surprised, attempted to take her hand; but, withdrawing it, she continued thus:—'Still I almost scruple to let you, unblasted as your prospects are, take to wife a beggar, blasted in reputation, broken in spirits, with a heart whose best affections lie buried in the grave, and which can offer you in return for your faithful tenderness nothing but cold respect and esteem; one too who is not only despicable to others, but also self-condemned.'

While Adeline said this, Berrendale, almost shuddering at the picture which she drew, paced the room in great agitation; and even the gratification of his passion, used as he was to the indulgence of

every wish, seemed, for a moment, a motive not sufficiently powerful
to enable him to unite his fate to that of a woman so degraded as
Adeline appeared to be; and he would, perhaps, have hesitated to
accept the hand she offered, had she not added, as a contrast to the
picture which she had drawn—'But if, in spite of all these
unwelcome considerations, you persist in your resolution of making
me yours, and I have resolution enough to conquer the repugnance
that I feel to make a second connection, you may depend on possessing in me one who will study your happiness and wishes in the
minutest particulars;—one who will cherish you in sickness and in
sorrow;—' (here a twinge of the gout assisted Adeline's appeal very
powerfully;) 'and who, conscious of the generosity of your attachment, and her own unworthiness, will strive, by every possible effort,
not to remain your debtor even in affection.'

Saying this, she put out her hand to Berrendale; and that hand,
and the arm belonging to it, were so beautiful, and he had so often
envied Glenmurray while he saw them tenderly supporting his head,
that while a vision of approaching gout, and Adeline bending over
his restless couch, floated before him, all his prudent considerations
vanished; and, eagerly pressing the proffered hand to his lips, he
thanked her most ardently for her kind promise; and, putting his
arm round her waist, would have pressed her to his bosom.

But the familiarity was ill-timed;—Adeline was already surprised,
and even shocked, at the lengths which she had gone; and starting
almost with loathing from his embrace, she told him it grew late, and
it was time for him to go to his lodgings. She then retired to her own
room, and spent half the night at least in weeping over the remembrance of Glenmurray, and in loudly apostrophizing his departed
spirit.

The next day Adeline, out of the money which she had earned,
discharged her lodgings; and having written a farewell note to Mrs
Beauclerc, begging to hear of her now and then, she and the mulatto
proceeded to town, with Berrendale, in search of apartments; and
having procured them, Adeline began to consider by what means, till
she could resolve to marry Berrendale, she should help to maintain
herself, and also contrive to increase their income if she became his
wife.

The success which she had met with in instructing children, led
her to believe that she might succeed in writing little hymns and tales

for their benefit; a method of getting money which she looked upon to be more rapid and more lucrative than working plain or fancy works:*—and, in a short time, a little volume was ready to be offered to a bookseller;*—nor was it offered in vain. Glenmurray's bookseller accepted it; and the sum which he gave, though trifling, imparted a balsam to the wounded mind of Adeline: it seemed to open to her the path of independence; and to give her, in spite of her past errors, the means of serving her fellow-creatures.

But month after month elapsed, and Glenmurray had been dead two years, yet still Adeline could not prevail on herself to fix a time for her marriage.

But next to the aversion she felt to marrying at all, was that she experienced at the idea of having no fortune to bestow on the disinterested Berrendale; and so desirous was she of his acquiring some little property by his union with her, that she resolved to ask counsel's opinion on the possibility of her claiming a sum of money which Glenmurray had bequeathed her, but without, as Berrendale had assured her, the customary formalities.

The money was near 300*l.*; but Berrendale had allowed it to go to Glenmurray's legal heir, because he was sure that the writing which bequeathed it would not hold good in law. Still Adeline was so unwilling to be under so many pecuniary obligations to a man whom she did not love, that she resolved to take advice on the subject, much against the will of Berrendale, who thought the money might as well be saved; but as a chance for saving the fee he resolved to let Adeline go to the lawyer's chambers alone, thinking it likely that no fee would be accepted from so fine a woman. Accordingly, more alive to œconomy than to delicacy or decorum, Berrendale, when Adeline, desiring a coach to be called, summoned him to accompany her to the Temple,* pleaded terror of an impending fit of the gout, and begged her to excuse his attendance; and Adeline, unsuspicious of the real cause of his refusal, kindly expressing her sorrow for the one he feigned, took the counsellor's address, and got into the coach, Berrendale taking care to tell her, as she got in, that the fare was but a shilling.

The gentleman, Mr Langley, to whom Adeline was going, was celebrated for his abilities as a chamber counsellor, and no less remarkable for his gallantries: but Berrendale was not acquainted with this part of his history; else he would not, even to save a lawyer's fee, have exposed his intended wife to a situation of such extreme impropriety; and Adeline was too much a stranger to the rules of general society, to feel any great repugnance to go alone on an errand so interesting to her feelings.

The coach having stopped near the entrance of the court to which she was directed, Adeline, resolving to walk home, discharged the coach, and knocked at the door of Mr Langley's chambers. A very smart servant out of livery answered the knock; and Mr Langley being at home, Adeline was introduced into his apartment.

Mr Langley, though surprised at seeing a lady of a deportment so correct and of so dignified an appearance enter his room unattended, was inspired with so much respect at sight of Adeline, whose mourning habit added to the interest which her countenance never failed to excite, that he received her with bows down to the ground, and leading her to a chair, begged she would do him the honour to be seated, and impart her commands.

Adeline embarrassed, she scarcely knew why, at the novelty of her situation, drew the paper from her pocket, and presented it to him.

'Mr Berrendale recommended me to you, sir,' said Adeline faintly.

'Berrendale, Berrendale, O, aye,—I remember—the cousin of Mr Glenmurray: you know Mr Glenmurray too, ma'am, I presume; pray how is he?'—Adeline, unprepared for this question, could not speak; and the voluble counsellor went on—'Oh!—I ask your pardon, madam, I see;—pray, might I presume so far, how long has that extraordinarily clever man been lost to the world?'

'More than two years, sir,' replied Adeline faintly.

'You are,—may I presume so far,—you are his widow?'—Adeline bowed. There was a something in Mr Langley's manner and look so like sir Patrick's, that she could not bear to let him know she was only Glenmurray's mistress.

'Gone more than two years, and you still in deep mourning!— Amiable susceptibility!—How unlike the wives of the present day! But I beg pardon.—Now to business.' So saying, he perused the paper which Adeline had given him, in which Glenmurray simply stated, that he bequeathed to Adeline Mowbray the sum of 260*l.* in the 5 per cents,* but it was signed by only one witness.

'What do you wish to know, madam?' asked the counsellor.

'Whether this will be valid, as it is not signed by two witnesses, sir?'

'Why,—really not,' replied Langley; 'though the heir at law, if he have either equity or gallantry, could certainly not refuse to fulfil what evidently was the intention of the testator:—but then, it is very surprising to me that Mr Glenmurray should have wished to leave any thing from the lady whom I have the honour to behold. Pray, madam,—if I may presume to ask,—Who is Adeline Mowbray?'

'I—I am Adeline Mowbray,' replied Adeline in great confusion.

'You, madam! Bless me, I presumed;—and pray, madam,—if I may make so bold,—what was your relationship to that wonderfully clever man?—his niece,—his cousin,—or—?'

'I was no relation of his,' said Adeline still more confused; and this confusion confirmed the suspicions which Langley entertained, and also brought to his recollection something which he had heard of Glenmurray's having a very elegant and accomplished mistress.

'Pardon me, dear madam,' said Mr Langley, 'I perceive now my mistake; and I now perceive why Mr Glenmurray was so much the envy of those who had the honour of visiting at his house. 'Pon my soul,' taking her hand, which Adeline indignantly withdrew, 'I am grieved beyond words at being unable to give you a more favourable opinion.'

'But you said, sir,' said Adeline, 'that the heir at law, if he had any equity, would certainly be guided by the evident intention of the testator.'

'I did, madam,' replied the lawyer, evidently piqued by the proud and cold air which Adeline assumed;—'but then,—excuse me,—the applicant would not stand much chance of being attended to, who is neither the *widow* nor *relation* of Mr Glenmurray.'

'I understand you, sir,' replied Adeline, 'and need trouble you no longer.'

'Trouble! my sweet girl!' returned Mr Langley, 'call it not trouble; I—' Here his gallant effusions were interrupted by the sudden entrance of a very showy woman, highly rouged, and dressed in the extremity of the fashion; and who in no very pleasant tone of voice exclaimed,—'I fear I interrupt you.'

'Oh! not in the least,' replied Langley, blushing even more than Adeline, 'my fair client was just going. Allow me, madam, to see you to the door,' continued he, attempting to take Adeline's hand, and accompanying her to the bottom of the first flight of stairs.

'Charming fine woman upon my soul!' cried he, speaking through his shut teeth, and forcibly squeezing her fingers as he spoke; 'and if you ever want advice I should be proud to see you here; at present I am particularly engaged,' (with a significant smile;) 'but—' Here Adeline, too angry to speak, put the fee in his hand, which he insisted on returning, and, in the struggle, he forcibly kissed the ungloved hand which was held out, praising its beauty at the same time, and endeavouring to close her fingers on the money: but Adeline indignantly threw it on the ground, and rushed down the remaining staircase; over-hearing the lady, as she did so, exclaim, 'Langley! is not that black mawkin* gone yet? Come up this moment, you devil!' while Langley obsequiously replied, 'Coming this moment, my angel!'

Adeline felt so disappointed, so ashamed, and so degraded, that she walked on some way without knowing whither she was going; and when she recollected herself, she found that she was wandering from court to court, and unable to find the avenue to the street down which the coach had come: while her very tall figure, heightened colour, and graceful carriage, made her an object of attention to every one whom she met.

At last she saw herself followed by two young men; and as she walked very fast to avoid them, she by accident turned into the very lane which she had been seeking: but her pursuers kept pace with her; and she over-heard one of them say to the other, 'A devilish fine girl! moves well too,—I cannot help thinking that I have seen her before.'

'And so do I.—O zounds! by her height, it must be that sweet creature who lived at Richmond with that crazy fellow, Glenmurray.'

Here Adeline relaxed in her pace: the name of Glenmurray—that name which no one since his death had ventured to pronounce in her presence,—had, during the last half-hour, been pronounced several times; and, unable to support herself from a variety of emotions, she stopped, and leaned for support against the wall.

'How do you do, my fleet and sweet girl?' said one of the gentle-men, patting her on the back as he spoke:—and Adeline, roused at the insult, looked at him proudly and angrily, and walked on. 'What! angry! If I may be so bold,' (with a sneering smile,) 'fair creature, may I ask where you live now?'

'No, sir,' replied Adeline; 'you are wholly unknown to me.'

'But were you to tell me where you live, we might cease to be strangers; but, perhaps your favours are all bespoken.—Pray who is your friend now?'

'Oh! I have but few friends,' cried Adeline mournfully.

'Few! the devil!' replied the young templar;* 'and how many would you have?' Here he put his arm round her waist: and his companion giving way to a loud fit of laughter, Adeline clearly understood what he meant by the term 'friend'; and summoning up all her spirit, she called a coach which luckily was passing; and, turning round to her tormentor, with great dignity said,—'Though the situation, sir, in which I once was, may, in the eyes of the world and in yours, authorize and excuse your present insulting address, yet, when I tell you that I am on the eve of marriage with a most respectable man, I trust that you will feel the impropriety of your conduct, and be convinced of the fruitlessness and impertinence of the questions which you have put to me.'

'If this be the case, madam,' cried the gentleman, 'I beg your pardon, and shall take my leave, wishing you all possible happiness, and begging you to attribute my impertinence wholly to my ignorance.' So saying, he bowed and left her, and Adeline was driven to her lodgings.

'Now,' said Adeline, 'the die is cast;—I have used the sacred name of wife to shield me from insult; and I am therefore pledged to assume it directly. Yes, HE was right—I find I must have a legal protector.'

She found Berrendale rather alarmed at her long absence; and, with a beating heart, she related her adventures to him: but when she said that Langley was not willing to take the fee, he exclaimed, 'Very genteel in him, indeed! I suppose you took him at his word?'

'Good Heavens!' replied Adeline, 'Do you think I would deign to owe such a man a pecuniary obligation?—No, indeed; I threw it with proud indignation on the floor.'

'What madness!' returned Berrendale: 'you had much better have put it in your pocket.'

'Mr Berrendale,' cried Adeline gravely, and with a look bordering on contempt, 'I trust that you are not in earnest: for if these are your sentiments,—if this is your delicacy, sir—'

'Say no more, dearest of women,' replied Berrendale pretending to laugh, alarmed at the seriousness with which she spoke: 'how could you for one moment suppose me in earnest? Insolent coxcomb!—I wish I had been there.'

'I wish you had,' said Adeline, 'for then no one would have dared to insult me:' and Berrendale, delighted at this observation, listened to the rest of her story with a spirit of indignant knight-errantry which he never experienced before; and at the end of her narration he felt supremely happy; for Adeline assured him that the next week she would make him her protector for life:—and this assurance opened his heart so much, that he vowed he would not condescend to claim of the heir at law the pitiful sum which he might think proper to withhold.

To be brief.—Adeline kept her word; and resolutely struggling with her feelings, she became the next week the wife of Berrendale.

For the first six months the union promised well. Adeline was so assiduous to anticipate her husband's wishes, and contrived so many dainties for his table, which she cooked with her own hands, that Berrendale, declaring himself completely happy for the first time in his life, had not a thought or a wish beyond his own fire-side; while Adeline, happy because she conferred happiness, and proud of the name of wife, which she had before despised, began to hope that her days would glide on in humble tranquillity.

It was natural enough that Adeline should be desirous of imparting this change in her situation to Mrs Pemberton, whose esteem she was eager to recover, and whose kind intentions towards her, at a moment when she was incapable of appreciating them, Savanna had, with great feeling, expatiated upon. She therefore wrote to her according to the address which Mrs Pemberton had left for her, and received a most friendly letter in return. In a short time Adeline had again an expectation of being a mother; and though she could not yet entertain for her husband more than cold esteem, she felt that as the father of her child he would insensibly become more dear to her.

But Berrendale awoke from his dream of bliss, on finding to what a large sum the bills for the half-year's house-keeping amounted. Nor was he surprised without reason. Adeline, more eager to gratify Berrendale's palate than considerate as to the means, had forgotten that she was no longer at the head of a liberal establishment like her mother's, and had bought for the supply of the table many expensive articles.

In consequence of this terrible discovery Berrendale remonstrated very seriously with Adeline; who meekly answered, 'My dear friend, good dinners cannot be had without good ingredients, and good ingredients cannot be had without money.'

'But, madam,' cried Berrendale, knitting his brows, but not elevating his voice, for he was one of those soft-speaking beings who in the sweetest tones possible can say the most heart-wounding things, and give a mortal stab to your self-love in the same gentle manner in which they flatter it:—'there must have been great waste, great mismanagement here, or these expenses could not have been incurred.'

'There may have been both,' returned Adeline, 'for I have not been used to œconomize, but I will try to learn;—but, I doubt, my dear Berrendale, you must endeavour to be contented with plainer food; for not all the œconomy in the world can make rich gravies and high sauces cheap things.'

'Oh! care and skill can do much,' said Berrendale;—'and I find a certain person deceived me very much when he said you were a good manager.'

'He only said', replied Adeline sighing deeply, 'that I was a good cook, and you yourself allow that: but I hope in time to please your appetite at less expense: as to myself, a little suffices me, and I care not how plain that food is.'

'Still, I think I have seen you eat with a most excellent appetite,' said Berrendale, with a very significant expression.

Adeline, shocked at the manner more than at the words, replied in a faltering voice, 'As a proof of my being in health, no doubt you rejoiced in the sight.'

'Certainly; but less robust health would suit our finances better.'

Adeline looked up, wishing, though not expecting, to see by his face that he was joking: but such serious displeasure appeared on it, that the sordid selfishness of his character was at once unveiled to her view; and clasping her hands in agony, she exclaimed, 'Oh, Glenmurray!' and ran into her own room.

It was the first time that she had pronounced his name since the hour of his death, and now it was wrung from her by a sensation of acute anguish; no wonder, then, that the feelings which followed completely overcame her, and that Berrendale had undisputed and solitary possession of his supper.

But he, on his side, was deeply irritated. The 'Oh, Glenmurray!' was capable of being interpreted two ways:—either it showed how much she regretted Glenmurray, and preferred him to his successor in spite of the superior beauty of his person, of which he was very vain; or it reproached Glenmurray for having recommended her to marry him. In either case it was an unpardonable fault; and this unhappy conversation laid the foundation of future discontent.

Adeline rose the next day dejected, pensive, and resolved that her appetite should never again, if possible, force a reproach from the lips of her husband. She therefore took care that whatever she provided for the table, besides the simplest fare, should be for Berrendale alone; and she flattered herself that he would be shamed into repentance of what he had observed, by seeing her scrupulous self-denial:—she even resolved, if he pressed her to partake of his dainties, that she would, to show that she forgave him, accept what he offered.

But Berrendale gave her no such opportunity of showing her generosity;—busy in the gratification of his own appetite, he never observed whether any other persons ate or not, except when by eating they curtailed his share of good things:—besides, to have an exclusive dish to himself was to him *tout simple;** he had been a pampered child; and being no advocate for the equality of the sexes, he thought it only a matter of course that he should fare better than his wife.

Adeline, though more surprised and more shocked than ever, could not help laughing internally, at her not being able to put her projected generosity in practice; but her laughter and indignation soon yielding to contempt, she ate her simple meal in silence: and while her pampered husband sought to lose the fumes of indigestion in sleep, she blessed God that temperance, industry and health went hand in hand; and, retiring to her own room, sat down to write, in order to increase, if possible, her means of living, and consequently her power of being generous to others.

But though Adeline resolved to forget, if possible, the petty conduct of Berrendale,—the mulatto, who, from the door's being open, had heard every word of the conversation which had so disturbed Adeline, neither could nor would forget it; and though she did not vow eternal hatred to her master, she felt herself very capable of indulging it, and from that moment it was her resolution to thwart him.

Whenever he was present she was always urging Adeline to eat some refreshments between meals, and drink wine or lemonade, and tempting her weak appetite with some pleasant but expensive sweetmeats. In vain did Adeline refuse them; sometimes they were bought, sometimes only threatened to be bought; and once when Adeline had accepted some, rather than mortify Savanna by a refusal, and Berrendale, by his accent and expression, showed how much he grudged the supposed expense,—the mulatto, snapping her fingers in his face, and looking at him with an expression of indignant contempt, exclaimed, 'I buy dem, and pay for dem wid mine nown money; and my angel lady sall no be oblige to you!'

This was a declaration of war against Berrendale, which Adeline heard with anger and sorrow, and her husband with rage. In vain did Adeline promise that she would seriously reprove Savanna (who had disappeared) for her impertinence; Berrendale insisted on her being discharged immediately; and nothing but Adeline's assurances that she, for slender wages, did more work than two other servants would do for enormous ones, could pacify his displeasure: but at length he was appeased. And as Berrendale, from a principle of œconomy, resumed his old habit of dining out amongst his friends, getting good dinners by that means without paying for them, family expenses ceased to disturb the quiet of their marriage; and after she had been ten months a wife Adeline gave birth to a daughter.

That moment, the moment when she heard her infant's first cry, seemed to repay her for all she had suffered; every feeling was lost in the maternal one; and she almost fancied that she loved, fondly loved, the father of her child: but this idea vanished when she saw the languid pleasure, if pleasure it could be called, with which Berrendale congratulated her on her pain and danger being passed, and received his child in his arms.

The mulatto was wild with joy: she almost stifled the babe with her kisses, and talked even the next day of sending for the tawny boy to come and see his new mistress, and vow to her, as he had done to her mother, eternal fealty and allegiance.

But Adeline saw on Berrendale's countenance a mixed expression,—and he had mixed feelings. True, he rejoiced in Adeline's safety; but he said within himself, 'Children are expensive things, and we may have a large family;' and, leaving the bed-side as soon as he could, he retired, to endeavour to lose in an afternoon's nap his unpleasant reflections.

'How different', thought Adeline, 'would have been HIS feelings and HIS expressions of them at such a time! Oh!—' but the name of Glenmurray died away on her lips; and hastily turning to gaze on her sleeping babe, she tried to forget the disappointed emotions of the wife in the gratified feelings of the mother.

Still Adeline, who had been used to attentions, could not but feel the neglect of Berrendale. Even while she kept her room he passed only a few hours in her society, but dined out; and when she was well enough to have accompanied him on his visits, she found that he never even wished her to go with him, though the friends whom he visited were married; and he met, from his own confession, other ladies at their tables. She therefore began to suspect that Berrendale did not mean to introduce her as his wife; nay, she doubted whether he avowed her to be such; and at last she brought him to own that, ashamed of having married what the world must consider as a kept mistress, he resolved to keep her still in the retirement to which she was habituated.

This was a severe disappointment indeed to Adeline: she longed for the society of the amiable and accomplished of her own sex; and hoped that, as Mr Berrendale's wife, that intercourse with her own sex might be restored to her which she had forfeited as the mistress of Glenmurray. Nor could she help reproaching Berrendale for the selfish ease and indifference with which he saw her deprived of those social enjoyments which he daily enjoyed himself, convinced as she was that he might, if he chose, have introduced her at least to his intimate friends.

But she pleaded and reasoned in vain. Contented with the access which he had to the tables of his friends, it was of little importance to him that his wife ate her humble meal alone. His habits of enjoyment had ever been solitary: the pampered school-boy, who had at school eaten his tart and cake by stealth in a corner, that he might not be asked to share them with another, had grown up with the same dispositions to manhood: and as his parents, though opulent, were vulgar in their manners and low in their origin, he had never been taught those graceful self-denials inculcated into the children of polished life, which, though taught from factitious and not real benevolence, have certainly a tendency, by long habit, to make that benevolence real which at first was only artificial.

Adeline had both sorts of kindness and affection, those untaught of the heart, and those of education;—she was polite from the situation into which the accident of birth had thrown her, and also from the generous impulse of her nature. To her, therefore, the uncultivated and unblushing *personnalité*,* as the French call it, of Berrendale, was a source of constant wonder and distress: and often, very often did she feel the utmost surprise at Berrendale's having appeared to Glenmurray a man likely to make her happy. Often did she wonder how the defects of Berrendale's character could have escaped his penetrating eyes.

Adeline forgot that the faults of her husband were such as could be known only by an intimate connection, and which cohabitation could alone call forth;*—faults, the existence of which such a man as Glenmurray, who never considered himself in any transaction whatever, could not suppose possible;—and which, though they inflicted the most bitter pangs on Adeline, and gradually untwisted the slender thread which had begun to unite her heart with Berrendale's, were of so slight a fabric as almost to elude the touch, and of a nature to appear almost too trivial to be mentioned in the narration of a biographer.

But though it has been long said that trifles make the sum of human things, inattention to trifles continues to be the vice of every one; and many a conjugal union which has never been assailed by the battery of crime, has fallen a victim to the slowly undermining power of petty quarrels, trivial unkindnesses and thoughtless neglect;—like the gallant officer, who, after escaping unhurt all the rage of battle by land and water, tempest on sea and earthquake on shore, returns perhaps to his native country, and perishes by the power of a slow fever.

But Adeline, who, amidst all the chimæras of her fancy and singularities of her opinions, had happily held fast her religion, began at this moment to entertain a belief that soothed in some measure the sorrows which it could not cure. She fancied that all the sufferings she underwent were trials which she was doomed to undergo, as punishments for the crime she had committed in leaving her mother and living with Glenmurray; and as expiations also. She therefore welcomed her afflictions, and lifted up her meek eyes to heaven in every hour of her trials, with the look of tearful but grateful resignation.

Meanwhile her child, whom, after her mother, she called Editha, was nursed at her own bosom, and thrived even beyond her expectations. Even Berrendale beheld its growing beauty with delight, and the mulatto was wild in praise of it; while Adeline, wholly taken up all day in nursing and in working for it, and every evening in writing stories and hymns to publish, which would, she hoped, one day be useful to her own child as well as to the children of others, soon ceased to regret her seclusion from society; and by the time Editha was a year old she had learnt to bear with patience the disappointment she had experienced in Berrendale. Soon after she became a mother she again wrote to Mrs Pemberton, as she longed to impart to her sympathizing bosom those feelings of parental delight which Berrendale could not understand, and the expression of which he witnessed with contemptuous and chilling gravity. To this letter she anticipated a most gratifying return; but month after month passed away, and no letter from Lisbon arrived. 'No doubt my letter miscarried,' said Adeline to Savanna, 'and I will write again:' but she never had resolution to do so; for she felt that her prospects of conjugal happiness were obscured, and she shrunk equally from the task of expressing the comfort which she did not feel, or unveiling to another the errors of her husband. The little regard, mean while, which she had endeavoured to return for Berrendale soon vanished, being unable to withstand a new violence offered to it.

Editha was seized with the hooping-cough: and as Adeline had sold her last little volume to advantage, Berrendale allowed her to take a lodging at a short distance from town, as change of air was good for the complaint.* She did so, and remained there two months. At her return she had the mortification to find that her husband, during her absence, had intrigued with the servant of the house:—a circumstance of which she would probably have remained ignorant, but for the indiscreet affection of Savanna, who, in the first transports of her indignation on discovering the connection, had been unable to conceal from her mistress what drove her almost frantic with indignation.

But Adeline, though she felt disgust and aversion swallowing up the few remaining sparks of regard for Berrendale which she felt, had one great consolation under this new calamity.—Berrendale had not been the choice of her heart: 'But, thank God! I never loved this man,' escaped her lips as she ran into her own room; and pressing her child to her bosom, she shed on its unconscious cheeks the tears which resentment and a deep sense of injury wrung from her. — 'Oh! had I loved him,' she exclaimed, 'this blow would have been mortal!'

She, however, found herself in one respect the better for Berrendale's guilt. Conscious that the mulatto was aware of what had passed, and afraid lest she should have mentioned her discovery to Adeline, Berrendale endeavoured to make amends for his infidelity by attention such as he had never shown her since the first weeks of his marriage: and had she not been aware of the motive, the change in his behaviour would have re-awakened her tenderness. However, it claimed at least complaisance and gentleness from her while it lasted: which was not long; for Berrendale, fancying from the apparent tranquillity of Adeline (the result of indifference, not ignorance) that she was not informed of his fault, and that the mulatto was too prudent to betray him, began to relapse into his old habits; and one day, forgetting his assumed liberality, he ventured, when alone with Savanna, who was airing one of Editha's caps, to expatiate on the needless extravagance of his wife in trimming her child's caps with lace.

This was enough to rouse the quick feelings of the mulatto, and she poured forth all her long concealed wrath in a torrent of broken English, but plain enough to be well understood. — 'You man!' she cried at last, 'you will kill her; she pine at your no kindness; — and if she die, mind me, man! never you marry aden. — You marry, forsoot! you marry a lady! true bred lady like mine! No, man! — You best get a cheap miss from de street and be content —'

As she said this, and in an accent so provoking that Berrendale was pale and speechless with rage, Adeline entered the room; and Savanna, self-condemned already for what she had uttered, was terrified when Adeline, in a tone of voice unusually severe, said, 'Leave the room; you have offended me past forgiveness.'

These words, in a great measure, softened the angry feelings of Berrendale, as they proved that Adeline resented the insult offered to him as deeply as he could wish; and with some calmness he exclaimed, 'Then I conclude, Mrs Berrendale, that you will have no objection to discharge your mulatto directly.'

This conclusion, though a very natural one, was both a shock and a surprise to Adeline; nor could she at first reply.

'You are *silent*, madam,' said Berrendale; 'what is your answer? Yes, or No?'

'Ye,—yes,—certainly,' faltered out Adeline; 'she—she ought to go—I mean that she has used very improper language to you.'

'And, therefore, a wife who resents as she ought to do, injuries offered to her husband, cannot hesitate for a moment to discharge her.'

'True, very true in some measure,' replied Adeline; 'but—'

'But what?' demanded Berrendale.

'O Berrendale!' cried Adeline, bursting into an agony of frantic sorrow, 'if she leaves me what will become of me! I shall lose the only person now in the world, perhaps, who loves me with sincere and faithful affection!'

Berrendale was wholly unprepared for an appeal like this; and, speechless from surprise not unmixed with confusion, staggered into the next chair. He was conscious, indeed, that his fidelity to his wife had not been proof against a few weeks' absence; but then, being, like most men, not over delicate in his ideas on such subjects, as soon as Adeline returned he had given up the connection which he had formed, and therefore he thought she had not much reason to complain. In all other respects he was sure that he was an exemplary husband, and she had no just grounds for doubting his affection. He was sure that she had no reason to accuse him of unkindness; and, unless she wished him to be always tied to her apron-string, he was certain he had never omitted to pay her all proper attention.

Alas! he felt not the many wounds he had inflicted by

> The word whose meaning kills; yet, told,
> The speaker wonders that you thought it cold:*

and he had yet to learn, that in order to excite or testify affection, it is necessary to seem to derive exclusive enjoyment from the society of the object avowed to be beloved, and to seek its gratification in preference to one's own, even in the most trivial things. He knew not that opportunities of conferring large benefits, like bank bills for 1000*l.*, rarely come into use; but little attentions, friendly participations and kindnesses, are wanted daily, and, like small change, are necessary to carry on the business of life and happiness.

A minute, more perhaps, elapsed, before Berrendale recovered himself sufficiently to speak; and the silence was made still more awful to Adeline, by her hearing from the adjoining room the sobs of the mulatto. At length, 'I cannot find words to express my surprise at what you have just uttered,' exclaimed Berrendale. 'My conscience does not reproach me with deserving the reproof it contained.'

'Indeed!' replied Adeline, fixing her penetrating eyes on his which shrunk downcast and abashed from her gaze. Adeline saw her advantage, and pursued it. 'Mr Berrendale,' continued she, 'it is indeed true, that the mulatto has offended both of us; for in offending *you* she has offended *me*; but, have you committed no fault, nothing for *me* to forgive? I know that you are too great a lover of truth, too honourable a man, to declare that you have not deserved the just anger of your wife: but you know that I have never reproached you, nor should you ever have been aware that I was privy to the distressing circumstance to which I allude, but for what has just passed: and, now, do but forgive the poor mulatto, who sinned only from regard for me, and from supposed slight offered to her mistress, and I will not only assure you of my forgiveness, but, from this moment, will strenuously endeavour to blot from my remembrance every trace of what has passed.'

Berrendale, conscious and self-condemned, scarcely knew what to answer; but, thinking that it was better to accept Adeline's offer even on her own conditions, he said, that if Savanna would make a proper apology, and Adeline would convince her that she was seriously displeased with her, he would allow her to stay; and Adeline having promised every thing which he asked, peace was again restored.

'But what can you mean, Adeline,' said Berrendale, 'by doubting my affection? I think I gave a sufficient proof of that, when, disregarding the opinion of the world, I married you, though you had been the mistress of another: and I really think that, by accusing me of unkindness, you make me a very ungrateful return.' To this indelicate and unfeeling remark Adeline vainly endeavoured to reply; but, starting from her chair, she paced the room in violent agitation.—'Answer me,' continued Berrendale, 'name one instance in which I have been unkind to you.' Adeline suddenly stopped, and, looking steadfastly at him, smiled with a sort of contemptuous pity, and was on the point of saying, 'Is not what you have now said an instance of unkindness?' But she saw that the same want of delicacy, and of that fine moral *tact* which led him to commit this and similar assaults on her feelings, made him unconscious of the violence which he offered.

Finding, therefore, that he could not understand her causes of complaint, even if it were possible for her to define them, she replied, 'Well, perhaps I was too hasty, and in a degree unjust: so let us drop the subject; and, indeed, my dear Berrendale, you must bear with my weakness: remember, I have always been a spoiled child.'

Here the image of Glenmurray and that of *home*, the home which she once knew, the home of her childhood, and of her *earliest* youth, pressed on her recollection. She thought of her mother, of the indulgences which she had once known, of the advantages of opulence, the value of which she had never felt till deprived of them; and, struck with the comparative forlornness of her situation—united for life to a being whose sluggish sensibilities could not understand, and consequently not sooth, the quick feelings and jealous susceptibility of her nature—she could hardly forbear falling at the feet of her husband, and conjuring him to behave, at least, with forbearance to her, and to speak and look at her with kindness.

She did stretch out her hand to him with a look of mournful entreaty, which, though not understood by Berrendale, was not lost upon him entirely. He thought it was a confession of her weakness and his superiority; and, flattered by the thought into unusual softness, he caught her fondly to his bosom, and gave up an engagement to sup at an oyster club, in order to spend the evening tête-à-tête with his wife. Nay, he allowed the little Editha to remain in the room for a whole hour, though she cried when he attempted to take her in his arms, and, observing that it was a cold evening, allowed Adeline her due share of the fire-side.

These circumstances, trivial as they were, had more than their due effect on Adeline, whose heart was more alive to kindness than unkindness; and those paltry attentions of which happy wives would not have been conscious, were to her a source of unfeigned pleasure—As sailors are grateful, after a voyage unexpectedly long, for the muddy water which at their first embarking they would have turned from with disgust.

That very night Adeline remonstrated with the mulatto on the impropriety of her conduct; and, having convinced her that in insulting her husband she failed in respect to her, Savanna was prevailed upon the next morning to ask pardon of Berrendale; and, out of love for her mistress, she took care in future to do nothing that required forgiveness.

As Adeline's way of life admitted of but little variety, Berrendale having persisted in not introducing her to his friends, on the plea of not being rich enough to receive company in return, I shall pass over in silence what occurred to her till Editha was two years old; premising that a series of little injuries on the part of Berrendale, and a quick resentment of them on the part of Adeline, which not even her habitual good humour could prevent, had, during that time, nearly eradicated every trace of love for each other from their hearts.

One evening Adeline as usual, in the absence of her husband, undressed Editha by the parlour fire, and, playing with the laughing child, was enjoying the rapturous praises which Savanna put forth of its growing beauty; while the tawny boy, who had spent the day with them, built houses with cards on the table, which Editha threw down as soon as they were built, and he with good-humoured perseverance raised up again.

Adeline, alive only to the maternal feeling, at this moment had forgotten all her cares; she saw nothing but the happy group around her, and her countenance wore the expression of recovered serenity.

At this moment a loud knock was heard at the door, and Adeline, starting up, exclaimed, 'It is my husband's knock!'

'O! no:—he never come so soon,' replied the mulatto running to the door; but she was mistaken—it was Berrendale: and Adeline, hearing his voice, began instantly to snatch up Editha's clothes, and to knock down the tawny boy's newly-raised edifice: but order was not restored when Berrendale entered; and, with a look and tone of impatience, he said, 'So! fine confusion indeed! Here's a fire-side to come to! Pretty amusement too, for a literary lady—building houses of cards! Shame on your extravagance, Mrs Berrendale, to let that brat spoil cards in that way!'

The sunshine of Adeline's countenance on hearing this vanished: to be sure, she was accustomed to such speeches; but the moment before she had felt happy, for the first time, perhaps, for years. She, however, replied not: but, hurrying Editha to bed, ordering the reluctant tawny boy into the kitchen, and setting Berrendale's chair, as usual, in the warmest place, she ventured in a faint voice to ask, what had brought him home so early.

'More early than welcome,' replied Berrendale, 'if I may judge from the bustle I have occasioned.'

'It is very true', replied Adeline, 'that, had I expected you, I should have been better prepared for your reception; and then you, perhaps, would have spoken more kindly to me.'

'There—there you go again.—If I say but a word to you, then I am called unkind, though, God knows, I never speak without just provocation: and, I declare, I came home in the best humour possible, to tell you what may turn out of great benefit to us both:— but when a man has an uncomfortable home to come to, it is enough to put him out of humour.'

The mulatto, who was staying to gather up the cards which had fallen, turned herself round on hearing this, and exclaimed, 'Home was very comfortable till you come;' and then with a look of the most angry contempt she left the room, and threw the door to with great violence.

'But what is this good news, my dear?' said Adeline, eager to turn Berrendale's attention from Savanna's insolent reply.

'I have received a letter,' he replied, 'which, by the by, I ought to have had some weeks ago, from my father-in-law in Jamaica, author- izing me to draw on his banker for 900*l.*, and inviting me to come over to him; as he feels himself declining, and wishes to give me the care of his estate, and of my son, to whom all his fortune will descend; and of whose interest, he properly thinks, no one can be so likely to take good care as his own father.'

'And do you mean that I and Editha should go with you?' said Adeline turning pale.

'No, to be sure not,' eagerly replied Berrendale; 'I must first see how the land lies. But if I go—as the old man no doubt will make a handsome settlement on me—I shall be able to remit you a very respectable annuity.'

Adeline's heart, spite of herself, bounded with joy at this discovery; but she had resolution to add,—and if duplicity can ever be pardonable, this was,—'So then the good news which you had to impart to me was, that we were going to be separated!' But as she said this, the consciousness that she was artfully trying to impress Berrendale with an idea of her feeling a sorrow which was foreign to her heart, overcame her; and affected also at being under the necessity of rejoicing at the departure of that being who ought to be the source of her comfort, she vainly struggled to regain composure, and burst into an agony of tears.

But her consternation cannot be expressed, when she found that Berrendale imputed her tears to tender anguish at the idea of parting with him: and when, his vanity being delighted by this homage to his attractions, he felt all his fondness for her revive, and, overwhelming her with caresses, he declared that he would reject the offer entirely if by accepting it he should give her a moment's uneasiness; Adeline, shocked at his error, yet not daring to set him right, could only weep on his shoulder in silence: but, in order to make real the distress which he only fancied so, she enumerated to herself all the diseases incident to the climate, and the danger of the voyage. Still the idea of Berrendale's departure was so full of comfort to her, that, though her tears continued to flow, they flowed not for his approaching absence. At length, ashamed of fortifying him in so gross an error, she made an effort to regain her calmness, and found words to assure him, that she would no longer give way to such unpardonable weakness, as she could assure him that she wished his acceptance of his father-in-law's offer, and had no desire to oppose a scheme so just and so profitable.

But Berrendale, to whose vanity she had never before offered such a tribute as her tears seemed to be, imputed these assurances to disinterested love and female delicacy, afraid to own the fondness which it felt; and the rest of the evening was spent in professions of love on his part, which, on Adeline's, called forth at least some grateful and kind expressions in return.

Still, however, she persisted in urging Berrendale to go to Jamaica: but, at the same time, she earnestly begged him to remember, that temperance could alone preserve his health in such a climate:—'or the use of pepper in great quantities,' replied he, 'to counteract the effects of good living?'*—and Adeline, though convinced temperance was the *best* preservative, was forced to give up the point, especially as Berrendale began to enumerate the number of delicious things for the table which Jamaica afforded.

To be brief: Berrendale, after taking a most affectionate leave of his wife and child, a leave which almost made the mulatto his friend, and promising to allow them 200*l.* a year till he should be able to send over for them, set sail for Jamaica; while Adeline, the night of his departure, endeavoured, by conjuring up all the horrors of a tempest at sea on his passage, and of a hurricane and an earthquake on shore when he arrived, to force herself to feel such sorrow as the tenderness which he had expressed at the moment of parting seemed to make it her duty to feel.

But morning came, and with it a feeling of liberty and independence so delightful, that she no longer tried to grieve on speculation as it were; but giving up her whole soul to the joys of maternal fondness, she looked forward with pious gratitude to days of tranquil repose, save when she thought with bitter regret of the obdurate anger of her mother, and with tender regret of the lost and ever lamented Glenmurray.

Berrendale had been arrived at Jamaica some months, when Adeline observed a most alarming change in Savanna. She became thin, her appetite entirely failed, and she looked the image of despondence. In vain did Adeline ask the reason of a change so apparent: the only answer she could obtain was, 'Me better soon;' and, continuing every day to give this answer, she in a short time became so languid as to be obliged to lie down half the day.

Adeline then found that it was necessary to be more serious in her interrogatories; but the mulatto at first only answered, 'No, me die, but me never break my duty vow to you: no, me die, but never leave you.'

These words implying a wish to leave her, with a resolution not to do so how much soever it might cost her, alarmed in a moment the ever disinterested sensibility of Adeline; and she at length wrung from her a confession that her dear William, who was gone to Jamaica as servant to a gentleman, was, she was credibly informed, very ill and like to die.

'You therefore wish to go and nurse him, I suppose, Savanna?'

'Oh! me no wish; me only tink dat me like to go to Jamaica, see if be true dat he be so bad; and if he die I den return, and die wid you.'

'Live with me, you mean, Savanna; for, indeed, I cannot spare you. Remember, you have given me a right to claim your life as mine; nor can I allow you to throw away my property in fruitless lamentations, and the indolent indulgence of regret. You shall go to Jamaica, Savanna: God forbid that I should keep a wife from her duty! You shall see and try to recover William if he be really ill,' (Savanna here threw herself on Adeline's neck,) 'and then you shall return to me, who will either warmly share in your satisfaction or fondly sooth your distress.'

'Den you do love poor Savanna?'

'Love you! Indeed I do, next to my child, and, and my mother,' replied Adeline, her voice faltering.

'Name not dat woman,' cried Savanna hastily; 'me will never see, never speak to her even in heaven.'

'Savanna, remember, she is my mother.'

'Yes, and Mr Berrendale be your husban; and yet, who dat love you can love dem?'

'Savanna,' replied Adeline, 'these proofs of your regard, though reprehensible, are not likely to reconcile me to your departure; and I already feel that in losing you—' here she paused, unable to proceed.

'Den me no go—me no go:—yet, dearest lady, you have love yourself.'

'Aye, Savanna, and can feel for you: so say no more. The only difficulty will be to raise money enough to pay for your passage, and expenses while there.'

'Oh! me once nurse the captain's wife who now going to Jamaica, and she love me very much; and he tell me yesterday that he let me go for noting, because I am good nurse to his wife, if me wish to see William.'

'Enough,' replied Adeline: 'then all I have to do is to provide you with money for your maintenance when you arrive; and I have no doubt but that what I cannot supply the tawny boy's generous patroness will.'

Adeline was not mistaken. Savanna obtained from her son's benefactress a sum equal to her wants; and almost instantly restored to her wonted health, by her mind's being lightened of the load which oppressed it, she took her passage on board her friend's vessel, and set sail for Jamaica, carrying with her letters from Adeline to Berrendale; while Adeline felt the want of Savanna in various ways, so forcibly, that not even Editha could, for a time at least, console her for her loss. It had been so grateful to her feelings to meet every day the eyes of one being fixed with never-varying affection on hers, that, when she beheld those eyes no longer, she felt alone in the universe,—nor had she a single female friend to whom she could turn for relief or consolation.

Mrs Beauclerc, to whose society she had expected to be restored by her marriage, had been forced to give up all intercourse with her, in compliance with the peremptory wishes of a rich old maid, from whom her children had great expectations, and who threatened to leave her fortune away from them, if Mrs Beauclerc persisted in corresponding with a woman so bad in principle, and so wicked in practice, as Adeline appeared to her to be.

But, at length, from a mother's employments, from writing, and, above all, from the idea that by suffering she was making atonement for her past sins, she derived consolation, and became resigned to every evil that had befallen, and to every evil that might still befall her.

Perhaps she did not consider as an evil what now took place: increasing coldness in the letters of Berrendale, till he said openly at last, that as they were, he was forced to confess, far from happy together, and as the air of Jamaica agreed with him, and as he was resolved to stay there, he thought she had better remain in England, and he would remit her as much money occasionally as his circumstances would admit of.

But she thought this a greater evil than it at first appeared; when an agent of Berrendale's father-in-law in England, and a friend of Berrendale himself, called on her, pretending that he came to inquire concerning her health, and raised in her mind suspicions of a very painful nature.

After the usual compliments:—'I find, madam,' said Mr Drury, 'that our friend is very much admired by the ladies in Jamaica.'

'I am glad to hear it, sir,' coolly answered Adeline.

'Well, that's kind and generous now,' replied Drury, 'and very disinterested.'

'I see no virtue, sir, in my rejoicing at what must make Mr Berrendale's abode in Jamaica pleasant to him.'

'May be so; but most women, I believe, would be apt to be jealous on the occasion.'

'But it has been the study of my life, sir, to endeavour to consider my own interest, when it comes in competition with another's, as little as possible;—I doubt I have not always succeeded in my endeavours: but, on this occasion I am certain that I have expressed no sentiment which I do not feel.'

'Then, madam, if my friend should have an opportunity, as indeed I believe he has, of forming a most agreeable and advantageous marriage, you would not try to prevent it?'

'Good heavens! sir,' replied Adeline; 'What can you mean? Mr Berrendale form an advantageous marriage when he is already married to me?'

'Married to you, ma'am!' answered Mr Drury with a look of incredulity. 'Excuse me, but I know that such marriages as yours may be easily dissolved.'

At first Adeline was startled at this assertion; but recollecting that it was impossible any form or ceremony should have been wanting at the marriage, she recovered herself, and demanded, with an air of severity, what Mr Drury meant by so alarming and ill-founded a speech.

'My meaning, ma'am,' replied he, 'must be pretty evident to you: I mean that I do not look upon you, though you bear Mr Berrendale's name, to be his lawful wife; but that you live with him on the same terms on which you lived with Mr Glenmurray.'

'And on what, sir, could you build such an erroneous supposition?'

'On Mr Berrendale's own words, madam; who always spoke of his connection with you, as of a connection which he had formed in compliance with love and in defiance of prudence.'

'And is it possible that he could be such a villain?' exclaimed Adeline. 'Oh my child! and does thy father brand thee with the stain of illegitimacy?—But, sir, whatever appellation Mr Berrendale might choose to give his union with me to his friends in England, I am sure he will not dare to incur the penalty attendant on a man's marrying one wife while he has another living; for, that I am his wife, I can bring pretty sufficient evidence to prove.'

'Indeed, madam! You can produce a witness of the ceremony, then, I presume?'

'No, sir; the woman who attended me to the altar, and the clergyman who married us, are dead; and the only witness is a child now only ten years old.'

'That is unfortunate!' (with a look of incredulity) 'but, no doubt, when you hear that Mr Berrendale is married to a West Indian heiress, you will come forward with incontrovertible proofs of your prior claims; and if you do that, madam, you may command my good offices:—but, till then, I humbly take my leave.' Saying this, with a very visible sneer on his countenance he departed, leaving Adeline in a state of distress—the more painful to endure from her having none to participate in it,—no one to whom she could impart the cause of it.

That Mr Drury did not speak of the possible marriage of Berrendale from mere conjecture, was very apparent; and Adeline resolved not to delay writing to her husband immediately, to inform him of what had passed, and to put before his eyes, in the strongest possible manner, the guilt of what he was about to do; and also the utter impossibility of its being successful guilt, as she was resolved to assert her claims for the sake of her child, if not for her own. This letter she concluded, and with truth too, with protestations of believing all Mr Drury said to be false: for, indeed, the more she considered Berrendale's character, the more she was convinced that, however selfish and defective his disposition might be, it was more likely Mr Drury should be mistaken, than Berrendale be a villain.

But, where a man's conduct is not founded on virtuous motives and immutable principles, he may not err while temptation is absent; but once expose him to her presence, and he is capable of falling into the very vices the most abhorrent to his nature: and though Adeline knew it not, such a man was Berrendale.

Adeline, having relieved her mind by this appeal to her husband, and being assured that Berrendale could not be married before her letter could reach him, as it was impossible that he should dare to marry while the mulatto was in the very town near which he resided, felt herself capable of attending to her usual employments again, and had recovered her tranquillity, when an answer to her letter arrived; and Adeline, being certain that the letter itself would be a proof of the marriage, had resolved to show it, in justification of her claims, to Mr Drury.

What then must have been her surprise, to find it exactly such a letter as would be evidence against a marriage between her and Berrendale having ever taken place! He thanked her for the expressions of fond regret which her letter contained, and for the many happy hours which he owed to her society; but hoped that, as Fate had now separated their destinies, she could be as happy without him as she had been with him; and assuring her that he should, according to his promise, regularly remit her 150*l.* a year if possible, but that he could at present only inclose a draft for 50*l.*

Adeline was absolutely stupefied with horror at reading this apparent confirmation of the villany of her husband and the father of her child; but roused to indignant exertion by the sense of Berrendale's baseness, and of what she owed her daughter, she resolved to take counsel's opinion in what manner she should proceed to prove her marriage, as soon as she was assured that Berrendale's (which she had no doubt was fixed upon) should have taken place; and this intelligence she received a short time after from the mulatto herself, who, worn out with sorrow, sickness and hardship, one day tottered into the house, seeming as if she indeed only returned to die with her mistress.

At first the joy of seeing Savanna restored to her swallowed up every other feeling; but tender apprehension for the poor creature's health soon took possession of her mind, and Adeline drew from her a narrative, which exhibited Berrendale to her eyes as capable of most atrocious actions.

CHAPTER II

It is very certain that when Berrendale left England, though he meant to conceal his marriage entirely, he had not even the slightest wish to contract another; and had any one told him that he was capable of such wicked conduct, he would have answered like Hazael, 'Is thy servant a dog that he should do this thing?'* But he was then unassailed by temptations:—and habituated as he was to selfish indulgence, it was impossible that to strong temptation he should not fall an immediate victim.

This strong temptation assailed him soon after his arrival, in the person of a very lovely and rich widow, a relation of his first wife, who, having no children of her own, had long been very fond of his child, then a very fine boy, and with great readiness transferred to the father the affection which she bore the son. For some time conscience and Adeline stood their ground against this new mistress and her immense property; but at length, being pressed by his father-in-law, who wished the match, to assign a sufficient reason for his coldness to so fine a woman, and not daring to give the true one, he returned the lady's fondness; and though he had not yet courage enough to name the marriage day, it was known that it would some time or other take place.

But all his scruples soon yielded to the dominion which the attractions of the lady, who was well versed in the arts of seduction, obtained over his senses, and to the strong power which the sight of the splendor in which she lived, acquired over his avarice; when, just as every thing was on the point of being concluded, the poor mulatto, who had found her husband dead, arrived almost broken-hearted at the place of Berrendale's abode, and delivered to him letters from Adeline.

Terrified and confounded at her presence, he received her with such evident marks of guilty confusion in his face, that Savanna's apprehensive and suspicious attachment to her mistress took the alarm; and, as she had seen a very fine woman leave the room as she entered, she, on pretence of leaving Berrendale alone to read his letters, repaired to the servants' apartments, where she learnt the intended marriage. Immediately forgetting her own distresses in those of Adeline, she returned to Berrendale, not with the languid, mournful pace with which she had first entered, but with the firm, impetuous and intrepid step of conscious integrity going to confound vice in the moment of its triumph.

Berrendale read his doom, the moment he beheld her, in her dark and fiery eye, and awaited in trembling silence the torrent of reproaches that trembled on her lip. But I shall not repeat what passed. Suffice that Berrendale pretended to be moved by what she said, and promised to break off the marriage,—only exacting from Savanna, in return, a promise of not imparting to the servants, or to any one, that he had a wife in England.

In the mean while he commended her most affectionately to the care of the steward; and confessing to his intended bride that he had a mistress in England, who had sent the mulatto over to prevent the match if possible, by persuading her he was already married, he conjured her to consent to a private marriage; and to prevent some dreadful scene, occasioned by the revenge of disappointed passion, should his mistress, as she had threatened, come over in person, he entreated her to let every splendid preparation for their nuptials be laid aside, in order to deceive Savanna, and induce her to return quietly to England.

The credulous woman, too much in love to believe what she did not wish, consented to all he proposed: but Berrendale, still fearful of the watchful jealousy of Savanna, contrived to find out the master to whom she belonged before she had escaped, early in life, with her first husband to England; and as she had never been made free, as soon as he arrived, he, on a summons from Berrendale, seized her as his property; and poor Savanna, in spite of her cries and struggles, was conveyed some miles up the country.

At length, however, she found means to escape to the coast; and, having discovered an old acquaintance in an English sailor on board a vessel then ready to sail, and who had great influence with the captain, she was by him concealed on board, with the approbation of the commander, and was on her way to England before Berrendale was informed of her escape.

I will not endeavour to describe Adeline's feelings on hearing this narration, and on finding also that Savanna before she left the island had been assured that Berrendale was really married, though privately, but that the marriage could not long be attempted to be concealed, as the lady even before it took place was likely to become a mother; and, that as a large estate depended on her giving birth to a son, the event of her confinement was looked for with great anxiety.

Still, in the midst of her distress, a sudden thought struck Adeline, which converted her anger into joy, and her sorrow into exultation. 'Yes, my mother may now forgive me without violating any part of her oath,' she exclaimed.—'I am now forsaken, despised and disgraced!'—and instantly she wrote to Mrs Mowbray a letter, calculated to call forth all her sympathy and affection. Then, with a mind relieved beyond expression, she sat down to deliberate in what manner she should act to do herself justice as a wife and a mother, cruelly aggrieved in both these intimate relations. Nor could she persuade herself that she should act properly by her child, if she did not proceed vigorously to prove herself Berrendale's wife, and substantiate Editha's claim to his property; and as Mr Langley was, she knew, a very great lawyer, she resolved, in spite of his improper conduct to her, to apply to him again.

Indeed she could not divest herself of a wish to let him know that she was become a wife, and no longer liable to be treated with that freedom with which, as a mistress, he had thought himself at liberty to address her. However, she wished that she had not been obliged to go to him alone: but, as the mulatto was in too weak a state of health to allow of her going out, and she could not speak of business like hers before any one else, she was forced to proceed unaccompanied to the Temple; and on the evening of the day after Savanna's return, she, with a beating heart, repaired once more to Mr Langley's chambers.

Luckily, however, she met the tawny boy on her way, and took him for her escort. 'Tell your master,' said she to the servant, 'that Mrs Berrendale wishes to speak to him:' and in a few minutes she was introduced.

'Mrs Berrendale!' cried Langley with a sarcastic smile; 'pray be seated, madam! I hope Mr Berrendale is well.'

'He is in Jamaica, sir,' replied Adeline.

'Indeed!' returned Langley. 'May I presume so far as to ask,—hem, hem,—whether your visit to me be merely of a professional nature?'

'Certainly, sir,' replied Adeline: 'of what other nature should it be?'

Langley replied to this only by a significant smile. At this moment the tawny boy asked leave to walk in the Temple gardens; and Adeline, though reluctantly, granted his request.

'Oh! à propos, John,' cried Langley to the servant, 'let Mrs Montgomery know that her friend miss Mowbray, Mrs Berrendale I mean, is here—she is walking in the garden.'

'My friend Mrs Montgomery, sir! I have no friend of that name.'

'No, my sweet soul? You may not know her by that name; but names change, you know. You, for instance, are Mrs Berrendale now, but when I see you again you may be Mrs somebody else.'

'Never, sir,' cried Adeline indignantly; 'but, though I do not exactly understand your meaning, I feel as if you meant to insult me, and therefore—'

'Oh no—sit down again, my angel; you are mistaken, and so apt to fly off in a tangent! But—so—that wonderfully handsome man, Berrendale, is off—heh? Your friend and mine, heh! pretty one!'

'If, sir, Mr Berrendale ever considered you as his friend, it is very strange that you should presume to insult his wife.'

'Madam,' replied Langley with a most provoking sneer, 'Mr Berrendale's wife shall always be treated by me with proper respect.'

'Gracious Heaven!' cried Adeline, clasping her hands and looking upwards with tearful eyes, 'when shall my persecutions cease! and how much greater must my offences be than even my remorse paints them, when their consequences still torment me so long after the crime which occasioned them has ceased to exist! But it is Thy will, and I will submit even to indignity with patience.'

There was a touching solemnity in this appeal to heaven, an

expression of truth, which it was so impossible for art to imitate, that Langley felt in a moment the injustice of which he had been guilty, and an apology was on his lips, when the door opened, and a lady, rouged like a French countess of the ancien régime,* her hair covered with a profusion of brown powder, and dressed in the height of the fashion, ambled into the room; and saying, 'How d'ye do, miss Mowbray?' threw herself carelessly on the sofa, to the astonishment of Adeline, who did not recollect her, and to the confusion of Langley, who now, impressed with involuntary respect for Adeline, repented of having exposed her to the scene that awaited her: but to prevent it was impossible; he was formed to be the slave of women, and had not courage to protect another from the insolence to which he tamely yielded himself.

Adeline at first did not answer this soi-disant* acquaintance of hers; but, in looking at her more attentively, she exclaimed, 'What do I see? Is it possible that this can be Mary Warner!'

'Yes, it is, my dear, indeed,' replied she with a loud laugh, 'Mary Warner, alias Mrs Montgomery; as you, you know, are miss Mowbray, alias Mrs Berrendale.'

Adeline, incapable of speaking, only gazed at her in silence, but with a countenance more in sorrow than in anger.*

'But, come, sit down, my dear,' cried Mary; 'no ceremony, you know, among friends and equals, you know; and you and I have been mighty familiar, you know, before now. The last time we met you called me *woman*, you know—yes, "woman!" says you—and I have not forgotten it, I assure you,' she added with a sort of loud hysterical laugh, and a look of the most determined malice.

'Come, come, my dear Montgomery,' said Langley, 'you must forget and forgive;—I dare say miss Mowbray, that is to say Mrs Berrendale, did not mean—'

'What should you know about the matter, Lang.?' replied Mary; 'I wish you would mind your own business, and let me talk to my dumb friend here. Well, I suppose you are quite surprised to see how smart I am!—seeing as how I once over-hard you say to Glenthingymy, "How very plain Mary is!" though, to be sure, it was never a barrel the better herring, and 'twas the kettle in my mind calling the pot*— heh, Lang.?'

Here was the clue to the inveterate dislike which this unhappy girl had conceived against Adeline. So true is it that little wounds inflicted on the self-love are never forgotten or forgiven, and that it is safer to censure the morals of acquaintances than to ridicule them on their dress, or laugh at a defect in their person. Adeline, indeed, did not mean that her observation should be over-heard by the object of it,—still she was hated: but many persons make mortifying remarks purposely, and yet wonder that they have enemies!

Motionless and almost lifeless Adeline continued to stand and to listen, and Mary went on—

'Well, but I thank you for one thing. You taught me that marriage was all nonsense, you know; and so thought I, miss Mowbray is a learned lady, she must know best, and so I followed your example— that's all you know.'

This dreadful information roused the feelings of Adeline even to phrensy, and with a shriek of anguish she seized her hand, and conjured her by all her hopes of mercy to retract what she had said, and not to let her depart with the horrible consciousness of having been the means of plunging a fellow-being into vice and ignominy.

A loud unfeeling laugh, and an exclamation of 'the woman is mad,' was all the answer to this.

'This then is the completion of my sufferings,' cried Adeline,— 'this only was wanted to complete the misery of my remorse.'

'Good God! this is too much,' exclaimed Langley. 'Mary, you know very well that—'

'Hold your tongue, Lang.; you know nothing about the matter: it is all nothing, but that miss Mowbray, like a lawyer, can change sides, you see, and attack one day what she defended the day before, you know; and she have made you believe that she think now being kept a shameful thing.'

'I do believe so,' hastily replied Adeline; 'and if it be true that my sentiments and my example led you to adopt your present guilty mode of life,—oh! save me from the pangs of remorse which I now feel, by letting my present example recall you from the paths of error to those of virtue.'

'Well pleaded,' cried the cold-hearted Mary—'Lang., you could not have done't so well—not up to that.'

'Mrs Montgomery,' said Langley with great severity, 'if you can-not treat Mrs Berrendale with more propriety and respect, I must beg you to leave the room; she is come to speak to me on business, and—'

'I sha'n't stir, for all that: and mark me, Lang., if you turn me out of the room, you know, curse me if ever I enter it again!'

'But your little boy may want you; you have left him now some time.'

'Aye, that may be true, to be sure, poor little dear! Have you any family, miss Mowbray?'—when, without waiting for an answer, she added, 'My little boy have got the small-pox very bad, and has been likely to die from convulsion fits, you know. Poor dear! I had been nursing it so long that I could not bear the stench of the room,* and so I was glad, you know, to come and get a little fresh air in the gardens.'

At this speech Adeline's fortitude entirely gave way. *Her* child had not had the small-pox, and she had been for some minutes in reach of the infection; and with a look of horror, forgetting her business, and every thing but Editha, she was on the point of leaving the room, when a servant hastily entered, and told Mary that her little boy was dead.

At hearing this, even her cold heart was moved, and throwing herself back on the sofa she fell into a strong hysteric; while Adeline, losing all remembrance of her insolence in her distress, flew to her assistance; and, in pity for a mother weeping the loss of her infant, forgot for a moment that she was endangering the life of her own child.

Mr Langley, mean time, though grieved for the death of the infant, was alive to the generous forgiving disposition which Adeline evinced; and could not help exclaiming, 'Oh, Mrs Berrendale! forgive us! we deserved not such kindness at your hands:' and Adeline, wanting to loosen the tight stays of Mary, and not choosing to undress her before such a witness, coldly begged him to withdraw, advising him at the same time to go and see whether the child was really dead, as it might possibly only appear so.

Revived by this possibility, Mr Langley left Mary to the care of Adeline, and left the room. But whether it was that Mary had a mind to impress her lover and the father of her child with an idea of her sensibility, or whether she had overheard Adeline's supposition, certain it is, that as soon as Langley went away, and Adeline began to unlace her stays, she hastily recovered, and declared her stays should remain as they were: but still exclaiming about her poor dear Benny, she kept her arms closely clasped round Adeline's waist, and reposed her head on her bosom.

Adeline's fears and pity for her being thus allayed, she began to have leisure to feel and fear for herself; and the idea, that, by being in such close contact with Mary, she was imbibing so much of the disease as must inevitably communicate it to Editha, recurred so forcibly to her mind, that, begging for God's sake she would loose her hold, she endeavoured to break from the arms of her tormentor.

But in vain.—As soon as Mary saw that Adeline wished to leave her, she was the more eager to hold her fast; and protesting she should die if she had the barbarity to leave her alone, she only hugged her the closer. 'Well, then, I'll try to stay till Mr Langley returns,' cried Adeline: but some minutes elapsed, and Mr Langley did not return; and then Adeline, recollecting that when he did return he would come fresh fraught with the pestilence from the dead body of his infant, could no longer master her feelings, but screaming wildly,—'I shall be the death of my child; for God's sake let me go,'—she struggled with the determined Mary. 'You will drive me mad if you detain me,' cried Adeline.

'You will drive me mad if you go,' replied Mary, giving way to a violent hysterical scream, while with successful strength she parried all Adeline's endeavours to break from her. But what can resist the strength of phrensy and despair? Adeline, at length worked up to madness by the fatal control exercised over her, by one great effort threw the sobbing Mary from her, and, darting down stairs with the rapidity of phrensy, nearly knocked down Mr Langley in her passage, who was coming to announce the restoration of the little boy.

She soon reached Fleet-street, and was on her road home before Langley and Mary had recovered their consternation: but she suddenly recollected that homewards she must not proceed; that she carried death about her; and wholly bewildered by this insupportable idea, she ran along the Strand,* muttering the incoherencies of phrensy as she went, till she was intercepted in her passage by some young men of *ton*,* who had been dining together, and, being half intoxicated, were on their way to the theatre.

Two of these gentlemen, with extended arms, prevented her further progress.

'Where are you going, my pretty girl,' cried one, 'in this hurry? shall I see you home? heh!'

'Home!' replied Adeline; 'name it not. My child! my child! thy mother has destroyed thee.'

'So!' cried another, 'an actress,* by all that's tragical!'

'Unhand me!' exclaimed Adeline wildly. 'Do not you know, poor babe, that I carry death and pollution about with me!'

'The devil you do!' returned the gentleman; 'then the sooner you take yourself off the better.'

'I believe the poor soul is mad,' said a third, making way for Adeline to pass.

'But,' cried the first who spoke, catching hold of her, 'if so, there is method and meaning in her madness; for she called Jaby here a poor babe, and we all know he is little better.'

By this time Adeline was in a state of complete phrensy, and was again darting down the street in spite of the gentleman's efforts to hold her, when another gentleman, whom curiosity had induced to stop and listen to what passed, suddenly seized hold of her arm, and exclaimed, 'Good Heavens! what can this mean? It is—it can be no other than miss Mowbray.'

At the sound of her own name Adeline started: but in a moment her senses were quite lost again; and the gentleman, who was no other than colonel Mordaunt, being fully aware of her situation, after reproving the young men for sporting with distress so apparent, called a coach which happened to be passing, and desired to know whither he should have the honour of conducting her.

But she was too lost to be able to answer the question: he therefore, lifting her into the coach, desired the man to drive towards Dover-street; and when there, he ordered him to drive to Margaret-street Oxford-street; when, not being able to obtain one coherent word from Adeline, and nothing but expressions of agony, terror, and self-condemnation, he desired him to stop at such a house, and, conducting Adeline up stairs, desired the first assistance to be procured immediately.

It was not to his own lodgings that colonel Mordaunt had conducted Adeline, but to the house of a convenient friend of his, who, though not generally known as such, and bearing a tolerably good character in the world, was very kind to the tender distresses of her friends, and had no objection to assist the meetings of two fond lovers.

It is to be supposed, then, that she was surprised at seeing colonel Mordaunt with a companion, who was an object of pity and horror rather than of love: but she did not want humanity; and when the colonel recommended Adeline to her tenderest care, she with great readiness ordered a bed to be prepared, and assisted in prevailing on Adeline to lie down on it. In a short time a physician and a surgeon arrived; and Adeline, having been bled and made to swallow strong opiates, was undressed by her attentive landlady; and though still in a state of unconsciousness, she fell into a sound sleep, which lasted till morning.

But colonel Mordaunt passed a sleepless night. The sight of Adeline, even frantic and wretched as she appeared, had revived the passion which he had conceived for her; and if on her awaking the next morning she should appear perfectly rational, and her phrensy merely the result of some great fright which she had received, he resolved to renew his addresses, and take advantage of the opportunity now offered him, while she was as it were in his power.

But to return to the Temple. Soon after Mr Langley had entered his own room, and while Mary and he were commenting on the frantic behaviour of Adeline, the tawny boy came back from his walk, and heard with marks of emotion, apparently beyond his age, (for though near twelve he did not look above eight years old,) of the sudden and frantic disappearance of Adeline.

'Oh! my dear friend,' cried he, 'if you are not gone home you will break my poor mother's heart!'

'And who is your mother?'

'Her name is Savanna; and she lives with Mrs Berrendale.'

'Mrs Berrendale!' cried Mary, 'miss Mowbray you mean.'

'No, I do not;—her name was Mowbray, but is now Berrendale.'

'What! is she really married?' asked Langley.

'Yes, to be sure.'

'But how do you know that she is?'

'Oh! because I went to church with them, and my mother cooked the wedding-dinner, and I ate plum-pudding and drank punch, and we were very merry,—only my mother cried, because my father could not come.'

'Very circumstantial evidence, indeed!' cried Langley, 'and I am very sorry that I did not know so much before. So you and your mother love this extraordinary fine woman, Mrs Berrendale, heh?'

'Love her! To be sure—we should be very wicked if we did not. Did you never hear the story of the pine-apple?' said the tawny boy.

'Not I. What was it?' and the tawny boy, delighted to tell the story, with sparkling eyes sat down to relate it.

'You must know, Mr Glenmurray longed for a pine-apple.'

'Mrs Glenmurray you mean,' said Mary laughing immoderately.

'I know what I say,' replied the tawny boy angrily; 'and so miss Adeline, as she was then called, went out to buy one;—well, and so she met my poor father going to prison, and I was crying after her, and so—' Here he paused, and bursting into tears exclaimed, 'And perhaps she is crying herself now, and I must go and see for her directly.'

'Do so, my fine fellow,' cried Langley: 'you had better go home, tell your mother what has passed, and to-morrow' (accompanying him down stairs, and speaking in a low voice) 'I will either write a note of apology or call on Mrs Berrendale myself.'

The tawny boy instantly set off, running as fast as he could, telling Langley first, that if any harm had happened to his friend, both he and his mother should lie down and die. And this further proof of Adeline's merit did not tend to calm Langley's remorse for having exposed her to the various distresses which she had undergone at his chambers.

CHAPTER III

Adeline awoke early the next morning perfectly sane, though weakened by the exertions which she had experienced the night before, and saw with surprise and alarm that she was not in her own lodging.

But she had scarcely convinced herself that she was awake, when Mrs Selby, the mistress of the house, appeared at her bed-side, and, seeing what was passing in her mind by her countenance, explained to her as delicately as she could the situation in which she had been brought there.

'And who brought me hither?' replied Adeline, dreadfully agitated, as the remembrance of what had passed by degrees burst upon her.

'Colonel Mordaunt of the life-guards,' was the answer; and Adeline was shocked to find that he was the person to whom she was under so essential an obligation. She then hastily arose, being eager to return home; and in a short time she was ready to enter the drawing-room, and to express her thanks to colonel Mordaunt.

But in vain did she insist on going home directly, to ease the fears of her family. The physician, who arrived at the moment, forbade her going out without having first taken both medicine and refreshment; and by the time that, after the most earnest entreaties, she obtained leave to depart, she recollected that, as her clothes were the same, she might still impart disease to her child, and therefore must on no account think of returning to Editha.

'Whither, whither then can I go?' cried she, forgetting she was not alone.

'Why not stay here?' said the colonel, who had been purposely left alone with her. 'O dearest of women! that you would but accept the protection of a man who adores you; who has long loved you; who has been so fortunate as to rescue you from a situation of misery and danger, and the study of whose life it shall be to make you happy.'

He uttered this with such volubility, that Adeline could not find an opportunity to interrupt him; but when he concluded, she calmly replied, 'I am willing to believe, colonel Mordaunt, from a conversation which I once had with you, that you are not aware of the extent of the insult which you are now offering to me. You probably do not know that I have been for years a married woman?'

Colonel Mordaunt started and turned pale at this intelligence; and in a faltering voice replied, that he was indeed a stranger to her present situation;—for that, libertine as he confessed himself to be, he had never yet allowed himself to address the wife of another.

This speech restored him immediately to the confidence of Adeline. 'Then I hope,' cried she, holding out her hand to him, which in spite of his virtue he passionately kissed, 'that, as a friend, you will have the kindness to procure me a coach to take me to a lodging a few miles out of town, where I once was before; and that you will be so good as to drive directly to my lodgings, and let my poor maid know what is become of me. I dread to think', added she bursting into tears, 'of the agony that my unaccountable absence must have occasioned her.'

The colonel, too seriously attached to Adeline to know yet what he wished, or what he hoped on this discovery of her situation, promised to obey her, provided she would allow him to call on her now and then; and Adeline was too full of gratitude to him for the service which he had rendered her, to have resolution enough to deny his request. He then called a coach for himself, and for Adeline, as she insisted on his going immediately to her lodgings; and also begged that he would tell the mulatto to send for advice, and prepare her little girl for inoculation directly.*

Adeline drove directly to her old lodgings in the country, where she was most gladly received; and the colonel went to deliver his commission to the mulatto.

He found her in strong hysterics; the tawny boy crying over her, and the women of the house holding her down on the bed by force, while the little Editha had been conveyed to a neighbour's house, that she might not hear the screams which had surprised and terrified her.

Colonel Mordaunt had opened the door, and was witnessing this distressing scene, before any one was conscious of his presence; but the tawny boy soon discovered him, and crying out—

'Oh! sir, do you bring us news of our friend?' sprang to him, and hung almost breathless on his arm.

Savanna, who was conscious enough to know what passed, though too much weakened from her own sufferings and anxieties to be able to struggle with this new affliction, started up on hearing these words, and screamed out 'Does she live? Blessed man! but say so, dat's all,' in a tone so affecting, and with an expression of agonized curiosity so overwhelming to the feelings, that colonel Mordaunt, whose spirits were not very high, was so choked that he could not immediately answer her; and when at last he faltered out, 'She lives, and is quite well,' the frantic joy of the mulatto overcame him still more. She jumped about his neck, she hugged the tawny boy; and her delight was as extravagant as her grief had been; till exhausted and silent she sunk upon the bed, and was unable for some minutes to listen quietly to the story which colonel Mordaunt came to relate.

When she was composed enough to listen to it, she did not long remain so; for as soon as she heard that colonel Mordaunt had met Adeline in her phrensy, and conveyed her to a place of safety, she fell at his feet, embraced his knees, and, making the tawny boy kneel down by her, invoked the blessing of God on him so fervently and so eloquently, that colonel Mordaunt wept like a child, and, exclaiming, 'Upon my soul, my good woman, I cannot bear this,' was forced to run out of the house to recover his emotion.

When he returned, Savanna said, 'Well—now, blessed sir, take me to my dear lady.'

'Indeed,' replied he, 'I must not; you are forbidden to see her.'

'Forbidden!' replied she, her eyes flashing fire; 'and who dare to keep Savanna from her own missess?—I will see her.'

'Not if she forbids it, Savanna; and if her child's life should be endangered by it?'

'O, no, to be sure not,' cried the tawny boy, who doted upon Editha, and, having fetched her back from the next house, was lulling her to sleep in his arms.

Colonel Mordaunt started at sight of the child, and, stooping down to kiss its rosy cheek, sighed deeply as he turned away again.

'Well,' cried Savanna, 'you talk very strange—me no understand.'

'But you shall, my excellent creature,' replied the colonel, 'immediately.' He then entered on a full explanation to Savanna; who had no sooner heard that her mistress feared that she had been so much exposed to the infection of the small-pox, as to make her certain of giving it to her child, than she exclaimed, 'Oh, my good God! save and protect her own self! She never have it, and she may get it and die!'

'Surely you must be mistaken,' replied the colonel, 'Mrs Berrendale must have recollected and mentioned her own danger if this be the case.'

'She!' hastily interrupted the mulatto, 'she tink of herself! Never—she only mind others' good.—Do you tink, if she be one selfish beast like her husban, Savanna love her so dear? No, Mr colonel, me know her, and me know though we may save the child we may lose the mother.' Here she began to weep bitterly; while the colonel, more in love than ever with Adeline from these proofs of her goodness, resolved to lose no time in urging her to undergo herself the operation which she desired for Editha.

Then, begging the mulatto to send for a surgeon directly, in spite of the tears of the tawny boy, who thought it cruel to run the risk of spoiling miss Editha's pretty face, he took his leave, saying to himself, 'What a heart has this Adeline! how capable of feeling affection! for no one can inspire it who is not able to feel it:* and this creature is thrown away on a man undeserving her, it seems!'

On this intelligence he continued to muse till he arrived at Adeline's lodgings, to whom he communicated all that had passed;

and from whom he learned, with great anxiety, that it was but too true that she had never had the small-pox; and that, therefore, she should probably show symptoms of the disease in a few days: consequently, as she considered it too late for her to be inoculated,* she should do all that now remained to be done for her security, by low living and good air.

That same evening colonel Mordaunt returned to Savanna, in hopes of learning from her some further particulars respecting Adeline's husband; as he felt that his conscience would not be much hurt by inducing Adeline to leave the protection of a man who was unworthy of possessing her. Fortunately for his wishes, he could not wish to hear more than Savanna wished to tell every thing relating to her adored lady: and colonel Mordaunt heard with generous indignation of the perfidious conduct of Berrendale; vowing, at the same time, that his time, his interest, and his fortune, should all be devoted to bring such a villain to justice, and to secure to the injured Editha her rightful inheritance.

The mulatto was in raptures:—she told colonel Mordaunt that he was a charming man, and infinitely handsomer than Berrendale, though she must own he was very good to look at; and she wished with all her soul that colonel Mordaunt was married to her lady; for then she believed she would have never known sorrow, but been as happy as the day was long.

Colonel Mordaunt could not hear this without a secret pang. 'Had I followed', said he mentally, 'the dictates of my heart when I saw Adeline at Bath, I might now, perhaps, instead of being a forlorn unattached being, have been a happy husband and father; and Adeline, instead of having been the mistress of one man, and the disowned wife of another, might have been happy and beloved, and as respectable in the eyes of the world as she is now in those of her grateful mulatto.'

However, there was some hope left for him yet.—Adeline, he thought, was not a woman likely to be over-scrupulous in her ideas; and might very naturally think herself at liberty to accept the protection of a lover, when, from no fault of hers, she had lost that of her husband.

It is natural to suppose that, while elevated with these hopes, he did not fail to be very constant in his visits to Adeline; and that at length, more led by passion than policy, he abruptly, at the end of ten days, informed Adeline that he knew her situation, and that he trusted that she would allow him to hope that in due time his love, which had been proof against time, absence, and disdain, would meet with reward; and that, on his settling a handsome income on her and her child for their joint lives, she would allow him to endeavour to make her as happy as she, and she only, could make him.

To this proposal, which was in form of a letter, colonel Mordaunt did not receive an immediate answer; nor was it at first likely that he should ever receive an answer to it at all, as Adeline was at the moment of its arrival confined to her bed, according to her expectations, with the disease which she had been but too fearful of imbibing: while the half-distracted mulatto was forced to give up to others the care of the sickening Editha, to watch over the delirious and unconscious Adeline.

But the tawny boy's generous benefactress gave him leave to remain at Adeline's lodgings, in order to calm his fears for Editha, and assist in amusing and keeping her quiet; and if attention had any share in preserving the life and beauty of Editha, it was to the affectionate tawny boy that she owed them; and he was soon rewarded for all his care and anxiety by seeing his little charge able to play about as usual.

Colonel Mordaunt and the mulatto meanwhile did not obtain so speedy a termination to their anxieties; Adeline's recovery was for a long time a matter of doubt; and her weakness so great after the crisis of the disorder was past, that none ventured to pronounce her, even then, out of danger.

But at length she was in a great measure restored to health, and able to determine what line of conduct it was necessary for her to pursue.—To return an answer to colonel Mordaunt's proposals was certainly her first business; but as she felt that the situation in which he had once known her made his offer less affronting than it would have been under other circumstances, she resolved to speak to him on the subject with gentleness, not severity; especially as during her illness, to amuse the anxiety that had preyed upon him, he had taken every possible step to procure evidence of the marriage, and gave into Savanna's hands, the first day that he was permitted to see her, an attested certificate of it.

CHAPTER IV

The first question which Adeline asked on her recovery was, Whether any letter had come by the general post during her illness; and Savanna gave one to her immediately.

It was the letter so ardently desired; for the direction was in her mother's hand-writing! and she opened it full of eager expectation, while her whole existence seemed to depend on the nature of its contents. What then must have been her agony on finding that the *enveloppe* contained nothing but her own letter returned! For some time she spoke not, she breathed not; while Savanna mixed with expressions of terror, at sight of her mistress's distress, execrations on the unnatural parent who had so cruelly occasioned it.

After a few days' incessant struggle to overcome the violence of her sorrow, Adeline recovered the shock, in appearance at least: yet to Savanna's self-congratulations she could not help answering (laying her hand on her heart), 'The blow is here, Savanna, and the wound incurable.'

Soon after she thought herself well enough to see colonel Mordaunt, and to thank him for the recent proof of his attention to her and her interest. But no obligation, however great, could shut the now vigilant eyes of Adeline to the impropriety of receiving further visits from him, or to the guilt of welcoming to her house a man who made open professions to her of illicit love.

She however thought it her duty to see him once more, in order to try to reconcile him to the necessity of the rule of conduct which she was going to lay down for herself; nor was she without hope that the yet recent traces of the disease, to which she had so nearly fallen a victim, would make her appearance so unpleasing to the eyes of her lover, that he would be very willing to absent himself from the house, for some time at least, and probably give up all thoughts of her.

But she did neither herself nor colonel Mordaunt justice.—She was formed to inspire a real and lasting passion—a passion that no external change could destroy—since it was founded on the unchanging qualities of the heart and mind: and colonel Mordaunt felt for her such an attachment in all its force. He had always admired the attractive person and winning graces of Adeline, and felt for her what he denominated love; but that rational though enthusiastic preference, which is deserving of the name of true love, he never felt till he had an opportunity to appreciate justly the real character of Adeline: still there were times when he felt almost gratified to reflect that she could not legally be his; for, whatever might have been the cause and excuse of her errors, she had erred, and the delicacy of his mind revolted at the idea of marrying the mistress of another.

But when he saw and heard Adeline this repugnance vanished; and he knew that, could he at those moments lead her to the altar, he should not have hesitated to bind himself to her for ever by the sacred ties which the early errors of her judgment had made her in his opinion almost unworthy to form.

At length a day was fixed for his interview with Adeline, and with a beating heart he entered the apartment; nor was his emotion diminished when he beheld not only the usual vestiges of her complaint, but symptoms of debility, and a death-like meagreness of aspect, which made him fear that though one malady was conquered, another, even more dangerous, remained. The idea overcame him; and he was forced to turn to the window to hide his emotion: and his manner was so indicative of ardent yet respectful attachment, that Adeline began to feel in spite of herself that her projected task was difficult of execution.

For some minutes neither of them spoke: Mordaunt held the hand which she gave him to his heart, kissed it as she withdrew it, and again turned away his head to conceal a starting tear; while Adeline was not sorry to have a few moments in which to recover herself, before she addressed him on the subject at that time nearest to the heart of both. At length she summoned resolution enough to say:—

'Much as I have been mortified and degraded, colonel Mordaunt, by the letter which I have received from you, still I rejoice that I did receive it:—in the first place, I rejoice, because I look on all the sufferings and mortifications which I meet with as latent blessings, as expiations required of me in mercy by the Being whom I adore, for the sins of which I have been guilty; and, in the second place, because it gives me an opportunity of proving, incontrovertibly, my full conviction of the fallacy of my past opinions, and that I became a wife, after my idle declamations against marriage, from change of principle, on assurance of error, and not from interest, or necessity.'

Here she paused, overcome with the effort which she had made; and colonel Mordaunt would have interrupted her, but, earnestly conjuring him to give her a patient hearing, she proceeded thus:—

'Had the change in my practice been the result of any thing but rational conviction, I should now, unfortunate as I have been in the choice of a husband, regret that ever I formed so foolish a tie, and perhaps be induced to enter into a less sacred connection, from an idea that that state which forced me to drag out existence in hopeless misery was contrary to reason, justice, and the benefit of society; and that the sooner its ties were dissolved, the better it would be for individual happiness and for the world at large.'

'And do you not think so?' cried colonel Mordaunt; 'cannot your own individual experience convince you of it?'

'Far from it,' replied Adeline; 'and I bless God that it does not: for thence, and thence only, do I begin to be reconciled to myself. I have no doubt that there is a great deal of individual suffering in the marriage state, from contrariety of temper and other causes; but I believe that the mass of happiness and virtue is certainly increased by it. Individual suffering, therefore, is no more an argument for the abolition of marriage, than the accidental bursting of a musquet would be for the total abolition of fire-arms.'

'But, surely, dear Mrs Berrendale, you would wish divorce to be made easier than it is?'

'By no means,' interrupted Adeline, understanding what he was going to say: 'To BEAR and FORBEAR I believe to be the grand secret of happiness, and ought to be the great study of life: therefore, whatever would enable married persons to separate on the slightest quarrel or disgust, would make it so much the less necessary for us to learn this important lesson; a lesson so needful in order to perfect the human character, that I believe the difficulty of divorce to be one of the greatest blessings of society.'

'What can have so completely changed your opinions on this subject?' replied colonel Mordaunt.

'Not my own experience,' returned Adeline; 'for the painful situations in which I have been placed, I might attribute, not to the *fallacy* of the system on which I have acted, but to those existing prejudices in society which I wish to see destroyed.'

'Then, to what else is the change in your sentiments to be attributed?'

'To a more serious, unimpassioned, and unprejudiced view of the subject than I had before taken: at present I am not equal to expatiate on matters so important: however, some time or other, perhaps, I may make known to you my sentiments on them in a more ample manner: but I have, I trust, said enough to lead you to conclude, that though Mr Berrendale's conduct to me has been atrocious, and that you are in many respects entitled to my gratitude and thanks, you and I must henceforward be strangers to each other.'

Colonel Mordaunt, little expecting such a total overthrow to his hopes, was, on receiving it, choked with contending emotions; and his broken sentences and pale cheek were sufficiently expressive of the distress which he endured. But I shall not enter into a detail of all he urged in favour of his passion; nor the calm, dignified, and feeling manner in which Adeline replied. Suffice that, at last, from a sort of intuitive knowledge of the human heart, as it were, which persons of quick talents and sensibilities possess, however defective their experience, Adeline resolved to try to sooth the self-love which she had wounded, knowing that self-love is scarcely to be distinguished in its effects from love itself; and that the agony of disappointed passion is always greater when it is inflicted by the coldness or false-hood of the beloved object, than when it proceeds from parental prohibition, or the cruel separation enjoined by conscious poverty. She therefore told colonel Mordaunt that he was once very near being the first choice of her heart: when she first saw him, she said, his person, and manners, and attentions, had so strongly prepos-sessed her in his favour, that he himself, by ceasing to see and converse with her, could alone have saved her from the pain of a hopeless attachment.

'For God's sake, spare me', cried Mordaunt, 'the contemplation of the happiness I might have enjoyed!'

'But you know you were not a marrying-man, as it is called; and forgive me if I say, that men who can on system suppress the best feelings of their nature, and prefer a course of libertine indulgence to a virtuous connection, at that time of life when they might become happy husbands and fathers, with the reasonable expectation of living to see their children grown up to manhood, and superintending their education themselves—such men, colonel Mordaunt, deserve, in the decline of life, to feel that regret and that self-condemnation which you this moment anticipate.'

'True—too true!' replied the colonel; 'but, for mercy's sake, torture me no more.'

'I would not probe where I did not intend to make a cure,' replied Adeline.

'A cure!—what mean you?'

'I mean to induce you, ere it be yet too late, to endeavour to form a virtuous attachment, and to unite yourself for life with some amiable young woman who will make you as happy as I would have endeavoured to make you, had it been my fortunate lot to be yours: for, believe me, colonel Mordaunt,' and her voice faltered as she said it, 'had *he*, whom I still continue to love with unabated tenderness, though years have elapsed since he was taken from me,—had he bequeathed me to you on his death-bed, the reluctance with which I went to the altar would have been more easily overcome.'

Saying this, she suddenly left the room, leaving colonel Mordaunt surprised, gratified, and his mind struggling between hopes and fears; for Adeline was not conscious that she imparted hope as well as consolation by the method which she pursued; and though she sent Savanna to tell the colonel she could see him no more that evening, he departed in firm expectation that Adeline would not have resolution to forbid him to see her again.

In this, however, he was mistaken: Adeline had learnt the best of all lessons,—distrust of her own strength;—and she resolved to put it out of her power to receive visits which a regard to propriety forbade, and which might injure her reputation, if not her peace of mind. Therefore, as soon as colonel Mordaunt was gone, she summoned Savanna, and desired her to proceed to business.

'What!' cried the delighted mulatto, 'are we going to prosecu massa?'

'No,' replied Adeline, 'we are going into the country: I am come to a determination to take no legal steps in this affair, but leave Mr Berrendale to the reproaches of his own conscience.'*

'A fiddle's-end!'* replied Savanna, 'he have no conscience, or he no leave you: better get him hang; if you can den you marry de colonel.'

'I had better hang the father of my child, had I, Savanna?'

'Oh! no, no, no, no,—me forget dat.'

'But I do not, nor can I even bear to disgrace the father of Editha: therefore, trusting that I can dispose of her, and secure her interest better than by forcing her father to do her justice, and bastardize the poor innocent whom his wife will soon bring into the world, I am going to bury myself in retirement, and live the short remainder of my days unknowing and unknown.'

CHAPTER V

Savanna was going to remonstrate, but the words 'short remainder of my days' distressed her so much, that tears choked her words; and she obeyed in silence her mistress's orders to pack up, except when she indulged in a few exclamations against her lady's cruelty in going away without taking leave of colonel Mordaunt, who, sweet gentleman, would break his heart at her departure, especially as he was not to know whither she was going. A post-chaise was at the door the next morning at six o'clock; and as Adeline had not much luggage, having left the chief part of her furniture to be divided between the mistresses of her two lodgings, in return for their kind attention to her and her child, she took an affectionate leave of her landlady, and desired the post-boy to drive a mile on the road before him; and when he had done so, she ordered him to go on to Barnet; while the disappointed mulatto thanked God that the tawny boy was gone to Scotland with his protectress, as it prevented her having the mortification of leaving him behind her, as well as the colonel.—'Oh! had I such a lover,' cried she, (her eyes filling with tears,) 'me never leave him, nor he me!' and for the first time she thought her angel-lady hard-hearted.

For some miles they proceeded in silence, for Adeline was too much engrossed to speak; and the little Editha, being fast asleep in the mulatto's arms, did not draw her mother out of the reverie into which she had fallen.

'And where now?' said the mulatto, when the chaise stopped.

'To the next stage on the high north road.' And on they went again: nor did they stop, except for refreshments, till they had travelled thirty miles; when Adeline, worn out with fatigue, staid all night at the inn where the chaise stopped, and the next morning they resumed their journey, but not their silence. The mulatto could no longer restrain her curiosity; and she begged to know whither they were going, and why they were to be buried in the country?

Adeline, sighing deeply, answered, that they were going to live in Cumberland; and then sunk into silence again, as she could not give the mulatto her true reasons for the plan that she was pursuing without wounding her affectionate heart in a manner wholly incurable. The truth was, that Adeline supposed herself to be declining: she thought that she experienced those dreadful languors, those sensations of internal weakness, which, however veiled to the eye of the observer, speak in forcible language to the heart of the conscious sufferer. Indeed, Adeline had long struggled, but in vain, against feelings of a most overwhelming nature; amongst which, remorse and horror, for having led by her example and precepts an innocent girl into a life of infamy, were the most painfully predominant: for, believing Mary Warner's assertion when she saw her at Mr Langley's chambers, she looked upon that unhappy girl's guilt as the consequence of her own; and mourned, incessantly mourned, over the fatal errors of her early judgment, which had made her, though an idolater of virtue, a practical assistant to the cause of vice. When Adeline imagined the term of her existence to be drawing nigh, her mother, her obdurate but still dear mother, regained her wonted ascendancy over her affections; and to her, the approach of death seemed fraught with satisfaction. For that parent, so long, so repeatedly deaf to her prayers, and to the detail of those sufferings which she had made one of the conditions of her forgiveness, had promised to see and to forgive her on her *death-bed*; and her heart yearned, fondly yearned, for the moment when she should be pressed to the bosom of a relenting parent.

To Cumberland, therefore, she was resolved to hasten, and into the very neighbourhood of Mrs Mowbray; while, as the chaise wheeled them along to the place of their destination, even the prattle of her child could not always withdraw her from the abstraction into which she was plunged, as the scenes of her early years thronged upon her memory, and with them the recollection of those proofs of a mother's fondness, for a renewal of which, even in the society of Glenmurray, she had constantly and despondingly sighed.

As they approached Penrith, her emotion redoubled, and she involuntarily exclaimed—'Cruel, but still dear, mother, you little think your child is so near!'

'Heaven save me!' cried Savanna; 'are we to go and be near dat woman?'

'Yes,' replied Adeline. 'Did she not say she would forgive me on my death-bed?'

'But you not there yet, dear missess,' sobbed Savanna; 'you not there of long years!'

'Savanna,' returned Adeline, 'I should die contented to purchase my mother's blessing and forgiveness.'

Savanna, speechless with contending emotions, could not express by words the feeling of mixed sorrow and indignation which overwhelmed her; but she replied by putting Editha in Adeline's arms; then articulating with effort, 'Look there!' she sobbed aloud.

'I understand you,' said Adeline, kissing away the tears gathering in Editha's eyes, at sight of Savanna's distress: 'but perhaps I think my death would be of more service to my child than my life.'

'And to me too, I suppose,' replied Savanna reproachfully. 'Well,—me go to Scotland; for no one love me but the tawny boy.'

'You first will stay and close my eyes, I hope!' observed Adeline mournfully.

In a moment Savanna's resentment vanished. 'Me will live and die vid you,' she replied, her tears redoubling, while Adeline again sunk into thoughtful silence.

As soon as they reached Penrith, Adeline inquired for lodgings out of the town, on that side nearest to her mother's abode; and was so fortunate, as she esteemed herself, to procure two apartments at a small house within two miles of Mrs Mowbray's.

'Then I breathe once more the same air with my mother!' exclaimed Adeline as she took possession of her lodging. 'Savanna, methinks I breathe freer already!'

'Me more choked,' replied the mulatto, and turned sullenly away.

'Nay, I—I feel so much better, that to-morrow I will—I will take a walk,' said Adeline hesitatingly.

'And where?' asked Savanna eagerly.

'Oh, to-night I shall only walk to bed,' replied Adeline smiling, and with unusual cheerfulness she retired to rest.

The next morning she arose early; and being informed that a stile near a peasant's cottage commanded a view of Mrs Mowbray's house, she hired a man and cart to convey her to the bottom of the hill, and with Editha by her side, she set out to indulge her feelings by gazing on the house which contained her mother.

When they alighted, Editha gaily endeavoured to climb the hill, and urged her mother to follow her; but Adeline, rendered weak by illness and breathless by emotion, felt the ascent so difficult, that no motive less powerful than the one which actuated her could have enabled her to reach the summit.

At length, however, she did reach it:—and the lawn before Mrs Mowbray's white house, her hay-fields, and the running stream at the bottom of it, burst in all their beauty on her view.—'And this is my mother's dwelling!' exclaimed Adeline; 'and there was I born: and near here—' shall I die, she would have added but her voice failed her.

'Oh! what a pretty house and garden!' cried Editha in the unformed accents of childhood;—'how I should like to live there!'

This artless remark awakened a thousand mixed and overpowering feelings in the bosom of Adeline; and, after a pause of strong emotion, she exclaimed, catching the little prattler to her heart—'You *shall* live there, my child!—yes, yes, you *shall* live there!'

'But when?' resumed Editha.

'When I am in my grave,' answered Adeline.

'And when shall you be there?' replied the unconscious child, fondly caressing her: 'pray, mamma—pray be there soon!'

Adeline turned away, unable to answer her.

'Look—look, mamma!' resumed Editha: 'there are ladies.—Oh! do let us go there now!—why can't we?'

'Would to God we could!' replied Adeline; as in one of the ladies she recognized Mrs Mowbray, and stood gazing on her till her eyes ached again: but what she felt on seeing her she will herself describe in the succeeding pages; and I shall only add, that, as soon as Mrs Mowbray returned into the house, Adeline, wrapped in a long and mournful reverie, returned, full of a new plan, to her lodgings.

There is no love so disinterested as parental love; and Adeline had all the keen sensibilities of a parent. To make, therefore, 'assurance doubly sure'* that Mrs Mowbray should receive and should love her orphan when she was no more, she resolved to give up the gratification to which she had looked forward, the hope, before she died, of obtaining her forgiveness—that she might not weaken, by directing any part of them to herself, those feelings of remorse, fruitless tenderness, and useless regret in her mother's bosom, which she wished should be concentrated in her child.

'No,' said Adeline to herself, 'I am sure that she will not refuse to receive my orphan to her love and protection when I am no more, and am become alike insensible of reproaches and of blessings; and I think that she will love my child the more tenderly, because to me she will be unable to express the compunction which, sooner or later, she will feel from the recollection of her conduct towards me: therefore, I will make no demands on her love for myself; but, in a letter to be given her after my decease, bequeath my orphan to her care;'—and with this determination she returned from her ride.

'Have you see her?' said Savanna, running out to meet her.

'Yes—but not spoken to her; nor shall I see her again.'

'What—I suppose she see you, and not speak?'

'Oh, no; she did not see me, nor shall I urge her to see me: my plans are altered,' replied Adeline.

'And we go back to town and colonel Mordaunt?'

'No,' resumed Adeline, sighing deeply, and preparing to write to Mrs Mowbray.

But it is necessary that we should for a short time go back to Berrendale, and relate that, while Adeline and Editha were confined with the small-pox, Mr Drury received a summons from his employer in Jamaica to go over thither, to be intrusted with some particular business: in consequence of this he resolved to call again on Adeline, and inquire whether she still persisted in styling herself Mrs Berrendale; as he concluded that Berrendale would be very glad of all the information relative to her and her child which he could possibly procure, whether his curiosity on the subject proceeded from fear or love.

It so happened, that as soon as Editha, as well as her mother, was in the height of the disorder, Mr Drury called; and finding that they were both very bad, he thought that his friend Berrendale was likely to get rid of both his encumbrances at once; and being eager to communicate good news to a man whose influence in the island might be of benefit to him, he every day called to inquire concerning their health.

The second floor in the house where Adeline lodged was then occupied by a young woman in indigent circumstances, who, as well as her child, had sickened with the distemper the very day that Editha was inoculated: and when Drury, just as he was setting off for Portsmouth, ran to gain the latest intelligence of the invalids, a char-woman, who attended to the door, not being acquainted with the name of the poor young woman and her little girl, concluding that Mr Drury, by Mrs Berrendale and miss who were ill with the small-pox, meant them, replied to his inquiries,—'Ah, poor things! it is all over with them, they died last night.'

On which, not staying for any further intelligence, Drury set off for Portsmouth, and arrived at Jamaica just as Berrendale was going to remit to Adeline a draft for a hundred pounds. For Adeline, and the injury which he had done her, had been for some days constantly present to his thoughts. He had been ill; and as indigestion, the cause of his complaints, is apt to occasion disturbed dreams, he had in his dreams been haunted by the image of Glenmurray, who, with a threatening aspect, had reproached him with cruelty and base ingratitude to him, in deserting in such a manner the wife whom he had bequeathed to him.

The constant recurrence of these dreams had depressed his spirits and excited his remorse so much, that he could calm his feelings in no other way than by writing a kind letter to Adeline, and inclosing her a draft on his banker. This letter was on the point of being sent when Drury arrived, and, with very little ceremony, informed him that Adeline was dead.

'Dead!' exclaimed Berrendale, falling almost senseless on his couch:—'Dead!—Oh! for God's sake, tell me of what she died!— Surely, surely, she—' Here his voice failed him.

Drury coolly replied, that she and her child both died of the small-pox.

'But *when*? my dear fellow!—when? Say that they died nine months ago' (that was previous to his marriage), 'and you make me your friend for life!'

Drury, so *bribed*, would have said *any thing*; and, with all the coolness possible, he replied, 'Then be my friend for life:—they died rather better than nine months ago.'

Berrendale, being then convinced that bigamy was not likely to be proved against him, soon forgot, in the joy which this thought occasioned him, remorse for his conduct to Adeline, and regret for her early fate: besides, he concluded that he saved 100*l.* by the means; for he knew not that the delicate mind of Adeline would have scorned to owe pecuniary obligations to the husband who had basely and unwarrantably deserted her.

But he was soon undeceived on this subject, by a letter which colonel Mordaunt wrote in confidence to a friend in Jamaica, begging him to inquire concerning Mr Berrendale's second marriage; and to inform him privately that his injured wife had zealous and powerful friends in England, who were continually urging her to prosecute him for bigamy.

This intelligence had a fatal effect on the health of Berrendale; for though the violent temper and overbearing disposition of his second wife* had often made him regret the gentle and compliant Adeline, and a separation from her, consequently, would be a blessing, still he feared to encounter the disgrace of a prosecution, and still more the anger of his West Indian wife; who, it was not improbable, might even attack his life in the first moment of ungoverned passion.

And to these fears he soon fell a sacrifice: for a frame debilitated by intemperance could not support the assaults made on it by the continued apprehensions which colonel Mordaunt's friend had excited in him; and he died in that gentleman's presence, whom in his last moments he had summoned to his apartment to witness a will, by which he owned Adeline Mowbray to be his lawful wife, and left Editha, his acknowledged and only heir, a very considerable fortune.

But this circumstance, an account of which, with the will, was transmitted to colonel Mordaunt, did not take place till long after Adeline took up her abode in Cumberland.

CHAPTER VI

But to return to colonel Mordaunt. Though Adeline had said that he must discontinue his visits, he resolved to disobey her; and the next morning, as soon as he thought she had breakfasted, he repaired to her lodgings; where he heard, with mixed sorrow and indignation, that she had set off in a post-chaise at six o'clock, and was gone no one knew whither.

'But, surely she has left some note or message for me!' exclaimed colonel Mordaunt.

'Neither the one nor the other,' was the answer; and he returned home in no very enviable state of mind.

Various, indeed, and contradictory were his feelings: yet still affection was uppermost; and he could not but respect in Adeline the conduct which drove him to despair. Nor was self-love backward to suggest to him, that had not Adeline felt his presence and attentions to be dangerous, she would not so suddenly have withdrawn from them; and this idea was the only one on which he could at all bear to dwell: for, when he reflected that day after day might pass without his either seeing or hearing from her, existence seemed to become suddenly a burthen, and he wandered from place to place with joyless and unceasing restlessness.

At one time he resolved to pursue her; but the next, piqued at not having received from her even a note of farewell, he determined to endeavour to forget her: and this was certainly the wiser plan of the two: but the succeeding moment he determined to let a week pass, in hopes of receiving a letter from her, and, in case he did not, to set off in search of her, being assured of succeeding in his search, because the singularity of Savanna's appearance, and the traces of the small-pox visible in the face of Adeline, made them liable to be observed, and easy for him to describe.

But before the week elapsed, from agitation of mind, and from having exposed himself unnecessarily to cold, by lying on damp grass at midnight, after having heated himself by immoderate walking, colonel Mordaunt became ill of a fever; and when, after a confinement of several weeks, he was restored to health, he despaired of being able to learn tidings of the fugitives; and disappointed and dejected, he sought in the gayest scenes of the metropolis and its environs to drown the remembrances, from which in solitude he had vainly endeavoured to fly. At this time a faded but attractive woman of quality, with whom he had formerly been intimate, returned from abroad, and, meeting colonel Mordaunt at the house of a mutual friend, endeavoured to revive in him his former attachment: but it was a difficult task for a woman, who, though capable of charming the senses, had never been able to touch the heart, to excite an attachment in a man already sentimentally devoted to another.

Her advances, however, flattered colonel Mordaunt, and her society amused him, till, at length, their intimacy was renewed on its former footing: but soon disgusted with an intercourse in which the heart had no share, tired of his mistress, and displeased with himself, he took an abrupt leave of her, and, throwing himself into his post-chaise, retired to the seat of a relation in Herefordshire.

Near this gentleman's house lived Mr Maynard and his two

sisters, who had taken up their abode there immediately on their return from Portugal. Major Douglas, his wife, and Emma Douglas, were then on a visit to them. Mordaunt had known major Douglas in early life; and as soon as he found that he was in the neighbourhood, he rode over to renew his acquaintance with him; and received so cordial a welcome, not only from the major, but the master of the house and his sisters, that he was strongly induced to repeat his visits, and not a day passed in which he was not, during some part of it, a guest at Mr Maynard's.

Mrs Wallington and miss Maynard, indeed, received him with such pointed marks of distinction and preference, as to make it visible to every observer that it was not as a friend only they were desirous of considering colonel Mordaunt; while, by spiteful looks and acrimonious remarks directed to each other, the sisters expressed the jealousy which rankled in their hearts, whenever he seemed by design or inadvertency to make one of them a particular object of his attention.

Of Emma Douglas's chance for his favour, they were not at all fearful:—they thought her too plain, and too unattractive, to be capable of rivalling them; especially in the favour of an officer, a man of fashion; and therefore they beheld without emotion the attention which colonel Mordaunt paid to her whenever she spoke, and the deference which he evidently felt for her opinion, as her remarks on whatever subject she conversed were formed always to interest, and often to instruct.

One evening, while major Douglas was amusing himself in looking over some magazines which had lately been bound up together, and had not yet been deposited in Mr Maynard's library, he suddenly started, laid down the book, and turning to the window, with an exclamation of—'Poor fellow!'—passed his hand across his eyes, as if meaning to disperse an involuntary tear.

'What makes you exclaim "Poor fellow?"' asked his lovely wife: 'have you met with an affecting story in those magazines?'

'No, Louisa,' replied he, 'but I met in the obituary with a confirmation of the death of an old friend, which I suspected must have happened by this time, though I never knew it before; I see by this magazine that poor Glenmurray died a very few months after we saw him at Perpignan.'

'Poor fellow!' exclaimed Mrs Douglas.

'I wish I knew what is become of his interesting companion, miss Mowbray,' said Emma Douglas.

'I wish I did too,' secretly sighed colonel Mordaunt: but his heart palpitated so violently at this unexpected mention of the woman for whom he still pined in secret, that he had not resolution to say that he knew her.

'Become of her!' cried miss Maynard sneeringly: 'you need not *wonder*, I think, what her fate is: no doubt Mr Glenmurray's *interesting companion* has not lost her companionable qualities, and is a companion still.'

'Yes,' observed Mrs Wallington; 'or, rather, I dare say that angel of purity is gone upon the town.'

It was the dark hour, else colonel Mordaunt's agitation, on hearing these gross and unjust remarks, must have betrayed his secret to every eye; while indignation now impeded his utterance as much as confusion had done before.

'Surely, surely,' cried the kind and candid Emma Douglas, 'I must grossly have mistaken miss Mowbray's character, if she was capable of the conduct which you attribute to her!'

'My dear creature!' replied Mrs Wallington, 'how should you know any thing of her character, when it was gone long before you knew her?—*Character*, indeed! you remind me of my brother... Mr Davenport,' continued she to a gentleman present, 'did you ever hear the story of my brother and an angel of purity whom he met with abroad?'

'No—never.'

'Be quiet,' said Maynard; 'I will not be laughed at.'

However, Mrs Wallington and miss Maynard, who had not yet forgiven the deep impression which Adeline's graces had made on their brother, insisted on telling the story; to which colonel Mordaunt listened with eager and anxious curiosity. It received all the embellishments which female malice could give it; and if it amused any one, certainly that person was neither Mordaunt, nor Emma Douglas, nor her gentle sister.

'But how fortunate it was,' added miss Maynard, 'that we were not with my brother! as we should unavoidably have walked and talked with this angel.'

Mordaunt longed to say, 'I think the good fortune was all on miss Mowbray's side.'

But Adeline and her cause were in good hands: Emma Douglas stood forth as her champion.—'We feel very differently on that subject,' she replied. 'I shall ever regret, not that I saw and conversed with miss Mowbray, but that I did not see and converse with her again and again.'

At this moment Emma was standing by colonel Mordaunt, who involuntarily caught her hand and pressed it eagerly; but tried to disguise his motive by suddenly seating her in a chair behind her, saying, 'You had better sit down; I am sure you must be tired with standing so long.'

'No; really, Emma,' cried major Douglas, 'you go too far there; though to be sure, if by seeing and conversing with miss Mowbray you could have convinced her of her errors, I should not have objected to your seeing her once more or so.'

'Surely,' said Mrs Douglas timidly, 'we ought, my love, to have repeated our visits till we had made a convert of her.'

'A *convert* of her!' exclaimed Mr Maynard's sisters, 'a convert of a kept mistress!' bursting into a violent laugh, which had a most painful effect on the irritable nerves of colonel Mordaunt, whose tongue, parched with emotion, cleaved to the roof of his mouth whenever he attempted to speak.

'Pray, to what other circumstance, yet untold, do you allude?' said Mr Davenport.

'Oh, we too had a rencontre with the philosopher and his charming friend,' said major Douglas, 'and—but, Emma, do you tell the story.—'Sdeath!—Poor fellow!—Well, but we parted good friends,' added the kind-hearted Caledonian,* dispersing a tear; while Emma, in simple but impressive language, related all that passed at Perpignan between themselves, Adeline, and Glenmurray; and concluded with saying, that, 'from the almost idolatrous respect with which Glenmurray spoke and apparently thought of Adeline, and from the account of her conduct and its motives, which he so fully detailed, she was convinced that, so far from being influenced by depravity in connecting herself with Glenmurray, Adeline was the victim of a romantic, absurd, and false conception of virtue; and she should have thought it her duty to have endeavoured, assisted by her sister, to have prevailed on her to renounce her opinions, and, by becoming the wife of Glenmurray, to restore to the society of her own sex, a woman formed to be its ornament and its example. Poor thing!' she added in a faltering voice, 'would that I knew her fate!'

'I can guess it, I tell you,' said Mrs Wallington.

'We had better drop the subject, madam,' replied Emma Douglas indignantly, 'as it is one that we shall never agree upon. If I supposed miss Mowbray happy, I should feel for her, and feel interest sufficient in her fate to make me combat your prejudices concerning her; but now that she is perhaps afflicted, poor, friendless, and scorned, though unjustly, by every "virtuous she that knows her story,"* I cannot command my feelings when she is named with sarcastic disrespect, nor can I bear to hear an unhappy woman supposed to be plunged in the lowest depths of vice, whom I, on the contrary, believe to be at this moment atoning for the error of her judgment by a life of lonely penitence, or sunk perhaps already in the grave, the victim of a broken heart.'

Colonel Mordaunt, affected and delighted, hung on Emma Douglas's words with breathless attention, resolving when she had ended her narration to begin his, and clear Adeline from the calumnies of Mrs Wallington and miss Maynard; but after articulating with some difficulty—'Ladies,—I—miss Douglas,—I—' he found that his feelings would not allow him to proceed: therefore, suddenly raising Emma's hand to his lips, he imprinted on it a kiss, at once fervent and respectful, and, making a hasty bow, ran out of the house.

Every one was astonished; but none so much as Emma Douglas.

'Why, Emma!' cried the major, 'who should have thought it? I verily believe you have turned Mordaunt's head;—I protest that he kissed your hand:—I suppose he will be here tomorrow, making proposals in form.'

'I wish he may!' exclaimed Mrs Douglas.

'It is not very likely, I think,' cried miss Maynard.

Mrs Wallington said nothing; but she fanned herself violently.

'How do you know that?' said Maynard. 'He kissed your hand very tenderly—did he not, miss Douglas? and took advantage of the dark hour: that looks very lover-like.'

Emma Douglas, who, in spite of her reason, was both embarrassed and flattered by colonel Mordaunt's unexpected mode of taking leave, said not a word; but Mrs Wallington, in a voice hoarse with angry emotion, cried:

'It was very free in him, I think, and very unlike colonel Mordaunt; for he was not a sort of man to take liberties but where he met with encouragement.'

'Then I am sure he would be free with *you*, sister, sometimes,' sarcastically observed miss Maynard.

'Nay, with both of you, I think,' replied Maynard, who had not forgiven the laugh at his expense which they had tried to excite; on which an angry dialogue took place between the brother and sisters: and the Douglases, disgusted and provoked, retired to their apartment.

'There was something very strange and uncommon', said Mrs Douglas, detaining Emma in her dressing-room, 'in colonel Mordaunt's behaviour—Do you not think so, Emma?—If it should have any meaning!'

'Meaning!' cried the major: 'what meaning should it have? Why, my dear, do you think Mordaunt never kissed a woman's hand before?'

'But it was so *particular.*—Well, Emma, if it should lead to consequences!'

'Consequences!' cried the major: 'my dear girl, what can you mean?'

'Why, if he should *really love* our Emma?'

'Why then I hope our Emma will love him.—What say you, Emma?'

'I say?—I—' she replied: 'really I never thought it possible that colonel Mordaunt should have any thoughts of me, nor do I now;—but it is very strange that he should kiss my hand!'

The major could not help laughing at the *naïveté* of this reply, and in a mutual whisper they agreed how much they wished to see their sister so happily disposed of; while Emma paced up and down her own apartment some time before she undressed herself; and after seeming to convince herself, by recollecting all colonel Mordaunt's conduct towards her, that he could not possibly *mean* any thing by his unusual adieu, she went to sleep, exclaiming, 'But it is very strange that he should kiss my hand!'

CHAPTER VII

The next morning explained the mystery: for breakfast was scarcely over, when colonel Mordaunt appeared; and his presence occasioned a blush, from different causes, on the cheeks of all the ladies, and a smile on the countenances of both the gentlemen.

'You left us very abruptly last night,' said major Douglas.

'I did so,' replied Mordaunt with a sort of grave smile.

'Were you taken ill?' asked Maynard.

'I—I was not quite easy,' answered he: 'but, miss Douglas, may I request the honour of seeing you alone for a few minutes?'

Again the ladies blushed, and the gentlemen smiled. But Emma's weakness had been temporary; she had convinced herself that colonel Mordaunt's action had been nothing more than a tribute to what he fancied her generous defence of an unfortunate woman, and with an air of unembarrassed dignity she gave him her hand to lead her into an adjoining apartment.

'This is very good of you,' cried colonel Mordaunt: 'but you are all goodness!—My dear miss Douglas, had I not gone away as I did last night, I believe I should have fallen down and worshipped you, or committed some other extravagance.'

'Indeed!—What could I say to excite such enthusiasm?' replied Emma, deeply blushing.

'What!—Oh, miss Douglas!'—Then after a few more ohs, and other exclamations, he related to her the whole progress of his acquaintance with and attachment to Adeline, adding as he concluded, 'Now then judge what feelings you must have excited in my bosom:—yes, miss Douglas, I reverenced you before for your own sake, I now adore you for that of my lost Adeline.'

'So!' thought Emma, 'the kiss of the hand is explained,'—and she sighed as she thought it; nor did she much like the word *reverenced:* but she had ample amends for her mortification by what followed.

'Really,' cried colonel Mordaunt, gazing very earnestly at her, 'I do not mean to flatter you, but there is something in your countenance that reminds me very strongly of Adeline.'

'Is it possible?' said Emma, her cheeks glowing and her eyes sparkling as she spoke: 'you may not mean to flatter me, but I assure you I am flattered; for I never saw any woman whom in appearance I so much wished to resemble.'

'You do resemble her indeed,' cried colonel Mordaunt, 'and the likeness grows stronger and stronger.'

Emma blushed deeper and deeper.

'But come,' exclaimed he, 'let us go; and I will—no, *you* shall—relate to the party in the next room what I have been telling you, for I long to shame those d——'

'Fye!' said Emma smiling, and holding up her hand as if to stop the coming word. And she did stop it; for colonel Mordaunt conveyed the reproving hand to his lips; and Emma said to herself, as she half-frowning withdrew it, 'I am glad my brother was not present.'

Their return to the breakfast-room was welcome to every one, from different causes, as colonel Mordaunt's motives for requesting a tête-à-tête had given rise to various conjectures. But all conjecture was soon lost in certainty: for Emma Douglas, with more than usual animation of voice and countenance, related what colonel Mordaunt had authorised her to relate; and the envious sisters heard, with increased resentment, that Adeline, were she unmarried, would be the choice of the man whose affections they were eagerly endeavouring to captivate.

'You can't think,' said colonel Mordaunt when Emma had concluded, leaving him charmed with the manner in which she had told his story, and with the generous triumph which sparkled in her eyes at being able to exhibit Adeline's character in so favourable a point of view, 'you can't think how much miss Douglas reminds me of Mrs Berrendale!'

'Lord!' said miss Maynard with a toss of the head, 'my brother told us that she was handsome!'

'And so she is,' replied the colonel, provoked at this brutal speech: 'she has one of the finest countenances that I ever saw,—a countenance never distorted by those feelings of envy, and expressions of spite, which so often disfigure some women,—converting even a beauty into a fiend; and in this respect no one will doubt that miss Douglas resembles her:

> '"What's female beauty—but an air divine,
> Thro' which the mind's all gentle graces shine?"*

says one of our first poets: therefore, in Dr Young's opinion, madam,' continued Mordaunt, turning to Emma, 'you would have been a perfect beauty.'

This speech, so truly gratifying to the amiable girl to whom it was addressed, was a dagger in the heart of both the sisters. Nor was Emma's pleasure unalloyed by pain; for she feared that Mordaunt's attentions might become dangerous to her peace of mind, as she could not disguise to herself, that his visits at Mr Maynard's had been the chief cause of her reluctance to return to Scotland whenever their journey home was mentioned. For, always humble in her ideas of her own charms, Emma Douglas could not believe that Mordaunt would ever entertain any feeling for her at all resembling love, except when he fancied that she looked like Adeline.

But however unlikely it seemed that Mordaunt should become attached to her, and however resolved she was to avoid his society, certain it is that he soon found he could be happy in the society of no other woman, since to no other could he talk on the subject nearest his heart; and Emma, though blaming herself daily for her temerity, could not refuse to receive Mordaunt's visits: and her patient attentions to his conversation, of which Adeline was commonly the theme, seemed to have a salutary effect on his wounded feelings.

But the time for their departure arrived, much to the joy of Mrs Wallington and her sister, who hoped when Emma was gone to have a chance of being noticed by Mordaunt.

What then must have been their confusion and disappointment, when colonel Mordaunt begged to be allowed to attend the Douglases on their journey home, as he had never seen the Highlands, and wished to see them in such good company! Major Douglas and his charming wife gave a glad consent to this proposal: but Emma Douglas heard it with more alarm than pleasure; for, though her heart rejoiced at it, her reason condemned it.

A few days, however, convinced her apprehensive delicacy, that, if she loved colonel Mordaunt, it was not without hope of a return.

Colonel Mordaunt declared that every day seemed to increase her resemblance to Adeline in expression and manner; and in conduct his reason told him that she was her superior; nor could he for a moment hesitate to prefer as a wife, Emma Douglas who had never erred, to Adeline who had.

Colonel Mordaunt felt, to borrow the words of a celebrated female

writer, that 'though it is possible to love and esteem a woman who
has expiated the faults of her youth by a sincere repentance; and
though before God and man her errors may be obliterated; still there
exists one being in whose eyes she can never hope to efface them, and
that is her lover or her husband.'[1] He felt that no man of acute
sensibility can be happy with a woman whose recollections are not
pure: she must necessarily be jealous of the opinion which he entertains of her; and he must be often afraid of speaking, lest he utter a
sentiment that may wound and mortify her. Besides, he was, on just
grounds, more desirous of marrying a woman whom he 'admired,
than one whom he forgave;'* and therefore, while he addressed
Emma, he no longer regretted Adeline.

In short, he at length ceased to talk of Emma's resemblance to
Adeline, but seemed to admire her wholly for her own sake; and
having avowed his passion, and been assured of Emma's in return,
by major Douglas, he came back to England in the ensuing autumn,
the happy husband of one of the best of women.

CHAPTER VIII

We left Adeline preparing to address Mrs Mowbray and recommend
her child to her protection:—but being deeply impressed with the
importance of the task which she was about to undertake, she timidly
put it off from day to day; and having convinced herself that it was
her duty to endeavour to excite her husband to repentance, and make
him acknowledge Editha as his legitimate child, she determined to
write to him before she addressed her mother, and also to bid a last
farewell to colonel Mordaunt, whose respectful attachment had
soothed some of the pangs which consciousness of her past follies
had inflicted, and whose active friendship deserved her warmest
acknowledgments.—Little did she think the fatal effect which one
instance of his friendly zeal in her cause had had on Berrendale;
unconscious was she that the husband, whose neglect she believed to
be intentional, great as were his crimes against her, was not guilty of
the additional crime of suffering her to pine in poverty without
making a single inquiry concerning her, but was convinced that both
she and her child were no longer in existence.

[1] Madame de Staël, *Recueil de Morceaux détachés*, page 208.

In her letter to him, she conjured him by the love which he *always* bore Glenmurray, by the love he *once* bore her, and by the remorse which he would sooner or later feel for his conduct towards her and her child, to acknowledge Editha to be his lawful heir, but to suffer her to remain under that protection to which she meant to bequeath her; and on these conditions she left him her blessing, and her pardon.

The letter to colonel Mordaunt was long, and perhaps diffuse: but Adeline was jealous of his esteem, though regardless of his love; and as he had known her while acting under the influence of a fatal error of opinion, she wished to show him that on conviction she had abandoned her former way of thinking, and was candid enough to own that she had been wrong.

'You, no doubt,' she said, 'are well acquainted with the arguments urged by different writers in favour of marriage. I shall therefore only mention the argument which carried at length full conviction to *my* mind, and conquered even my deep and heartfelt reverence for the opinions of one who long was, and ever will be, the dearest object of my love and regret. But *he*, had he lived, would I am sure have altered his sentiments; and had he been a parent, the argument I allude to, as it is founded on a consideration of the interest of children, would have found its way to his reason, through his affections.

'It is evident that on the education given to children must depend the welfare of the community; and, consequently, that whatever is likely to induce parents to neglect the education of their children must be *hurtful* to the welfare of the community. It is also certain, that though the agency of the *passions* be necessary to the existence of all society, it is on the cultivation and influence of the *affections* that the happiness and improvement of social life depend.

'Hence it follows that marriage must be more beneficial to society in its consequences, than connections capable of being dissolved at pleasure; because it has a tendency to call forth and exercise the affections, and control the passions.—; It has been said, that, were we free to dissolve at will a connection formed by love, we should not wish to do it, as constancy is natural to us,* and there is in all of us a tendency to form an exclusive attachment. But though I believe, from my own experience, that the few are capable of unforced constancy, and could love for life one dear and honoured object, still I believe that the many are given to the love of change;—that, in men

especially, a new object can excite new passion and, judging from the
increasing depravity of both sexes, in spite of existing laws, and in
defiance of shame,—I am convinced, that if the ties of marriage were
dissolved, or it were no longer to be judged infamous to act in contempt of them, unbridled licentiousness would soon be in general
practice.—What then, in such a state of society, would be the fate of
the children born in it?—What would their education be?—Parents
continually engrossed in the enervating but delightful egotism of a
new and happy love, lost in selfish indulgence, the passions awake,
but the affections slumbering, and the sacred ties of parental feeling
not having time nor opportunity to fasten on the heart,—their offspring would either die the victims of neglect, and the very existence
of the human race be threatened; or, without morals or instruction,
they would grow up to scourge the world by their vices, till the whole
fabric of civilized society was gradually destroyed.

'On this ground, therefore, this strong ground, I venture to build
my present opinion, that marriage is a wise and ought to be a sacred
institution; and I bitterly regret the hour when, with the hasty and
immature judgment of eighteen, and with a degree of presumption
scarcely pardonable at any time of life, I dared to think and act
contrary to this opinion and the reverend experience of ages, and
became in the eyes of the world an example of vice, when I believed
myself the champion of virtue.'

She then went on to express the following sentiments. 'You will
think, perhaps, that I ought to struggle against the weakness which is
hurrying me to the grave, and live for the sake of my child.—Alas! it
is for her sake that I most wish to die.

'There are two ways in which a mother can be of use to her
daughter: the one is by instilling into her mind virtuous principles,
and by setting her a virtuous example: the other is, by being to her
in her own person an awful warning,—a melancholy proof of the
dangers which attend a deviation from the path of virtue. But, oh!
how jealous must a mother be of her child's esteem and veneration!
and how could she bear to humble herself in the eyes of the beloved
object, by avowing that she had committed crimes against society,
however atoned for by penitence and sorrow! I can never, now, be
a correct example for my Editha, nor could I endure to live to
be a warning to her.—Nay, if I lived, I should be most probably a
dangerous example to her; for I should be (on my death-bed I think

I may be allowed the boast) respected and esteemed; while the society around me would forget my past errors, in the sincerity of my repentance.

'If then a strong temptation should assail my child, might she not yield to it from an idea that "one false step may be retrieved,"* and cite her mother as an example of this truth? while, unconscious of the many secret heart-aches of that repentant mother, unconscious of the sorrows and degradations she had experienced, she regarded nothing but the present respectability of her mother's life, and contented herself with hoping one day to resemble her.

'Believe me, that were it possible for me to choose between life and death, for my child's sake, the choice would be the latter. Now, when she shall see in my mournful and eventful history, written as it has been by me in moments of melancholy leisure, that all my sorrows were consequent on one presumptuous error of judgment in early youth, and shall see a long and minute detail of the secret agonies which I have endured,—those agonies wearing away my existence, and ultimately hurrying me to an untimely grave; she will learn that the woman who feels justly, yet has been led even into the practice of vice, however she may be forgiven by others, can never forgive herself; and though she may dare to lift an eye of hope to that Being who promises pardon on repentance, she will still recollect with anguish the fair and glorious course which she might have run; and that, instead of humbly imploring forbearance and forgiveness, she might have demanded universal respect and esteem.

'True it is, that I did not act in defiance of the world's opinion, from any depraved feelings, or vicious inclinations: but the world could not be expected to believe this, since motives are known only to our own hearts, and the great Searcher of hearts: therefore, as far as example goes, I was as great a stumbling block to others as if the life I led had been owing to the influence of lawless desires; and society was right in making, and in seeing, no distinction between me and any other woman living in an unsanctioned connection.

'But methinks I hear you say, that Editha might never be informed of my past errors. Alas! wretched must that woman be whose happiness and respectability depend on the secrecy of others! Besides, did I not think the concealment of crime in itself a crime, how could I know an hour of peace while I reflected that a moment's malice, or inadvertency, in one of Editha's companions might cause her to blush at her mother's disgrace?—that, while her young cheek was flushed perhaps with the artless triumphs of beauty, talent, and virtue, the parent who envied me, or the daughter who envied her, might suddenly convert her joy into anguish and mortification, by artfully informing her, with feigned pity for my sorrows and admiration of my penitence, that I had once been a *disgrace* to that family of which I was now the pride?—No—even if I were not for ever separated in this world from the only man whom I ever loved with passionate and well-founded affection, united for life to the object of my just aversion, and were I not conscious (horrible and overwhelming thought!) of having by my example led another into the path of sin,—still, I repeat it, for my child's sake I should wish to die, and should consider, not early death, but lengthened existence, as a curse.'

So Adeline reasoned and felt in her moments of reflection: but the heart had sometimes dominion over her; and as she gazed on Editha, and thought that Mrs Mowbray might be induced to receive her again to her favour, she wished even on any terms to have her life prolonged.

CHAPTER IX

Having finished her letter to colonel Mordaunt and Berrendale, she again prepared to write to her mother; a few transient fears overcoming every now and then those hopes of success in her application, which, till she took up her pen, she had so warmly encouraged.

Alas! little did she know how erroneously for years she had judged of Mrs Mowbray. Little did she suspect that her mother had long forgiven her; had pined after her; had sought, though in vain, to procure intelligence of her, and was then wearing away her existence in solitary woe, a prey to self-reproach, and to the corroding fear that her daughter, made desperate by her renunciation of her, had, on the death of Glenmurray, plunged into a life of shame, or sunk, broken-hearted, into the grave! for not one of Adeline's letters had ever reached Mrs Mowbray; and the mother and the daughter had both been the victims of female treachery and jealousy.

Mrs Mowbray, as soon as she had parted with Adeline for the last time, had dismissed all her old servants, the witnesses of her sorrows and disgrace, and retired to her estate in Cumberland,—an estate where Adeline had first seen the light, and where Mrs Mowbray had first experienced the transports of a mother. This spot was therefore ill calculated to banish Adeline from her mother's thoughts, and to continue her exclusion from her affections. On the contrary, her image haunted Mrs Mowbray:—whithersoever she went, she still saw her in an attitude of supplication; she still heard the plaintive accents of her voice;—and often did she exclaim, 'My child, my child! wretch that I am! must I never, never see thee more!'

These ideas increased to so painful a degree, that, finding her solitude insupportable, she invited an orphan relation in narrow circumstances to take up her abode with her.

This young woman, whose ruling passion was avarice, and whose greatest talent was cunning, resolved to spare no pains to keep the situation which she had gained, even to the exclusion of Adeline, should Mrs Mowbray be weak enough to receive her again. She therefore intercepted all the letters which were in or like Adeline's hand-writing; and having learnt to imitate Mrs Mowbray's, she enclosed them in a blank cover to Adeline; who, thinking the direction was written in her mother's hand, desisted, as the artful girl expected she would do, from what appeared to her a hopeless application.

And she exulted in her contrivance;—when Mrs Mowbray, on seeing in a magazine that Glenmurray was dead, (full a year after his decease,) bursting into a passion of tears, protested that she would instantly invite Adeline to her house.

'Yes,' cried she, 'I can do so without infringement of my oath.— She is disgraced in the eye of the world by her connection with Glenmurray, and she is wretched in love; nay, more so, perhaps, than I have been; and I can, I will invite her to lose the remembrance of her misfortunes in my love!'

Thus did her ardent wish to be reunited to Adeline deceive her conscience; for, by the phrase 'wretched in love,' she meant, forsaken by the object of her attachment,—and that Adeline had not been: therefore her oath remained in full force against her. But where could she seek Adeline?—Dr Norberry could, perhaps, give her this information; and to him she resolved to write—though he had cast her from his acquaintance: 'but her pride', as she said, 'fell with her fortunes; ' and she scrupled not to humble herself before the zealous friend of her daughter. But this letter would never have reached him, had not her treacherous relation been ill at the time when it was written.

Dr Norberry had recovered the illness of which Adeline supposed him to have died: but as her letter to him, to which she received no answer, alluded to the money transaction between her and Mrs Norberry; and as she commented on the insulting expressions in Mrs Norberry's note, that lady thought proper to suppress the second letter as well as the first; and when the doctor, on his recovery, earnestly demanded to know whether any intelligence had been received of miss Mowbray, Mrs Norberry, with pretended reluctance, told him that she had written to him in great distress, while he was delirious, to borrow money; that she had sent her *ten pounds*, which Adeline had returned, reproaching her for her parsimony, and saying that she had found a friend who would not suffer her to want.

'But did you tell her that you thought me in great danger?'

'I did.'

'Why, zounds, woman! did she not, after that, write to know how I was?'

'Never.'

'Devil take me if I could have thought it of her!' answered the doctor—who could not but believe this story for the sake of his own peace, as it was less destructive to his happiness to think Adeline in fault, than his wife or children guilty of profligate falsehood: he therefore, with a deep sigh, begged Adeline's name might never be mentioned to him again; and though he secretly wished to hear of her welfare, he no longer made her the subject of conversation.

But Mrs Mowbray's letter recalled her powerfully both to his memory and affections, while, with many a deep-drawn sigh, he regretted that he had no possible means of discovering where she was;—and with a heavy heart he wrote the following letter, which miss Woodville, Mrs Mowbray's relation, having first contrived to open, and read it, ventured to give into her hands, as it contained no satisfactory information concerning Adeline.

' "I look on the separation of my mother and me in this world to be eternal," said the poor dear lost Adeline to me, the last time we met. "You do!" replied I: "then, poor devil! how miserable will your mother be when her present resentment subsides!—Well, when that time comes, I may perhaps see her again," added I, with a d——d queer something rising in my throat as I said it, and your poor girl blessed me for the kind intention.—(Pshaw! I have blotted the paper: at my years it is a shame to be so watery-eyed.) Well,—the time above mentioned is come—you are miserable, you are repentant—and you ask me to forget and forgive.—I do forget, I do forgive: some time or other, too, I will tell you so in person; and were the lost Adeline to know that I did so, she would bless me for the act, as she did before for the intention. But, alas! where she is, what she is, I know not, and have not any means of knowing. To say the truth, her conduct to me and mine has been devilish *odd*, not to say *wrong*. But, poor thing! she is either dead or miserable, and I forgive her:—so I do you, as I said before, and the Lord give you all the consolation which you so greatly need!

'Yours once more,

'In true kindness of spirit,

'JAMES NORBERRY.'

This letter made Mrs Mowbray's wounds bleed afresh, at the same time that it destroyed all her expectations of finding Adeline; and the only hope that remained to cheer her was, that she might perhaps, if yet alive, write sooner or later, to implore forgiveness. But month after month elapsed, and no tidings of Adeline reached her despairing mother.

She then put an advertisement in the paper, so worded that Adeline, had she seen it, must have known to whom it alluded; but it never met her eyes, and Mrs Mowbray gave herself up to almost absolute despair; when accident introduced her to a new acquaintance, whose example taught her patience, and whose soothing benevolence bade her hope for happier days.

One day as Mrs Mowbray, regardless of a heavy shower, and lost in melancholy reflections, was walking with irregular steps on the road to Penrith, with an unopened umbrella in her hand, she suddenly raised her eyes from the ground, and beheld a quaker-lady pursued by an over-driven bullock, and unable any longer to make an effort to escape its fury. At this critical moment Mrs Mowbray, from a sort of irresistible impulse, as fortunate in its effects as presence of mind, yet scarcely perhaps to be denominated such, suddenly opened her umbrella; and, approaching the animal, brandished it before his eyes. Alarmed at this unusual appearance, he turned hastily and ran towards the town, where she saw that he was immediately met and secured.

'Thou hast doubtless saved my life,' said the quaker, grasping Mrs Mowbray's hand, with an emotion which she vainly tried to suppress; 'and I pray God to bless thine!'

Mrs Mowbray returned the pressure of her hand, and burst into tears; overcome with joy for having saved a fellow-creature's life; with terror, which she was now at leisure to feel for the danger to which she had herself been exposed; and with mournful emotion from the consciousness how much she needed the blessing which the grateful quaker invoked on her head.

'Thou tremblest even more than I do,' observed the lady, smiling, but seeming ready to faint; 'I believe we had better, both of us, sit down on the bank: but it is so wet that perhaps we had better endeavour to reach my house, which is only at the end of yon field.' Mrs Mowbray bowed her assent; and, supporting each other, they at length arrived at a neat white house, to which the quaker cordially bade her welcome.

'It was but this morning,' said Mrs Mowbray, struggling for utterance, 'that I called upon Death to relieve me from an existence at once wretched and useless.'—Here she paused:—and her new acquaintance, cordially pressing her hand, waited for the conclusion of her speech;—'but now,' continued Mrs Mowbray, 'I revoke, and repent my idle and vicious impatience of life. I have saved your life, and something like enjoyment now seems to enliven mine.'

'I suspect', replied the lady, 'that thou hast known deep affliction; and I rejoice that at this moment, and in so providential a manner, I have been introduced to thy acquaintance:—for I too have known sorrow, and the mourner knows how to speak comfort to the heart of the mourner. My name is Rachel Pemberton; and I hope that when I know thy name, and thy story, thou wilt allow me to devote to thy comfort some hours of the existence which thou hast preserved.' She then hastily withdrew, to pour forth in solitary prayer the breathings of devout gratitude:—while Mrs Mowbray, having communed with her own thoughts, felt a glow of unwonted satisfaction steal over her mind; and by the time Mrs Pemberton returned, she was able to meet her with calmness and cheerfulness.

'Thou knowest my name,' said Mrs Pemberton as she entered, seating herself by Mrs Mowbray, 'but I have yet to learn thine.'

'My name is Mowbray,' she replied, sighing deeply.

'Mowbray!—The lady of Rosevalley in Gloucestershire; and the mother of Adeline Mowbray?' exclaimed Mrs Pemberton.

'What of Adeline Mowbray? What of my child?' cried Mrs Mowbray, seizing Mrs Pemberton's hand. 'Blessed woman! tell me,—Do you indeed know her?—can you tell me where to find her?'

'I will tell thee all that I know of her,' replied Mrs Pemberton in a faltering voice; 'but thy emotion overpowers me.—I—I was once a mother, and I can feel for thee.' She then turned away her head to conceal a starting tear; while Mrs Mowbray, in incoherent eagerness, repeated her questions, and tremblingly awaited her answer.

'Is she well? Is she happy?—say but that!' she exclaimed, sobbing as she spoke.

'She was well and contented when I last heard from her,' replied Mrs Pemberton calmly.

'Heard from her? Then she writes to you! Oh, blessed, blessed woman! show me her letters, and tell me only that she has forgiven me for all my unkindness to her—' As she said this, Mrs Mowbray threw her arms round Mrs Pemberton, and sunk half-fainting on her shoulder.

'I will tell thee all that has ever passed between us, if thou wilt be composed,' gravely answered Mrs Pemberton; 'but this violent expression of thy feelings is unseemly and detrimental.'

'Well—well—I will be calm,' said Mrs Mowbray; and Mrs Pemberton began to relate the interview which she had with Adeline at Richmond.

'How long ago did this take place?' eagerly interrupted Mrs Mowbray.

'Full six years.'

'Oh, God!' exclaimed she, impatiently,—'Six years! By this time then she may be dead—she may—'

'Thou art incorrigible, I fear,' said Mrs Pemberton, 'but thou art afflicted, and I will bear with thy impatience:—sit down again and attend to me, and thou wilt hear much later intelligence of thy daughter.'

'How late?' asked Mrs Mowbray, with frantic eagerness;—and Mrs Pemberton, overcome with the manner in which she spoke, could scarcely falter out, 'Within a twelvemonth I have heard of her.'

'Within a twelvemonth!' joyfully cried Mrs Mowbray: but, recollecting herself, she added mournfully—'but in that time what—what may not have happened!'

'I know not what to do with thee nor for thee,' observed Mrs Pemberton; 'but do try, I beseech thee, to hear me patiently!'

Mrs Mowbray then re-seated herself; and Mrs Pemberton informed her of Adeline's premature confinement at Richmond; of her distress on Glenmurray's death, and of her having witnessed it.

'Ah! you acted a mother's part—you did what I ought to have done,' cried Mrs Mowbray, bursting into tears,—'but, go on—I will be patient.'

Yet that was impossible; for, when she heard of Adeline's insanity, her emotions became so strong that Mrs Pemberton, alarmed for her life, was obliged to ring for assistance.

When she recovered,—'Thou hast heard the worst now,' said Mrs Pemberton, 'and all I have yet to say of thy child is satisfactory.'

She then related the contents of Adeline's first letter, informing her of her marriage:—and Mrs Mowbray, clasping her hands together, blessed God that Adeline was become a wife. The next letter Mrs Pemberton read informed her that she was the mother of a fine girl.

'A mother!' she exclaimed, 'Oh, how I should like to see her child!'—But at the same moment she recollected how bitterly she had reviled her when she saw her about to become a mother, at their last meeting; and, torn with conflicting emotions, she was again insensible to aught but her self-upbraidings.

'Well—but where is she now? where is the child? and when did you hear from her last?' cried she.

'I have not heard from her since,' hesitatingly replied Mrs Pemberton.

'But can't you write to her?'

'Yes;—but in her last letter she said she was going to change her lodgings, and would write again when settled in a new habitation.'

Again Mrs Mowbray paced the room in wild and violent distress: but her sorrows at length yielded to the gentle admonitions and soothings of Mrs Pemberton, who bade her remember, that when she rose in the morning she had not expected the happiness and consolation which she had met with that day; and that a short time might bring forth still greater comfort.

'For', said Mrs Pemberton, 'I can write to the house where she formerly lodged, and perhaps the person who keeps it can give us intelligence of her.'

On hearing this, Mrs Mowbray became more composed, and diverted her sorrow by a thousand fond inquiries concerning Adeline, which none but a mother could make, and none but a mother listen to with patience.

While this conversation was going on, a knock at the door was heard, and miss Woodville entered the room in great emotion; for she had heard, on the road, that a mad bullock had attacked a lady; and also that Mrs Mowbray, scarcely able to walk, had been led into the white house in the field by the road side.

Miss Woodville was certainly as much alarmed as she pretended to be: but there was a somewhat in the expression of her alarm which, though it gratified Mrs Mowbray, was displeasing to the more penetrating Mrs Pemberton. She could not indeed guess that miss Woodville's alarm sprung merely from apprehension lest Mrs Mowbray should die before she had provided for her in her will: yet, notwithstanding, she felt that her expressions of concern and anxiety had no resemblance to those of real affection; and in spite of her habitual candour, she beheld miss Woodville with distrust.

But this feeling was considerably increased on observing, that when Mrs Mowbray exultingly introduced her, not only as the lady whose life she had been the means of preserving, but as the friend and correspondent of her daughter, she evidently changed colour; and, in spite of her habitual plausibility, could not utter a single coherent sentence of pleasure or congratulation:—and it was also evident, that, being conscious of Mrs Pemberton's regarding her with a scrutinizing eye, she was not easy till, on pretence of Mrs Mowbray's requiring rest after her alarm, she had prevailed on her to return home.

But she could not prevent the new friends from parting with eager assurances of meeting again and again: and it was agreed between them, that Mrs Pemberton should spend the next day at the Lawn.

Mrs Pemberton, who is thus again introduced to the notice of my readers, had been, as well as Mrs Mowbray, the pupil of adversity. She had been born and educated in fashionable life; and she united to a very lovely face and elegant form, every feminine grace and accomplishment.

When she was only eighteen, Mr Pemberton, a young and gay quaker,* fell in love with her; and having inspired her with a mutual passion, he married her, notwithstanding the difference of their religious opinions, and the displeasure of his friends. He was consequently disowned by the society: but being weaned by the happiness which he found at home from those public amusements which had first lured him from the strict habits of his sect, he was soon desirous of being again admitted a member of it; and in process of time, he was once more received into it; while his amiable wife, having no wish beyond her domestic circle, and being disposed to think her husband's opinions right, became in time, a convert to the same profession of faith, and exhibited in her manners the rare union of the easy elegance of a woman of the world with the rigid decorum and unadorned dress of a strict quaker.

But in the midst of her happiness, and whilst looking forward to a long continuance of it, a fever, caught in visiting the sick bed of a cottager, carried off her husband, and next two lovely children; and Mrs Pemberton would have sunk under the stroke, but for the watchful care and affectionate attentions of the friend of her youth, who resided near her, and who, in time, prevailed on her to receive with becoming fortitude and resignation the trials which she was appointed to undergo.

During this season of affliction, as we have before stated, she became a teacher in the quaker's society: but at the time of her meeting Adeline at Richmond, she had been called from the duties of her public profession to watch over the declining health of her friend and consoler, and to accompany her to Lisbon.

There, during four long years, she bent over her sick couch, now elated with hope, and now sunk into despondence; when, at the beginning of the fifth year, her friend died in her arms, and she returned to England, resolved to pass her days, except when engaged in the active duties of her profession, on a little estate in Cumberland, bequeathed to her by her friend on her death-bed. But ill health and various events had detained her in the west of England since her return; and she had not long taken possession of her house near Penrith, when she became introduced in so singular a manner to Mrs Mowbray's acquaintance—an acquaintance which would, she hoped, prove of essential service to them both; and as soon as her guest departed, Mrs Pemberton resolved to inquire what character Mrs Mowbray bore in the neighbourhood, and whether her virtues at all kept pace with her misfortunes.

Her inquiries were answered in the most satisfactory manner; as, fortunately for Mrs Mowbray, with the remembrance of her daughter had recurred to her that daughter's benevolent example. She remembered the satisfaction which used to beam from Adeline's countenance when she returned from her visits to the sick and the afflicted; and she resolved to try whether those habits of charitable exertion which could increase the happiness of the young and light-hearted Adeline, might not have power to alleviate the sorrows of her own drooping age, and broken joyless heart.

'Sweet are the uses of adversity!'*—She who, while the child of prosperity, was a romantic, indolent theorist, an inactive speculator, a proud contemner of the dictates of sober experience, and a neglecter of that practical benevolence which can in days produce more benefit to others than theories and theorists can accomplish in years—this erring woman, awakened from her dreams and reveries to habits of useful exertion by the stimulating touch of affliction, was become the visitor of the sick, the consoler of the sorrowful, the parent of the fatherless, while virtuous industry looked up to her with hope; and her name, like that of Adeline in happier days, was pronounced with prayers and blessings.

But, alas! she felt that blessing could reach her only in the shape of her lost child: and, though she was conscious of being useful to others, though she had the satisfaction of knowing that she had but the day before been the means of preserving a valuable life, she met Mrs Pemberton, when she arrived at the Lawn, with a countenance of fixed melancholy, and was at first disposed to expect but little success from the project of writing to Adeline's former lodgings in order to inquire.

The truth was, that miss Woodville had artfully insinuated the improbability of such an inquiry's succeeding; and, though Mrs Mowbray had angrily asserted her hopes when miss Woodville provokingly asserted her *fears*, the treacherous girl's insinuations had sunk deeply into her mind, and Mrs Pemberton saw, with pain and wonder, an effect produced of which the cause was wholly unseen. But she at length succeeded in awakening Mrs Mowbray's

hopes; and in a letter written by Mrs Pemberton to the mistress of
the house whence Adeline formerly dated, she inclosed one to her
daughter glowing with maternal tenderness, and calculated to speak
peace to her sorrows.

These letters were sent, as soon as written, to the post by Mrs
Mowbray's footman; but miss Woodville contrived to meet him near
the post-office, and telling him she would put the letter in the
receiver, she gave him a commission to call at a shop in Penrith for
her, at which she had not time to call herself.

Thus was another scheme for restoring Adeline to her afflicted
mother frustrated by the treachery of this interested woman; who,
while Mrs Pemberton and Mrs Mowbray looked anxiously forward
to the receipt of an answer from London, triumphed with malignant
pleasure in the success of her artifice.—But, spite of herself, she
feared Mrs Pemberton, and was not at all pleased to find that, till the
answer from London could arrive, that lady was to remain at the
Lawn.

She contrived, however, to be as little in her presence as possible;
for, contrary to Mrs Pemberton's usual habits, she felt a distrust of
miss Woodville, which her intelligent eye could not help expressing,
and which consequently alarmed the conscious heart of the culprit.
Being left therefore, by miss Woodville's fears, alone with Mrs
Mowbray, she drew from her, at different times, ample details of
Adeline's childhood, and the method which Mrs Mowbray had
pursued in her education.

'Ah! 'tis as I suspected,' interrupted Mrs Pemberton during one
of these conversations. 'Thy daughter's *faults* originated in thee! her
education was cruelly defective.'

'No!' replied Mrs Mowbray with almost angry eagerness, 'whatever my errors as a mother have been, and for the rash marriage
which I made I own myself culpable in the highest degree, I am sure
that I paid the greatest attention to my daughter's education. If you
were but to see the voluminous manuscript on the subject, which I
wrote for her improvement—'

'But where was thy daughter; and how was she employed during
the time that thou wert writing a book by which to educate her?'

Mrs Mowbray was silent; she recollected that, while she was
gratifying her own vanity in composing her system of education,
Adeline was almost banished her presence; and, but for the humble

instruction of her grandmother, would, at the age of fifteen, have run a great risk of being both an ignorant and useless being.

'Forgive me, friend Mowbray,' resumed Mrs Pemberton, aware in some measure of what was passing in Mrs Mowbray's mind— 'forgive me if I venture to observe, that till of late years, a thick curtain of self-love seems to have been dropped between thy heart and maternal affection. It is now, and now only that thou hast learned to feel like a true and affectionate mother!'

'Perhaps you are right,' replied Mrs Mowbray mournfully, 'still, I always meant well; and hoped that my studies would conduce to the benefit of my child.'

'So they might, perhaps, to that of thy second, third, or fourth child, hadst thou been possessed of so many; but, in the mean while, thy first-born must have been fatally neglected. A child's education begins almost from the hour of its birth; and the mother who understands her task, knows that the circumstances which every moment calls forth, are the tools with which she is to work in order to fashion her child's mind and character.—What would you think of the farmer who was to let his fields lie fallow for years, while he was employed in contriving a method of cultivating land to increase his gains ten-fold?'

'But I did not suffer Adeline's mind to lie fallow.—I allowed her to read, and I directed her studies.'

'Thou didst so; but what were those studies? and didst thou acquaint thyself with the deductions which her quick mind formed from them? No—thou didst not, as parents should do, inquire into the impressions made on thy daughter's mind by the books which she perused. Prompt to feel, and hasty to decide, as Adeline was, how necessary was to her the warning voice of judgment and experience!'

'But how could I imagine that a girl so young should dare to act, whatever her opinions might be, in open defiance of the opinions of the world?'

'But she had not lived in the world; therefore, scarcely knew how repugnant to it her opinions were; nor, as she did not mix in general society, could she care sufficiently for its good opinion, to be willing to act contrary to her own ideas of right, rather than forfeit it: besides, thou ownest that thou didst openly profess thy admiration of the sentiments which she adopted; nor, till they were confirmed irrevocably hers, didst thou declare, that to act up to them was, in thy opinion, vicious. And then it was too late: she thought thy timidity, and not thy wisdom, spoke, and she set thee the virtuous example of acting up to the dictates of conscience. But Adeline and thou are both the pupils of affliction and experience; and I trust that, all your errors repented of, you will meet once more to expiate your past follies by your future conduct.'

'I hope so too,' meekly replied Mrs Mowbray, whose pride had been completely subdued by self-upbraidings and distress: 'Oh! when—when will an answer arrive from London?'

CHAPTER X

Alas! day after day elapsed, and no letter came; but while Mrs Mowbray was almost frantic with disappointment and anxiety, Mrs Pemberton thought that she observed in miss Woodville's countenance a look of triumphant malice, which ill accorded with the fluent expressions of sympathy and regret with which she gratified her unsuspicious relation, and she determined to watch her very narrowly; for she thought it strange that Adeline, however she might respect her mother's oath, should never, in the bitterness of her sorrows, have unburthened her heart by imparting them to her: one day, when, as usual, the post had been anxiously expected, and, as usual, had brought no letter from London concerning Adeline; and while miss Woodville was talking on indifferent subjects with ill suppressed gaiety, though Mrs Mowbray, sunk into despondence, was lying on the sofa by her; Mrs Pemberton suddenly exclaimed— 'There is only one right way of proceeding, friend Mowbray,—thou and I must go to London, and make our inquiries in person, and then we shall have a great chance of succeeding.' As she said this, she looked stedfastly at miss Woodville, and saw her turn very pale, while her eye was hastily averted from the penetrating glance of Mrs Pemberton; and when she heard Mrs Mowbray, in a transport of joy, declare that they had better set off that very evening, unable to conceal her terror and agitation, she hastily left the room.

Mrs Pemberton instantly followed her into the apartment to which she had retired, and the door of which she had closed with great violence.—She found her walking to and fro, and wringing her hands, as if in agony. On seeing Mrs Pemberton, she started, and sinking into a chair, she complained of being very ill, and desired to be left alone.

'Thou art ill, and thy illness is of the worst sort, I fear,' replied Mrs Pemberton; 'but I will stay, and be thy physician.'

'*You*, my physician?' replied miss Woodville, with fury in her looks; 'You?'

'Yes—*I*—I see that thou art afraid lest Adeline should be restored to her paternal roof.'

'Who told you so, officious, insolent woman?' returned miss Woodville.

'Thy own looks—but all this is very natural in thee: thou fearest that Adeline's favour should annihilate thine.'

'Perhaps I do,' cried miss Woodville, a little less alarmed, and catching at this plausible excuse for her uneasiness; 'for, should I be forced to leave my cousin's house, I shall be reduced to comparative poverty, and solitude again.'

'But why shouldest thou be forced to leave it? Art thou not Adeline's friend?'

'Ye—yes,' faltered out miss Woodville.

'But it is uncertain whether we can find Adeline—still we shall be very diligent in our inquiries; yet it is so strange that she should never have written to her mother, if alive, that perhaps—'

'Oh, I dare say she is dead,' hastily interrupted miss Woodville.

'Has she been dead long, thinkest thou?'

'No—not long—not above six months, I dare say.'

'No!—Hast thou any reason then for knowing that she was alive six months ago?' asked Mrs Pemberton, looking steadily at miss Woodville, as she spoke.

'I?—Lord—no—How should I know?' she replied, her lip quivering, and her whole frame trembling.

'I tell thee how.—Art thou not conscious of having intercepted letters from thy cousin, to her relenting parent?'

Mrs Pemberton had scarcely uttered these words, when miss Woodville fell back nearly *insensible* in her chair—a proof that the accusation was only too well founded. As soon as she recovered, Mrs Pemberton said, with great gentleness, 'Thou art ill,—ill indeed, but, as I suspected, thy illness is of the mind; there is a load of guilt on it; throw it off then by a full confession, and be the sinner that repenteth.'

In a few moments miss Woodville, conscious that her emotion had betrayed her, and suspecting that Mrs Pemberton had by some means or other received hints of her treachery, confessed that she had intercepted and destroyed letters from Adeline to her mother; and also owned, to the great joy of Mrs Pemberton, that Adeline's last letter, the letter in which she informed Mrs Mowbray that all the conditions were then fulfilled, without which alone she had sworn never to forgive her, had arrived only two months before; and that it was dated from such a street, and such a number, in London.

'My poor friend will be so happy!' said Mrs Pemberton; and, her own eyes filling with tears of joy, she hastened to find Mrs Mowbray.

'But what will become of *me*?' exclaimed miss Woodville, detaining her—'*I* am ruined—ruined for ever!'

'Not so,' replied Mrs Pemberton, 'thou art *saved*,—saved, I trust, *for ever*.—Thou hast confessed thy guilt, and made all the atonement now in thy power. Go to thine own room, and I will soon make known to thee thy relation's sentiments towards thee.'

So saying, she hastened to Mrs Mowbray, whom she found giving orders, with eager impatience, to have post horses sent for immediately.

'Then thou art full of expectation, I conclude, from the event of our journey to town?' said Mrs Pemberton smiling.

'To be sure I am,' replied Mrs Mowbray.

'And so am I,' she answered—'for I think that I know the present abode of thy daughter.'

Mrs Mowbray started—her friend's countenance expressed more joy and exultation than she had ever seen on it before; and, almost breathless with new hope, she seized her hand and conjured her to explain herself.

The explanation was soon given; and Mrs Mowbray's joy, in consequence of it, unbounded.

'But what is thy will', observed Mrs Pemberton, 'with regard to thy guilty relation?'

'I cannot—cannot see her again now, if ever;—and she must immediately leave my house.'

'Immediately?'

'Yes,—but I will settle on her a handsome allowance; for my

conscience tells me, that, had I behaved like a mother to my child, no one could have been tempted to injure her thus.—I put this unhappy woman into a state of temptation, and she yielded to it:—but I feel only too sensibly, that no one has been such an enemy to my poor Adeline as I have been; nor, conscious of my own offences towards her, dare I resent those of another.'

'I love, I honour thee for what thou hast now uttered,' cried Mrs Pemberton with unusual animation.—'I see that thou art now indeed a christian; such are the breathings of a truly contrite spirit; and, verily, she who can so easily forgive the crimes of others may hope to have her own forgiven.'

Mrs Pemberton then hastened to speak hope and comfort to the mind of the penitent offender, while Mrs Mowbray ran to meet her servant, who, to her surprise, was returning without horses, for none were to be procured; and Mrs Mowbray saw herself obliged to delay her journey till noon the next day, when she was assured of having horses from Penrith. But when, after a long and restless night, she arose in the morning, anticipating with painful impatience the hour of her departure, Mrs Pemberton entered her room, and informed her that she had passed nearly all the night at miss Woodville's bed-side, who had been seized with a violent delirium at one o'clock in the morning, and in her ravings was continually calling on Mrs Mowbray, and begging to see her once more.

'I will see her directly,' replied Mrs Mowbray, without a moment's hesitation; and hastened to miss Woodville's apartment, where she found the medical attendant whom Mrs Pemberton had sent for just arrived. He immediately declared the disorder to be an inflammation on the brain, and left them with little or no hope of her recovery.

Mrs Mowbray, affected beyond measure at the pathetic appeals for pardon addressed to her continually by the unconscious sufferer, took her station at the bed-side; and, hanging over her pillow, watched for the slightest gleam of returning reason, in order to speak the pardon so earnestly implored: and while thus piously engaged, the chaise that was to convey her and her friend to London, and perhaps to Adeline, drove up to the gate.

'Art thou ready?' said Mrs Pemberton, entering the room equipped for her journey.

At this moment the poor invalid reiterated her cries for pardon, and begged Mrs Mowbray not to leave her without pronouncing her forgiveness.

Mrs Mowbray burst into tears; and though sure that she was not even conscious of her presence, she felt herself almost unable to forsake her:—still it was in search of her daughter that she was going—nay, perhaps, it was to her daughter that she was hastening; and, as this thought occurred to her, she hurried to the door of the chamber, saying she should be ready in a moment.

But the eye of the phrensied sufferer followed her as she did so, and in a tone of unspeakable agony she begged, she entreated that she might not be left to die in solitude and sorrow, however guilty she might have been.—Then again she implored Mrs Mowbray to speak peace and pardon to her drooping soul; while, unable to withstand these solicitations, though she knew them to be the unconscious ravings of the disorder, she slowly and mournfully returned to the bed-side.

'It is late,' said Mrs Pemberton—'we ought ere now to be on the road.'

'How can I go, and leave this poor creature in such a state?—But then should we find my poor injured child at the end of the journey! Such an expectation as that!—'

'Thou must decide quickly,' replied Mrs Pemberton gently.

'Decide! Then I will go with you.—Yet still, should Anna recover her senses before her death, and wish to see me, I should never forgive myself for being absent—it might sooth the anguish of her last moments to know how freely I pardon her.—No, no:—after all, if pleasure awaits me, it is only delaying it a few days; and this, this unhappy girl is on her *death-bed*.—You, you must go *without* me.'

As she said this, Mrs Pemberton pressed her hand with affectionate eagerness, and murmured out in broken accents, 'I honour thy decision, and may I return with comfort to thee!'

'Yet though I wish you to go,' cried Mrs Mowbray, 'I grieve to expose you to such fatigue and trouble in your weak state of health, and—'

'Say no more,' interrupted Mrs Pemberton, 'I am only doing my duty; and reflect on my happiness if I am allowed to restore the lost sheep to the fold again!'*—So saying she set off on her journey, and arrived in London only four days after Adeline had arrived in Cumberland.

Mrs Pemberton drove immediately to Adeline's lodgings, but received the same answer as colonel Mordaunt had received; namely, that she was gone no one knew whither. Still she did not despair of finding her: she, like the colonel, thought that a mulatto, a lady just recovered from the small-pox, and a child, were likely to be easily traced; and having written to Mrs Mowbray, owning her disappointment, but bidding her not despair, she set off on her journey back, and had succeeded in tracing Adeline as far as an inn on the high North road,—when an event took place which made her further inquiries needless.

CHAPTER XI

Adeline, after several repeated trials, succeeded in writing the following letter to her mother:

'Dearest of Mothers,

'WHEN this letter reaches you, I shall be no more; and however I may hitherto have offended you, I shall then be able to offend you no longer; and that child, whom you bound yourself by oath never to see or forgive but on the most cruel of conditions while living, dead you may perhaps deign to receive to your pardon and your love.— Nay, my heart tells me that you will do more,—that you will transfer the love which you once felt for me, to my poor helpless orphan; and in full confidence that you will be thus indulgent, I bequeath her to you with my dying breath.—O! look on her, my mother, nor shrink from her with disgust, although you see in her my features; but rather rejoice in the resemblance, and fancy that I am restored to you pure, happy, and beloved as I once was.—Yes, yes,—it will be so: I have known a great deal of sorrow—let me then indulge the little ray of pleasure that breaks in upon me when I think that you will not resist my dying prayer, but bestow on my child the long arrears of tenderness due to me.

'Yes, yes, you will receive, you will be kind to her; and by so doing you will make me ample amends for all the sorrow which your harshness caused me when we met last.—That was a dreadful day! How you frowned on me! I did not think you could have frowned so dreadfully—but then I was uninjured by affliction, unaltered by illness. Were you to see me now, you would not have the heart to frown on me: and yet my letters, being repeatedly returned, and even the last unnoticed and unanswered, though it told you that even on your own conditions I could now claim your pardon, for that I had been "wretched in love," and had experienced "the anguish of being forsaken, despised, and disgraced in the eye of the world," proves but too surely that the bitterness of resentment is not yet past!—But on my *death-bed* you promised to see and forgive me—*and I am there, my mother!!* Yet will I not claim that promise;—I will not weaken, by directing it towards myself, the burst of sorrow, of too late regret, of self-upbraidings, and long-restrained affection, which must be directed towards my child when I am not alive to profit by it. No:—though I would give worlds to embrace you once more, for the sake of my child I resign the gratification.

'Oh, mother! you little think that I saw you, only a few days ago, from the stile by the cottage which overlooks your house: you were walking with a lady, and my child was with me (my Editha, for I have called her after you). You seemed, methought, even cheerful, and I was so selfish that I felt shocked to think I was so entirely forgotten by you; for I was sure that if you thought of me you could not be cheerful. But your companion left you; and then you looked so very sad, that I was wretched from the idea that you were then thinking too much of me, and I wished you to resume your cheerfulness again.

'*I* was not cheerful, and Editha by her artless prattle wounded me to the very soul.—She wished, she said, to live in that sweet house, and asked why she should not live there? *I could* have told her why, but dared not do it; but I assured her, and do not for mercy's sake prove that assurance false! that she *should* live there *one day*.

'"But when—when?" she asked.

'"When I am in my grave," replied I: and, poor innocent! throwing herself into my arms with playful fondness, she begged me to go to my grave directly. I feel but too sensibly that her desire will soon be accomplished.

'But must I die unblest by you? True, I am watched by the kindest of human beings! but then she is not my mother—that mother, who, with the joys of my childhood and my home, is so continually recurring to my memory. Oh! I forget all your unkindness, my mother, and remember only your affection. How I should like to feel your hand supporting my head, and see you perform the little offices which sickness requires.—And must I never, never see you more? Yes! you will come, I am sure you will, but come, come quickly, or I shall die without your blessing.

'I have had a fainting fit—but I am recovered, and can address you again.—Oh! teach my Editha to be humble, teach her to be slow to call the experience of ages contemptible prejudices; teach her no opinions that can destroy her sympathies with general society, and make her an alien to the hearts of those amongst whom she lives.

'Be above all things careful that she wanders not in the night of scepticism. But for the support of religion, what, amidst my various sorrows, what would have become of *me*?

'There is something more that I would say. Should my existence be prolonged even but a few days, I shall have to struggle with poverty as well as sickness; and the anxious friend (I will not call her servant) who is now my all of earthly comfort, will scarcely have money sufficient to pay me the last sad duties; and I owe her, my mother, a world of obligation! She will make my last moments easy, and *you* must reward her. From her you will receive this letter when I am no more, and to your care and protection I bequeath her. She is—my eyes grow dim, and I must leave off for the present.'

On the very evening in which Adeline had written this address to her mother, Mrs Mowbray had received Mrs Pemberton's letter; and as miss Woodville had been interred that morning, she felt herself at liberty to join Mrs Pemberton in her search after Adeline, while various plans for this purpose presented themselves to her mind, and each of them was dismissed in its turn as fruitless or impracticable. Full of these thoughts she pensively walked along the lawn before her door, till sad and weary she leaned on a little gate at the bottom of it; which, as she did so, swung slowly backwards and forwards, responsive as it were to her feelings.

But, as she continued to muse, and to recall the varied sorrows of her past life, the gate on which she leaned began to vibrate more quickly; till, unable to bear the recollections which assailed her, she was hastening with almost frantic speed towards the house, when she saw a cottager approaching, to whose sick daughter and helpless family she had long been a bountiful benefactress.

'What is the matter, John?' cried Mrs Mowbray, hastening forward to meet him—'you seem agitated.'

'My poor daughter, madam!' replied the man, bursting into tears.

At the sight of his distress, his *parental* distress, Mrs Mowbray sighed deeply, and asked if Lucy was worse.

'I doubt she is dying,' said the afflicted father.

'God forbid!' exclaimed Mrs Mowbray, throwing her shawl over her shoulders; 'I will go and see her myself.'

'What, really?—But the way is so long, and the road so miry!'

'No matter—I must do my duty.'

'God bless you, and reward you!' cried the grateful father—'that is so like you! Lucy said you would come!'

Mrs Mowbray then filled a basket with medicine and refreshments, and set out on her charitable visit.

She found the poor girl in a very weak and alarming state; but the sight of her benefactress, and the tender manner in which she supported her languid head, and administered wine and other cordials to her, insensibly revived her; and while writhing under the feelings of an unhappy parent herself, Mrs Mowbray was soothed by the blessings of the parent whom she comforted.

At this moment they were alarmed by a shriek from a neighbouring cottage, and a woman who was attending on the sick girl ran out to inquire into the cause of it.

She returned, saying that a poor sick young gentlewoman, who lodged at the next house, was fallen back in a fit, and they thought she was dead.

'A young gentlewoman,' exclaimed Mrs Mowbray, 'at the next cottage!' rising up.

'Aye sure,' cried the woman, 'she looks like a lady for certain, and she has the finest child I ever saw.'

'Perhaps she is not dead,' said Mrs Mowbray:—'let us go see.'

CHAPTER XII

Little did Mrs Mowbray think that it was her own child whom she was hastening to relieve; and that, while meditating a kind action, recompense was so near.

Adeline, while trying to finish her letter to her mother, had scarcely traced a few illegible lines, when she fell back insensible on her pillow; and at the moment of Mrs Mowbray's entering the cottage, Savanna, who had uttered the shriek which had excited her curiosity, had convinced herself that she was gone for ever.

The woman who accompanied Mrs Mowbray entered the house first; and opening a back chamber, low-roofed, narrow, and lighted only by one solitary and slender candle, Mrs Mowbray beheld through the door the lifeless form of the object of her solicitude, which Savanna was contemplating with loud and frantic sorrow.

'Here is a lady come to see what she can do for your mistress,' cried the woman, while Savanna turned hastily round:—'Here she is—here is good madam Mowbray.'

'Madam Mowbray!' shrieked Savanna, fixing her dark eyes fiercely on Mrs Mowbray, and raising her arm in a threatening manner as she approached her: then snatching up the letter which lay on the bed,—'Woman!' she exclaimed, grasping Mrs Mowbray's arm with frightful earnestness, 'read dat—'tis for you!'

Mrs Mowbray, speechless with alarm and awe, involuntarily seized the letter—but scarcely had she read the first words, when uttering a deep groan she sprung forward, to clasp the unconscious form before her, and fell beside it equally insensible.

But she recovered almost immediately to a sense of her misery; and while, in speechless agony, she knelt by the bed-side, Savanna, beholding her distress, with a sort of dreadful pleasure exclaimed, 'Ah! have you at last learn to feel?'

'But is she, is she *indeed* gone?' cried Mrs Mowbray, 'is there *no* hope?' and instantly seizing the cordial which she had brought with her, assisted by the woman, she endeavoured to force it down the throat of Adeline.

Their endeavours were for some time vain: at length, however, she exhibited signs of life, and in a few minutes more she opened her sunk eye, and gazed unconsciously around her.

'My God! I thank you!' exclaimed Mrs Mowbray, falling on her knees; while Savanna, laying her mistress's head on her bosom, sobbed with fearful joy.

'Adeline! my child, my dear, dear child!' cried Mrs Mowbray, seizing her clammy hand.

That voice, those words which she had so long wished to hear, though hopeless of ever hearing them again, seemed to recall the fast fading recollection of Adeline; she raised her head from Savanna's bosom, and, looking earnestly at Mrs Mowbray, faintly smiled, and endeavoured to throw herself into her arms,—but fell back again exhausted on the pillow.

But in a few minutes she recovered so far as to be able to speak; and while she hung round her mother's neck, and gazed upon her with eager and delighted earnestness, she desired Savanna to bring Editha to her immediately.

'Will you, will you—,' said Adeline, vainly trying to speak her wishes, as Savanna put the sleeping girl in Mrs Mowbray's arms: but she easily divined them; and, clasping her to her heart, wept over her convulsively—'She shall be dear to me as my own soul!' said Mrs Mowbray.

'Then I die contented,' replied Adeline.

'Die!' exclaimed Mrs Mowbray hastily: 'no, you must not, shall not die; you must live to see me atone for—'

'It is in vain,' said Adeline faintly. 'I bless God that he allows me to enjoy this consolation—say that you forgive me.'

'Forgive you! Oh, Adeline! for years have I forgiven and pined after you: but a wicked woman intercepted all your letters; and I thought you were dead, or had renounced me for ever.'

'Indeed!' cried Adeline. 'Oh! had I suspected that!'—'Nay more, Mrs Pemberton is now in London, in search of you, in order to bring you back to happiness!' As Mrs Mowbray said this, Savanna, drawing near, took her hand and gently pressed it.

Adeline observed the action, and seeing by it that Savanna's heart relented towards her mother, said, 'I owe that faithful creature more than I can express; but to your care I bequeath her.'

'I will love her as my child,' said Mrs Mowbray, 'and behave to her better than I did to—'

'Hush!' cried Adeline, putting her hand to Mrs Mowbray's lips.

'But you *shall* live! I will send for Dr Norberry; you shall be moved to my house, and all will be well—all our past grief be forgotten,' returned Mrs Mowbray with almost convulsive eagerness.

Adeline faintly smiled, but repeated that every hope of that kind was over, but that her utmost wish was gratified in seeing her mother, and receiving her full forgiveness.

'But you must live for my sake!' cried Mrs Mowbray: 'and for mine,' sobbed out Savanna.

'Could you not be moved to my house?' said Mrs Mowbray. 'There every indulgence and attention that money can procure shall be yours. Is this a place,—is this poverty—this—' here her voice failed her, and she burst into tears.

'Mother, dearest mother,' replied Adeline, 'I see you, I am assured of your love again, and I have not a want beside. Still, I could like, I could wish, to be once more under a *parent's roof.*'

In a moment, the cottager who was present, and returning with usury to Mrs Mowbray's daughter the anxious interest which she had taken in his, proposed various means of transporting Adeline to the Lawn; a difficult and a hazardous undertaking; but the poor invalid was willing to risk the danger and the fatigue; and her mother could not but indulge her. At length the cottager, as it was for the *general benefactress*, having with care procured even more assistance than was necessary, Adeline was conveyed on a sort of a litter, along the valley, and found herself once more in the house of her mother; while Savanna, sharing in the joy which Adeline's countenance expressed, threw herself on Mrs Mowbray's neck, and exclaimed, 'Now I forgive you!'

'Mother, dear mother,' cried Adeline, after having for some minutes vainly endeavoured to speak—'I am so happy! no more an outcast, but under my mother's roof!—Nay, I even think I *can* live now,' added she with a faint smile.

Had Adeline risen from her bed in complete health and vigour, she would scarcely have excited more joy in her mother, and in Savanna, than she did by this expression.

'Can live!' cried Mrs Mowbray, 'O! you shall, you must live.'— And an express was sent off immediately to Dr Norberry too, who was removed to Kendal, to be near his elder daughter, lately married in the neighbourhood.

Dr Norberry arrived in a few hours. Mrs Mowbray ran out to meet him; but a welcome died on her tongue, and she could only speak by her tears.

'There, there, my good woman, don't be foolish,' replied he: 'it is cursed silly to blubber, you know: besides, it can do no good,'— giving her a kiss, while tears trickled down his rough cheek.—'So, the lost sheep is found?'

'But, O! she will be lost again,' faltered Mrs Mowbray; 'I doubt nothing can save her!'

'No!' cried the old man, with a gulp, 'no! not my coming so many miles on purpose?—Well, but where is she?'

'She will see you presently, but begged to be excused for a few minutes.'—'You see,' said he, 'by my dress, what has happened,' gulping as he spoke. 'I have lost the companion of thirty years!—and—and—' here he paused, and after an effort went on to say, that his wife in her last illness had owned that she had suppressed Adeline's letters, and had declared the reason of it—'But, poor soul!' continued the doctor, 'it was the only sin against me, I believe, or any one else, that she ever committed—so I forgave her; and I trust that God will.'

Soon after they were summoned to the sick room, and Dr Norberry beheld with a degree of fearful emotion, which he vainly endeavoured to hide under a cloak of pleasantry, the dreadful ravages which sorrow and sickness had made in the face and form of Adeline.

'So, here you are at last!' cried he, trying to smile while he sobbed audibly, 'and a pretty figure you make, don't you?—But we have you again, and we will not part with you soon, I can tell you,' (almost starting as the faint but rapid pulse met his fingers,) 'that is, I mean,' added he, 'unless it please God.'—Mrs Mowbray and Savanna, during this speech, gazed on his countenance in breathless anxiety, and read in it a confirmation of their fears.—'But who's afraid?' cried the doctor, forcing a laugh, while his tone and his looks expressed the extreme of apprehension, and his laugh ended in a sob.

Mrs Mowbray turned away in a sort of desperate silence; but the mulatto still kept her penetrating eye fixed upon him, and with a look so full of woe!

'I'll trouble you, mistress, to take those formidable eyes of yours off my face,' cried the doctor, pettishly; 'for, by the Lord, I can't stand their inquiry!—But who the devil are you?'

'She is my nurse, my consoler, and my friend,' said Adeline.

'Then she is mine of course,' cried the doctor, 'though she has a devilish terrible stare with her eyes:—but give me your hand, mistress. What is your name?'

'Me be name Savanna,' replied the mulatto; 'and me die and live wid my dear mistress,' she added, bursting into tears.

'Zounds!' cried the doctor, 'I can't bear this—here I came as a physician, and these blubberers melt me down into an old woman.—

Adeline, I must order all these people out of the room, and have you to myself, or I can do nothing.'

He was obeyed; and on inquiring into all Adeline's symptoms, he found little to hope and every thing to fear—'But your mind is relieved, and you have youth on your side; and who knows what good air, good food, and good nurses may do for you!'

'Not to mention a good physician,' added Adeline, smiling, 'and a good friend in that physician.'

'This it be to have money,' said Savanna, as she saw the various things prepared and made to tempt Adeline's weak appetite:—'poor Savanna mean as well—her heart make all these, but her hand want power.'

During this state of alarming suspense Mrs Pemberton was hourly expected, as she had written word that she had traced Adeline into Lancashire, and suspected that she was in her mother's neighbourhood.—It may be supposed that Mrs Mowbray, Adeline, and Savanna, looked forward to her arrival with eager impatience; but not so Dr Norberry—he said that no doubt she was a very good sort of woman, but that he did not like pretensions to righteousness over much, and had a particular aversion to a piece of formal drab-coloured morality.

Adeline only laughed at these prejudices, without attempting to confute them; for she knew that Mrs Pemberton's appearance and manners would soon annihilate them. At length she reached the Lawn; and Savanna, who saw her alight, announced her arrival to her mistress, and was commissioned by her to introduce her immediately into the sick chamber.—She did so; but Mrs Pemberton, almost overpowered with joy at the intelligence which awaited her, and ill fortified by Savanna's violent and mixed emotions against the indulgence of her own, begged to compose herself a few moments before she met Adeline: but Savanna was not to be denied; and seizing her hand she led her up to the bed-side of the invalid.—Adeline smiled affectionately when she saw her; but Mrs Pemberton started back, and, scarcely staying to take the hand which she offered her, rushed out of the room, to vent in solitude the burst of uncontrollable anguish which the sight of her altered countenance occasioned her.—Alas! her eye had been but too well tutored to read the characters of death in the face, and it was some time before she recovered herself sufficiently to appear before the anxious watchers by the bed of Adeline with that composure which on principle she always endeavoured to display.—At length, however, she re-entered the room, and, approaching the poor invalid, kissed in silence her wan yet flushed cheek.

'I am very different now, my kind friend, to what I was when you *first* saw me,' said Adeline, faintly smiling.

To the moment when they *last* met, Adeline had not resolution enough to revert, for then she was mourning by the dead body of Glenmurray.

Mrs Pemberton was silent for a moment; but, making an effort, she replied, 'Thou art now more like what thou wert in *mind*, when I *first* saw thee at Rosevalley, than when I first met thee at Richmond. At Rosevalley I beheld thee innocent, at Richmond guilty, and here I see thee penitent, and, I hope, resigned to thy fate.'—She spoke the word *resigned* with emphasis, and Adeline *understood* her.

'I am indeed resigned,' replied Adeline in a low voice: 'nay, I feel that I am much favoured in being spared so long. But there is one thing that weighs heavily on my mind; Mary Warner is leading a life of shame, and she told me when I last saw her, that she was corrupted by my precept and example: if so—'

'Set thy conscience at rest on that subject,' interrupted Mrs Pemberton: 'while she lived with me, I discovered, long before she ever saw thee, that she had been known to have been faulty.'

'Oh! what a load have you removed from my mind!' replied Adeline. 'Still it would be more relieved, if you would promise to find her out; and she may be heard of at Mr Langley's chambers in the Temple. Offer her a yearly allowance for life, provided she will quit her present vicious habits; I am sure my mother will gladly fulfil my wishes in this respect.'

'And so will I,' replied Mrs Pemberton. 'Is there any thing else that I can do for thee?'

'Yes: I have two pensioners* at Richmond,—a poor young woman, and her orphan boy,—an illegitimate child,' she added, deeply sighing, as she recollected what had interested her in their fate. 'I bequeath them to your care; Savanna knows where they are to be found. And now, all that disturbs my thoughts at this awful moment is, the grief which my poor mother and Savanna will feel;—nay, they will be quite unprepared for it; for they persist to hope still, and

I believe that even Dr Norberry allows his wishes to deceive his judgment.'

'They will suffer, indeed!' cried Mrs Pemberton: 'but I give thee my word, that I will never leave thy mother, and that Savanna shall be our joint care.'

'It is enough—I shall now die in peace,' said Adeline; and Mrs Pemberton turned away to meet Mrs Mowbray, who with Dr Norberry at that moment entered the room. Mrs Mowbray met her, and welcomed her audibly and joyfully: but Mrs Pemberton, aware of the blow which impended over her, vainly endeavoured to utter a congratulation; but throwing herself into Mrs Mowbray's extended arms, she forgot her usual self-command, and sobbed loudly on her bosom.

Dr Norberry gazed at the benevolent quaker with astonishment. True, she was '*drab-coloured*'; but where was the repulsive formality that he had expected? 'Zounds!' thought he, 'this woman can feel like other women, and is as good a hand at a crying-bout as myself.' But Mrs Pemberton did not long give way to so violent an indulgence of her feelings; and gently withdrawing herself from Mrs Mowbray's embrace, she turned to the window, while Mrs Mowbray hastened to the bedside of Adeline. Mrs Pemberton then turned round again, and, seizing Dr Norberry's hand, which she fervently pressed, said in a faltering voice, 'Would thou couldst *save* her!' 'And—and *can't* I? can't I?' replied he, gulping. Mrs Pemberton looked at him with an expression which he could neither mistake nor endure; but muttering in a low tone, 'No! dear, sweet soul! I doubt I can't, I doubt I can't, by the Lord!' he rushed out of the room.

From that moment he never was easy but when he could converse with Mrs Pemberton; for he knew that she, and she only, sympathized in his feelings, as she only knew that Adeline was not likely to recover. The invalid herself observed his attention to her friend, nor could she forbear to rally him on the total disappearance of his prejudices against the fair quaker; for, such was the influence of Mrs Pemberton's dignified yet winning manners, and such was the respect with which she inspired him, that, if he had his hat on, he always took it off when she entered the room, and never uttered any thing like an oath, without humbly begging her pardon; and he told Adeline, that were all quakers like Mrs Pemberton, he should be tempted to cry, 'Drab is your only wear.'

Another, and another day elapsed, and Adeline still lived.—On
the evening of the third day, as she lay half-slumbering with her head
on Savanna's arm, and Mrs Mowbray, lulling Editha to sleep on her
lap, was watching beside her, glancing her eye alternately with satisfied and silent affection from the child to the mother, whom she
thought in a fair way of recovery; while Dr Norberry, stifling an
occasional sob, was contemplating the group, and Mrs Pemberton,
her hands clasped in each other, seemed lost in devout contemplation, Adeline awoke, and as she gazed on Editha, who was fondly
held to Mrs Mowbray's bosom, a smile illumined her sunk countenance. Mrs Mowbray at that moment eagerly and anxiously pressed
forward to catch her weak accents, and inquire how she felt. 'I have
seen that fond and anxious look before,' she faintly articulated, 'but
in happier times! and it assures me that you love me still.'

'Love you still!' replied Mrs Mowbray with passionate
fondness:—'never, never were you so dear to me as now!'

Adeline tried to express the joy which flushed her cheek at these
words, and lighted up her closing eyes: but she tried in vain. At
length she grasped Mrs Mowbray's hand to her lips, and in
imperfect accents exclaiming 'I thank thee, gracious Heaven!' she
laid her head on Savanna's bosom, and expired.

THE END

TEXTUAL NOTES

This list contains a selection of substantive variants between the 1805 and 1844 editions. Minor changes in punctuation, capitalization, and paragraph starts are omitted. Changes made in the 1810 edition are noted in brackets (e.g. [*as in 3rd*]) after the 1844 variants. (It appears that the 1844 edition was set from a corrected third edition of the novel.) As these instances demonstrate, Opie's revisions consist of a systematic removal of words and phrases that might be considered indecorous, 'coarse', or blasphemous.

11.34	Lord bless me!] *omitted*
11.36	Lord] *omitted*
12.6–7	And God forgive me, and you too, Lina] And forgive me, Lina
12.13	Lord help us and save us!] *omitted*
16.17	Zounds!] Why
18.12	Zounds!] Pshaw
18.14	devilish] sadly
18.27	God] Heaven
24.33	My good gracious!] *omitted*
29.1	Upon my soul] Really
29.36	chastity] purity
29.38	chastity] purity
30.14	, thank God] *omitted*
32.26	love] dear
33.3	Aye, by all means] No, indeed
37.9	that God] He
37.18	to confine himself within] *omitted*
48.15	'Thank God!' replied Adeline. The girl sighed still more deeply.] *omitted*
55.20	Candide] romances
55.33–56.17	till she opened the Nouvelle Heloise . . . fate of her devoted daughter] *omitted*
59.21–2	not doubting . . . wishes] *omitted*
60.37	Great God!] *omitted*
61.17	My master have sent you] My master has sent you
75.25	confounded] *omitted*
84.9	, and be hanged to you] *omitted*
84.18	Lord] Heaven
85.11–12	(an old blockhead!)] *omitted*
88.33	the devil] *omitted*
88.37	d——d] vile [*omitted entirely in 3rd*]
89.3	Zounds] Why

90.4	Zounds!] *omitted*
90.16	'Sdeath] *omitted*
90.19	cursed] great
90.25	by the Lord] *omitted*
90.37	Odzooks] Why
93.19	But God grant] *omitted*
95.32	was suspected of being] was suspected, though unjustly, of being
96.4	Zounds,] *omitted*
96.9	of a bastard child] *omitted*
96.10	sdeath] *omitted*
96.26–7	(pushing her pillow vehemently towards the valence as she spoke,)] *omitted*
96.30	rose unrefreshed the next morning] rose the next morning
97.4	Zounds] Hold
97.21	Zounds!] *omitted*
97.21	bluntly] *omitted*
98.30	devilish] very
99.8	d——d dog]—but I forbear [*as in 3rd*]
99.9–10	the good lad looks as ashamed of what he has done as any modest miss in Christendom] *omitted*
99.23	Why, zounds!] Why!
99.32	Zounds!] There,
101.10	'Gadzooks,'] *omitted*
101.25	'It is d——d ill, sir'] *omitted* [it is very ill (*3rd*)]
101.35	and—Lord have mercy upon us!' cried the doctor] and here the doctor,
101.36–7	and seeing the situation into which his words had thrown Adeline who was then] saw Adeline
103.26	devilish] pretty
103.27	friend. Zounds,] friends; and
106.12	and I call on God to witness my oath] *omitted*
106.14–15	being forsaken and despised as I have been] having lost the man you adore
106.15–16	disgraced in the eye of the world] disgraced in the eye of the world as I have been
106.27	God's] Pity's
109.19	, but of misery] *omitted*
109.30–3	'Yet—no. Girl, . . . I have done.'] *omitted*
110.9	Zounds,] *omitted*
110.15	d——d] *omitted* [*as in 3rd*]
110.20–1	God knows when] I know not when
110.39	d——d] *omitted* [*as in 3rd*]
115.38	God] Heaven
129.36	ardently] evidently
132.2	my dearest life] my dearest love

137.34	six pounds] ten pounds [*as in 3rd*]
137.35	half] part [*as in 3rd*]
137.36	half] part [*as in 3rd*]
138.4	b——h] toad
144.17	noting] nothing
171.34	wat will appen] what will happen [wat will happen (*in 3rd*)]
178.3–4	at present I am particularly engaged] *omitted*
178.27	And so do I.—O zounds!] And I think so too!—
178.35	patting her on the back as he spoke] *omitted*
179.2	but perhaps your favours are all bespoken.—] *omitted*
179.4–6	'Oh! I have but few friends,' . . . 'how many would you have'] *omitted*
179.6	Here, he put his arm round her waist: and] Here, as
182.19	was to him *tout simple*] seemed to him quite natural and proper
184.30	pampered] *omitted*
185.36	heaven] God and Saviour,
186.38	God] Heaven
192.7	God knows,] *omitted*
193.32	preservative] preservation
194.37	God] Heaven
204.22	Good God!] *omitted*
204.27	she have] she has
205.2	curse] hang [*as in 3rd*]
206.5	for God's sake] *omitted*
206.15	for God's sake] *omitted*
207.3	pollution] infection
216.32	latent blessings] merciful chastisements
218.29	For God's sake] In pity
227.30–1	, though capable of charming the senses] *omitted*
227.35–6	disgusted with an intercourse in which the heart had no share] *omitted*
236.15	passion] attachment
241.5	exclusion] seclusion
242.19	zounds,] what
242.22	Devil take me if I could] I could not have
243.2	d——d] *omitted* [*as in 3rd*]
243.12	devilish] *omitted*
244.7	God to bless thine] that thine may be blest
248.26	teacher] minister
248.34	engaged in the active duties of her profession,] engaged in active duties,
253.1	great] much
260.7	God] Heaven
264.30	, by the Lord] *omitted*
264.34	devilish] *omitted*

264.38   Zounds] Pshaw
267.16   'Zounds! thought he,] *omitted*
268.20   gracious Heaven] blessed Lord!

EXPLANATORY NOTES

4 *history, biography, poetry, and discoveries in natural philosophy*: Editha rejects precisely those subjects of study recommended for young women by conservative writers. Jane West, in *Letters Addressed to a Young Lady*, suggests natural history (or biology) and experimental natural philosophy (science) as subjects that 'open a delightful field of instructive entertainment to every young woman' (3 vols., 2nd edn. (London, 1806), ii. 424); she also mentions history and biography as suitable subjects for study (ii. 427, 431). James Fordyce, in his much reprinted *Sermons to Young Women*, also notes 'History, in which I include Biography and Memoirs, ought to employ a considerable share of your leisure', and adds that girls should also read 'Poetry of all kinds, where strict regard is paid to decorum': 2 vols., newly rev. edn. (London, 1775), ii. 10, 14.

new theories in politics: some writers specifically warned against girls reading political theory: 'In retirement they are haunted by another species of enemies, no less alarming to their understandings, to their morals, and to their repose. . . . Under the former description may be ranked all those systems of ethics, and treatises on education, which are founded on the false doctrine of human perfectibility, and consequently reject the necessity of divine revelation and supernatural agency' (West, *Letters*, i. 15). Mary Wollstonecraft, on the other hand, specifically encourages it: 'They might, also, study politics, and settle their benevolence on the broadest basis; for the reading of history will scarcely be more useful than the perusal of romances, if read as mere biography; if the character of the times, the political improvements, arts, etc. be not observed': *A Vindication of the Rights of Woman*, ed. Janet Todd and Marilyn Butler, *The Works of Mary Wollstonecraft*, 7 vols. (London 1989), v. 218.

5 *'turn to a tory in her elbow chair'*: William Hayley, *The Triumphs of Temper; A Poem in Six Cantos*, 'Yet every day, by transmutation rare, | Turn'd to Tory in his elbow-chair' (i. 33–4).

like an animal in an exhausted receiver: a receiver is 'the bell-glass of an air pump' (*OED*) of the kind used in eighteenth-century laboratories for experiments on animal respiration; hence, Adeline is like a creature in a sealed jar from which the air has been exhausted or extracted. The image appears to have been vivid for Opie; in *Detraction Displayed* (London 1828), she refers to an act being 'nearly as cruel as to exclude the air necessary for respiration' (p. ii).

the experimental philosophy of her mother: the phrase is perhaps a pun; 'experimental philosophy' in ordinary discourse referred to the study of nature or natural phenomena, which suits the sense of the bell-glass, but Editha's interest in the social experiments of radical political philosophers may also be suggested.

6 *pudding without butter*: keeping butter from children because of its 'relaxing' or laxative qualities was an eighteenth-century commonplace. In *Domestic Medicine*, Dr William Buchan advises that 'Butter ought likewise to be sparingly given to children. It both relaxes the stomach and produces gross humours' (19th edn. (London, 1805), 19). Wollstonecraft, in a letter to William Godwin, reminds him 'Do not give Fanny butter with her pudding': *Collected Letters of Mary Wollstonecraft*, ed. Ralph M. Wardle (Ithaca, NY, 1979), 390.

7 *flannel, or no flannel*: like diet, clothing was a subject of intense debate in child-rearing, especially the weight of the fabric. In April 1796 the author writes to Wollstonecraft that 'a very amiable clever friend of mine who is on the point of bringing forth a first child . . . is desirous of knowing *in detail*, your means of inuring Fanny to a thin dress in this cold climate—I have sent her all the information on the subject which I am in possession of, with my testimony as eye witness of the success of your plan, as exhibited in the strong, well-formed limbs, & florid complexion of your child—but I wish to receive from you, the particulars she requests—will you favour me with them?' (Bodleian Library, Abinger deposit, dep. b. 210/6).

'whether children require any clothing at all for their feet': J. J. Rousseau, in *Émile* (1762), writes 'Why must my pupil be forced always to have a cow's skin under his feet? What harm would there be if in case of need his own skin were able to serve him as sole . . . let Émile run barefoot in all seasons . . .' (trans. Allan Bloom (New York, 1979), 139). Locke, in *Some Thoughts Concerning Education* (1693), advises that the child 'have his *shoes* so thin, that they might leak and *let in water*, when ever he comes near it', as part of a toughening regime (ed. James L. Axtell (Cambridge, 1968), sec. 3, p. 118). On the other hand, Dr Buchan, in *Advice to Mothers* (1769), advises that soon after children begin to walk they be supplied 'with easy shoes, adapted to the natural shape of the foot, neither too large . . . nor too small. . . . A well made shoe answers the two-fold purpose of cleanliness, and of defence against external injuries, including cold and moisture': *The Physician and Child-Rearing: Two Guides 1809–1894*, reprint edn. (New York, 1972), 49.

10 *arithmetic*: this old-fashioned skill taught by Mrs Woodville is also one of the skills advocated by contemporary conservative writers on female education. Jane West, in *Letters to a Young Lady*, stresses the importance of this subject, especially as it pertains to charity and domestic order: 'To return to the subject of early *œconomic* habits . . . Though I profess to abstain, in this letter, from what is called *scientific* instruction, I must recommend one branch of knowledge, on which sensible men ever set a great value in women; I mean, that every girl ought to possess a

competent knowledge of arithmetic. It is also desirable that this knowledge should be practical as well as theoretical . . .' (iii. 258–9).

11 *'to watch, and weep, beside a parent's bed'*: Anna Letitia Barbauld, 'To Miss R[igby], on her Attendance upon her Mother at Buxton' (l. 7).

12 *Mr Locke on the conduct of the human understanding*: John Locke's principal philosophical work, his *Essay Concerning Human Understanding* (1690), established him, in J. S. Mill's words, as the 'unquestioned founder of the analytic philosophy of the mind'.

13 *draughts*: 'a game played by two persons on a board of the same kind as that used in chess, which game it somewhat resembles, though of much simpler character, all the pieces or "men" being of equal value and moving alike diagonally' (*OED*); also known in North America as checkers.

I doubt: 'to doubt' is 'to anticipate with apprehension, to apprehend (something feared or undesired)' (*OED*). Opie uses the word in this sense throughout the novel.

14 *no conjuror*: 'one who is far from clever' (*OED*).

as Mr Shandy did his grief : a reference to Laurence Sterne's *Tristram Shandy*, in which Tristram's father, Walter, turns his attention to producing a detailed system for educating his son, in part as a means of assuaging his grief over the death of his first son, Bobby, and the ill-fortune which had so far dogged Tristram's life. Editha's desire to codify her child-rearing theories and subsequent failure to educate Adeline despite her interest in education places this novel in a recognized tradition; as T. G. A. Nelson notes, 'In novels, there are moments when a parent's interest in educational theory is made to seem like a substitute for direct involvement in the life of the child. The most flagrant example, of course, is *Tristram Shandy*, a book notoriously influenced by Locke, where Walter Shandy writes a "TRISTRA-paedia, or system of education" for Tristram, but is always somewhere else whenever a crisis occurs in his son's life': *Children, Parents, and the Rise of the Novel* (Newark, 1995), 91.

attacked the institution of marriage: William Godwin had vehemently challenged marriage in one brief segment of his *Enquiry Concerning Political Justice* (1793). In his discussion 'Of Property', he refers to 'the evil of marriage, as it is practised in European countries' and calls it 'a system of fraud'; he concludes by noting that 'The abolition of the present system of marriage appears to involve no evils': ed. Isaak Kramnick, Penguin edn. (Harmondsworth, 1985), VIII. viii. app., pp. 762–3.

15 *the American war*: this reference dates the setting of the early part of the novel to the years of the American Revolution (War of Independence), 1775–83.

the astrologer in the fable: in Aesop's fable 'An Astrologer and a Traveller', the astrologer, while gazing at the distant stars, falls into a nearby ditch, the moral being that focusing on problems far away should not blind one to those close at hand.

15 *a showing-off woman*: no epithet could be more pejorative concerning female intellect in the period. James Fordyce writes 'A woman that affects to dispute, to decide, to dictate on every subject; that watches or makes opportunities of throwing out scraps of literature, or shreds of philosophy, in every company; that engrosses the conversation, as if she alone was qualified to entertain; that betrays, in short, a boundless intemperance of tongue, together with an inextinguishable passion for shining by the splendour of her supposed talents; such a woman is truly insufferable. At first, perhaps, she may be considered merely as an object of ridicule; but she soon grows into an object of aversion': *Sermons*, ii. 33. Similarly, Hannah More, in *Strictures on the Modern System of Female Education*, jibes at women who pride themselves on their intellect: 'women who are so puffed up with the conceit of talents as to neglect the plain duties of life, will not frequently be found to be women of the best abilities': (London, 1799), ii. 7. Opie herself, in *Detraction Displayed* (1828), refers to such a person as 'a *woman of display*', but goes on to assert 'I have more respect for *women of display*, than for women of real acquirements, who, from the terror of being called Blues [blue-stockings or women of intellect], deny their right to be deemed so' (p. 265). Opie attributes to Editha the qualities most frequently criticized by conservative writers on women's education, in order to highlight Adeline's ability to combine intellect with modesty and domestic responsibility.

16 *bouts rimés*: 'Words rhyming in accordance with a given rhyme scheme, ordinarily that of the sonnet, and used as the basis of a verse-making game. The object . . . was to write a poem which would utilize the given words as end rhymes yet achieve an effect of naturalness and ease. Accordingly the list of words was made as bizarre and incongruous as possible. The diversion became highly fashionable and remained so in both France and England, until the 19th c.': Alex Preminger (ed.), *Princeton Encyclopedia of Poetry and Poetics*, enlarged edn. (Princeton, 1974), 81–2.

a politician: 'one versed in the theory or science of government' (*OED*). In terms of gender, however, the word may have had greater political resonance for Opie's readers. Hannah More, while encouraging women to support the government patriotically, qualified her call, noting 'I am not sounding an alarm to female warriors, or exciting female politicians: I hardly know which of the two is the most disgusting and unnatural character': *Strictures*, i. 6.

season at Bath: the 'season' is that period of the year during which fashionable people gather at a location; it was an important part of the social—especially the courtship—ritual of the elite in the eighteenth century. The London season was the most important, but Bath, noted for its curative waters, was still a fashionable destination.

assize-balls: dances held to coincide with the periodic meeting of the assize court in a community.

17 *'Such things, 'tis true, are neither new nor rare,* | *The only wonder is, how they got there'*: cf. Alexander Pope, 'Epistle to Dr. Arbuthnot': 'The things, we know, are neither rich nor rare, | But wonder how the Devil they got there?' (ll. 171–2). A similar version of this line appears in Pope's 'Fragment of a SATIRE' (ll. 21–2).

19 *'something than beauty dearer'*: James Thomson, *The Seasons*, 'Spring', 'Something than beauty dearer, should they look | Or on the mind, or mind-illumined thus' (ll. 1141–2).

24 *Rochefoucault's maxim*: François, Duc de la Rochefoucauld (1613–80) was the author of *Maximes* (first published in a pirated edition in 1664). The maxims in general illustrate Rochefoucauld's belief that self-interest is the fundamental basis of human behaviour, even of those actions which may appear to be most altruistic or disinterested. Although this passage does not appear to be linked to a specific maxim, it agrees with the general tenor of the work, and is close to two: no. 168 'What is commonly called Friendship is only a Partnership; a reciprocal regard for one another's Interests; and an Exchange of good Offices; in a word 'tis a mere Traffic, wherein Self-love always proposes to be a Gainer'; and no. 172 'We cannot love any Thing but on our own account; and we only follow our Taste and Inclination when we prefer our friends to ourselves: And yet 'tis this preference that alone constitutes true and perfect friendship': *Moral Maxims: by the Duke de la Rochefoucault*, translated from the French with notes (London, 1749), 69, 71.

rout: 'A fashionable gathering or assembly, a large evening party or reception, much in vogue in eighteenth and early nineteenth centuries' (*OED*).

25 *his prize*: to claim an article of apparel as a courtship trophy was an intimate gesture. Brightwell records a similar incident when Godwin was involved in a flirtation with the then Amelia Alderson. Alderson writes 'It would have entertained you highly to have seen him bid me farewell. He wished to salute [kiss] me, but his courage failed him. . . . "Will you give me nothing to keep for your sake, and console me during my absence," murmured out the philosopher, "not even your slipper? I had it in my possession once and need not have returned it!" This was true; my shoe had come off and he had put it in his pocket some time. You have no idea how gallant he is become': *Memorials of the Life of Amelia Opie*, 59–60.

26 *minauderies*: 'Coquettish airs' (*OED*), often pejorative. Hannah More, in *Strictures*, notes 'They had refined elegance into insipidity, frittered down delicacy into frivolousness, and reduced manner into *minauderie*' (i. 73).

28 *like the orator of old . . . this applause*: the orator is Phocian: Plutarch records that 'when once he gave his opinion to the people, and was met with the general approbation and applause of the assembly, turning to some of his friends, he asked them, "Have I inadvertently said something

foolish?"': *Plutarch's Lives*, Dryden edn. revised, 3 vols. (London, 1910), iii. 7.

30 *he has written a volume to prove the absurdity of the custom*: treatises against duelling were not rare at the end of the eighteenth century, but the most immediate context is 'Of Duelling', an appendix to Book II (Principles of Society) in Godwin's *Political Justice*. He argues against the practice from the worth to society of the individuals involved, deeming it contrary to the good of society to risk useful lives. But almost equal space is devoted to the concern a man might feel that to refuse a duel would be to risk his reputation for courage and personal honour. Godwin redefines personal courage as the courage to defy social convention: 'He that would break through a received custom because he believes it to be wrong must no doubt arm himself with fortitude. . . . If courage have any intelligible nature, one of its principal fruits must be the daring to speak truth at all times, to all persons, and in every possible situation in which a well informed sense of duty may prescribe it. What is it but the want of courage that should prevent me from saying, "Sir, I will not accept your challenge . . . I should be a notorious criminal were I to attempt your life, or assist you in an attempt upon mine"' (II. ii. app. ii, p. 180). It is this aspect that Adeline focuses on in her discussion of the issue with Glenmurray. For more on duelling, see V. G. Kiernan, *The Duel in European History* (Oxford, 1988).

33 *poltroon*: 'A spiritless coward; a mean-spirited, worthless wretch' (*OED*).

34 *he determined on having no second*: it was customary for each duellist to be accompanied by a friend or 'second' whose role was to observe that proper rules were followed and no foul play occurred. Glenmurray hopes to involve as few people as possible, perhaps in part to limit the number who know of his choice to fight in spite of his professed principles. In this instance Sir Patrick's honour towards men is revealed in his refusal to procure a service he believes Glenmurray is unable to obtain for himself.

35 *whether he ought to stay, or fly his country*: homicide by duel was a capital crime, though offenders were seldom convicted; nevertheless, in duels resulting in death the surviving combatant usually fled the country to voluntary exile.

36 *like the eagle in the song . . . cried 'Quarter!'*: to cry 'quarter' is to surrender. The song itself is untraced.

38 *from the dread . . . a wife*: in his biography of Godwin, William St Clair gives an account of the awkwardness Godwin felt in explaining his decision to marry the pregnant Wollstonecraft: 'With everyone enjoying jokes about his marriage, Godwin felt the embarrassment deeply, and in several letters he defended himself vigorously against the easy accusation that he had contravened his own principles': *The Godwins and the Shelleys* (London, 1989), 172.

the dearest of all monopolies: in *Political Justice* Godwin had described marriage as 'the worst of all monopolies' (VIII. viii. app., p. 762); Opie was sceptical of the high-minded absence of jealousy (and indeed almost all emotion) in Godwin's work, and here, playing on the phrase, suggests that Glenmurray similarly refuses to recognize the role of passion in his attachment.

44 *'punctual as lovers to the moment sworn'*: Edward Young, *The Complaint: or, Night-Thoughts on Life, Death, and Immortality*, 'Punctual as lovers to the moment sworn, | I keep my assignation with my woe' (Night III, ll. 4–5).

Verbum sapienti: a word is sufficient to the wise.

chains of Hymen: bonds of matrimony; Hymen was the classical god of marriage.

45 *Now, had I said that, it would have been called a bull*: i.e. an Irish bull, 'an expression containing a manifest contradiction in terms or involving a ludicrous inconsistency unperceived by the speaker' (*OED*).

47 *quietus*: 'a discharge or acquittance given on payment of sums due, or clearing of accounts' (*OED*).

49 *there have been no writings . . . and so sir Pat have got all:* according to English Common Law in this period, a woman's legal existence was suspended on marriage, and her husband acquired complete control of her property. Separate contracts, however, drawn up as pre-nuptial settlements could allow a woman to retain control of some money, either through pin-money, a fixed sum to be provided annually for her use by the husband, or through married women's separate property, an estate for her sole use and not under the control of her husband or available to his creditors. Since no such settlement has taken place, Sir Patrick has full legal control of Editha's property. For more on this topic see Susan Staves, *Married Women's Separate Property in England, 1660–1833* (Cambridge, Mass., 1990).

54 *disciples of Epicurus*: those who follow Epicurean philosophy which holds that pleasure is the chief good and goal of life; often, as here, popularly interpreted as hedonistic, though Epicurus taught that intellectual pleasures were preferable to sensual ones.

Æolian harps: stringed instruments sounding by the action of the wind.

55 *Scuderi's and other romances*: Madeleine de Scudéry (1607–1701), author of French romances; Editha's taste in literature runs to the heroic romance rather than the contemporary novel. This may simply indicate that her taste in literature is somewhat old-fashioned, or it may suggest that such romances have informed her infatuation with Sir Patrick, for they offer a portrait of courtly love and some women readers found in them a fantasy of female empowerment through being an object of desire to whom the lover pays court. Charlotte Lennox's *The Female Quixote* (1752) offers a satiric portrait of such a reader.

Rousseau's Contrat Social . . . pages of his Candide: Jean-Jacques Rousseau (1712–78), Charles-Louis Montesquieu (1689–1755), and Voltaire

(François-Marie Arouet, 1694–1778), three key writers in eighteenth-century France whose works were also influential in England. Rousseau's *Contrat Social* (*Social Contract*, 1762) is a work of political theory whose opening assertion that sovereignty rests with the people marks it as a central document underpinning the French Revolution. His *Julie, ou La Nouvelle Héloïse* (*Julie, or the New Heloise*, 1761) is an epistolary novel that explores human passion and social responsibility. Montesquieu's *Esprit des Loix* (*Spirit of the Laws*, 1748) offers a methodical analysis of political institutions and ends by advocating liberal constitutional monarchy. His *Lettres Persanes* (*Persian Letters*, 1721) is an epistolary novel in which he uses the device of the outsider, in this case a Persian ruler visiting France, to comment on and satirize contemporary social, legal, and political institutions. Voltaire's *Brutus* (1730) is a heroic tragedy. *Candide* (1759) is a philosophical tale or *conte*, and perhaps his best-known work; it reflects his scepticism of philosophical systems which deal in abstractions and bear no relation to life as the individual experiences it, through a satire of Leibniz's philosophy of optimism. Editha's library thus provided Adeline with ample exposure to works of social theory, but not to literary critiques of social ideas.

56 *till she opened the Nouvelle Heloise . . . the fate of her devoted daughter*: at this period most conservative writers vilified Rousseau and his works, especially this novel. Hannah More says of it 'He does not paint an innocent woman, ruined, repenting, and restored; but with a far more mischievous refinement, he annihilates the value of chastity, and with pernicious subtlety attempts to make his heroine appear almost more amiable without it. He exhibits a virtuous woman, the victim not of temptation but of reason, not of vice but of sentiment, not of passion but of conviction; and strikes at the very root of honour by elevating a crime into a principle': *Strictures*, i. 32–3. Here Opie asserts the potential value of fiction to educate the sentiments, and of readers to learn lessons of restraint as well as expression of the passions from Julie's experience. This substantial passage was omitted by Opie in her changes to the text for the 1844 Grove Edition of the novel. The suppression of support for the education derived from sentiment in Rousseau's novel marks more than anything else the conservative nature of the changes made.

57 *en attendant!*: in the mean time.

59 *ferme ornée*: a combination of working farm and garden, modelled on the classical ideal of uniting philosophical retreat with profitable agriculture; its peak of popularity was in England in the eighteenth century.

65 *violent emotions . . . alarming symptoms*: according to Buchan, 'Consumptions are often occasioned, and always aggravated, by a melancholy cast of mind', and he lists as a cause of the disease 'Violent passions, exertions, or affections of the mind; as grief, disappointment, anxiety, or close application to the study of abstruse arts or sciences' (*Domestic Medicine*, 174, 167). As a young man of slender build given to meditation

on abstruse social theories and rendered anxious by the situation of his lover, Glenmurray is a prime candidate for a serious bout of consumption.

66 *you are to be governed by no other law but your desire to promote general utility . . .*: Adeline's comments here echo several statements in *Political Justice*, sharpening the comparison between Glenmurray and Godwin. In this political tract, Godwin asserts, 'I am bound to employ my talents, my understanding, my strength and my time, for the protection of the greatest quantity of general good. Such are the declarations of justice, so great is the extent of my duty' (III. ii. 175). He later goes on to say that 'Men are capable, no doubt, of preferring an inferior interest of their own to a superior interest of others; but this preference arises from a combination of circumstances and is not the necessary and invariable law of our nature' (IV. x. 386). Instead, individuals should act through a 'system of disinterested benevolence' (IV. x. 387) in which narrow, individual interest is replaced by rational reflection upon the larger demands of liberty, knowledge, equality, virtue and justice. He contends that 'Neither philosophy, nor morality, nor politics will ever show like itself till man shall be acknowledged for what he really is, a being capable of rectitude, virtue and benevolence, and who needs not always be led to actions of general utility, by foreign and frivolous considerations' (IV. x. 387).

67 *nabob*: 'A person of great wealth, usually one who has returned from India with a large fortune' (*OED*).

70 *a young man of twenty-eight, and . . . a girl of nineteen*: though the novel was recognized at the time as a *roman à clef* based on Godwin and Wollstonecraft, the resemblances are indirect at best. Opie exercises considerable licence in assigning ages to her characters: Godwin was 37 when he published *Political Justice* (1793) and 41 when he married Wollstonecraft; she was 38. By shifting the ideology of maturity to the enthusiasm of youth, she gains a sympathetic response to the actions of the characters, which are constructed as the results of a naive idealism rather than a more mature philosophy open to charges of moral depravity.

76 *in a pet*: taking 'Offence at being (or feeling) slighted or not made enough of; a fit of ill humour from this cause' (*OED*).

poste restante: 'A direction written upon a letter which is to remain at the post office until called for' (*OED*).

88 *in Moorfields*: in an asylum for the insane. Bedlam (Bethlem Hospital for the Care of the Insane) moved to new quarters at Moorfields in 1676, where it became one of the leading landmarks of London. See Jonathan Andrews *et al.*, *The History of Bethlem* (London, 1997), esp. 230–59.

90 *But no more could I a Malabar widow, who . . . throws herself on the funeral pile of her husband*: the reference is to the ritual of *sati*, or 'suttee' as English writers of the period called it, in which, according to popular

understanding, a virtuous Hindu wife follows her husband to her
death by immolation on his funeral pyre. The practice fascinated
Western travel writers, who usually showed a horror of the event but
also an admiration for the courage of the woman involved. In 1791
Mariana Stark published a tragedy, *The Widow of Malabar*, based on
Antoine-Marin Lemierre's 1770 tragedy *La Veuve du Malabar*, which
was the subject of a number of imitations and parodies. See John Stratton
Hawley (ed.) *Sati, the Blessing and the Curse* (Oxford, 1994).

90 *Old Hummums*: a Coffee House in Covent Garden, established around
1700, and in 1801–3 'described as adjoining the Tavistock Coffee House
and Public Breakfast Room ... "a good house, much frequented by
the theatrical and other gentlemen. Famous for good beds and other
conveniences; warm baths"': Bryant Lillywhite, *London Coffee Houses*
(London, 1963), 418.

93 *a dawdle*: one who idles or wastes time, usually feminine.

95 *Dr Norberry was suspected of being a very gallant man*: to be 'gallant' was
to be involved in amorous affairs; Opie adds the phrase 'though unjustly'
in 1844, to make clear the unfounded nature of these suspicions.

96 *can see into a mill-stone*: proverbial, 'I can see as far into a millstone as
another man'; the phrase is 'a claim to acuteness, often used ironically':
Morris Tilley, *Dictionary of Proverbs in England in the Sixteenth and
Seventeenth Centuries* (Ann Arbor, 1950), 462.

99 *no one ought to do evil that good may come*: Romans 3: 8 'And not *rather*,
(as we be slanderously reported, and as some affirm that we say,) Let us
do evil, that good may come?'

'The murder is out': 'now the murder's out', Farquhar, *The Recruiting
Officer* (1706), III. i.

100 *'But thou, oh Hope! with eyes so fair, | What was thy delighted measure!'*:
William Collins, 'The Passions: An Ode for Music,' (ll. 29–30).

102 *hectic*: 'the kind of fever which accompanies consumption or other
wasting diseases' (*OED*).

103 *it has broke its knees—never to be sound again*: Norberry uses an equestrian
metaphor; a horse with broken knees shows scarring of the joint from a
previous injury (usually a fall), and is often lame or unsound and therefore not fit to ride. Hence, Editha's pride has been damaged irreparably.

112 *'curst with every granted prayer'*: Alexander Pope, 'Epistle to a Lady':
'Atossa, curs'd with ev'ry granted pray'r' (l. 147).

118 *of what great importance a strict adherence to veracity is, to the interests of
society*: another echo of *Political Justice*. Central to the abolition of vice in
society and the construction of a utopia from the best of individual
expression is the 'strict adherence to veracity', or what Godwin terms
'The Cultivation of Truth' (IV. v. 296) and its appearance in 'the incidents
and commerce of ordinary life' (IV. vi. 311) as 'sincerity'. Of 'the
value and energy of truth', Godwin writes, 'There is no topic more

fundamental to the principles of political science, or to the reasonings of this work' (IV. v. 296). Sincerity he describes as 'the most powerful engine of human improvement' (IV. vi. 320). Without the cultivation of truth and the practice of sincerity, all the utopian dreams expressed in *Political Justice* would be doomed to failure. His comments on infidelity in marriage are particularly relevant to *Adeline Mowbray*. While stating that 'Certainly no ties ought to be imposed upon either party, preventing them from quitting the attachment, whenever their judgement directs them to quit it', he expressly notes that 'the point of principal importance is a determination to have recourse to no species of disguise. . . . What, at present, renders it . . . peculiarly loathsome is its being practised in a clandestine manner. It leads to a train of falsehood and a concerted hypocrisy, than which there is scarcely anything that more eminently depraves and degrades the human mind' (VIII. viii. app., p. 764).

119 *Mrs Pemberton*: Rachel Pemberton's speech, specifically her use of 'thy', 'thee', and 'thou', marks her as a Quaker. Opie's friend Joseph Gurney referred to 'the humbling sacrifice of plainness of speech, behaviour and apparel' that attended his entry into the strict order of Friends; when Opie joined the Society of Friends in 1825, remembering to practise plain speech appears to have been an effort. Mary Russell Mitford notes that 'Mr Haydon told me that, in about a quarter of an hour's chat, she forgot her thou's and thee's and became altogether as merry as she used to be' (quoted in Jacobine Menzies-Wilson and Helen Lloyd, *Amelia: The Tale of a Plain Friend* (Oxford, 1937), 142, 218).

122 *straining at a gnat, and swallowing a camel*: Matthew 23: 24, 'Ye blind guides, which strain at a gnat, and swallow a camel'; both the camel and the gnat are unclean animals—the phrase suggests that in trying to avoid a trifling defilement, the Pharisees are subject to a greater one.

125 *'The conscious mind is its own awful world!'*: James Thomson, *Tancred and Sigismundo. A Tragedy*, 'The World approve!—What is the World to me? | The conscious Mind is its own awful world': *The Plays of James Thomson, 1700–1748: A Critical Edition*, ed. John C. Greene, 2 vols. (New York, 1987), v. vi. 94–5.

126 *'things as they are'*: part of the original title of Godwin's political novel: *Things as they Are; or, The Adventures of Caleb Williams* (1794); the title suggests the concern with examining society as it functioned at the time.

128 *by-blow*: 'One who comes into the world by a side stroke; an illegitimate child, a bastard' (*OED*).

129 *'Alas! regardless of their doom, | The little victims play!'*: Thomas Gray, 'Ode on a Distant Prospect of Eton College' (ll. 51–2).

134 *'hope though hope were lost'*: Anna Laetitia Barbauld, 'Come here fond youth, whoe'er thou be', 'It is to hope, though hope were lost' (l. 19).

136 *pine-apple*: Glenmurray's craving for this fruit accords with contemporary medical understanding of his illness. In the section 'Of

Consumptions' in *Domestic Medicine*, Dr Buchan writes 'Acids seem to have peculiarly good effects in this disease; they both tend to quench the patient's thirst and to cool the blood. The vegetable acids, as apples, oranges, lemons, &c appear to be the most proper. I have known patients suck the juice of several lemons a day with manifest advantage, and would for this reason recommend acid vegetables to be taken in as great a quantity as the stomach will bear them' (p. 175). The hot-house pine-apples produced in England in this period were reported to have been particularly acidic.

138 *that ugly black b——h!*: changed to 'ugly black toad' in 1844 edition.

140 *dun*: a pressing creditor or debt-collector.

141 *Sterne's dear Jenny*: Laurence Sterne, in *Tristram Shandy*, writes 'Now this I like;—when we cannot get at the very thing we wish,——never to take up with the next best in degree to it;——no; that's pitiful beyond description', and then provides the example of his 'dear, dear *Jenny*' who, when she cannot get the expensive silk fabric she desires, selects instead the cheapest cloth available (vol. 1, ch. 18).

142 *the Magdalen*: an institution for the reformation of prostitutes, so called after the woman in the Bible referred to as Mary Magdalene, who came to be represented in Western culture as a prostitute restored to virtue through repentance and faith. Magdalen Hospital opened in London in 1758, and other communities subsequently established similar institutions. One of the earliest uses cited in the *OED* is from Wollstonecraft's argument in *A Vindication of the Rights of Woman*: 'many innocent girls become the dupes of a sincere, affectionate heart, and still more are, as it may emphatically be termed, *ruined* before they know the difference between virtue and vice:—and thus prepared by their education for infamy, they become infamous. Asylums and Magdalenes are not the proper remedies for these abuses. It is justice, not charity, that is wanting in the world!' (p. 140).

143 *flannels . . . gouty couch*: again, Berrendale's fantasies concerning his ill-ness accord with contemporary medical practice. In the section 'Of Gout' in *Domestic Medicine*, Dr Buchan notes 'As the most safe and efficacious method of discharging the gouty matter is by perspiration, this ought to be kept up by all means, especially in the affected part. For this purpose the leg and foot should be wrapt in soft flannel, fur, or wool' (p. 359). Adeline warming the flannels before wrapping the affected limb would only increase their alleged curative powers.

145 *Savanna*: possibly derived from Alderson family lore, the name recalls that of the black nurse, Savannah, who accompanied the author's mother on her return to England as an orphaned child from India.

148 *the 'Change*: the Royal Exchange; rebuilt in 1669 following the Great Fire which destroyed the first Royal Exchange, the structure housed shops and financial offices, and was the centre of one of the chief commercial districts of London.

annuity of 300l. for life: Berrendale's £300 annuity establishes him firmly in the ranks of gentility, but should by no means be seen as untold wealth. The sum might make a man 'comfortable as a bachelor', but would not have been sufficient to support a household or an extravagant life-style. Copeland notes that 'John Trusler in *The Economist* (1774) claims that precisely £370 16s. a year would be needed to support a household with two servants': *Women Writing About Money: Women's Fiction in England 1790–1820* (Cambridge, 1995), 29. If Berrendale also invested the £2,000 he recovered from his father's business, this would be his approximate annual income.

150 *Four years cannot have added much to the maturity of my judgment . . . rules of their conduct*: Glenmurray's position is very similar to that articulated by Godwin in the preface to his novel *Fleetwood* (1805), published just a month after *Adeline Mowbray*. Recognizing that his critics would accuse him of contradicting his principles in the positive view of marriage represented in the novel, he notes '[*Political Justice*] was a treatise, aiming to ascertain what new institutions in political society might be found more conducive to general happiness than those which at present prevail. In the course of this disquisition it was enquired, whether marriage, as it stands described and supported in the laws of England, might not with advantage admit of certain modifications? Can any thing be more distinct, than such a proposition on the one hand, and a recommendation on the other that each man for himself should supersede and trample upon the institutions of the country in which he lives? A thousand things might be found excellent and salutary, if brought into general practice, which would in some cases appear ridiculous, and in others be attended with tragical consequences, if prematurely acted upon by a solitary individual': *Fleetwood: or The New Man of Feeling*, ed. Pamela Clemit in *Collected Novels and Memoirs of William Godwin*, general editor Mark Philip (London, 1982), v. 14–15.

158 *'Father, if it be possible, permit this cup to pass by me untasted'*: Adeline conflates two verses from Matthew: 26: 39, 'And he went a little further, and fell on his face, and prayed, saying, O my Father, if it be possible, let this cup pass from me: nevertheless, not as I will, but as thou *wilt*', and 26: 42, 'O my father, if this cup may not pass away from me, except I drink it, thy will be done.'

162 *Adeline in a state of insanity*: according to Helen Small, 'Between about 1770 and about 1810, stories about bereaved or deserted women fallen into insanity were the subject of an extraordinary vogue in sentimental prose, poetry, drama, and painting. For a culture which placed great emphasis on the visible expression of sentiment and on the dramatic staging of "feeling", the established iconography of love-madness was attractive material': *Love's Madness: Medicine, the Novel, and Female Insanity 1800–1865* (Oxford, 1996), 11.

167 *quondam*: 'That formerly was or existed' (*OED*).

167 *a getting-up*: a return to health; 'To get up again: to reach its former good
     condition' (*OED*). Mary follows up her query concerning the child with
     one about Adeline's recovery from childbirth.

171 *the heads of Adeline's story*: i.e. its main points.

175 *plain or fancy works*: plain work is plain sewing, distinct from fancy work
     which is embroidery; needlework was often the only potential source of
     income for destitute women.

     a little volume was ready to be offered to a bookseller: like many women in
     the period, including Wollstonecraft who published *Original Stories from
     Real Life* (1788) and later Opie herself with *Tales of the Pemberton Family*
     (1825) and *The Black Man's Lament* (1826), Adeline tries to support
     herself through writing for the market in books for children that had
     begun to open in the mid-eighteenth century and expanded rapidly in
     the nineteenth.

     the Temple: 'name of two of the Inns of Court in London' (*OED*), hence
     the legal district.

176 *260l. in the 5 per cents*: such an investment would yield Adeline an annual
     income of only £13. In an age when a common labourer might earn £25
     in a year, Glenmurray's attempted legacy is pitifully slight. See Copeland
     Woman Writing About Money, 24–5.

178 *black mawkin*: a form of the word 'malkin', in its general sense, 'Used as a
     female personal name; applied typically to a woman of the lower classes',
     here in the sense of an 'unworthy female . . . a servant or country wench;
     a slut, slattern, drab' (*OED*). She is described as black because she is still
     dressed in mourning.

179 *young templar*: a young lawyer; a templar is 'a barrister or other person
     who occupies chambers in the Inner or Middle Temple' (*OED*).

182 *tout simple*: Opie translates this in the 1844 edition as 'quite natural and
     proper'.

185 *personnalité*: the quality of always being preoccupied with one's self; used
     in this sense by Mme de Staël in *Corinne* (see note to p. 236 below).

     which cohabitation could alone call forth: in *Political Justice* Godwin
     attaches to his chapter 'On Property' an appendix entitled 'Of
     Cooperation, Cohabitation, and Marriage', in which he points out that
     contemporary courtship patterns led to marriage between people
     who had no idea of the other's real character. Opie stresses here that
     only prolonged close contact could reveal the essential selfishness of
     Berrendale's nature.

186 *hooping-cough . . . complaint*: in the section 'Of the hooping-cough, or,
     chin-cough' Buchan notes 'One of the most effectual remedies in the
     chin-cough is change of air' (*Domestic Medicine*, 271).

188 *'The word . . . thought it cold'*: Hannah More, 'Sensibility: A Poetical
     Epistle to the Hon. Mrs. Boscawen', ll. 337–8, slightly misquoted.

193 *'the use of pepper in great quantities . . . to counteract the effects of good*

living': F. S. Cozzens notes in *Sayings* (1870) 'There is a maxim there [in the tropics], that people who eat cayenne pepper will live forever. Like variety, it is the spice of life, sir, at the equator' (p. 15). Opie may have known this maxim, or she may simply be drawing on a much earlier tradition of pepper as an aid to digestion. Walter Bailey, in *A Short Discourse of the Three Kinds of Pepper in Common Use* (1588), asserts that it 'doth concoct and expell not onely the crudities of the belly and of the first veines, but also doth digest, extenuate, discusse, and by urine carieth the excrements of the inner veines, clenseth the bloud, and keepeth clean the habite of the body by sweate and perspiration through the skin'.

199 *Hazael, 'Is thy servant a dog that he should do this thing?'*: 2 Kings 8: 13.

203 *ancien régime*: 'system of government in France before the Revolution of 1789' (*OED*).

    soi-disant: 'self-styled'; 'would-be'.

    with a countenance more in sorrow than in anger: Shakespeare, *Hamlet*, I. ii. 232.

    it was never a barrel the better herring, and 'twas the kettle . . . calling the pot—: Mary combines two proverbial sayings, 'never a barrel the better herring', meaning 'not to know which to shun or to chuse, which to leave, or which to take', and 'the pot calling the kettle black-arse', which is 'spoken when others up braid us with those faults that they are guilty of themselves' (Tilley, *Dictionary of Proverbs*, 30, 353). Mary suggests that she and Adeline are equivalent, with nothing to choose between them. Opie implies, but stops short of, the vulgarity of the full version of the latter expression.

205 *the stench of the room*: a foul-smelling sickroom may have been commonly associated with poor children afflicted with this disease. Buchan notes 'A very dirty custom prevails among the lower classes of people, of allowing children in the small-pox to keep on the same linen, during the whole period of that loathsome disease. This is done lest they should catch cold; but it has many ill consequences. The linen becomes hard by the moisture which it absorbs, and frets the tender skin. It likewise occasions a bad smell, which is very pernicious both to the patient and those about him' (*Domestic Medicine*, 209).

206 *Fleet Street . . . the Strand*: Fleet Street runs east–west just north of the legal district of the Temple; immediately to the west it becomes the Strand. During the mid- to late eighteenth century 'the Strand and the alleys leading off it, were also a favourite haunt of pickpockets and prostitutes': Ben Weinreb and Christopher Hibbert (eds.), *London Encyclopaedia* (London, 1983), 830.

    men of ton: men of fashion or mode.

207 *an actress*: Drury Lane, famous for its theatre and notorious as a rowdy district in the eighteenth century, leads north from the Strand. During this period actresses were still generally considered to be women of questionable morals.

211　*prepare her little girl for inoculation directly*: although Opie wrote at a time
of increasing confidence in vaccination (i.e. protection from smallpox
through cowpox, first documented by Jenner in 1793), she is true to the
temporal setting of the novel in her use of inoculation, the earlier
developed practice of deliberate infection with a mild strain of live
smallpox virus. Dr Buchan offers the following description: 'The present
method of inoculating in Britain is to make two or three slanting incisions
in the arm, with a lancet wet with fresh matter taken from a ripe pustule
[of someone infected with smallpox]; afterwards the wounds are
closed up, and left without any dressing' (*Domestic Medicine*, 218). The
Tawny Boy's subsequent fears for Editha's beauty are well-founded, for
though inoculation reduced mortality rates, the likelihood of permanent
disfigurement remained.

212　*What a heart has this Adeline . . . for no one can inspire it who is not able to
feel it*: this quality in Adeline is reminiscent of the sensibility which the
author found compelling in Wollstonecraft; she writes to her 'Will you
help me to account for the *strong desire* I always feel when with you, to say
affectionate things to you? Perhaps it is because you, like [Rousseau's]
Julie, appear so capable of feeling affection that you cannot fail to excite
it' (letter to Mary Wollstonecraft, 28 August 17[96]; Abinger deposit,
dep. b. 210/6).

213　*too late for her to be inoculated*: unless inoculation took place prior to or
immediately on exposure to the disease it would not be effective.

219　*I am come to a determination . . . his own conscience*: Adeline refrains from
the suit for Editha's sake, but Opie also may have felt that such an action
would have been indelicate. Cf. her letter to Mrs Taylor 1794: 'What is a
woman made of, think you, that can *sue* a man for inconstancy? Truly of
very coarse materials; yet I really believe Miss Mann's trial would have
attracted me more than that for sedition. It would have given me so many
new ideas' (quoted in Brightwell, *Memorials*, 47).

　　　'*A fiddle's-end*': a fiddlestick's end. 'Something insignificant or absurd,
a mere nothing. Often substituted for another word when derisively
repeating a remark' (*OED*).

223　'*assurance doubly sure*': Shakespeare, *Macbeth*, IV. i. 83.

226　*his second wife*: this designation is confusing; Berrendale was first married
to the West Indian heiress, then to Adeline, and thirdly (bigamously) to
the rich widow who was a relation of his first wife. Opie may simply
mean his second (simultaneous) living wife, or she may have slipped in
the count.

230　*Caledonian*: a native of Scotland; '*humorously* = Scotchman' (*OED*).

231　'*virtuous she that knows her story*': untraced.

234　'*What's female beauty—but an air divine,* | *Thro' which the mind's all gentle
graces shine?*': Edward Young, *Love of Fame, The Universal Passion in
Seven Characteristic Satires*, Satire VI, 'On Women', ll. 151–2.

236 *though it is possible to love . . . admired than one whom he forgave*: Anne-Louise Germaine de Staël (1766–1817) was one of the leading woman intellectuals of late eighteenth-century France. Her *Recueil de morceaux détachés* (*Collection of Detached Pieces*, 1796) includes the novella 'The Story of Pauline', which tells the story of a young woman in Saint-Domingue married at 13 for the sake of her dowry to a man who subsequently arranges for her seduction by his cousin. Eventually rescued by a sympathetic older woman, she travels to France where she begins life anew and attracts the affection of a young man who believes her always to have been as virtuous as she now is. Pauline, in love but wracked by guilt concerning her past conduct, resists him. When her mentor asks him whether 'he did not believe it possible to love and respect a woman who had recovered from the early wildness of her young days and had expiated it through her repentance', he replies at length in a passage Opie paraphrases in her novel: ' "I believe her misdeeds are all obliterated before God and men," he answered. "There is only one person in whose eyes she cannot make amends, and that is her lover or husband. I am not considering this question as a moralist—it should generally be resolved by indulgence. But as a sensitive man capable of a love verging on idolatry, I do not hesitate to say that there can be no happiness with a woman whose memories are not pure. A woman like that is always anxious about the opinion her lover has of her; he himself is afraid of pronouncing a single word that might humiliate her, and this mutual distrust makes them feel that they are two separate beings. . . . I want to marry someone I admire, not someone I forgive." ': *An Extraordinary Woman: Selected Writings of Germaine de Staël*, trans. Vivian Folkenflik (New York, 1987), 127–8.

237 *constancy is natural to us*: Godwin speculates in *Political Justice* that 'It is a question of some moment whether the intercourse of the sexes, in a reasonable state of society, would be promiscuous, or whether each man would select for himself a partner to whom he will adhere as long as that adherence shall continue to be the choice of both parties. Probability seems to be greatly in favour of the latter' (VII. viii. app. p. 763).

239 *'one false step may be retrieved'*: Thomas Gray's 'Ode on the Death of a Favourite Cat' presents a moral fable, using the cat's demise to remind female readers to guard their virtue: 'From hence, ye beauties, undeceived, | Know, one false step is ne'er retrieved, | And be with caution bold' (ll. 37–9). Here Adeline fears that if her own 'false step' of loving Glenmurray out of wedlock were to be recouped through her reintegration into society, her daughter might learn to think from her example that the reverse of Gray's warning is true.

248 *a young and gay quaker*: members of the Society of Friends were divided into 'strict' and 'gay' according to the rigour with which they adhered to principles of plain speech and dress. Gay Quakers elected not to wear the drab clothing that distinguished Friends from the rest of society, choosing instead to mix more freely with the worldly. Strict Quakers wore drab

and used 'thee' and 'thou' instead of 'you' in their speech. See also note to p. 119.

249 *'Sweet are the uses of adversity!'*: Shakespeare, *As You Like It*, II. i. 12.

256 *restore the lost sheep to the fold again!*: Luke 15: 16, 'Rejoice with me; for I have found my sheep which was lost.' Dr Norberry also alludes to this parable at p. 263.

266 *pensioners*: Adeline has continued to support the unwed mother who attracted her attention earlier in the novel, p. 129.

TROLLOPE IN OXFORD WORLD'S CLASSICS

ANTHONY TROLLOPE

An Autobiography
Ayala's Angel
Barchester Towers
The Belton Estate
The Bertrams
Can You Forgive Her?
The Claverings
Cousin Henry
Doctor Thorne
Doctor Wortle's School
The Duke's Children
Early Short Stories
The Eustace Diamonds
An Eye for an Eye
Framley Parsonage
He Knew He Was Right
Lady Anna
The Last Chronicle of Barset
Later Short Stories
Miss Mackenzie
Mr Scarborough's Family
Orley Farm
Phineas Finn
Phineas Redux
The Prime Minister
Rachel Ray
The Small House at Allington
La Vendée
The Warden
The Way We Live Now

The Oxford World's Classics Website

www.worldsclassics.co.uk

- Information about new titles
- Explore the full range of Oxford World's Classics
- Links to other literary sites and the main OUP webpage
- Imaginative competitions, with bookish prizes
- Peruse *Compass*, the Oxford World's Classics magazine
- Articles by editors
- Extracts from Introductions
- A forum for discussion and feedback on the series
- Special information for teachers and lecturers

www.worldsclassics.co.uk

American Literature

British and Irish Literature

Children's Literature

Classics and Ancient Literature

Colonial Literature

Eastern Literature

European Literature

History

Medieval Literature

Oxford English Drama

Poetry

Philosophy

Politics

Religion

The Oxford Shakespeare

A complete list of Oxford Paperbacks, including Oxford World's Classics, OPUS, Past Masters, Oxford Authors, Oxford Shakespeare, Oxford Drama, and Oxford Paperback Reference, is available in the UK from the Academic Division Publicity Department, Oxford University Press, Great Clarendon Street, Oxford OX2 6DP.

In the USA, complete lists are available from the Paperbacks Marketing Manager, Oxford University Press, 198 Madison Avenue, New York, NY 10016.

Oxford Paperbacks are available from all good bookshops. In case of difficulty, customers in the UK can order direct from Oxford University Press Bookshop, Freepost, 116 High Street, Oxford OX1 4BR, enclosing full payment. Please add 10 per cent of published price for postage and packing.